To Megan,
Love
Catherine Sabatina x

Sweet Jasmine, Cakes and Magic
By Catherine Sabatina

Published by Catherine Sabatina
A Catherine Sabatina book 9780957112605
First published in Great Britain
© copyright Catherine Sabatina 2011

This work is registered with UK Copyright Service registration number 341775

This work is a work of fiction and except in the case of historical fact, any resemblance to actual persons living or dead is purely coincidental.
This book is sold subject to the condition that it shall not, by way of trade or otherwise, be lent out, resold, hired out, or otherwise circulated without the publisher's prior consent in any form of binding or cover other than that in which it is published and without similar condition, including this condition, being imposed on the subsequent publisher.

For more information about Catherine Sabatina visit
www.catherinesabatina.com

ISBN
978-0-9571126-0-5 Paperback
978-0-9571126-1-2 ebook, Kindle
978-0-9571126-2-9 ebook, ipad

Thank you to our sponsor

Little Kit Bags

www.littlekitbags.co.uk

Catherine Sabatina was born in 1978 and works as an exercise to music teacher. She has dedicated her first book **Sweet Jasmine, Cakes and Magic** *to her mother Maureen because she loved to read and to her father 'Bob' because of the way he's nurtured her imagination all throughout her life.*

Special thanks to Anne Jennings, Dani Bright, Rakhi Mawkin, Carly Marsh and Steve Miles

"A white witch is a very good witch indeed; we refrain from using our magical abilities from causing harm unto others"
(Adrianna Jasmine Poppleapple Mariposa Forthright-Punch, 2008)

Introduction

The witch was petite, yet beautifully put together. She was precisely five feet and five inches of sheer perfection. Her glossy hair was dark and rich and cascaded halfway down her back into gentle, shiny waves. Her breasts were large and round, accentuated by the fact that she was graced with a tiny, toned waist and a bottom on par with a Latin ballroom goddess. She possessed the sort of figure that packed a punch, evoked sexual fantasies and even made you want to cry out 'mama mia!' or literally cry in general. Her gorgeous lips were round and full, utterly kissable and from the moment you laid eyes on them, you couldn't help but dream of falling into their pillow-like plumpness. She had a small gap between her two front teeth, which is commonly known for being lucky, so when she had the opportunity to wear a brace for her gap in her early teens, she point blank refused. Still, it suited her face and kept her in with a chance of winning the odd scratch card every now and then. Her olive skin beamed with health and radiance, as if sprayed with some magical shimmer and her little nose wiggled with charm whenever she chuckled. The witch's eyes were two different colours. Her right eye brown, her left blue. Quite similar to David Bowie (Google him if your under 25!) Furthermore, if you were ever lucky enough to stare deeply into those multi-coloured eyes: pupil, cornea and white liquidly stuff would be the last thing that you'd notice. For those eyes were special. They were almost a doorway to another world, a world that not many humans would ever have the opportunity to encounter. All things considered, she was a pretty unique specimen physically and mentally. However, as if her physical attributes weren't enough, she possessed other abilities that were most certainly deeper than skin.

The witch you are reading about is named Adrianna Jasmine Poppleapple Mariposa Forthright-Punch. She is 26 years of age and dwells in a roomy two-bedroom apartment in Islington, London. She lives alone with her three-year-old black cat named Jupiter 10, who is the replacement of many Jupiters before him. Adrianna Jasmine runs her own catering company called 'The Magic of Food.' She is intelligent, beautiful and confident, however, extremely modest. For she knows full well that she's a bit of a strudel, but does not spend hours in front of a mirror. She simply has better things to do. She's happy and content with who she is, and what she is and most importantly, the things that she can do.

Adrianna Jasmine is highly organised, writes everything down and makes lists. She is never late; never mixes up times and dates. Her kitchen cupboards are spotlessly clean and all her jars of food and packets are lined up neatly in rows and labelled accordingly. Her fridge is sparkling and her oven could easily shelve cashmere sweaters if one required the cupboard space. It really is that clean.

Adrianna Jasmine is a cook. Her catering company keeps her doing what she loves best - cooking, creating and bringing a touch of magic into a person's life. And she can certainly bring enchantment into a person's life with her food. To evoke special feelings from consuming her moreish morsels, Adrianna Jasmine adds very 'special' ingredients to her cooking. Her favourite magic ingredients are 'natural endorphins,' similar to those found in exquisite Belgian chocolates. 'Being a bit tipsy' is the merry feeling one experiences after a nice glass of wine and 'aphrodisiac' commonly found in oysters. Therefore, if you're ever likely to swallow any of Adrianna Jasmine's extraordinary delights, don't be alarmed if you experience an overwhelming sensation to ravish your partner after consumption.

Adrianna Jasmine is a witch. She is a modern witch living in a modern world and thoroughly enjoys life to boot. She has a thriving business (obviously), a loyal cat (Jupiter 10) and no complicated love in her life (bliss). She is a very careful witch, keeping a low profile, trusts only those close to her and keeps her workload fairly modest and secluded. She would never tell anyone that she is a witch - never, never! 'Why?' you might ask. Well, the reason is quite simple. As we have established, Adrianna Jasmine is indeed a witch and her moreish morsels are all the rage because of her magical powers. Now the world must not know this, otherwise she could be called all sorts of nasty names, chased through the streets of London, burned at the stake, or even arrested and sued for adding dodgy chemicals to a Christmas party spread. Not that her ingredients are at all dodgy. On the contrary, they are fresh and natural. But they could pose a problem with the mere mortals of the Food Standards Agency. More importantly, her status as a witch must be kept secret for far greater reasons than being caught for spiking potato gratin with happy- go- lucky feelings.

Jupiter 10 is named that because he is the tenth cat named Jupiter that she has owned. Adrianna Jasmine has always owned a black cat simply because she is a witch and it is customary. However, there is more to it than that. Ever heard of shape shifting? Shape-shifting is a common craft in the world of witches and every now and then a witch may wish to disappear from prying eyes or even indulge in a little sporting activity such as spying. So whenever she feels the urge for a spot of eavesdropping the witch can shape-shift into her cat and wander freely and unnoticed, gathering information and gossip. Although, there is a catch...The witch can only shape shift into her cat up to nine times during a cat's life, otherwise the cat snuffs it (Hence the nine lives belief). And yes, you guessed it - that's how the little Jupiters numbers one to nine snuffed it. Unfortunately our sweet Adrianna Jasmine has a little problem when it comes to shape shifting into her cats. Well, actually, it's a little more than a problem. Adrianna Jasmine is addicted to shape-shifting and therefore keeps killing her cats. The worst thing is, she feels absolutely terrible about it, but simply can't kick the habit. She was thinking about checking herself into the Priory to tackle her problem once and for all, but she thought her reason for checking in could have sounded a little weird, so she decided to go cold turkey all by herself. Anyway, Jupiter 10 is three human years old and has five cat lives left intact. Things are certainly looking up!

Oh well, no one's purrrrfect! Still, if you are a black cat living in Islington right now, be afraid; be very afraid as you may just feel the end of her wand!

Adrianna Jasmine does not have a boyfriend; she is young, free and single - best way to be in her eyes, as she most certainly does not want to complicate her life with love and nutty menfolk. Love is the most powerful emotion in the world and can therefore cause all sorts of problems, even for the most skilled of witches. Love can tie a person into knots; throw you off your guard; put you off your dinner and turn you into nothing but a giant mush ball. No, no, Adrianna Jasmine prefers to keep her wits about her, to keep her head firmly on her shoulders and out of the pink fluffy love clouds, thank you very much.

Anyway, in regards to love she *loves* being a witch and she believes that if she projects all her love into her craft, her craft will most certainly give her a great, great deal back.

Love spells, in Adrianna Jasmine's eyes, are also out of the question. They are much too powerful and sooner or later they will simply backfire and leave a terrible mess in their wake. A witch must never cast a raw love spell on another human being; it could drive the wretched human to drink, or worse still, to death!

Adrianna Jasmine has a mother, Sicily, who is a she also has a curious habit of calling her daughter the most unusual pet names, such as Pickle Flower Poppet, Sorbet Surprise, or Twinkle Tambourine. Sicily taught the art of Witchcraft to Adrianna Jasmine just as her mother had previously taught her and her mother before that and *her* mother before that.

Sicily, as far back as Adrianna Jasmine could remember, sported a short, sharp black, bob. It resembled the look of a 1920s silent film star, all dramatic, cut to a perfect edge and somewhat staccato. The style suited Sicily's beautiful face, as she could indeed carry off such an unforgiving cut. However, the style mirrored the witch's personality too. For you see, Adrianna Jasmine's mother was a little short in height, (five foot three inches) sometimes a little sharp (would say what she thought) and at times very dramatic (ostentatious, eccentric and worked as a drama teacher at the London Academy of Prestigious Arts) and even aged 52, possessed a body that was cut to perfection! (Think Selma Hayek meets Shirley McClain).

Now if you ever have the pleasure of meeting the lovely Sicily, you would be right to detect certain dark aspects in her nature. We are not comparing her naughty side to the deluded manifestations of Heinrich Krame, who simply wrote beastly things about witches in The Malleus Maleficarum. In his opinion, witches were lustful, sex-crazed nymphomaniacs (Sicily was a seductive siren), feeble-brained (she was sharp as a sharpened pencil), obtained the intelligence of a six year old (BA Honours in theatre and dance and Certificate in Post Graduate Education), impressionable (she set the rules!), had terrible memories (Sicily remembered everything), were perpetual liars by nature (twisted the truth on many an occasion), and addicted to evil superstitions (respected the Threefold Law: What you send out will return to you three times over). What a ridiculous man he was. Back in the dark ages, if a woman found a herb that could be used for medicinal purposes and worked, they would simply say:

"Thank you very much, now burn her at the stake! WITCH, WITCH, WITCH!"

So there you have it. Sicily was not evil, just naughty, and very dedicated to her craft. So much so, just like her daughter, that she put love on a back burner for years in order to stay committed to it. Until, that was, when she desired a handsome and accomplished 33 year-old pianist named Henry Forthright Punch.

Sicily has an older sister of two years, Kristobella, who is also a witch. However, Kristobella lives in Chelsea and owns a stylish fashion boutique called Simply Kristobella's. Sicily and Kristobella were born in East Finchley in the 1950's. Their father, Luca Mariposa, owned a bakery in Long Lane and they all lived in the two bedroom flat above it. Their mother, Lilliana Poppleapple, was a gifted and brilliant seamstress and ran a business making clothes. Honestly, there wasn't anything that woman couldn't make. Kristobella seemed to take after her mother, for she adored sewing and designing Hollywood inspired dresses and dreamed that one day she would own a sophisticated shop in a swanky part of London. Well, she grew up and owns a sophisticated shop in Chelsea and frequents top fashion shows.

Sicily however, although she did enjoy the occasional sewing, had dreams of acting and dancing, a life on the stage. The family were never quite sure where Sicily's theatrical talents hailed from. They believed it *may* have spawned from her grandmother Clovis Poppleapple, who apparently enjoyed the odd glass of stout down at the local public house before entertaining the punters by swaying drunkenly on an old wooden crate, reciting uncouth poetry and belting out old sea shanties. It was said she was quite the extrovert and a fine talent that was wasted on top of a dusty box! So perhaps it was Clovis who Sicily took after, although Sicily has never recited anything but Shakespeare and Oscar Wilde, and certainly not in a pub!

Over her school years Adrianna Jasmine would be visited by other witches (Sicily's theatrical friends) so that they could pass on their knowledge to the younger generation and tell fascinating stories about their ancestors who were burnt at the stake: they were gifted women, wrongly accused of worshipping the horny devil. These stories would make Adrianna Jasmine's toes curl with excitement and her heart swell with pride that she, too, was one of these gifted women. She would also learn some great tips about the craft on these occasions, as each witch who came to see her always seemed to be specialised in a certain subject. Like old Mrs Berry, who was an expert on herbal remedies and did actually boast that she had the cure for the cold virus, and the sprightly Bella Bell, whose strongest craft was levitation and could make anything levitate. Then there was Carolina Plum, her main discipline was potion making: she was able brew and bottle the most unimaginable things, such as, lust, happy Christmas memories, unhappy thoughts and even a creature's soul. But Adrianna Jasmine has more fond memories of Carolina Plum. Adrianna Jasmine adored the blonde-haired woman. She was so calm, sexy and sultry. Words seemed to pour from her mouth like silken honey; she wore lovely feminine clothes and smelt delicious. More importantly, Adrianna Jasmine loved it when she received a hug from Carolina Plumb, as they were very special and magical.

Adrianna Jasmine's favourite colours were the colours of autumn. Her flat was filled with these beautiful colours; her floors were of polished wood, the settees dark red and covered in cushions and throws. Her curtains were made of fabulous brown velvet and her scattered rugs threaded in gold, burgundy and richness. Her bathroom walls were the colour of purple grape (very relaxing) which set off her porcelain Victorian bath tub and thick creamy church candles to perfection. Her dark wooden shelves housed delightful bottles of exquisite smelling oils, creams and gels, which she would gladly enjoy from time to time to create the most relaxing and heavenly bath a woman could only dream about.

Her kitchen, however, was somewhat clinical in appearance, for this was where she worked and it had to be kept spotless. Nonetheless, the walls were painted orange (for brightness and to evoke energy) and there was plenty of natural light

Her bedroom did not favour the colours of autumn; it was the purist of white. To Adrianna Jasmine her bedroom was a sanctuary, where thoughts of the day should be released and peace and tranquillity should take over the mind without any distraction. Moreover, most of Adrianna Jasmine's spells were cast from her bedroom, due to its calming influence and it was also where one would discover her beautiful magic altar and find a plethora of fascinating magical tools.

An additional attractive feature in Adrianna Jasmine's bedroom was her bed. It looked like a giant marshmallow that engulfed her into warmth, comfort and softness. She adored it and sometimes couldn't wait for sleep to call for her sink into its deliciousness, but being a witch, sleep is a rarity. Witches simply don't need to do it. Still, it was nice to lounge on it every now and then.

A Future Event

Two witches are huddled together in a dark corner, hidden by shadow and smoke.

Witch 1: She's very beautiful, isn't she?

Witch 2: Who?

Witch 1: The younger one!

Witch 2: Yes. I suppose she is.

Witch 1: She looks like her, that's why.

(Witch 2 pulls a look of disgust)

Witch 1: Now don't be like that, they're both stunning specimens. Although I must say the younger one does seem to be rather…unique. She exudes a power of the purist form, that one.

Witch 2: So her aura is white?

Witch 1: As white as angel wings.

Witch 2: What about the older one? I'll bet my gold tooth hers is as black as jet.

Witch 1: Hmmm. Not quite. More like a dark grey.

Witch 2: Unbelievable! How's she managed to do that!

Witch 1: She obviously directs her black magic into that of white. That's why her aura is grey, although I think it's confused. It's obviously a mix of the two colours. Oh, that's interesting…

Witch 2: What is?

Witch 1: The blonde's aura is red!

Witch 2: Why do you suppose that is?

Witch 1: She's saucy, I suppose. There's darkness there as well. How they've managed to get away with it after all these years is beyond me.

Witch 2: They all make me sick. They shouldn't be allowed to practice anymore, the time has come to teach the cackle a lesson they'll never forget.

Witch 1: Ooh, someone's touchy! Careful, witchy, or you'll be suspected.

Witch 2: I know. I'm just full of aggression and hatred at the moment. I walked past a florist the other day and all the wretched flowers shrivelled up and died. Honestly, it was very unfortunate for the owner.

Witch 1: Very unfortunate!

Witch 2: Goddess, I want her punished.

Witch 1: You're not thinking about making a move tonight! It'll be suicide!

Witch 2: Don't be ridiculous. We'd never survive. There's enough power in that circle to light up New York City. No, we need to stay amongst the shadows for now and then I'll pounce. Are you keeping an eye on that glass, Missus?

Witch 1: Yes, of course I am. It's the glass with the vodka and coke, the one furthest away from us.

Witch 2: Good. Make sure you snatch it before the waiter takes it away. I need her saliva for my next move.

Witch 1: Hmmm… I'm intrigued. Oh, I bet it's delicious. What *are* you thinking of doing? Some sort of deluded curse?

Witch 2: Don't be a fool. I'm not thinking anything and neither are you. Idiot! You know damn well that there's a possibility the cackle could detect the darkness of our thoughts. Keep your mind clear and try not to think about the glass. Just keep an eye on it, we'll talk next week.

*

Vanilla Charm Cup Cakes

8oz softened butter
8oz Caster Sugar
1tsp vanilla essence
4 large free range eggs
8oz self-raising flour
4tbsp milk

Butter icing
6 oz unsalted butter
12oz icing sugar
1tsp vanilla essence

Whisk everything up in a bowl until light and fluffy and then spoon the mixture into delightfully coloured cupcake cases
Bake in a pre-heated oven, gas mark 4, between 15-20 min
(Make sure cakes are firm to touch)

Once cooled, cream the butter icing by whisking the butter, vanilla and icing sugar together. Then using a piping bag, whirl the icing onto the cakes, sprinkle with 'hundreds and thousands' and enjoy with a nice cup of tea on a lazy afternoon

Chapter 1
The Menu

It was October 27th 2008 and Adrianna Jasmine was in her kitchen cooking up her moreish morsels for a large party in honour of some up-and-coming popsicle, Chrystal Rose. The party was to be held at the famous music producer, Byron Pigwell's, seven storey house in London's Mayfair and *everyone* who was *anyone* was going to be there! As she stirred and sautéed, beat and kneaded, the witch cast her mind back to when she first received the call from Pigwell's camp. A call, unbeknown to her, that would result in more than just a catering gig!

Byron Pigwell was a man of medium build (five foot ten inches) and in fairly good shape, for someone creeping up into their 50's, and possessed a full head of hair, although some were inclined to believe that the hair was implanted. He had a reputation for being a little forceful, sarcastic, sometimes uncouth, smarmy and arrogant. But he was damn good at his job, boasted a great eye for talent and more importantly, knew how to sell records. Pigwell had heard about Adrianna Jasmine's 'cooking' from a friend who had sampled the witch's culinary talents at 'The Lemon Drop' magazine's launch party. The chap had apparently raved about Adrianna Jasmine's sumptuous moreish morsels with such fanaticism, Pigwell felt almost compelled to hire her. So, as a result, Adrianna Jasmine landed a rather large and unexpected catering contract. The swanky affair was Byron Pigwell's idea. He had firmly stated to Adrianna Jasmine that Chrystal Rose was going to be 'the next best thing' and that the party's main target was to kick-start the girl's assets into the limelight and warm up the engine of the evil media machine. Lots of influential people would be there: journalists, photographers, actors, singers etc. So, he sought something fabulous.

The party's theme was to be fun, yet classy (Adrianna hated that word - it made her think of people who obtained little or no taste, trying to be delicately tasteful), different, sexy and Burlesque! For the guests' entertainment, Pigwell had hired six giant champagne glasses filled with water, bubbles and girlies. The girlies were apparently top of the range dancers/models and their job was to wear nothing but skimpy diamond bikinis whilst frolicking about in foam and slippery, slurpy suds for all to gaze. He had mentioned to Adrianna Jasmine that he was a fan of Dita Von Tease, Betty Page and the whole burlesque scene and thought it would be a great theme for Chrystal Rose's party. Now Adrianna Jasmine had not met or seen Chrystal Rose; however, she did not imagine the girl to resemble a sultry, mysterious Burlesque performer who demonstrated curious skills of flexibility. For some reason the colour pink, hair extensions, fake bake, poodles, juicy tracksuits and voice tweaking came to mind. Surely something more bubble gum and less satirical with a kinky edge would be better for a young pop princess's party?

"Oh well, its Pigwell's cash that's paying for the party," shrugged Adrianna Jasmine whilst talking out loud to herself, "I guess he can have what he jolly well wants."

And it seemed that on his wish list were skimpy bikinis, sparkling basques, pearl necklaces, six inch expensive stilettos and endless pairs of legs dangling over the top of bubble-filled giant champagne glasses. As Byron Pigwell excitedly set the scene, Adrianna Jasmine couldn't help picturing soggy swim suits, pruned bodies, spiky heels cracking the glass and pneumonia! Still it's what some people would find a turn on and what some girls would put themselves through these days in order to be noticed by model scouts. Adrianna Jasmine wasn't stupid, she had watched America's Next Top Model. Nonetheless, the witch told Pigwell that she found his party theme to be totally inspirational and nothing short of pure genius. (A little praise goes a long way!). She could sense Pigwell smiling down the phone,

"Well, yes," he said, trying to sound modest, "that's bang on the money. Anyway, call my PA when you come up with a menu, will you? I've got a Shih Tzu massage in ten minutes," and with that he hung up.

"Did he just say what I thought he said?" pondered the witch, and then she shook her head in disbelief, "unbelievable, he's launched hundreds of careers into stardom and has a string of hit television shows, but he can't tell the difference between an ancient massage technique and a miniature fluffy dog!"

13

Laughing to herself, she sat down in her living room and began to plan her masterpiece of a menu and, as always, began with the desserts. You see, whenever Adrianna Jasmine wrote out a party menu, or a menu in general, she always began with the dessert. Thinking about desserts simply enticed *her* natural endorphins to flow. The thought of chocolate, strawberries, sponge and cream, stimulated her creative brain cells and once they were stimulated, her creative juices simply flowed.

"Ok...," she contemplated, "let's start off with the *fun*" She began to make notes.

"Individual cupcakes decorated with rich butter icing in colours such as blue, pink, yellow and orange. The pink butter icing will taste of strawberries; the yellow will taste of lemon; the blue will taste of blueberry and the orange...well orange! They will be light and fluffy and decorated with edible candy diamonds, Very Marilyn Monroe! They should all be sprinkled with a little *tipsy* in order to evoke the fun. Hmmm..." she mused, "OK, how about scrumptious Belgian chocolate petit fours, poured into little individual silver paper cups? I'll make a batch of caramelized pecan and caramelized orange zest. The rest I'll simply leave au natural. Oh! What about mini Baileys, white and dark chocolate cheesecakes? They're simply heaven! Then for the piece de resistance my famous fruits of the forest crème brûlée. Everyone loves a crème brûlée, especially the part when you crack the sugar open and spoon the rich, creamy loveliness into one's utterly lucky mouth. Perfect!"

Adrianna Jasmine then came up with the clever idea of browning and burning the sugar into hard caramel in front of the salivating guests with a small blowtorch. "It would be part of the entertainment!" she thought enthusiastically. "Perhaps I could wear a velvet bikini and six inch heels whilst I'm at it." She giggled to herself at the idea before rapidly coming to her senses. "On second thoughts, Pigwell would probably like the idea of me tottering about in skimpy underwear, blowtorching his crème brûlée. Better not even joke. Onto the main! Ok, *classy*. I'm thinking, a hot buffet laid out in silver dishes resting on candle-lit hot trays, similar to those found at the local Indian! Hmmm...what shall I do?" She reflected hard for a few moments then began to write out more notes. "A sweet potato and aubergine curry, using the finest aromatic herbs and spices found in London, sprinkled with flaked almonds and fresh sweet coconut (to support the curry lovers). Mini Beef Wellingtons, using the leanest and best of local British filleted beef, spread with my delectable homemade chicken liver pate and melt- in- the- mouth 'home made' all butter pastry (in consideration for the carnivores and sophisticates). Individual creamy fish pies with saffron and wine and oh yes! A spaghetti bolognese, accompanied with angel hair rainbow pasta (to support the bright, young, hip things and the middle aged men who are trying to look hip in front of the bright young things). A batch of fragrant, sticky jasmine rice, potatoes roasted in goose fat, creamy potato and cheese gratin, caramelized carrots, mange tout and long green beans cooked al dente!"

She was about to make a note to sprinkle her main courses with 'aphrodisiac,' but thought better of it. For all she knew Chrystal Rose could really be 14 and you could bet your bottom dollar, what with the sloppy soap sudded Burlesque dancers, there would be enough testosterone and horn at the party already, thank you very much. No need to add any more fuel to the fire! So she quite wisely left it out for health and safety reasons. Instead, she opted for the choice of 'Harmony' which would sensibly evoke relaxation and comfort. There would be no attitude at this party!

Onto the starters, and here she regarded the *different* request from Byron Pigwell.

"OK here goes...what about scallops sautéed in garlic butter, wrapped in Parma ham with a béarnaise dip (for the seafood fans); crispy bacon wrapped around stuffed dates, utterly salty, sweet and delicious, ooh, and escargots!" She clapped her hands in excitement.

"I could stuff them with walnuts and herbs. It would stir up conversation about the French and well...snails! I'll buy a load down at the market today and start with the force-feeding of garlic and coriander. Yes, that should fatten them up all plump and juicy, they'll be fit to burst by the time I'm finished with them." Then her face rapidly began to fall.

"Ugh, now to support those pesky vegetarians," thought Adrianna Jasmine. She was not a fan of non-meat eaters, she found them dull. "I guess they'll just have to make do with a nice batch of rosemary and parmesan shortbread with black olives, slow- roasted cherry tomatoes and goat's cheese. They've got the sweet potato curry, gratin and mixed vegetables and I suppose I could do some nice vegetarian pasta salads...Anyway, I think I'll add my world-famous *endorphins* to the starters in order to rev up a few engines." Adrianna Jasmine giggled to herself mischievously.

Once complete she studied her menu to make sure that it was nothing less than perfect. However, the witch unfortunately came to the conclusion that something was missing and that it was not perfect. What was it? She contemplated: an additional dessert, possibly? No, her dessert menu was looking delicious. More fish perhaps? What about extra support for the veggies? They always take it so personally if there isn't enough vegetarian choice on a menu and start chaining themselves to trees and things. What if there were vegans at the party? They were always a thorn in a caterer's side.

"I'll add some celery sticks and spike them with *inebriated*," she thought wickedly, "ha! That'll teach them to be so fussy!!!"

Then she had it. Espresso Martinis made from fine Cuban coffee, flaming coffee beans and high quality vodka, no 'tipsy' required with these babies, they packed enough alcoholic punch. Perfect again.

Later, Adrianna Jasmine ran the menu plan past Pigwell's abrupt, yet highly efficient PA Hannah, via telephone, who then ran it past Pigwell. In less than two minutes Hannah had re-contacted Adrianna Jasmine with the exciting news of the go ahead.

"He decided he liked it," she calmly said in her cosmopolitan London voice. "He told me to tell you he is a great fan of spag bol and wished that restaurant menus took a leaf out of your book and offered a more varied choice of food in order to suit individual tastes. Not everyone desires Beluga. Some people just want bangers. Those were Mr. Pigwell's very own words."

"Oh, right," said Adrianna Jasmine, not quite knowing whether to take this as a compliment, "That's great...well, I'll see you Saturday 28th October. Oh, and just to let you know, Sparkling China will be delivering the cutlery, china wear, centre pieces and tables at ten thirty that morning."

"I'll be there personally to greet them," said Hannah abruptly, barked a goodbye and swiftly hung up the phone.

Adrianna Jasmine was busy cooling the crème brûlée, last minute force-feeding the snails with herbs and garlic, pouring out chocolate, simmering bolognese and icing cakes. She had been up since 5am and was flagging a little. *Time for a coffee*, she thought, *and maybe one of my little cakes*. She decided to indulge in a lemon flavoured cake, no tipsy included, as she needed a clear head, and made her way into the living room to recuperate. Just as she sat down, the phone rang. It was her mother.

"Toot, Toot little star, its mother," sang Sicily, "just wanted to know if you're alright? I haven't spoken to you in absolutely ages."

"Mother," Adrianna Jasmine groaned with a sigh, "I spoke to you last night!" *Ugh, you're so dramatic*, thought the witch silently! There was a short pause.

"Oh yes, of course. We did munch bum," said Sicily eventually, "but it was hardly what I'd call a full on conversation, darling." (One hour.) "I feel as if your life is a total mystery to me." Adrianna Jasmine exhaled and rubbed her forehead.

"My life isn't a mystery, mother; you know more about me than I know about me. And right now I'm preparing for that party I'm catering for, we spoke about it last night, remember!"

"Of course I remember, darling, yes, the Burlesque party," said Sicily enthusiastically, "oh what fun that should be, and very chic, darling. Why, it's almost a waste *you* going. Goddess, I'd give up my powers for a whole day for a chance to party Burlesque style again, in some fabulous house in Mayfair."

"Hmmm,' said the younger witch, slightly offended that her mother had insinuated that she was boring! The cheek! *"I'm* there to work, mother, not to enjoy myself!" she said firmly.

"I know that, darling!" Said Sicily with a chuckle. "Goddess, it would take a spell and a half to get *you* to enjoy yourself at the moment. It's not all work and witchcraft, you know. You can let your hair down once in a while! Wicca is joyful and fun, darling, it's meant to be celebrated. So for Goddess sake, go out and enjoy the fact that you're a witch!'

"Mother!" warned Adrianna Jasmine sharply, "Wicca is also meant to be serious and well respected, not abused for ill-gotten gains."

"Oh piff puff, darling," said Sicily dismissing Adrianna Jasmine's tee-total approach to the ancient art. *Goddess* she thought, *what the girl really needs to do is strip off to her birthday suit, dance naked under the full moon and embrace her Pagan roots. And fast!*

"Why don't you slip on a sexy dress and a slick of Chanel red lippy when you're there?" suggested her mother eagerly, "go on, and flaunt your body as well as your cooking skills. I tell you, the other women wouldn't stand a chance next to my petite butterscotch moose."

Adrianna Jasmine heaved a long sigh.

"Mother, I've got a perfectly suitable uniform to wear for the party, thank you very much. And it's not as fuddy duddy as you may think."

"Hmmm," said her mother unconvinced, "all I'm saying is you should make the most of yourself. Goddess, honey pie, sometimes you turn me into nothing but a bundle of crackling frustration."

"Mother!" warned her daughter again, "stop, now!"

"Well, OK darling," said Sicily sulkily, "I've said my piece. Anyway, so the party's burlesque?"

"You know it is," said Adrianna Jasmine, sipping her coffee.

"Oh those were the days," said Sicily dreamily as she cast her mind back to the days of her youth. Adrianna Jasmine rolled her eyes.

"You know I was a fabulous Burlesque dancer, in my time." *'Here we go'* thought Adrianna Jasmine silently. "I had the hair cut, the attitude, and if I remember rightly, a purple boa, too...oh, I had it all! Actually, darling, I've still got that boa somewhere. Maybe you should take it along with you to the party? Use it to be a little risqué! You could drape it over you all seductively whilst sashaying about in one of those champagne glasses you told me they've hired. Oh, it's a shame you're hiding away in the kitchen, darling. You should get out there and show those girls a thing or two!"

"Mother," Goddess she was incorrigible, "I am not walking about in some old moth-ridden feather boa and frolicking in a soggy giant champagne glass, just for pervy guests to, well, PERVE! I am the caterer, a professional caterer, not some two-bit dancer!"

"Well, *I'll* give it a go!" tinkled Sicily, "you just hand me a pair of pasties and a diamante thong!" Adrianna Jasmine had to swallow back the bile.

Ugh, I feel a vomit coming on!

"I am *not* taking you."

"I wasn't suggesting that you should, darling," exclaimed Sicily innocently, "I would never dream..."

"You're too old, anyway," broke in Adrianna Jasmine. "Besides, all the dancers have already been hired *and* they're professional, from professional institutes."

"Don't be ridiculous, darling," said Sicily, sounding almost bored. *"Oh help me!"* implored Adrianna Jasmine. "You are talking to *thee* professional. Goddess! You know when I was a young girl living in Paris as a *dancer* in The Moulin Rouge, The Moulin Rouge, darling can you believe it! I was so exceptionally brilliant that I used to drive this young artist chap to drink because he was so infatuated with me."

"Infuriated, more like," mumbled Adrianna Jasmine under her breath.

"He would buy a table at the front of the stage every night, without fail," Sicily twittered on, "simply to watch me dance. He would then send me a bunch of red roses after every performance and endless bottles of champagne. He was captivated by me. He practically begged me to be his muse. He didn't want to paint anything else and wanted nothing more in life than to have me hanging up on his wall."

"Obviously!" said Adrianna Jasmine.

"He said art was dead unless my beauty was captured on canvas and expressed in swirls of oily paint, to re-awaken the art world once more. Apparently my face was the key! I often wondered what Michelangelo's opinion would have been on the subject; after all, he did a spectacular job on that ceiling. But still, what's aesthetically pleasing to one isn't always to another. I was eventually broken down of course and I allowed him to paint me until *his* paint ran out, if you know what I mean. Ha, ha! No, no, I was splashing about in champagne before those amateurs were even born. Professionals. Pah!"

"Mother!" said Adrianna Jasmine sounding more like the adult, "Firstly, keep your disgusting escapades of your youth to yourself. I really don't want to know. And secondly, you were his muse when the plague hit Europe; times have changed."

Unperturbed by her daughter's insults, Sicily continued to plough on.

"And," she added with forced assurance, "I was a dancer at the Moulin Rouge, the Moulin Rouge, darling. Can you believe it! And what *we* did was a damned site sexier and more risqué than those so called Pussy Cat Dollies, or anything those two-bit boppers will ever do at that silly little party tomorrow night. What they need is me, twenty years ago, and a couple of Russians. Oh, they wouldn't know what'd hit them!'

"Yes, mother," sighed Adrianna Jasmine, "but it's not twenty years ago and you're now a middle-aged witch!"

"Oh, you're a cruel girl," said Sicily, her voice low and pained at her daughter's spiteful comment, she hated being reminded that she was no longer 25. Still, she thought with content, even at her age she still had it!

"Anyway," said Sicily flippantly changing the subject, "will you be using 'magic' in your cooking?"

"Yes!" said Adrianna Jasmine firmly, "why?"

"Oh, nothing, blueberry pancake," said Sicily toying with her daughter, "I just don't want anything coming back upon on you thrice now, do I? So watch where you point that wand!"

Adrianna Jasmine sucked in a soothing waft of air, in the hope it would calm her down.

"And why would anything come back upon me thrice, mother?"

"Well," said Sicily her voice now serious, "you are using magic to put people under the influence, darling. Some people get sent down for things like that."

That's it! Thought Adrianna Jasmine, *I've had enough, she's comparing me to some loser in a club who has to spike women's drinks in order to get laid.*

"I don't spike my menu so I can bed some underage youth in a night club, mother, I do it to help people, to spread a little cheer in a miserable world, to evoke laughter and good will and believe it or not, I don't want anything in return, just a happier world for all to live in!" Goddess, why was she explaining herself? Her mother was a fine one to talk in regards to appeasing the universe! The things that woman has used magic for in her time, it's a wonder she's not on the black witch list. Adrianna Jasmine continued with her rant. "I sat at my altar last night and said my prayers to the Goddess like a good little witch, explained my actions of manipulating people's subconscious and I am now at one with the divine powers, now was there anything else, mother? A recipe you wanted or something? Come on, I've got to get back into the kitchen."

"No," answered her mother.

"Thank Goddess!" said her daughter.

"How's that lovely cat of yours?"

"Grrr!"

"Is he still alive? I do hope he is, I rather like Jupiter 102"

"Yes," Adrianna Jasmine answered through clenched teeth, "Jupiter *ten* is very much alive and meowing."

"That's good, flip flop, because you must come to terms with the fact that you have a little…problem?"

"Bye, mother!" Snapped Adrianna Jasmine and hung up the phone.

Once the phone was safely switched off, Adrianna Jasmine took in a deep lung-full of air, exhaled slowly and repeated the process a few times until her blood pressure returned to its customary status of normal. The witch took a large gulp of her delicious hazel nut mochaccino and felt comforted by its sweet creamy richness. She then heard a little "meow," and peered down to find Jupiter 10 coiling around her ankles. She picked him up and cuddled his soft silky fur into her cheek.

"OK, all calm again now," sighed the witch, then the phone rang. With an exasperated huff, she dropped Jupiter 10 onto the floor with a thud, resulting in the cat grumpily skulking off into the hallway.

I don't believe her, she thought angrily, *what now?* Maddened by her mother's infuriating persistence and ever growing ability to frustrate her, Adrianna Jasmine answered the phone.

"What mother? What, what, what?! No, I haven't been misusing my broom…" "Honey, it's me, Sarah!"

Adrianna Jasmine immediately felt her anger disperse.

"Oh, sorry, Sarah,' said Adrianna Jasmine with relief, "I thought you were the big bad witch coming to finish me off."

Sarah chuckled knowingly,

"Ah, don't tell me," said Sarah with a gentle calmness to her voice, "the lovely Sicily has been on the phone to you and now completely ruined what was, only moments ago, a perfectly happy day?"

Adrianna Jasmine sighed, "Spot on!" Sarah, who was an extremely cheerful person with a real zest for life, was Adrianna Jasmine's best friend, who, along with her parents, owned a large coffee shop called "Princess Sarah's Magic and Coffee House". Sarah, like Adrianna Jasmine, is also a witch. "Yes, your conclusion is correct. My mother has just irritated the living hell out of me and I need to calm down."

"So, calm down," said Sarah impassively, "anyway, I've called for two things: one is to order a box of chocolate chip cupcakes, a large coffee-walnut and maple syrup cake, a batch of scrumptious Rocky Road and a simple Victoria Sponge for Monday morning please." (As we have just recently established, Sarah owns a magic-come-coffee shop, and just to let you know, Adrianna Jasmine makes all their cakes!) "Also, to confirm that I will be at your beck and call tomorrow night, at Pigwell's party." (Sarah helps Adrianna Jasmine out from time to time with her business.)

"That's great, thanks for that, Sarah," Adrianna Jasmine sounded relived. "That's a huge weight off my mind. This party is going to be packed full of pretentious popsicles, wannabes, skinny minis frolicking in giant Champagne flutes and so much testosterone that you could bottle it. I need all the… oh, Goddess!" Adrianna Jasmine cried out, slapping a hand across her forehead.

"What?" said Sarah clearly startled.

"It gets worse."

Sarah pulled her eyebrows together. "How could it get worse? It sounds like it's going to be nothing short of fabulous, to think, all those famous people there." Adrianna Jasmine winced. "*I* like celebrities," stated Sarah firmly, "and glamour. *You're* the one who has a problem with them and believes that celebrity magazines are harmful to one's mental health and... oh, Goddess!" The penny had dropped with a bang. Sarah felt horror rise up through her toes. "Oh, you didn't," tested Sarah, "you haven't called "Serve up a Storm," have you? Please tell me you didn't." Adrianna Jasmine just about managed to muster a squeak down the phone.

"OK, we're doomed," said Sarah dramatically, "have you forgotten the last time we hired the services of that bumbling, incompetent agency?! "Serve up a Storm" only employs the worst catering staff in the history of civilization, we are absolutely done for!"

"Yes, yes, I know," Adrianna Jasmine agreed pathetically. "If you just let me explain..."

"*And* you do realize that the waitresses will be too busy slapping on lip gloss to serve the guests?"

"I know, I know," groaned Adrianna Jasmine, "but like I said, if you just..."

"*And* terrified of breaking their acrylic nails. So you do realize that they won't actually be carrying anything, we'll have to do it *and* my Goddess you can forget about serving up the snails. You might as well face it now, they won't make it out of the kitchen, do you really think they'd go anywhere near them?"

Adrianna Jasmine let out a long sigh. She hadn't forgotten the last time she painstakingly used the agency that supplies waiters who are actually out of work actors and models. Ugh, especially the bumbling blonde aspiring actress Salome, who dropped her lippy into the giant chocolate fountain and all hell broke loose. Although in all fairness, she did dive in and retrieve it with the skill of an elite athlete (probably due to it being a Mac). Goddess, how did this day turn into such a hellish nightmare?

"And the men are worse," Sarah battled on with the force of Napoleon, she wasn't even coming up for air, "all they seem to do is pose, like they're living in the Littlewoods catalogue or something, and it takes them about an hour to put one pea on a plate!"

"I'm not serving peas tomorrow!" Adrianna Jasmine added quickly, hoping her little announcement would appease her friend. It didn't!

For what appeared to be an age, the two witches argued down the telephone, with Sarah almost threatening to quit unless they came up with alternative staffing arrangements. She suggested that they hired from some other agency, which would provide them with something a bit more professional. However, Adrianna Jasmine explained that there was no other agency available that evening, hence the reason as to why she had hired "Serve up a Storm". They were literally the last resort. Sarah huffed and puffed, she was very close to throwing in the towel, there was absolutely no way on this mortal realm she would be prepared to work with a group of precious, and precocious, brats. Then she had a brain wave.

"I know!" she announced, her eyes gleaming like the She Devil, "We'll drug them."

At first, Adrianna Jasmine thought that Sarah was stark staring raving bonkers and she didn't exactly appreciate the malice in Sarah's voice either, but then again...Adrianna Jasmine thought for a moment. "Drug them? That's a bit harsh, don't you think? My mother has already compared my liking for sprinkling food with happy mood enhancing magic to some weasel faced loser slipping something nasty into an unsuspecting girl's drink at a night club, so maybe not, Sarah."

Sarah snorted. "Pah! What does she know? I say we do it! These are desperate times, Jazzy and desperate times call for desperate magic." Adrianna Jasmine contemplated for a few moments, it was true they were desperate. Besides, it wouldn't be hard, just a little spell..."No, it's obscene, Sarah, the three-fold law would never allow it!"

Sarah sighed heavily. "Yes- it-would!" She practically said through her teeth.

"Wow, you're full of the joys of spring today, aren't you? If you become any darker you'll disappear. Okay then, explain how we can fool the great law. I'm dying to know!"

"Easy," said Sarah coolly, "we clear it with them." Now Adrianna Jasmine was really confused. "We just explain to the law *why* we are drugging the hired help without bringing us into the equation."

"Err, how?" quizzed the confused Adrianna Jasmine, "the whole reason why we're even considering performing some kind of mind meddling spell is to make life easier for *us*! Oh, we are *so* going to pay!"

"Like I said," Sarah continued ignoring the alarm bells Adrianna Jasmine was so clearly hearing, "we won't pay if you leave us out of it." Sarah treated herself to a deep breath. "Look, we just explain to the Goddess during potion time that the whole reason those idiots are at that party at all is not to earn a decent wage but to network so they can mingle with record producers and model scouts."

"And..." said Adrianna Jasmine still confused.

"Well, no one likes an overzealous wannabe, do they? It can put you right off! You can bet your Book of Shadows they'll be pestering all the big names, they could even get thrown out into the cold for being a nuisance. So this is where our potion comes into play. We create the potion to manufacture a more professional, courteous team, which in turn will indeed help our night run much more smoothly. But we don't mention that bit."

"We don't?"

"No we don't! During brewing time we'll tell the three-fold law that the purpose of the spell is purely to help the team on their way to stardom." Adrianna Jasmine raised her eyebrows. "Like I said before, no model or talent scout likes an overzealous wannabe, or a body dripping in attitude, it puts you right off. This little spell will offer the crew the ability to appear more poised, graceful, cool and elegant, much more appealing. Who knows? They just might catch the eye of some bigwig in the entertainment business, thanks to their new *temporary* personality. Plus, they'll learn the value of a good honest night's graft; it'll be fine. A piece of your cake!"

Adrianna Jasmine still wasn't convinced, but as they concluded earlier, what choice did they have?

Do it yourself Citrus Bang-Bang Boom!

Treat yourself to a citrus scented candle, such as orange or lime. Run a bath and add 3 drops of rosemary essential oil, 2 drops of lemon essential oil and 2 drops of frankincense essential oil to the water. Now get in, you'll be zinging in no time!

'Make sure you are not allergic to any of the essential oils, hives are so unattractive, darling!'
(Sicily Poppleapple Mariposa Forthright Punch 2008)

Chapter 2
Tallulah Toffee

It was the day of the party and Adrianna Jasmine was on track. She had prepared her tidbits and was now storing them safely away in high quality Tupperware boxes, ready to be transported to Pigwell's house. Her vegetables were all sliced and nipped to perfection, the crème brûlée all cooled and set, the Beef Wellingtons wrapped up neatly in their all butter pastry coat and the beautiful rich spaghetti sauce simmered to excellence. All her little cakes had been artistically iced and neatly placed into large, lined cardboard boxes, the chocolate petit fours were chilling in the fridge and the snails were plump and fit to burst from their monstrous diet of garlic and herbs. So far, so good!

However, as Adrianna Jasmine continued working on, she was suddenly struck down with an overwhelming sense of nausea: her tummy appeared to be full of butterflies desperately flying about trying to make their escape.

"That's strange," she thought out loud, "what's brought this on? I haven't eaten anything that I shouldn't. Am I ill or just nervous about tonight? No, no," she dismissed, "everything is under control, my best friend will be there with me, I'm drugging the hired help, I've magically spiked the food and I've catered for parties like this many a time. Piece of my scrumptious pistachio rocky road cheese cake! Besides, it's usually Sarah who works herself up into a tizzy at events such as these, not me!"

Sarah, unlike Adrianna Jasmine, worships and admires celebrities. She pours over everything from Heat to Hello, watches re-runs of E Entertainment and is a member of no less than 20 celebrity web sites, including Jordan's! *Hmmm...so why all the butterflies?*

It was approaching 10.00am and it was time for Adrianna Jasmine to transfer her tidbits into her ice blue catering van. She loved her van, she loved the colour (ice blue was a very cool and calming colour, very soothing for a city cursed with such heavy traffic) and the fact that it bore her company's name "The Magic of Food," along with her web address.

The van was fitted with two refrigerators, an oven, storage units and a sink! Adrianna Jasmine had fallen head over heels with the van the moment she saw it at The Catering Show at London's Earls Court, almost three years earlier. Disappointingly, she was unable to purchase the dreamy kitchen on wheels due to the little matter of cost; it was way out of the young witch's price range. Enter Sicily to the financial rescue! Every now and then Sicily surprises her daughter with some sort of random announcement, decision or gesture, rather like the time she decided to take on a second job as a live nude model for aspiring art students. Although this particular surprise was rather nice: she picked up the cheque! Yep, Sicily treated her daughter to her trusty van and is partly the reason as to why Adrianna Jasmine is in business!

Now, you may be wondering how on earth Sicily could afford a second-hand, but very well-conditioned ice blue catering van on a teacher's and part time nude life model salary. Surely, they don't pay *that* well? Perhaps she sells spells to dark witches in order to raise a little extra capital, or other things…? Don't be foolish! Sicily maybe a little wild and free spirited, it's her pagan roots you know, but she's not a brazen hussy. No, the reason is far less sinister. You see when Adrianna Jasmine was in her early teens, Henry Forthright Punch had become very suspicious about Sicily. She was spending far too much time at her flat in Islington, and he came to the conclusion that she was up to all sorts of tricks with another fellow. So in order to convince her husband she was not up to foul play and, more importantly, witchcraft, poor Sicily had to reluctantly sacrifice Wicca for a happy marriage, resulting in letting her beloved flat.

On a more positive note, letting the property worked out rather well financially, as she made a tidy monthly profit, although she never touched a penny of it. Sicily felt too guilty for losing the sanctuary that allowed her and her daughter, who was at a critical learning age, to perform magic in privacy. As a result Sicily let the money simply flourish in a high interest rate savings account, perfect for when her lovely daughter needed it. It was indeed *needed* by the lovely Adrianna Jasmine when she decided to go into business for herself and consequently was able to purchase her trusty van along with other pieces of equipment: a Kenwood Chef for example, and a melon ball scoop!

The weather was cool and dry, Adrianna Jasmine felt hot and sticky as she loaded up the van. She was perspiring and her long hair was sticking itself onto her baking neck. So she twisted her mane into a wispy knot and secured tightly with two chop sticks. The effect was instantly cooling, her skin could breathe again.

She couldn't wait to have a nice shower and wash away all the hard work and toil that was sticking to her body like dead fingers, causing the witch to feel sluggish.

As she loaded up the last of the Tupperware boxes, Adrianna Jasmine glanced at her watch and considered the time.

"Hmmm...10.30pm. I must jump into the shower soon and get a move on. Oh, I hope Sarah isn't late getting over here."

She slammed shut the door to her van, locked it and took her mobile phone out of her jeans. She needed to contact Sarah and inform her that they would be leaving for Pigwell's in approximately one hour. She decided to text Sarah opposed to phoning her friend, otherwise they would waste time gossiping.

Will B leaving in 1hr, u ok to get here for then? LV AJ

With luck, hopefully Sarah was already on her way, and not caught up in a rush at the coffee house. Apparently Sarah's mother, Blaire, was a little put out that her daughter would not be working today and in her stead was a 16 year old school-leaver, named Iggy.

Moments later a text arrived; **will be there! S x.**

Good, thought Adrianna Jasmine with a satisfied grin and went back into her flat to enjoy a nice hot shower.

Adrianna Jasmine walked into her heavenly bathroom and began to run her shower. She set the temperature to hot, then stepped away and began to undress. As the water jets splashed from the shower head into the free-standing Victorian bath, the bathroom itself began to steam up, creating a light, soft mist. She reached for her puff and squeezed lemon, lime and orange shower gel (Citrus Bang-Bang-Boom!) on top of it.

"Gorgeous," she cooed as she breathed in the gel's fruity aroma. The shower gel was very special, not only did it smell as if it had been directly squeezed from the fruit itself, but this shower gel was *magically* invigorating. Citrus fruit shower gels, which are commonly found in most popular high street shops, are known for their *supposed* ability to perk one up and liven up the senses. However, they are nothing compared to the gel Adrianna Jasmine uses. This stuff is special, it packs a punch! It could energize your body, even if it was racked full of flu or alcohol! Plus it could keep you revitalized throughout the hardest day of your life, due to its slow releasing, spirit lifting aromas (similar to slow releasing carbohydrates!). You would never smell of BO, as the offensive odor would be terminated without mercy by the adorable whiff of lemon and lime soufflé drizzled in a sweet orange sauce.

Now you're probably thinking, "Hey *I* could do with some of that!" and yes, you would be right. Although, dear reader, Citrus Bang-Bang-Boom! is a *Tallulah Toffee* product and consequently only available to Witching folk. Tallulah Toffee products have been around for about 50 years and Tallulah herself is now in her eighties. She has been, and still is, creating the most marvelous and delicious beauty products ever seen on the face of the earth and if mere mortals could get their hot little hands on them they would never buy anything from the shops again. You see, Tallulah's products really do work, no, they REALLY DO WORK!!! Toffee Products obtain very special ingredients and top scientists of the mortal world would love to know all about them. Well tough!!! You see, when Tallulah was a young sprightly thing she travelled deep into the heart of the Brazilian rain forest to explore its rich natural habitat. By all accounts, her exploration went exceptionally well. Due to using a little magic on her journey - for example, good guidance spells and location spells - Tallulah was able to unearth extraordinary fruits, plants, animals and insects that were later revealed to be proficient in improving one's skin. Moreover, due to the ever-increasing destruction of the rain forest, these beauties of the natural world would never be discovered again: they are now all extinct, and her secrets will never be discovered by anyone else. More power to the witch! These new findings were taken back to Tallulah's private palace on her remote island in the South Pacific (she is unquestionably rich) and were studied, squeezed, juiced, milked and freeze dried; then blended with more well-known ingredients, such as aloe vera, essential oils, boswolox and pentapeptides. So this, dear reader, along with chanting secret magic during the mixing process, is how the woman is capable of creating the most stupendous beauty products on the face of the earth.

Her work, however, is top secret; all her employers are under strict magical surveillance spells, in order to prevent any mischief or disloyal behaviour! These spells are truly wondrous, they simply disallow an employee of Tallulah Toffee Products from spilling the beans about her product secrets, and believe me, she has covered every angle.

Her most triumphant spell is the Muddling Memory Spell. The spell disallows her employees to remember any chant or ingredients used to create Toffee Products outside Tallulah's factory. Once they step out of the Toffee Factory, they can barely remember what they do for a living, let alone remember long lists of ingredients and incantations. There are also other types of security spells used to protect Toffee's wonders. For example, one silly chap named Hector was caught writing notes about a certain face mask formula inside the factory. His paper kept turning into ash every time he wrote anything down. The spell knew he was writing out the formula in order to sell it to a mortal cosmetic company; the spell wasn't having any of it.

Or there was another occasion when an equally silly woman, Eudora Gem-Stone, tried to tape-record the chant used for the Ever Lasting Youth Night Cream. When she played it back, the spell had recorded her words in gobble-dee-gook, which is a completely unrecognizable language. Both employees' positions were terminated without references.

All Tallulah Toffee products are truly remarkable and are the greatest on the planet. Most witches of the world use them, including Sicily, which is partly the reason why the fifty-two-year-old witch looks so fabulous. Some witches, however, simply can't be bothered with all that and therefore don't look particularly glamorous or good for their age. If they simply bathed in Toffee's Aqua Marine Dream

Age Recovery Bath Oil, exfoliated with Toffee's Back to Baby Skin Exfoliation Scrub and smothered their body head to toe in Toffee's Wrinkle Dissolve Dark Chocolate and Marshmallow, *it's a miracle* Cream, they would soon look a million dollars! Ohh...and the Toffee's Everlasting Hair Removing Ointment wouldn't go amiss, either; perfect for those stubborn sprouts of hair on ones chin and upper lip! The products are renowned for their ability to dissolve blackheads, dry up white heads within seconds of application, smooth out wrinkles before your very eyes and tighten tired, old skin to look like a six month old baby's botty. All creams, gels, mousses, lotions, scrubs and masks smell utterly divine and are packaged in delightful bottles. Some are carved out of semi-precious stones or tough plastics that change colour simply because they can, and so they look delightful on a bathroom shelf. So there you have it, Toffee Products. Some believe the products to be the greatest find the world has ever seen and they could possibly be right. Some will never have the chance to sample them. One thing is for sure, Adrianna Jasmine is Citrus Bang-Bang-Boom's biggest fan!

"The air disturbance by the wings of a single butterfly is enough to change the weather"
(Marc Perkel)

Chapter 3
The Mystic Odessa

"I'm in here," called Adrianna Jasmine, stepping into her matching underwear.

Sarah made her way into her friend's bedroom and found the witch pulling up her jeans. "Hi, Jazzy, how's tricks?" Sarah enquired in her usual happy-go-lucky mood; her blazing red curls were bouncing about excitedly on her head.

"Hmm, OK-ish," Adrianna Jasmine answered in a lengthened sigh, her tummy was still in knots and she was concerned why it hadn't unravelled itself.

"Really?" enquired Sarah, concerned, as she plonked herself down on the big marshmallow of a bed. "What's up?"

"I'm not too sure," answered Adrianna Jasmine distantly, applying some pink blusher to her cuter than a button face. "My tummy feels a bit upset, you know, similar to how yours felt before your driving test!"

Sarah winced and shuddered at the memory. She cast her mind back to 3.52pm almost six years earlier as the driving examiner loomed menacingly towards her. "Hmmm… I bet it's not *that* bad. Anyway, it's probably diarrhoea."

"No, it's not!" Adrianna Jasmine said, laughing. "It's like nerves or something." "You sure?" teased Sarah, "I can nip out and buy an emergency supply of Imodium if you like?"

Adrianna Jasmine giggled again, "No, you don't have to!"

"Ok, well don't say I didn't offer when you come up short as you bend over into the oven to retrieve your beef wellingtons! Anyway, tell me where my uniforms are."

Adrianna Jasmine sidled across to her wardrobe and pulled out two sets of uniforms. The first uniform was a light weight and casual ensemble consisting of grey slacks and an ice blue fitted baby T, with "the magic of food" written across the front. The second uniform was a black Karen Millen fitted shift dress.

"I take it we're wearing the casual stuff now and the little black number later on tonight?"

Adrianna Jasmine nodded and Sarah slipped into her casual uniform. Moments later, she stood up and admired her image in the mirror. Sarah was an athletic size 12, medium height, graced with attractive features, blessed with the most creamy, blemish free skin on the planet, speckled with golden freckles, and of course, her head was adorned with thick, rich, red bouncy curls that sprung around with all the energy of a pogo stick. She reminded Adrianna Jasmine of the colours of autumn.

"Not bad at all," said Sarah as she admired her reflection in the mirror, "If I were a bloke, I wouldn't say no!"

Adrianna Jasmine rolled her eyes and giggled at her fabulous friend, "You wouldn't?"

"Nope," said Sarah confidently, "However, the problem is they don't say yes either, at the moment!"

"Oh…why's that?" asked Adrianna Jasmine, who was pinning up her hair into a soft cascading French twist.

"I'm just a bit unlucky in love right now," sighed Sarah, "I can't seem to attract any suitable beau."

Love wasn't the best conversational subject to engage in with Adrianna Jasmine. However, she sympathized with her friend, as she knew love was important for Sarah (Sarah wasn't as dedicated to witchcraft as Adrianna Jasmine and most certainly would put love before magic).

"You will, sweetie," soothed Adrianna Jasmine, "perhaps if you don't look so hard, it'll find you."

"Perhaps," pondered Sarah, "anyway, it looks like you're the one who's going to be lucky in love at the moment, not me. Bloody typical!"

Adrianna Jasmine nearly stabbed herself in the eye with a kirby grip.

"Ouch!" she wailed. "Look what you made me do!"

Sarah giggled, ignoring her friend's eye-watering pain. "Yep, pretty soon too," said Sarah with assurance, "Odessa told…"

"Odessa?" broke in Adrianna Jasmine sharply, still clutching her watery eye, "What? You went to see Odessa? Goddess you are desperate, my girl!" (Odessa was a psychic, medium, tarot card, crystal ball and tea leaves reader from Russia who had set up shop in the corner of Princess Sarah's Magic and Coffee House, next to the aromatherapy candle collections).

Sarah ignored Adrianna Jasmine's insubordinate remark and continued on regardless. "No, I didn't go to *see* Odessa: *she* tracked *me* down. She believes that she has learnt some important information concerning someone close to my heart with the initials A and J."

"So?" scoffed Adriana Jasmine, "that doesn't necessarily mean that's me!"

"Yeah, right!" said Sarah sarcastically, "Like I know twenty other people whose first name begins with an A and then a J! She shook her head. Unbelievable! "Anyway, she also declared that the particular person in question has a little *addiction* problem?"

"An addiction problem!" yelled Adrianna Jasmine, "I don't have an addiction problem. Am I a junkie heroin addict?! What's the woman talking about? I'll sue, I'll curse, I'll hex…oh, she could be talking about *anybody*!"

Sarah stared blankly at her friend, "Yeah like I said before, there are sooo many other people I know whose initials are A and J *and* who enjoy *shape shifting into their cats*? She was very specific, you know."

"What?" snapped Adrianna Jasmine. "Great. Now it seems everyone knows about my little…hobby."

Ignoring the steam dangerously rising from Adrianna Jasmine's head, Sarah ploughed on with her tale. "According to the Mystic Odessa, who described you to a Tee, by the way…"

"I know the blasted woman!" shot Adrianna Jasmine, "of course she would describe me to a Tee, she sees me every day at the blinking coffee house, I'm hardly a psychic vision!"

Sarah, who simply blocked out her friend's high pitched screeching and hysteria, continued on calmly.

"According to Odessa, you're heading straight down the love road, my girl, and by all accounts there's no service station stop either!"

Feeling almost dizzy from hyperventilation, Adrianna Jasmine sat on the bed and tried to calm herself down with a soothing breathing technique she had learnt at yoga. It wasn't working! Goddess, love really did terrify her.

"Well," said Adrianna Jasmine, her arms folded across her chest and huffing so hard it almost cut off her blood supply to her heart, "I think it's a load of rubbish. I personally believe the Mystique Odessa to be a little...vague in regards to her psychic skills. It's all nonsense."

Sarah raised her eyebrows. "I'm dying to hear this one!" Her eyes gleaming with intrigue.

"Well, I'm no physic," said Adrianna Jasmine matter-of-factly, "but don't you think somehow *I* would have clocked on to the fact that something inappropriate was about to happen to me? A sign or something, perchance? I am a witch, you know."

"Err, so what are you saying?" asked Sarah, "you know full well Odessa is a gifted fortune teller and if she says you're going to meet someone you are jolly well going to meet someone!"

"Oh, really?" Adrianna Jasmine snorted, "I don't believe it for a second."

Sarah's mouth nearly hit the floor. "Are you insinuating that the woman is not authentic?"

"No...well, not exactly, but..." fumbled Adrianna Jasmine.

"How dare you!" Sarah boomed.

"Whoa there, take some unflustered floss, will you, Sarah and calm down...Goddess!" *Bloody love,* she thought, look what trouble it was causing and they were only talking about it! "All I'm saying is," said Adrianna Jasmine trying to keep calm, "that it *has been known*, from time to time, that psychics get it wrong and in the worst cases, the psychics aren't even...genuine? These people are clever you know!"

That was it, Sarah felt as if she would burst with fury. Her nostrils flared out and her eyes became stony.

"So, you think my family has allowed some hoax to rent a space in our shop, then, do you?"

"No, no, of course not…" said Adrianna Jasmine, frustration and fluster rising up through her voice.

"So we can con innocent people out of their money, then, do you?"

"What? Now that's going a bit too far… I didn't say…"

"Because I know my family isn't quite in the same league as *your* family when it comes to the craft, but there is one thing that we're not, and that's *dishonest*."

"I didn't say that you were," tried Adrianna Jasmine desperately, "Sarah this is becoming silly now," but Sarah had not quite finished with her rant.

"My family are still witches and *we* can tell if a person is lying about their supernatural ability and the Mystic Odessa is most certainly not a fraud, give her a little credit."

Adrianna Jasmine looked down at the floor, feeling ashamed of herself. "Sorry," she mumbled, "I just don't like what I'm hearing." Adrianna Jasmine expressed a long well overdue sigh. "I don't crave or long for love in my life, Sarah, it almost…repulses me if I'm honest, I don't want to hear this, any of this! I live for my craft; my craft is my passion, it's my soul, my everything! Why complicate things?" Sarah shrugged her shoulders; she decided to not say another word, what was the point? If there were any truth in the prediction, Adrianna Jasmine would soon know about it. "Anyway," said Adrianna Jasmine with forced enthusiasm, "let's not talk so much rubbish, we need to think about making a move soon."

Adrianna Jasmine padded out of the room into the kitchen: she needed to feed Jupiter 10 so he wouldn't go hungry while she was out. As she opened the can of cat food, she spoke quietly to herself.

"The Mystique Odessa is *wrong*, love in the conventional form is not for me, it's not my destiny, never has been, never will be."

She smiled to herself as she forked Jupiter 10's food into his little bowl, then looked up at the door to see Sarah standing there leaning against the frame, arms crossed loosely.

"OK, look," she suggested in a more diplomatic voice, "I know you're not looking for love, but what if love is looking for *you*?"

Adrianna Jasmine turned to face her friend. "That's impossible," she scoffed, "I don't put myself into any positions where love can find me."

Sarah smiled knowingly. "Even *your* powers are no match for love Adrianna Jasmine, if it wants you it *will* find you."

Sarah's words ran a chill through Adrianna Jasmine's spine, it was true, love could find her if it wanted to, love was the strongest power on the face of the earth.

"Why are we having this conversation again, Sarah?" asked Adrianna Jasmine clearly upset, "I'm aware of what Odessa said, but it's a bit ridiculous now, so can we stop? We've got a busy night ahead of us and I'm up to here already! So Sarah *please,* just leave it alone."

Feeling slightly guilty that she had provoked her friend into feeling unhappy, she apologized by offering her a hug. "Sorry, Jazzy. I didn't mean to go over the top, you know what I'm like!"

Adrianna Jasmine smiled and nodded a vigorous "YES!" Sarah threw her arms up in surrender. "OK. I'll say no more," she said, then offered to help Adrianna Jasmine unload the rest of the fridge.

"By the way…" inquired Sarah, her voice creepy with curiosity. "How's that stomach of yours, still churning?"

"It's OK," answered Adrianna Jasmine weakly, "I'm going to have a little ginger beer before we go, that should ease it."

"Yeah, why don't you do that?" suggested Sarah with a patronizing smile, "ginger's good for upset tums…still, I wonder what brought it on?"

Adrianna Jasmine shrugged and walked out of the kitchen.

Sarah looked on after her friend and smiled wryly to herself.

"Anticipation, my little witch, that's what brought it on, anticipation."

'Grab a piece of cotton wool and put droplets of vanilla extract onto it, or perhaps lemon oil if you prefer, place it in the middle of your fridge, and say farewell to nasty niffs and odours'
(A tip from Adrianna Jasmine)

Chapter 4
What a Splendid Kitchen!

As Adriana Jasmine and Sarah drove through the impressive and somewhat intimidating driveway to Casa Pigwell, they couldn't help but feel slightly overwhelmed. The house was enormous.

"Wow, wow, wow," exclaimed Sarah, who was simply fizzing with excitement, "it's huge! I can't believe we're actually about to go into such a gigantic house! Goddess, I thought my Grandma's house was big, it had four bedrooms; to me it was like a mansion and I always remember," she added hurriedly talking quicker than the speed of light, "I was never allowed in *the best* room for fear of dirtying the carpet, she was a right old cow! I bet he's got at least ten bedrooms, all en suite and definitely a state-of-the-art gym, sauna, steam room. Goddess, he's got to have a pool and his own cinema and…"

"Whoa, calm down, little miss star struck," said Adrianna Jasmine, who appeared to be completely unfazed by the splendor of the house. "We need to give the impression that we cater in places like this all the time, no big deal, so say goodbye to the mesmerized country bumpkin image and hello to the sophisticated professional, OK?"

With eyes on stalks Sarah nodded vigorously, Adrianna Jasmine rolled her eyes, "Yeah, just like that," she mumbled to herself.

As the witches pulled up outside the main entrance, they came face to face with a prickly looking woman holding a clipboard. She was abruptly signalling to them to take the van around the side of the house towards the tradesmen's entrance. The woman was about the same age as Adrianna Jasmine, slim and stylishly dressed. Her face was attractive, although spoilt by her somewhat angry expression.

"Oh, that's charming that is, being made to go around to the unloading entrance," said Sarah with a huff, "now I *do* feel like the hired help!"

"Sarah!" Said Adrianna Jasmine firmly, "we *are* the hired help!"

"And don't I know it!" shot back Sarah grumpily and then she turned her attention back towards the prickly woman with the clipboard. "Goddess if she scrunches her face up any harder she'll be crippled with crinkles before she hits 30. Actually, she'll probably use Botox."

"That charming specimen of a woman is none other than Pigwell's PA, Hannah. As far as I can recall, I found her to be rather spiky on the phone the other day. Perhaps she's had a bad day?"

"More like a bad life!" remarked Sarah frostily, and then to Adrianna Jasmine's astonishment, Sarah unexpectedly let out a loud screech.

Adrianna Jasmine jumped.

"What? What's going on?"

It seemed that Sarah had turned towards the passenger window, to open the van door, and like a scene from a horror movie, Hannah's glowering face had appeared from out of nowhere, inches away from Sarah's nose. The unexpected image of the PA caused Sarah to scream out in fright and sheer shock. Adrianna Jasmine had to turn away to stifle a laugh.

'Goddess, that was hilarious!' she thought wickedly.

Sarah, whose heart was beating faster than a raver on amphetamines, was not impressed, and so left it to her "boss" to deal with the demonic creature with the possessed clip board and poisoned pen.

"I can't talk to her," grumbled Sarah under rapid breath, her heart still beating dangerously fast, "I'll vex her if I do, so help me, Goddess."

A few moments later, her door was gently opened by a sympathetic Adrianna Jasmine.

"Come on you," she coaxed, "it's all right. She's gone now."
Sarah heaved a sigh of relief and slid out of the van.
"She's a right bitch that one, what *is* her problem?"
"Lack of sex," said Adrianna Jasmine nonchalantly, "come on, help me carry this stuff up these stairs; they lead into the kitchen."

Over in London's Canary Wharf, Taylor Jameson was sitting at his desk in the offices of Fantastico Banquetto, the famous and critically acclaimed food magazine. As he gazed out of his window onto the river, Taylor lazily let out a large yawn. Following a heavy night of rich food and wine, the food critique was flagging. He was craving nothing more than disappearing home, putting his feet up in front of the TV, sipping a cold bottle of beer and tucking into a large stuffed-crust pizza. But, alas, that was never going to happen, not tonight, anyway. He was assigned to critique the food and drink at some pop tarts launch party.

To cap it off, Taylor's boss, Archie Soams, had personally requested that he babysit Fantastico Banquetto's top Italian food critic, Luca Placidi that night, who was notoriously well known for his love of fast cars, fast women and fine food. The little pocket dynamo was simply filled to the brim with energy and Taylor was worried that his own poor, wornout body wouldn't keep up. Apparently, at this precise moment in time, Luca was zooming round London like Michel Schumacher in a hired red Ferrari.

Taylor shook his head and laughed at the thought of Luca living it up in his red babe-magnet, with La Traviata blaring out from the speakers, whilst peering through Armani sunglasses. Shame it was grey and cloudy out.

He sighed again. Luca had actually called him this morning, offering a day out in the hot car, in order to tear after hot women, but Taylor had politely declined. Eighteen months earlier, given half the chance, Taylor would have happily joined Luca in the offer of tearing around London in a Ferrari, sashaying into all best bars and restaurants and flirting with young nubile things, but, as it was, Taylor could think of nothing less appealing.

Drowsily, he tapped away at his keyboard: he still hadn't completed his write up about the restaurant he had sampled last night.

He had eaten at The Oyster Pearl, a swanky new restaurant over in Knightsbridge and although he couldn't fault the fresh seafood platter, sumptuous monkfish thermador and the trio of delectable chocolate desserts that he had enjoyed for pudding, the whole experience had been exhausting.

This was thanks to the nauseating Lexi Howler, the owner of The Oyster Pearl, smothering herself all over him like a rash. She was unconditionally and categorically head over heels in lust with Taylor and boy didn't she let him know it! It was embarrassing. To add to Taylor's gloom, Lexi Howler had informed him, in between attempts to stick her tongue in his ear, that she was attending a little party the following night at her good friend Byron Pigwell's house, if he cared to join her.

'Oh blast', he thought miserably, *'that's the same party I've got to attend tomorrow night, great, that's two nights of the Howl I'll have to endure. I wonder if they still sell chastity belts? Ear plugs wouldn't go amiss, either'!*

"So what do you think, baby?" probed Lexi, trying to sound young, cool and sexy and missing it by a landslide, "you and me tomorrow night, at chez Pigwell's: champagne, caviar, glitz and glamour. You fancy coming along for the ride?"

Due to impeccable manners and not wishing to offend Lexi by telling her that he would rather eat his own brain with a spoon than attend a party with her, he dealt with the situation in the most tactile way he could possibly think of. He lied, told her he had a very important engagement to attend to that night and made a mental note to himself to hide from her at the party.

As I languished inside the exquisite setting of The Oyster Pearl in London's up-market Knightsbridge, I immediately felt as if I were being transported back into art deco 1930s. The interior decoration is a cross between film noir meets under the deep blue sea, as plush dark plum sofas cushion the derrière, the crisp black and white tiled floors simply scream tango with Rudolf Valentino and the unusual tropical fish tanks create an element of tranquility and explosive colour. The food is exquisitely presented and in addition to an eloquently splendid meal, the ladies are offered the opportunity to pick an oyster from one of the gigantic tanks in the hope of discovering their very own pearl! Although watch out for the man-eating owner, the famous Lexi Howler, who finds it hard to keep her hands to herself and is the cause of sudden, 'unexpected lack of appetite.' So be warned ladies, keep your men on a leash and if you're a bachelor, be afraid, be very afraid. Unless you're looking for a sugar mama that is!

Taylor laughed to himself, "God, if only I could!"

"My Goddess," breathed Adrianna Jasmine, as she entered Pigwell's kitchen, "I'm in heaven."

The kitchen was nothing short of spectacular. As one stepped onto the cream polished floor tiles, the underfloor heating instantly warmed your tootsies and pretty spotlights that were peppered about constantly changed colour.

Two gigantic black and white crystal chandeliers hung dramatically from the high ceilings and the granite work surfaces, speckled with sapphire blue flecks, sparkled like star dust.

"It looks like your own personal galaxy," said Sarah, clearly mesmerized by the spectacular sparkles. "It's so shiny."

Adrianna Jasmine agreed, she was definitely on another kitchen planet and she had fallen in love with every delicious square inch.

The witch marvelled at the giant wood and marble chopping boards, copper pots and pans that dangled from every available nook and cranny, the impressive collection of kitchen knives and the humongous plasma TV carved into the wall. There were state-of-the-art mixers, blenders, coffee and bread makers and a candyfloss machine, just like the ones you see at the fair. The kitchen also boasted two industrial size ovens (one being steam) and a giant top-of-the-range fridge and freezer. Two giant sinks, which could quite easily be mistaken for hot tubs and an industrial size dishwasher, so you wouldn't even need to use them! Pigwell even had an original Coke vending machine in his kitchen, like the ones used back in the 50s.

"And I bet all this stuff hardly ever gets used," said Adrianna Jasmine with a sigh, "what a waste."

"Okay, girls, this is your office for now." The formidable Hannah had just entered snapping the witches out of their wonderland. Sarah looked positively terrified. "Help yourself to anything in order to make your food amazing, and I mean amazing," she added sternly. "Byron Pigwell is not a man of halves; the main objective today is to impress, got it?"

Adrianna Jasmine remained cool, she wasn't too keen on this belittling skinny figured, and fashion obsessed diva, who appeared to look down upon every living creature within her spitting distance.

"Of course, Hannah," she calmly replied, "I completely understand, a good impression is of the upmost importance."

"Yes it is!" hissed Hannah, "the people who are attending this party are very significant and influential. They could bring you down missus, bring you down to Chinatown, just like that!" She then clicked her fingers with a loud snap that popped through the ears, easily setting tinnitus into overkill. Adrianna Jasmine stared back at the prickly PA, her face was expressionless, yet her eyes were dancing with wicked amusement.

"Be sure to pop into the kitchen at some point, Hannah," suggested Adrianna Jasmine with an eerie calmness to her voice, "before it all becomes too crazy."

Hannah scoffed. "And why prey should I do that?"

Adrianna Jasmine smiled sweetly, a plan had popped into her head, "so you can enjoy a special good luck cocktail with us," she said with a casual shrug.

Hannah was hugging her clipboard so tightly to her chest that it looked almost ready to crumble, looked down at the witch with utter disdain.

"What? Drink with you two?" Hannah mocked cruelly, "oh sure, that would be as appealing as…" she trailed off and fell silent.

Her facial muscles began to soften and her eyes curiously glazed over, she became freakishly still.

Adrianna Jasmine's mouth curled into a wicked smile.

"Yes?" asked the witch, "you were saying...?"

Sarah, cowering by the stove, immediately came forward with a new found courage. *Ha! Not so mean now, are you*! She thought.

Hannah eventually completed her sentence: "as appealing as being offered a cool drink in the middle of the burning desert."

Adrianna Jasmine's lips held her a devious smile. A picture of a cool, refreshing, pink cocktail in a tall frosted glass, laden with ice, mint and strawberries and a thin black straw had just surprisingly popped into Hannah's head. She could literally *feel* the sweet fluid trickling down her dry throat like liquid heaven, quenching her thirst and easing built up stress in its wake. Adrianna Jasmine watched the PA continue to stare into space as she licked her lips; the witch knew exactly what Hannah was thinking as they were Adrianna Jasmine's very own thoughts, transmitted from her brain into Hannah's. Adrianna Jasmine remained totally focused, her eyes motionless, her breath calm.

"Yes, a nice sweet cocktail," she whispered with an eerie chill to her voice, "that's what you want, that's what you need."

Hannah responded with a dopey nod.

"That's what I neeeeed!"

Hannah remained zombified for a few more lingering moments, until Adrianna Jasmine believed the frosty PA had seen enough and subsequently allowed the image to fade gently from Hannah's mind. Unfortunately, as the image disappeared, the harshness to Hannah's face reappeared with vengeance.

"Well, If I'm not too busy with the *hundreds* of guests that are attending the party," she snapped, "I may be able to spare a moment or two; I do work for one of the greatest men in the music business, you know!"

"I know, Hannah," smiled Adrianna Jasmine sweetly, "and that's why you deserve a little treat."

Hannah, who was feeling a little discombobulated, to say the least, turned awkwardly on her spiky heels and left the witches to their cooking.

"Nice work," praised Sarah with an air of smugness, "how long before she's begging for it?"

"I give her an hour," replied Adrianna Jasmine coldly, "after that she won't be able to fight the thirst."

"Everything has a home, everything has a place, tidy as you go and never put off till tomorrow what you can do today."
(Adrianna Jasmine)

Chapter 5
Operation Stepford Staff

"Goddess, the snails are huge!" Adrianna Jasmine deliberated as she peered into the enormous tub. They were plump; fit to burst and smelled of garlic herbs.

"Yuck, they're revolting!" spat Sarah, who had approached the tub for a quick peek. "I can't believe people actually eat those things." She peered down again and had a change of heart.

"Hmm… I think I'll try that one, if that's okay. Well, when they've been cooked of course!" Impressed at her friend's keenness to try a snail, she offered Sarah the pick of the bunch.

"In that case," she suggested with a happy grin, "why don't you pick him out? You know, like they do at lobster restaurants!"

"Goddess, that's barbaric," screeched Sarah. She peered back into the tub. "Anyway, mustn't dwell. Yes, I'll take him. He does look positively huge!"

"OK, he's yours, my dear. Put him somewhere safe or he'll get mixed up with the others, or worse, accidentally spiked with endorphins."

"Hey, I don't care if he's sprinkled with a few endorphins," Sarah considered, "I could do with a few more endorphins tonight, I'll be like the Road Runner on speed!"

"Hmmmm…" Adrianna Jasmine reflected. Her friend was hyperactive at the best of times; she didn't need any more encouragement.

"Ok. Well, don't eat him all at once," Adrianna Jasmine warned. "Or you'll be bouncing off the walls."

"Hurray," yelled Sarah and she clapped her hands excitedly.

The first and fifth floors of Pigwell's palace were open for the guest's pleasure. The fifth floor had been designed purely for entertainments. It was the size of a nightclub, decked out with a DJ stand, top-of-the-line musical sound systems, light show equipment, fully stocked bar, locker room and water closets. The first floor designed mainly for relaxation, what with its Grecian inspired swimming pool, giant hot tub, sauna and aromatherapy steam room, mini beauty salon and ambient lighting. Therefore a perfect location for the party guests to sit, relax and unwind with a cocktail, whilst watching the National British Synchronized Swimming Team performing a burlesque style water ballet extravaganza! Only Pigwell!

The two witches decided to take a trip up to the fifth floor to familiarize themselves with the area in which the party was to be held. They stepped onto the elevators plush cream carpet, and within a twinkling of an eye arrived at their destination. The doors slid silently open. The two witches were once again blown away by the sheer splendour of Pigwell's abode. They stepped into a gigantic room surrounded by glass windows and onto the finest cream marble flooring imported from the quarries of Italy. A beige suede sofa encircled the room, and could probably seat a hundred people. It appeared as though it could seat over one hundred people. At the far end of the room was an enormous fire place set behind thick glass. Above it was a state-of-the-art plasma screen set into a giant gold gilt picture frame.

The walls were painted a soft cream, which set off the black and white crystal chandeliers to perfection, and humungous fish tank built into the walls, providing spellbinding views and vibrant colours to the neutral toned room.

"It's unbelievable," Sarah gushed standing next to one of the fish tanks, clearly hypnotized by the motions of an electric blue coral, swaying and dancing gently amongst the crystal clear water, "I do hope no one spills wine on the sofa!"

Sparkling China, the company that provided everything from plates to cutlery for the most eloquent and exclusive parties in town, had left in its wake an impressive collection of party wear.

As the witches wandered over to where Sparkling China had deposited their treasure trove of goodies, they couldn't help but coo in delight as they discovered beautiful black china plates trimmed with rose quartz, elegant pink crystal glasses, glistening sterling silver cutlery and chic black napkins stamped with a dark pink glittery rose.

"Oh, look at those gigantic vases filled with rose petals, Jazzy!" said Sarah, clearly impressed. "Would you look at all those beautiful colours? I can see salmon pink, dark pink and Bordeaux. Ooh… and they smell divine too. Sparkling China has really outdone itself! You were absolutely right to suggest to Pigwell that he hire them and...Oh, look at the tea candles, they're shaped like black roses flecked with glitter!"

Impressed, Adrianna Jasmine nodded in agreement. The company had even supplied the buffet tables, stiffly starched black linen table cloths, hot plates and black sparkling coasters.

Time turned to 5.30pm and the witches were busy boiling water, baking, roasting and steaming. However, for security reasons all foodstuffs had been pre-spiked at Adrianna Jasmine's home: well, she didn't want anyone spying on her now, did she? However, there was still the little matter of whizzing up Hannah's magic drink, which most certainly included unusual, never before seen ingredients.

"Goddess!" cried Adrianna Jasmine aloud, "she'll be here soon like a crazed vampire, thirsty for blood. Better get a move on."

She then turned her attention away from brushing the beautiful beef wellingtons with glistening butter for a few moments and began to create the PA's magical brew. Firstly, she dug out her first aid box, which wasn't really a first aid box at all, well, at least not the conventional kind; she plucked out a few herbs and spices of the mystical variety and added them to a small saucepan of boiling water. As she stirred the magical brew the witch began to chant under her breath:

Appease her torment and twisted face,
Touch her soul with respect and grace.
Soften her anger, set her free,
With the powers of earth and one, two, three.
Songs are for singing; life is for living.
Air is for breathing; a gift is for giving
Goddess of wonder, relieve her strife.
Help this woman to live her life.

    Adrianna Jasmine poured the potion into a little bottle and reserved it for later.

The giant glasses, soon to be filled with bubble and trouble, had been lent to Pigwell by Spun Gold Music Video Productions. The glasses were previously designed for a certain RNB music starlet, Leticia Vendetta's, latest music video. However, at the last minute the director changed his mind in regards to the genre of music video.
    It had somehow gone from a typical James Bond style frolic, to a Jungle themed romp which included real leopards, snakes, giant spiders, tigers and elephants.
    At the time, it had sounded like a great idea, but prior to the first hour of shooting, all the crew, including the director, wished that they had stuck to the James Bond frolic. The jungle-themed romp turned out to be more like a jungle flop, as the unreliability, unpredictability and smelliness of the animals meant shooting was a complete nightmare.
    Spiders escaped from their cages and giant centipedes ran away to a new life in London. In addition to the fiasco, Miss Vendetta found herself to be allergic to fur and had to be rushed to hospital with a vicious asthma attack and the worst case of hives ever seen. She was also petrified of creepy crawlies and had to be placed on medication to calm her down. Disaster!
    The giant champagne glasses were merrily scattered about the living area of the fifth floor and dangerously loaded up with industrial strength bubble bath, water and itchy-looking glitter.

At six o' clock, the dancers/models and waiters/actors/models had arrived. Hannah, of course, greeted them all, but with the warmth of Frosty the Snowman, holding her arm Hitler-fashion, yelling a slicing, "silence!"

The large group, who now resembled rabbits caught in headlights, stared, a little shocked at the dragon lady.

"When you hear your name," she barked, "shout 'present' and respond quickly."

A beautiful brunette began to giggle, she found this neurotic, strict headmistress-like figure rather amusing. Hannah unfortunately caught the girl giggling.

"Err, let me warn you," said Hannah menacingly, "it will *pay* to listen and respect, young lady. Byron Pigwell is not man who employs amateurs and silly giggling little girls."

As to be expected, the girl at first appeared a little shocked at Hannah's sharpness. However, her beauty had obviously made her thick skinned and prior to the initial shock, she simply flicked her long luscious hair, shrugged her gorgeous shoulders and brushed off Hannah's curtness.

There was a stir from the group and more giggles began to erupt. This, of course, infuriated Hannah immensely and she was just about to respond with a list of verbal abuse when one of the men from the group, who resembled a male Latino supermodel, spoke up. He had been observing the mistress of evil from residence a la door frame and found himself to be totally unimpressed with the young woman's attitude towards the hired help.

The Sexy Latino slowly uncrossed his toned, caramel coloured arms and looked straight towards Hannah.

"And it will *pay* to respect us, miss."

Immediately Hannah turned towards the one who had dared to speak, ready to unleash hell.

Unfazed by the gaze of death, the gorgeous Latino hunk, who looked rather on par with a young Antonio Banderas, continued.

"Because in all due respect," he said whilst staring deeply into her eyes, "the way you are speaking to these people, including myself, is totally unacceptable, disrespectful and unnecessary.

Change your attitude, Miss or you won't *have* any staff to order about tonight, comprendé?"

Hannah looked incensed, how very dare he! It was bad enough being backchatted by staff, but what made the situation worse was that the man with the warm, rich brown eyes, seemed to be stirring her loins up into a fiery frenzy.

Hannah cleared her throat, and then proceeded to erupt into a coughing fit. The wrecking crew rolled their eyes in boredom and began to talk amongst themselves.

When Hannah finally composed herself, *God, the thought of that cocktail would go down a treat right now*, she attempted to battle on.

"Lacy Quantro?"

"Present," responded a leggy, well-spoken blonde.

"Occupation for this evening?"

"Well, err," said leggy blonde, "to slip into an itsy-bitsy bikini and spend the night in a champers glass."

Hannah was not amused. "Upstairs: fourth door on the right."

"Thanks," purred leggy blonde, "by the way this is Eden, Dominique, Sadie, Estelle, Meredith and Antonella, Rodrigo, Kirk, Jive and Joules, we're *all* dancers, just thought it would save you time darrrrling!"

Hannah now looked furious and was just about to spit something acid-like towards the bold blonde when she caught a look of warning from Antonio Banderas. For some reason, dare she even dream of it, Hannah wished to impress him and opted to keep her mouth shut. "Costumes are hanging up," she said, through gritted teeth.

"Thanks," chorused the girls and boys as they departed for the stairs, leaving a mass smell of perfume, aftershaves, giggles and chewing gum pops in their wake.

Hannah sighed deeply before focusing back to her list. "Angelo Di Angelo?"

"Present," answered the smoldering voice of her Latino honey bomb, "your orders, your Highness?"

Hannah could feel her cheeks burning, she falsely laughed in attempt to shroud her embarrassment.

How dare he do this to me, she thought angrily, *and where's that bloody cocktail?* She was beginning to feel neurotic, never so much had Hannah desired a drink.

"Err..." she forgot what she was about to say, or what she was doing here, or her very own name, for that matter, "oh yes; um what are you doing here tonight, Antonio?"

"It's Angelo," corrected the lovely Latino smoothly.

"I-I meant An-Angelo, s-s-sorry," fumbled the flustered Hannah.

"It's quite alright, Miss," said Angelo politely, "I am part of the catering crew assigned by the agency, Serve up a Storm."

"Of course you are," Hannah almost whispered, "and, err, who else is from Serve up a Storm?"

About half a dozen hands went up.

"Ok, well, um, off you pop to the kitchen: it's on the ground floor," she pointed towards the lift, "the two ladies in there will tell you what to do I expect," and with that she scuttled off like a scarab beetle as far away from Angelo Di Angelo as possible, in order to re compose and to hopefully turn back into the woman she once was!

As the two witches had predicted, their waiters for the night, except Angelo, were nothing but a complete and utter let down. Serve up a Storm had done it again!

First of all there was Freddie Von Zerger, who was a 20 year old, 6'3" wannabe model/movie star from Cambridge, on a gap year from Uni (studying media in Bournemouth), said "yah" instead of "yes," never looked you in the eye, never listened to a word you said, constantly flicked his blonde floppy hair and believed every moment was a Kodak moment. He probably posed on the loo. (Poisoned!)

Then there was Valantina Valentine, a curvaceous Selma Hayek look alike. However, she spoke very little English and possessed a fiery temper. Sarah proposed that Valantina Valentine was a volatile and explosive person due to being a ho- blooded Latin woman. Adrianna Jasmine put it down to the fact that Valantina Valentine was a complete and utter bitch. (Poisoned.) It got worse, too.

Kiki Reece Kookie was a 26 year old mature student. Her daddy, Teddy Reece Kookie, owned an exclusive chain of health spas/country hotels. However, Teddy had cut off Kiki's monthly allowance to teach her the struggles of the real world. So Kiki had to work temporarily as a waitress to make the rent. But Kiki Reece Kookie was undeterred by this little blip, as she was perfectly aware that when Teddy popped his clogs she would one day become a very wealthy Kookie indeed. She also admitted to the other waiters (Adrianna Jasmine just so happened to overhear), that she didn't give a 'rat's arse' about working tonight and that she was only there to network, just like the others. (Poisoned!)

Oh, and how could we forget Raul Crook, a 19 year old cockney geezer from north London who dreamt of pop stardom? Raul pronounced words like, alright "Au wite," and hello, "allow," walked liked a penguin and irksomely broke into bursts of song at any goddess given opportunity. Apparently, it was just in case a music producer was within proximity of his vocal chords. (Poisoned!)

Then there was Poppy Pilchard, a beautiful fellow redhead wannabe model, who unfortunately was only 5'2", and therefore too short to become a catwalk queen. She was a nice enough girl but a little self-absorbed for the witches likening, (so.... poisoned!).

Then last but not least the Perez Twins. Utter Adonis's, the stuff threesome dreams were made of, but totally thick! (Poisoned!)

Sarah welcomed the motley crew as they gathered, dripping with attitude, into the kitchen whilst Adrianna Jasmine was busy assembling their "welcome cocktails" quietly in the corner.

"Hi, everyone," Sarah greeted the gruesome group with as much chirpiness as she could muster. "I'm Sarah and this lovely lady over here is Adrianna Jasmine, the owner of The Magic of Food."

Simultaneously they turned towards Adrianna Jasmine.

Without stirring a facial muscle, Valantina Valentine expertly scanned Adrianna Jasmine's body from top to toe and check out her feline competition. Valantina Valentine realized she immediately felt intimidated by this sexy chef and hated her. Freddie Von Zerger looked positively bored, Kiki Reece Kookie looked deranged, and

Raul Crook looked greasy. Poppy Pilchard flashed teeth and tits and the Adonis boys turned towards the witch as if a photographer had yelled out their names at a film premier.

Adrianna Jasmine managed a small smile and greeted them all with a polite, "Hi there," then resumed back to her special brew. Sarah continued.

"Thank you for all wearing black fitted jeans as requested, your T shirts and aprons are all ready for you to change into, so err…if you wouldn't mind collecting them and then popping them on…there are bathrooms on the next floor for you to change…if you like…" she trailed off.

The group was staring at Sarah as if she were stark staring raving bonkers. The adonis boys appeared to be dazed and confused, whereas Kiki Reece Kookie looked as if the mere mention of uniforms were an insult to her religion.

From the blank look on their faces, Sarah wondered if the group hadn't been able to decode her instructions. She decided to repeat herself again, but much slower this time and then hand them their uniforms one at a time.

She was just about to try again, when luckily Adrianna Jasmine came to the rescue.

"OK, forget the uniforms for the moment," Adrianna Jasmine said breezily, "have a little drink instead, that way we can *really* get this party started!"

At first, there was not even a stir of emotion. Sarah began to panic.

"What're we meant to do, force it down their throats?" Then, for the first time since the tedious crew had congregated in the kitchen, life was apparent!

Facial muscles were roused, eyebrows scrunched, thought lines furrowed deep into the brow, lips curled into smiles and fists rested on chins, in the style of thoughtful professors contemplating the laws of physics.

Adrianna Jasmine acted quickly upon this response and shook the luscious cocktail vigorously in her special cocktail shaker. She poured the potent pink liquid over ice, strawberries, lime, mint and caster sugar. The glasses were chilled and let off a smoking effect, similar to something out of The Munsters. Long black straws sprouted from the top of each smoking glass, waiting to be sucked.

"Come and get it," thought Adrianna Jasmine wickedly and she handed each and every one the intriguing cocktail.

When she reached Angelo Di Angelo, Adrianna Jasmine had accidentally on purpose not made enough; she had sensed from the moment he had entered the room that his aura was *normal.*

"Oops. Sorry there," she apologized batting her eyelids, "I'll just whiz you up another one, it won't take long"

"Thank you, miss," said Angelo politely, "you are very kind. But I prefer not to drink when I work." You had to love him!

"Very sensible," commented Adrianna Jasmine, "why don't I make you a non-alcoholic one instead! It'll be just as good and totally refreshing." Adrianna Jasmine smiled encouragingly at Angelo Di Angelo. She liked this guy; he was a good soul.

"If it's not too much trouble… then yes, thank you, miss."

Adrianna Jasmine smiled, gave Angelo a wink, and glided off to whiz up an exotic cocktail suitable for an equally exotic person.

As Adrianna Jasmine poured fresh liquids into the cocktail shaker, little moans of appreciation could be heard from around the kitchen. The Serve up a Storm crew was certainly enjoying its sweet, mind-meddling Adrianna Jasmine specialty! However, Adrianna Jasmine had no interest in observing the foolish group suck up their liquid fate, she was confident that it would do the trick. Sarah, on the other hand, watched the carnage with great pleasure and with, some may say, slightly freaky, overzealous eyes.

"Go on, drink up my pretties," she coaxed darkly, "mmm… yummy. That's it."

Adrianna Jasmine completed the non-poisoned version of the cocktail and poured it into a beautifully prepared tall glass for the lovely Angelo de Angelo.

"Ah, thank you, miss." said Angelo de Angelo graciously as he accepted the glass from the sweet Adrianna Jasmine. He took a hearty suck.

"Wow, this is really very nice," he complimented, "in fact… it's perfect!"

Adrianna Jasmine smiled warmly towards the handsome yet humble hunk.

"Your very welcome, Angelo," she said staring deeply into his eyes, "help yourself to more if you wish."

Angelo was just about to say, "don't mind if I do," when his voice became stuck and his words were trapped. Suddenly he was unable to break away from Adrianna Jasmine's mysterious gaze.

Whoa, this is strange!

Their eyes locked in an intense, transfixed and expressionless stare, neither one moving nor barely breathing; Adrianna Jasmine was at it again.

She was planting a little thought into the unsuspecting head of Angelo de Angelo and he became so fixated that blinking was no longer an option.

Three minutes later, the curious stare off was broken by Raul Crook belting out a surprisingly good rendition of Take That's 'Could It Be Magic' and Angelo was able to blink once more.

"How dare his music career distract him from his all-important sucking!" thought Sarah angrily and pounced towards the wannabe Gary Barlow like a demented cat. "Err, very good, Raul. However, drink up, drink up, strawberries are wondrous for the vocal chords you know!"

Raul suddenly stopped singing and looked interested, "Are they?"

"Oh yes…very, they're full of antioxidants, helps keep the throat free of infection and full of vitality."

Raul pouted in thought.

"Well, in that case," he said, "bottoms up!"

Sarah licked her lips and twisted her fingers in excitement, as she watched Raul, the X Factor's dream contestant, slurp his way to the bottom of the glass.

"Wow," commented Sarah impressed, "not even a hint of ice-cream headache syndrome."

"Strawberries, hey? I'll remember that one for next time!" And with that, he put his glass down and was just about to burst into an additional song, (Oh Ho, Ho It's Magic!) when Raul Crook suddenly began to act rather strangely. The aspiring singer proceeded to sharply straighten his back, in the manner of a pole being shoved up one's backside, depressed his shoulder blades, similar to that of a member of the Bolshoi Ballet, engaged his pelvic floor, similar to a dedicated pilates student and sucked in his abdominals, similar to a size twelve attempting to wear size ten pair jeans.

"It's happening!" thought Sarah as she licked her lips with wicked excitement, for not only was Raul Crook showing signs that the potion was starting to work, so were the rest of the crew. Team Serve up a Storm were ready for action.

Like an elite marine core, team Serve up a Storm were simultaneously organizing themselves into a line according to height. (Freddie Von Zerger down to Poppy Pilchard.) They stood to perfect attention, chins up, shoulders back and pure concentration carved into their dedicated faces.

Sarah then began to march up and down in front her troop, in style of captain Mainwaring in Dad's Army and barked out her orders. Firstly, she ordered them to put on their costumes. The team immediately stripped and changed into their work uniforms. Then she ordered them to brush and tidy their hair and scrub their nails to a gleam. She then ordered the girls to lose their heavy slap and to apply subtle, classic make up to their faces. Minutes later, they were ready.

Freddie Von Zerger oozed discipline, opposed to disorder, Valantina Valentine did no longer resemble a volatile volcano, but a beautiful Spanish missionary and Kiki Reece Kookie appeared to be going for the waitress of the year award. Raul didn't sing another note; Poppy Pilchard resembled a living saint, purely dedicated to serve the goddesses and the Perez twins were in the belief that the whole world was at stake unless the party went off without a hitch. Therefore, they needed to concentrate like they had never concentrated before. Wow, they would have head ache tomorrow!

Angelo De Angelo who had been sipping his cocktail quietly next to Adrianna Jasmine, looked on totally bemused; why was there sudden change to his fellow Serve up a Stormers?

"It's Sarah," Adrianna Jasmine informed him, "she was born to lead, a Leo, you know, what else is there to say...!"

Suddenly the door to the kitchen burst open and a rather crazed and desperate looking Hannah came thundering towards Adrianna Jasmine, her eyes blazing with psychotic rage. Goddess help anyone who stood in her path, she'd mow them down without a moment's thought. Breathlessly she demanded, "Where's-that-drink?"

Angelo shook his head disapprovingly; she was too rude for words.

"Here it is," Adrianna Jasmine tinkled and handed the distressed PA a tall glass filled with ice, tangerine coloured liquid, lemon and lime slices along with the infamous black straws.

Hannah all but snatched the glass from Adrianna Jasmine and aggressively hurled the straws to the ground. She dramatically tossed her head back and gulped the drink down with ravenous thirst. Moments later the glass was bare and Hannah shut her eyes in utter content.

"Wow," she said still breathing heavily. "Now I know how a vampire must feel when he's dying for blood to quench his eternal thirst."

"Nutter!" thought Angelo shaking his head once more. This was turning out to be the strangest job ever!

As the warm and tingling liquid made its journey around Hannah's body, a change began to happen. Her eyes softened into doe-like charm and her stiff lips melted into soft cushions of plump loveliness. Her wrinkled brow seemed literally to iron itself out and the muscles around her shoulders and neck loosened as if some miraculous masseuse had performed nothing short of magic. Hannah had become nice!

Miraculously the highly strung and unapproachable PA was now all but glowing with the warmth of an angel.

At first she was a little confused, she wasn't feeling her normal angry and neurotic self.

"This isn't right," she contemplated, "why aren't I feeling enraged, hurried, stressed and unattractive? Why is it I feel calm, content, pretty in my own skin and comfortable with my surroundings? This isn't me at all!"

Thrilled with the results, Adrianna Jasmine walked over to Hannah, so she could encourage the new and improved woman out of her shell.

"Would you like another?" Adrianna Jasmine gently asked, "are you feeling...well?"

At first there was no response; however, Adrianna Jasmine was patient and sure enough after a few moments, Hannah eventually found her voice.

"Oh no, thank you," Hannah replied graciously, "that was just what the doctor ordered. Anyway," she said looking around the room, "can I get *you* something, do you need help with anything, is there anything I can do...?"

Adrianna Jasmine smiled at Hannah with utter content, *Bingo!* She thought triumphantly, *goodbye ice queen and hello living saint!*

"Actually...," said Adrianna Jasmine, her voice etched in craftiness, "there *is* something I'd like you do."

"Anything!" said Hannah

"Oh, good," beamed Adrianna Jasmine, "come and meet our head waiter, Angelo."

At the sound of his name and the horror that loopy Hannah was striving towards him, a dreaded fear spread over Angelo de Angelo's rippled body.

"Great, that's all I need," he grumbled under his breath, "but...hang on, did I hear her say... head waiter?"

As the two women walked over to Angelo, Adrianna Jasmine met his bemused expression and winked confidently at him.

"Head waiter, miss?"

"Ah, you heard that then?" said Adrianna Jasmine smiling.

Modestly Angelo shrugged his shoulders.

"I have very good hearing, Adrianna Jasmine," he teased.

"You most certainly do, and yes, I would like it very much if you took on the role of head waiter tonight. I think you're just the man for the job."

Angelo presented Adrianna Jasmine with a small bow, "I would be honoured," he said, sounding more like Zorro excepting the noble responsibility of defending a small, wretched village.

"Good," said Adrianna Jasmine happily, "that's settled then. By the way, have you met…Hannah?"

Angelo struggled to keep his facial expression from crumbling up in disgust at the mere mention of the woman's name.

"Because I don't think you have, not this one anyway," she added quietly, "let me introduce you both."

"Oh, we've already met!" Angelo darkly confirmed.

"Really? Are you sure?" Adrianna Jasmine asked with enforced surprise, "Well... have you met *this* Hannah?"

Hannah stepped forward as if making a grand entrance through a plush, plum, velvet curtain out onto a stage.

At first, all Angelo saw was the same nauseating woman who had welcomed him in Chez Pigwell with all the warmth of a penguin's back side, however…she looked the same, was dressed the same, but seemed to be a completely different person.

What is *going on?*

Delightful Chocolate Flinty

250 grams Milk chocolate
250grams fruit and nut chocolate
2oz Unsalted butter
A good handful of torn up marshmallows
110g digestive biscuits broken up
A good handful of de shelled Pistachio nuts

Method

Melt the chocolate and butter in a bowl over a pan of simmering water. Meanwhile, line a non-stick 18 inch round cake tin with greaseproof paper. Stir the rest of the ingredients into the chocolate mixture and pour into the cake tin. Press down gently, until mixture is even. Leave to chill for at least four hours. Remove from cake tin and slice when ready to serve

Chapter 6
The Course of True Love

At 7pm pandemonium erupted as the beautiful people began to arrive. The paparazzi snapped away furiously at slender women glancing over their left shoulders whilst arching their spines (apparently it's the most flattering angle for a woman to be photographed), the glamour models erotically thrusting out their chests and the pop singers cheekily poking out their tongues. The footballers strutted through the doors with moody coolness and discreetly scanned the room in the search of the lucky lady who could very well be offered the chance to frolic in their bed, or possibly their vomit, post-party. The beautiful models of the fashion world glided through the doors with the grace of figure skaters and millionaire businessmen entered the room ready for a night out of the office. Then, just when it seemed it was impossible to fit anymore stars into one place, the judging panel from Strictly Come Dancing burst in through the doors and the place simply erupted. The party had begun!

Beautiful girls in glittery bikinis splashed about seductively in the champagne glasses and the male dancers walked around on stilts dressed in mobster-style pinstripe suits, brandishing fake machine guns filled with flavoured vodka, which they playfully squirted down the guests' throats the moment they appeared through the doors.

Six-foot near-naked female models sashayed around the room draped in feather boas, just hiding their somewhat struggling dignity and team Serve up a Storm offered the guests chilled crystal champagne on arrival.

Master of ceremony, DJ Charlie Fresco, was rigged up on a high platform pumping out remix versions of famous Frank Sinatra, Dean Martin, and Ella Fitzgerald classics. It was a like listening to a cross between rat pack and house music.

The lighting was out of this world. The room constantly changed colour from soft ambient moods of blues and purples, to vibrant oranges and reds. It was total magic!

At 7.30pm, team Serve up a Storm began to serve the starters.

The shortbreads, olives, scallops, dates wrapped in bacon and snails were placed decoratively onto silver platters and handed around to guests. (The snails, of course, were greeted with mixed reviews, especially from a group of models who squealed like mice at the very thought of consuming such creepy critters). However, the snails were all consumed and yes, France was mentioned a few times. The crystal rose napkins were offered to guests along with tiny silver sparkling forks and loving, courteous smiles exuded from the waiting staff's angelic little faces. The joyful sounds of culinary bliss erupted from the party peoples' mouths, as they experienced the heavenly crumbliness of the savoury shortbreads and plump, juiciness from the succulent sweet scallops accompanied with the salty combination of the wafer thin Parma ham.

All over the room you could hear sounds of approval as the witch's food danced on tongues and taste buds. Even the skinny ones were indulging in a nibble or two; something about this food stuff was rather good! The endorphins, it seemed, were kicking in!

Adrianna Jasmine glanced at her watch.

"Not bad!" she noted, with a satisfied grin, "not even an hour into the party and the magic, it appears, has already kicked in. You could power a small country with the positive energy exuding from this very room!"

Taylor Jameson and his work colleague, Luca Placidi, entered the enormous room on the fifth floor. Luca, a short chap with a large enthusiastic personality, immediately zoomed in on the bikini-clad models and shot off like a bullet towards their taut little bottoms.

Taylor, on the other hand, who was feeling tired and grouchy, immediately scanned the room for Lexi Howler. His mission for the evening was to keep well away from the man-eater and protect his dignity.

I hope the food doesn't take forever to arrive, he thought, *and then I can taste it and get the hell out of here.*

"This is fantastico!" shouted Luca jubilantly as he came charging back towards his workmate, giddy as a school boy, "look at all of these beautiful women. I 'ave ah died and gonna to heaven!"

Taylor forced a weak smile. Sure, the place was filled with beautiful bodies, but when you've seen one, you've seen them all! Besides, they were all as shallow as a baby's bath. They were here for one thing and one thing only: to further their career. None of them were interesting, intelligent or genuine, they were all out to screw you one way or the other, and frankly he was bored of it.

"I don't know about you, my friend," announced Luca rubbing his hands together, "but I'm heading straight for the champagne!"

And with that, Luca Placidi sprinted over to the nearest champagne glass filled to the brim with a sexy girl, splashing about in a diamante bikini.

Taylor, who wasn't in the mood for champagne, stayed rooted to the spot. Although he did find it rather amusing when one of the guys on stilts shot vodka from his faux Tommy gun over Luca's stunned face: a warning to stay *out* of the champagne glass.

As Taylor looked out toward the seeming mass of party-goers, a tray of delicious nibbles were heading straight his way.

"Escargot?" offered Freddie Von Zerger politely.

Taylor, who hadn't eaten escargots in quite some time, nodded and the waiter expertly placed the lifeless plump lump smothered in garlic and herbs onto a plate. Moments later, more delectable delights were offered and soon the food critique was munching his way through a feast of savoury feast.

As he popped the medley of treats into his mouth, he was taken aback by the wondrous medley of tastes: the escargots were tender and bursting with flavor; the shortbreads were the lightest he had ever sampled and the scallops tasted as if they had been caught by King Neptune himself. Moreover, the food not only *tasted* supreme, but it seemed to have some sort of positive effect on him. He was beginning to feel happy and more relaxed. As a result, he opted for seconds.

"Wow this is good!" he commented aloud, stunned by the sheer brilliance of the tastes dancing about vibrantly on his tongue, "bring on the main!"

"It's going great Adrianna Jasmine, just great," gushed Sarah as she raced back into the kitchen to deposit an empty tray. "Not only is the food a success, but you won't believe the amount of celebrities that are out there: it's like E Entertainment in 3D! They're all living, breathing, talking!"

Adrianna Jasmine, who was leaning rather precariously into the large oven tying to retrieve her prize-winning beef wellingtons, laughed at her friend.

"Glad you're having a ball, witchy, and touch wood, the rest of the night'll be pretty amazing, too!"

Once the wellingtons were out the oven, the witches began to dish up the vegetables onto hot plates.

"Sarah, get the pasta on," asked Adrianna Jasmine, not mucking around, "the water's boiling and once you've done that, please find Angelo and a couple of the others to get the rest of the bits out onto the tables, then tell the others to get to their stations. We are ready to go, go, go!"

With military efficiency, team Serve up a Storm were at action stations looking smart, helpful and organized.

Angelo proudly carried out the beef wellingtons to the allotted table; Raul followed suit with the tray of crispy potatoes roasted in goose fat, whilst Adrianna Jasmine transported the mange tout and caramelized carrots.

The banquet was placed onto food warmers, powered by little candles and the waiters/waitresses stood patiently with ladles in arm, ready to spoon and scoop.

Soon additional food began to appear from the elevator. Out came the rainbow pasta and the beautiful rich red bolognese sauce magically sprinkled with, *comforting thoughts of hot summer nights in southern Italy*; the vegetable curry, magically sprinkled with, *mystical sensations of a magic carpet ride*; the lightly fragrant fluffy jasmine rice sprinkled with, "harmonic sensations whilst meditating on a Thai beach" and two beautiful, creamy, cheese and potato gratins magically sprinkled with, *comfort and joy*.

Basically folks, each dish made everyone feel very, very happy.

As the party-goers tucked into their delicious main course, the room was a haven of goodwill and contentment. The glamour models no longer felt the need for a second breast augmentation, their breasts were good as they were, thank you very much, and the footballers felt inspired to try harder to make it to a world cup final.

Raul Crook made himself busy by handing out ice-cold glasses of champagne and resisted the urge to hum or do-ray-me at the thirsty guests.

Valantina Valentine spooned out rich gratin to the masses. Her big breasts and radiant smile certainly added to the dishes *flavour* and even the two witches were bemused as to how one could look so virginal yet so sluttish. Still, it helped plonk cheese and potatoes onto empty plates.

The Perez twins were stationed with the rainbow pasta and Bolognese sauce. Apparently this dish went down rather well with Luca, who, yes, did manage to tear himself away from the glitter girls. He had nothing but praise for Adrianna Jasmine's sumptuous sauce.

More and more people were lining up to eat, it was going very well. Adrianna Jasmine was relieved when the second batch of beef wellingtons was ready; the first batch had disappeared rapidly.

Usually at this sort of bash, food is teased and prodded, a second thought to the free alcohol, but this was an Adrianna Jasmine party; things were different. The food proved to be similar to a drug. It enticed you and made you feel good about yourself. However, unlike hard core drugs, it was only mildly addictive, totally natural, and heavily laden with vitamins and minerals. It would not cause bad trips, rotten come downs, bankruptcy, bad skin or death!

Thirty minutes after dishing out the main, the crowd had thinned a little from the serving stations and the waiters were able to catch their breath. The Perez twins, however, remained on guard, even though there was no sauce left to dish out and a pathetic six strands of spaghetti remained in the bowl.

Angelo took the opportunity to place his serving tongs down for a few moments and stretch out his fingers - they had actually cramped from serving up so many beef wellingtons - when a little charming voice brought him back to attention.

"Is there any left for me?" inquired a sweet little voice, "They look delicious."

"Yes, certainly miss," Angelo said attentively, "one or two…?"

He trailed off mid-sentence, totally stunned at who he was talking to.

The girl standing before him was the epitome of sheer delight. Her hair was sandy blonde, thick, long and gently cascaded over her lightly tanned breasts. Her eyes shone like dark blue sapphires and the divine scent wafting from her glowing skin drifted like silky spirits into his appreciative nostrils.

At first he was confused, he had to think for a moment. It *was* her.

"Hannah?" he tested, "is that you?"

Hannah smiled shyly and simply nodded. She was wearing a dark emerald green dress made from chiffon and silk, she was a dream in green.

"You look…beautiful," he commented, his eyes devouring every square inch of her delicious body.

"Thank you," she said graciously and softly reached out towards Angelo. She embraced his warm, masculine hands, clutching them in her own and gently squeezing them with affection.

"I'm sorry about earlier," she said with utter sincerity, "there was no excuse for my behaviour, but I think I was…stressed!" As she said the word *stressed,* Hannah shook her head, it seemed so ridiculous to her now that she should have behaved in such a ghastly manor. "Forgive me?" she asked, searching his eyes for some sign of amnesty.

Angelo still couldn't quite believe that this goddess before him, who, only an hour ago, was the PA from hell, was actually asking if *he* would accept *her* apology. What was going on! He remained silent; his brain was scrambling for a decent explanation.

His thoughts drifted briefly back to the kitchen. Just before he was offered a drink by Adrianna Jasmine, he remembered a vision that had entered his mind, a vision surrounded in green and a scent. He recalled an overwhelming sense of lime, basil and mandarin wafting into his nasal passages. At the time he thought it was one of Adrianna Jasmine's heavenly sauces. Little did he know, he had actually pre-sniffed Hannah's perfume, the perfume Hannah so happened to be wearing now. What was this? Some sort of witchcraft?!

Who cares! he thought wildly, *she smells good enough to eat.* "Angelo!" He shook out of his daze a little; his name sounded like it had never sounded before, "is everything ok? Do you forgive me?"

Hannah's voice was so sweet and sincere; Angelo couldn't help but turn to a quivering state of mush.

He decided to compose himself and return once more to the strong, passionate Latino he once was. He stared deeply into her eyes.

"Of course I do, Hannah. As far as I'm concerned there is nothing to forgive." With textbook Hollywood style, Angelo lowered his head towards her soft little hand and planted a perfect kiss onto the back of it.

As the sexual electricity passed from his lips onto her tender, sensitive skin, Hannah couldn't help but swoon.

Angelo didn't want to let go, he was lost in Hannah's charm, her aroma, her sexuality, his lust, his confusion, his passion, he would stay there forever, unable to move. He would quite willingly stay in this moment, forever trapped in torturous ecstasy. Just then, like a thunderbolt from the heavens, an announcement came from above.

"My God," he whispered, as he raised his eyes skyward, "is it really you?" Alas, it was not God, but Charlie Fresco making an announcement to the party guests and Angelo reluctantly let go of Hannah's hand.

Fruits of the Forest Crème Brûlée

One packet of frozen forest fruit
600ml double cream
5 egg yolks
50g caster sugar
4 drops vanilla extract
caster sugar (for topping)
6 ramekin dishes

Whisk the egg yolks, sugar, cream and vanilla into a bowl until light and fluffy. Place a few berries into the bottom of each of the six ramekin dishes and pour the creamy mixture over the top. Place in a roasting tin and carefully add boiling water until the water comes halfway up the sides of the ramekins. Place the roasting tin in an oven pre-heated to 170°C and bake for about 40 minutes. Once cooked, remove the ramekins from the roasting tin and allow to cool at room temperature.
When ready to serve sprinkle a level teaspoon of caster sugar evenly over the surface of each ramekin. Place under a hot grill to caramelize or use a blowtorch. Wait until the sugar forms a hard crust then serve. Enjoy that delectable crack!

Chapter 7
Like Being Bathed in Honey

"Ladies and Gentlemen," announced Charlie Fresco over the microphone, "pray silence for the star of tonight's festivities: the sparkling, the dazzling, the latest phenomenon to explode into the pop world, the gorgeous, the talented, Chrystal Rose!"

There was a hushed silence from the guests as they eagerly waited for the arrival of their star.

Gradually the lights began to fade and the sound of wind and the twinkling of stars, rather similar to that found in a planetarium, appeared from nowhere. Slowly, the eager crowd were transported into a state of hypnosis and guided into the mysteries of deep space.

Soft white rose petals began to fall from the ceiling and the delighted guests gently raised their hands in the hope that a delicate petal would land softly onto their fingertips.

The beautiful, haunting sound of violins complimented the planetarium symphony, stroking the nervous system and causing the hairs on one's arm to stand on end.

People's very souls were awash with bliss, never had music proven to be so deep, so sensitive and so evocative.

Angelo was most certainly feeling it! He was still transfixed by the vision in green before him, yet totally overwhelmed by the music and ambiance, his body squirming in a mixture of agony and ecstasy.

"My God," he said, his voice etched with torment, "my body is not strong enough to withhold such excruciating rapture."

Then, like a cherry on one of Adrianna Jasmine's cupcakes, the most beautiful female voice, which could only be likened to "being bathed in honey," threw fuel onto the fire and the ecstasy intensified.

The voice was strong, yet pure; it obtained the power to tantalize, hypnotize and even make you cry. The voice would undoubtedly be the voice of the angel that guided your spirit to the gates of heaven and into eternal paradise.

As her voice drifted amongst the enchanted guests, planets and stars ingeniously began to appear on the ceiling and the walls of the gigantic room. It was miraculous, as if Michelangelo himself had painted a symphony of stars and planets out of multi-coloured, florescent, 21st century lighting at Chez Pigwell. The effect was breathtaking. Perhaps Pigwell had been in contact with the planetarium after all! Had David Copperfield intervened?

Then to the guests delight, the body to the voice suddenly appeared and Chrystal Rose made her debut entrance.

Suspended from virtually invisible wires, she appeared like a luminous angel descending from heaven, decorated in the palest of pink chiffon that shimmered with hundreds of Swarovski crystals, capturing the light and twinkling similarly to the Milky Way. Her skin was the colour of creamy caramel and her figure like a lithe young dear; she was breathlessly beautiful. As the guests applauded, Chrystal Rose hovered silently amongst the stars and planets, her blonde hair billowing like a mermaids against the artificial wind machine. Adrianna Jasmine was knocked for six, her perception of the popsicle was completely wrong; she would never judge a book by a cover again, as long as she lived.

The guests settled themselves into a hushed silence, mesmerized and eager to hear her perform once more. Slowly, she began. The billowing angel softy opened her lips and out poured the most beautiful version of the famous aria, One Fine Day from Madame Butterfly. She was pitch perfect all the more remarkable as she sang without accompaniment. As the stunned crowd hung on her every angelic breath, Charlie Fresco expertly introduced tack, the effect was overwhelming.

Watching the show from the buffet station, Adrianna Jasmine felt someone squeeze her hand. It was Sarah.

"My Goddess," whispered Sarah, "it's so beautiful, she's officially my new favorite celebrity."

Adrianna Jasmine nodded in agreement and whispered back, "Mine, too!"

As the aria drew near to a crescendo, Chrystal Rose hit the high note and filled the room with sheer wonder and delight. People cheered at the classical pop sensation and couldn't help but wonder how a pop star could sing opera so majestically! What would she sing in the charts: Ave Maria, Nessun Dorma, Carmen, or Aqua's Barbie Girl? Both ways, she could sing and her voice wasn't even studio enhanced!

When Chrystal Rose completed her masterpiece, the lights went out to blackness and the crowd erupted into applause. A few moments later, the lights went back up and Chrystal Rose was gone. Charlie Fresco hit the decks and funky music began to play. Life in the room began to stir once more and people slowly turned their attention back towards one another.

"OK," signalled Adrianna Jasmine to Angelo, "desserts."

Angelo was still frozen to the spot, totally spellbound by Hannah. He had to be poked and prodded by Sarah to snap back into reality.

"Excuse me, Hannah, I have to go," apologized Angelo, clearly upset that he had to abandon his Juliet, "but I'll be back momentarily."

Hannah beamed and informed Angelo that it was quite alright as she really had to circulate the room and check on all the guests; therefore they would meet anon. Unfortunately, she did not receive any beef wellington and was quite ravenous, however, she decided not to make a fuss, as her Latin lovely was busy and she could always just go straight to dessert!

Adrianna Jasmine loved this part of the party, the desserts. Not only because she loved puddings and all things sweet, but this is where she got to go front of house and meet the crowd. The serving stations had been cleared away and new plates and cutlery lay ready for the fruits of the forest crème brûlée and Espresso Martinis. Team Serve up a Storm were set to work carrying out the multi-coloured cupcakes and chocolate petit fours on glass trays and offering them to the crowd.

Jack Bryce, the new teen football sensation educated his fellow party guests as to why one should mix a chocolate petit fours and strawberry cupcake simultaneously in the mouth. Apparently it was like experiencing an orgasm: the overwhelming cacophony of flavours was too much to handle and resulted in some kind of oral explosion.

A fellow, much older football icon, stated that he was surprised that the sixteen year old Jack actually knew what an orgasm felt like and that he had not experienced one until his mid-thirties. He finished with the mind-pondering theory that kids were growing up too fast these days and missing out on good old fashioned fun. Jack, however, heard the comment and scoffed. His idea of fun was divulging in a threesome with a pair of Ukrainian hot-assed twins; not sitting at home putting together a week-by-week build-it-yourself model airplane. The older footballer didn't say a word, he had enjoyed many a happy afternoon with his model airplane; bloody kids these days!

As the desserts were being gobbled down by satisfied guests, Byron Pigwell and his young protégé made their appearance and worked the room. Chrystal Rose, who was holding a glass of pink champers, whilst nibbling on a strawberry cupcake, graciously accepted compliments from her party guests, whilst Pigwell stood beside her like a proud Don. He jeered up her greatness with rousing speeches about how she was going to take over the world, be more famous than Mariah Carey and that one should expect the Chrystal Rose doll out on the shelves at Christmas. Apparently if you pressed her hand her dress would light up and she'd belt out song!

As Adrianna Jasmine set up her brûlée and Martini station, she looked over towards Poppy Pilchard who was standing in the middle of a group of strapping young footballers and rugby players. She was explaining the rules of some sort of drinking game and pouring a bottle of Cointreau into empty shot glasses. The players had to knock back the orange liquid from a shot glass, swill it in their mouths for 30 seconds, swallow, and then suck air in through their teeth. It looked revolting, but rings of laughter could be heard as the boys gave it a go.

Adrianna Jasmine was impressed, not only had Poppy Pilchard proved to be using her initiative; in addition, she proved herself to be an excellent drinks master. She held a tight grip on the bottle, kept everything in good humour and controlled the alcohol consumption to just one shot per person.

Freddie Von Zerger had been busy throughout the evening keeping stations clean, whacking dishes into the dishwasher, serving food and tirelessly offering tidbits amongst the chaotic throng. He was an incredibly good looking chap, although due to being under a spell, he totally ignored a top model scout when she caught his dazzling eye. The scout for, Luminary Limited simply believed that the young waiter "had it." She was desperate for the chiselled god-like creature to pop down to the office for an informal chat. Freddie had politely turned down the shocked woman, never once had she experienced a young, good-looking man at an event like this - where networking was the main reason to exist - turn down the chance of fame and fortune. He had said that right now he was very busy and didn't have time to stop and talk. Luckily she slipped a card into his jeans back pocket, so he would find it in the morning.

The queen of food, Adrianna Jasmine, was now stood firmly, blowtorch in hand and ready to caramelize. She was thrilled with the way the night had flowed. It could only be, in her eyes, described as a joyous, emotional, uphill expedition. First flatness, then heightened spirits, pursued with contentment, finishing with complete joviality! Similar to that of an aerobic curve during a group exercise session! It made her smile to think that she had something to do with the pleasurable mood about the place.

The witch was also additionally delighted to see Hannah walking towards her, politely asking to sample one of her delicious crème brûlées. She had confessed that she was hungry due to missing out on the starter and main course, although omitted the information that it was actually Angelo's fault! Adrianna Jasmine was happy to oblige and set to dusting the creamy delight with sugar, before lighting her blowtorch and caramelizing.

"Ouch!" winced Adrianna Jasmine, and painfully rubbed her belly with her free hand. Concerned at the thought that the witch might be in discomfort; Hannah asked if she was alright.

Adrianna Jasmine braved a smile.

"Yes, I'm fine," she explained weakly, "I had a little tummy trouble earlier and it's just flared up again."

The witch then handed the dessert to Hannah, who still appeared to look concerned.

"Hey, if you need a break, just take it, your team are more than capable of holding the fort, in fact I've never witnessed such a proficient team, whatever you gave them in that drink earlier, certainly did the trick!"

Adrianna Jasmine laughed uneasily, "Yes, who would have thought that strawberries could be so effective!"

She then quickly turned her attention to a pretty young girl in a purple coloured leopard print mini-dress that appeared to be interested in a fruits of the forest crème brûlée.

"Fruits of the forest crème brûlée?"

The girl looked a little puzzled, she knew what a brûlée was, although was a little muddled as to what fruits of the forest were.

Adrianna Jasmine smiled and patiently explained to purple leopard print what the vibrant forest dwelling berries were. The girl licked her lip gloss and decided to try one. She watched in awe as Adrianna Jasmine sprinkled white sugar on top of the yummy looking dessert and then proceeded to transform the white sugar into golden, crunchy caramel with her blowtorch. Adrianna Jasmine then instructed the girl to wait a couple of minutes for the sugar to harden in order to experience the "crack" of caramel, before delving into the creamy bottom. Purple leopard skin promised to allow the caramel to set, and then merrily skipped off amongst the fellow party revelers.

"Well, she looks cheerful," concluded Adrianna Jasmine with a satisfied gin, "I do like bringing a little joy to people via their food."

She wiped down her station, and then decided to make a start on the Espresso Martinis. She put two scoops of ice, vodka and coffee into her cocktail shaker, shook the contents vigorously, then expertly tossed the shaker into air and caught it one-handed behind her back.

"Wow, that's pretty impressive!" said an unfamiliar, rich, deep voice, "Tom Cruise's got nothing on you!"

Adrianna Jasmine smiled, "Espresso...Martini?"

A handsome man with dark blonde hair and sumptuous chocolate brown eyes had momentarily frozen the witch to the spot. Her tummy gripped sharply again and for a second she wasn't actually sure where she was. The man was about 5 foot, 11 inches tall, well built, appeared as though he enjoyed a few sessions at the gym, along with the odd spin class and absolutely gorgeous. As a result the witch was momentarily speechless. His aura, commonly known as the electromagnetic field that surrounds the human body, and can be detected by magical sensitive folk, appeared to Adrianna Jasmine in the colour of blue, corn flower blue; if you want to get finicky about it. This made Adrianna Jasmine very happy indeed as a blue aura was always a frontrunner. She learnt that he was a sturdy vocal communicator, open-minded and free thinking, possessed strong male energies, great for the bedroom, sensitive and caring, and filled with positive possibilities – perfect, he would never grow to be predictable and dull.

How wonderful, she breathed, *not only does he appear physically beautiful, but his aura has confirmed that he's an all-round decent human being, too.* The witch sighed with contentment, *I feel myself drawing towards you like a cat to tuna.*

As a result, the witch found her frozen state suddenly developing into a flustered state of disarray. Her belly stirred sharply once more and her heart began to flutter wildly. She flushed pink and her bottom lip quivered like jelly in a bowl.

The man smiled genially at the delightful creature standing before him and asked if she was the reason behind this magnificent spread. At first she didn't answer, she was literally lost in his ambiance. As an alternative to answering his questions, she opted to silently guess his age and surprisingly, if he was married. He looked about mid-thirties, very healthy and wore no band on his wedding finger. *Phweeeeeew,* she thought with surprising relief. Recognizing the fact that she was now embarrassing herself by not actually speaking; she momentarily came to and forced herself to speak.

"Yes," she practically squeaked, "I'm the Magic of food!"

"You certainly are!" the man quipped cheekily, the witch giggled all a fluster.

"Well, I must say," said the man with genuine enthusiasm, "not only does the food taste great, but I don't think I've ever felt so *happy* whilst eating in my whole life. It's quite extraordinary. May I ask what your secret ingredient is?"

Adrianna Jasmine's face dropped like a stone prior to hearing the words, "secret" and "ingredient."

Okay just relax, she told herself, *calm, calm, calm. How would he know that I was a witch, spiked food with magic potions and stayed up into the dead of night chanting over sauces and strips of beef?* She opted to play it cool. "Now that would be telling," she teased, "but I can assure you, only the finest ingredients and knowledge one can buy goes into a Magic of Food spread."

He smiled again at this beautiful looking woman and found himself locked into her eyes. They were spectacularly unusual. Not because one eye appeared to be a different colour to the other, but they were deep and full mystery. Why, you could write a ten thousand word thesis on their captivating charm and spend years trying to unlock their mystery, similar to a historian trying to unlock the mystery of the Dead Sea scrolls.

Adrianna Jasmine felt her body swoon, she liked this man very much. "Well...," she tantalized, "would you like to try one of my Espresso Martini's...or perhaps a crème brûlée? They're very...creamy."

The man felt a stir in his Armani Exchange designer jeans. Was she flirting with him?

"Tempt me," he virtually whispered, flirting back. He could imagine doing a lot more with that crème brûlée than eating it!

She stretched out towards the sugar with a graceful arm and soft fingers, picked up a little silver spoon, scooped up some sugar and began to sprinkle it over the dessert. She then set the spoon down and lit the blowtorch. As the flame whirred into action, she took a moment to stare deep and seductive into the stranger's eyes, before expertly browning the sugar into sweet caramel.

"I suggest," she said after switching the blowtorch off, "you allow it to go hard before diving in...Mr...?"

The man was literally squirming like a worm on a hook.

"T...Taylor," he fumbled, "my name is Taylor."

"Because Mr. Taylor, otherwise it's not quite as, err...pleasurable?"

The man, who was reduced to rubble by Adrianna Jasmines alluring charm, managed to nod.

"That's good advice," he breathed, not taking his eyes off of hers for one precious moment, although *it's just Taylor. I should have* been more specific. My name," he started again, "is *Taylor Jameson*."

"Ah!" said the witch with a smile, "I see," and she complimented him on his lovely name.

Taylor graciously accepted the compliment, and then asked her name was.

"Adrianna Jasmine," she told him proudly, she wasn't about to reveal her full name, she didn't want to frighten the poor boy off.

"That's the prettiest name I've ever heard," complimented Taylor, taken aback by its charm.

"Thank you," said the witch modestly, "now, what do you think of my crème brûlée?"

Taylor picked up a little silver spoon and, still trapped within her eyes, tapped his spoon onto the burnt caramel and scooped the luscious fusion of sweetness and cream into his mouth. He closed his eyes as the orgasmic sumptuousness enveloped his very existence. Honestly, he could taste it in his toes it was so good.

"Well…what do you think?" Adrianna Jasmine asked seductively, although the cheeky witch knew full well what he thought of her excellent dessert, she just wanted to hear it.

He was silent for a moment, then opened his eyes and looked straight into hers.

"It's like paradise," he praised, "I want to close my eyes and allow my tongue to explore every corner of my mouth; it's the most lusciously creamy, dexterously decadent and irresistibly scrumptious dessert that I have ever had the pleasure of eating."

Adrianna Jasmine tinkled with giggles at his response, and then Taylor cleared his throat and put on a faux professional voice.

"Well, that's what I'd have written in my article, anyway, Miss Jasmine. It is *Miss* Jasmine?"

Adrianna Jasmine shook her head, "actually it's Adrianna Jasmine Poppleapple…" She decided that was all he needed to know for now, "but you can just call me Adrianna Jasmine."

They continued chatting between Adrianna Jasmine's sugar sprinkling and caramel burning. She discovered that Taylor Jameson was a food critic for the leading food magazine Fantastico Banquetto. He spent his working days sampling tidbits, from leading restaurants to national food chains, high quality posh nosh to ethnic family run corporations. He enjoyed going to the gym and keeping fit, as he used to play semi-pro rugby until a tackle to his knee put an end to his career at the tender age of 20. Therefore, although mortified and crushed by the prospect of never playing for England, he read English at university, managed to do a bit of travelling after he received an honours degree; then on a whim, prior to returning from his travels, applied for a job at Fantastico Banquetto. He unexpectantly got a job as a very junior journalist on a very junior pay roll. However, after years of working as a junior, he stuck to his guns and made his way up to senior food critic for the top food magazine and has been sent all over the world, to eat!

"Sounds wonderful and very interesting," said Adrianna Jasmine dreamily. "It must be nice to do all the eating and not have to cook! And to top it off you get to travel, too!"

Taylor smiled and shrugged his shoulders. "Well, when it comes to it, I just want my money's worth, a good enjoyable meal and the basis to write something positive. I hate having to write a bad review."

"Really?" questioned the witch, "why, you're only stating your opinion, everyone has the right to that, even if it is a powerful one in a leading food magazine..." She paused as the horrid realization of whom she was actually talking to rushed over her. Why, he could use his powerful pen to either launch the Magic of Food into stardom or completely obliterate it. She wished she hadn't been quite so Mrs Pankhurst.

Taylor sensed the witch's flirty and friendly behaviour shift to uncomfortable and stiff.

Oh sweetheart! he thought tenderly. "I've frightened you. Relax," Taylor soothed, "I'm not going to write anything that could compromise your business, why on earth would I do that? You're terrific if were to write about the Magic of Food's leading lady, the pages would be filled with nothing but lovely stuff. So don't think for one moment I'd ever write anything but positive praise for you. In fact..." he added as if he were washed over with some sort of ingenious brain wave, "if you were to permit me, I would love to write about your triumph in the December issue, next month. Just imagine what it would do for your business!"

Adrianna Jasmine took a moment to drink it all in. Did he really say what she thought he said? An article in Fanatastico Banquetto! No, he couldn't have. Why, the opportunity for someone like her to appear in Fantastico Banquetto was the equivalent to a young aspiring model appearing in Vogue: it was a dream come true! Think of the opportunities it could unfold, the prospect of more catering gigs, perhaps finally splurging out on more appropriate premises to cook in! Her flat really was not suitable anymore, it was way too small.

"Wow," she finally managed to say, her heart pounding in excitement. "I never thought... I never dreamed, wow! *And* I would get to see you again," she added, although silently.

She adored his eyes, his humbleness, his smile and the way he looked at her. She had not experienced a man gazing upon her with such admiration and curiosity before. It was as if he was studying a magnificent piece of art that had been unveiled for the first time, longing to be touched and explored. She liked this very much and longed to touch his fingertips, and entwine her fingers into his hand. She longed for their cheeks to melt into one another's, to breathe in his aftershave, experience his strong arms around her body and slowly embark on that soft, tentative first kiss.

Adrianna Jasmine had not blinked for almost thirty seconds, she was entranced. Even when Taylor ceased to talk, she stood there, dumbstruck. Now she felt like a moron!

"Err," she quickly landed back onto earth, "wow, yes," she said repeating herself, "that would be amazing, truly, gosh could you do that?! I never expected...wow. Me, in Fantastico Banquetto."

Taylor beamed with happiness, he had to love her.

"It's already done. Listen, do you have a business card, I would really like to interview you as well as write about your success tonight, I think the public would love you. Where do you work?"

Adrianna flinched a little, being interviewed meant talking about her private life and well...the fact that she had to work out of her own kitchen. For some reason she felt embarrassed about it.

However, Taylor seemed to think that this added to her charm. This girl didn't need a fancy kitchen; all she needed was a hob!

"I have a health inspection certificate, she added, "you can print a copy of it if you like, you know, in case people think: yuck, she cooks at home! Not that you would think that if you saw my home," she added talking ten to the dozen, "It's spotless."

Taylor chuckled.

"Listen, I have an idea!" he said.

"Oh?" enquired the witch, a date, she hoped.

"Forget about the certificate, how about I present a whole feature on you, I can see the headline now, why, with your charm, you'd make the front cover!"

"Front cover of what?" questioned a familiar voice. Adrianna Jasmine turned around. It was Sarah. She repeated her question,

"Front cover of what?"

Adrianna Jasmine felt too overwhelmed to explain. Luckily Taylor took control.

"Of course she would *love* to do it," winked the redhead, "she'd be spectacular."

Adrianna Jasmine, who was now slowly returning back to earth, managed to smile. "Yes, I think I'd love to do it!" she confessed blissfully

Taylor looked thrilled.

"It seems like we need to set a date, then!" He said cheerfully, and polished off the crème brûlée with gusto. What a night it was turning out to be!

'Spend a few moments a day calming down, you owe it to yourself. Find a quiet spot, close your eyes, relax the muscles of your face, and soften your jaw and brow. Allow your shoulders to become heavy and relaxed. Breathe in deeply, allowing your rib cage to rise, and breathe out slowly, allowing your ribcage to fall. Clear your mind and after ten minutes you will feel refocused, refreshed and re-energised.'
(Adrianna Jasmine, 2008)

Chapter 8
Chaos

The night swept on in a blur of champagne, music and laughter and everyone appeared to be in fine spirits. Probably due to Adrianna Jasmine's tipsy potion, magically sprinkled into the scrumptious puddings, generating the effects of champagne merriment. In addition, Adrianna Jasmine had expertly whizzed up more of her famous espresso Martini glasses before flamboyantly setting them alight. The glow from the flames attracted plenty of curiosity and soon a flock of people were lining up, eager to try out the fun-looking beverage.

"Try this," suggested Adrianna Jasmine to Taylor, once the throng had dispersed, if you like my crème brûlée then I'm sure you'll enjoy this."

Keenly he accepted and took a hearty sip. The sweet brown liquid kissed his lips, drizzled like honey down his throat then settled, all warm and cozy in his tummy.

"Ooh, that's good," he said with a chuckle, "very impressive." He licked his sweet, sticky lips and went in for another. "That," he said holding up the half empty glass as if it were a fine heirloom, "is truly incredible...rather like the lady who made it."

Adrianna Jasmine smiled shyly; she was falling hook, line and sinker for her tanned, blonde honey-pot.

How can this be? she pondered. *This wasn't the plan, relationships, cooking, witchccraft plus, my strange family, they just don't go together...but he does smell divine!*

Taylor, too, was falling hook, line and sinker. Little did Adrianna Jasmine know, he had already mentally undressed her, kissed every inch of her sensual body, made her moan in delight, held her tight, deep into the night and even brought her breakfast in bed the following morning: pain au chocolate, granola, Earl Grey, and a single red rose.

She appeared to be earthy and natural, yet possessed an air of sophistication and worldly knowledge. He didn't know whether to wrap her up in a big fluffy warm towel, or take her white water rafting.

He chuckled to himself. He was rather enjoying this flirting business; it was fun, then again, this girl was actually *worth* flirting with.

Thank God I came now, he mused to himself gratefully, *to think I could have missed out on meeting her, plus all this fine food, alcohol and...oh no!!!*

"Taylor, honey!"

Adrianna Jasmine looked up and witnessed a fifty-something year old blonde woman, wearing a white crisp designer shirt, Versace Jeans, killer heals and even more killer nails, in the process of wildly throwing her arms around the rather horrified-looking Taylor. The woman was caked in San Tropez and appeared to be a fan of Botox and collagen. Her cheeks were puffed out with fillers, as if she were sucking on cotton buds. She looked like a melon on a stick.

"Hey, Lexi!" said Taylor with strained enthusiasm, "you're...here!"

"Of course I'm here, babes," she said with a screech laugh, "wouldn't have missed this for the world! And I must say you're looking gorgeous as ever, ooh yes! Anyhoo, I thought you weren't coming tonight, you naughty boy!"

"Oh, err..." he fumbled trying to find an appropriate excuse as to why he was attending the party, "it was a last minute decision really, the magazine was insistent, I couldn't get out of it..." he could feel bile rising from the back of his throat, Lexi Howler really did repulse him.

She then proceeded to fling her arms around him once more and hung from his neck like a chimpanzee, albeit dipping in designer wear and diamonds. Taylor's eyes flickered towards Adrianna Jasmine,

Please don't think for one moment I condone this infuriating behaviour, he silently implored, but Adrianna Jasmine's face was unreadable.

"Now, you hunky devil," pouted Lexi, "where's my kiss?"

Oh Christ! he thought with horror, *I want to be kissing Adrianna Jasmine, not you!*

Despite the feeling of utter revulsion, Taylor Jameson acted like the perfect gentleman smiled graciously and then painfully kissed the woman on her bouncy castle cheeks.

"Well, that'll do…for now," she sulked, then unravelled her boa constrictor bejewelled arms from around Taylor's neck. He sighed in relief.

"You having a good time?" she asked in her cockney accent. Taylor nodded, well he *had* been!

"It's fabulous, isn't it," she gushed, "and my God, wasn't the little Chrystal Rose amazing! Tonight is utterly amazing, the service, amazing, the alcohol, amazing and my God!" She dramatically stepped back to take a better look, "I have to say it again, y*ou* look amazing!"

She trussed her surgically enhanced double D's forward towards the uncomfortable-looking food critic, placed her hands dramatically onto her hips, cocked her head to one side and stared in awe at the specimen standing before her.

Taylor smiled and rubbed his eyebrows, Lexi was a very tiring woman, especially after knocking back a few sherbets. He cast his mind back to a time when he astonishingly found himself handcuffed to Lexi, who was nothing short of inebriated, at some restaurant launch party a few years back. It had been an uncomfortably embarrassing moment in itself, made worse by a picture of the outrageous moment printed in The News of The World! And pictures like those are not forgotten easily.

"Don't move a muscle," she said trying to sound seductive, and turned towards Adrianna Jasmine.

"Can I get a couple of those, lovie?" Lexi was gesturing towards the espresso Martinis.

"Certainly," answered Adrianna Jasmine politely and handed the woman two pre-made drinks.

Not taking her eyes off Taylor, Lexi took a large gulp then licked the rim of the glass, her tongue swishing about like a wet snake.

You look about as sexy as a dead hedgehog, thought Taylor, but ever the gentleman, proceeded to engage in conversation.

"They're good, aren't they?" he said trying to hold back his repugnance for her.

Lexi chortled

"Well, honey, as long as it's got alcohol in it, it could be rhino pee for all I care!" Lexi then proceeded to erupt into high pitched laughter, causing Adrianna Jasmine to wince, and Taylor to screw his eyes up in pain.

"No, seriously," she said in a more serious tone, "it's good stuff and the food is very good, still mustn't praise too much, got to keep the competition at bay."

With that, Adrianna Jasmine's ears pricked up and then she realized who this ghastly woman was. Yes, she was Lexi Howler. The owner of a rather swanky restaurant in the west end called The Oyster Pearl, so named because each paying customer is allowed to choose an oyster from the gigantic restaurant's tank before they leave in the hope to find a pearl.

Genius concept, mused Adrianna Jasmine, *but how do these type of women end up such good businesswomen?*

However, Adrianna Jasmine decided not let Lexi intimidate her. She, too, was a successful businesswoman, practically half Lexi's age and was not cosmetically enhanced to popping point. Moreover, poor Taylor didn't seem to be the slightest bit interested in the fact that Lexi was wet and wild for his affections. So there was nothing to worry about, yet whilst looking about the room, something did worry the witch.

As Lexi persisted to tempt Taylor into her bed that night, Adrianna Jasmine tuned her attentions towards the Perez twins. They were not in mission impossible mode anymore; they seemed to be clutching each other practically in tears!

Adrianna Jasmine quietly slipped away from her station; she needed to enquire why the twins were acting in such a peculiar manner.

En route to the Perez twins, she also happened to detect a certain blip in the newly reformed character of Freddie Von Zerger, was he…flirting? Yes, Freddie was clearly flirting with a cute, dark-haired model type, opposed to Serving up a Storm!

"My Goddess," she breathed with dread, "the spell, it's wearing off."

Panicked, the witch scanned the room for Sarah. Where was she? She had only been with her at the dessert station ten minutes ago.

Then Adrianna Jasmine looked at her watch, it was nearly 1am and to her horror she realized she had been flirting and caramelizing so avidly, that she had forgotten to keep an eye on the time.

With 1am rapidly approaching, she now had her work cut out.

Damn love and mush, she fumed angrily, *look what it's done and I was only bloody flirting!* That's why, she scolded herself, *you should never, never fall in love, oh, how could I have been so stupid?*

She grabbed hold of the Perez twins, then burst in between Freddie and the hottie.

"Excuse me, sorry," she said and grabbed Freddie's arm. She frog-marched him into the lift and took him down into the kitchen. Freddie squirmed and protested, but due to the spell still weakening his natural persona, along with the sheer determination of the witch, he didn't stand a chance.

Once in the kitchen, Adrianna Jasmine thrust some pre-made drinks into glasses and began to frantically chant over them.

Oh liquid cool, fresh and clear,

Soften their blow and their fear.
Bring them back gently to earth,
Complete with health, joy and mirth.

Gradually they sense where they are,
They have not travelled very far.
Their minds muddle free, librated of shock;
Their hearts tick steadily, like the hands of a clock.

She mumbled a quick grovelling to the Goddess and prayed that the bloody spell worked.

"Here, drink that," she half coaxed, half threw at them. "Drink!" *Goddess, if you don't,* she thought in horror, *you'll find yourself suddenly waking up from a ghastly nightmare, that you won't actually remember having, the trauma could possibly kill you.*

The trembling threesome at first shunned their drinks. Adrianna Jasmine started to panic.

"Come on now, you lot, drink up," she tried to coax, it was useless.

The group stared at her startled and confused as to why they needed desperately to drink, and then the Perez twins began to cry again.

"Oh Goddess," cried the witch. "OK, right, don't panic."

She reached into her pocket, retrieved her mobile and dialed for a taxi.

"Where do you three live?" She asked assertively, she was considering the possibility of bundling them all off home in a taxi, then praying for their wellbeing and sanity at her altar tonight.

"Str...stre...Stratham," sobbed the two twins, "number 4, Bright Field Way, we live with our mum."

Freddie, however, was not crying and to Adrianna Jasmine's delight was sipping his drink quietly, his mind misty and muddled. Adrianna Jasmine sighed in relief.

"Where to please?" Thank Goddess, it was the taxi firm.

High-pitched sobs erupting from the fretful twins made it difficult for the cabby to hear Adrianna Jasmine's instructions and as a result she had to shout down the phone.

"Right away, miss. About forty-five minutes?"

"What!" she cried, in alarm, "haven't you got anything sooner?"

The cabby explained that that was the best he could do, so take it or leave it. Adrianna Jasmine decided to leave it, what was the point they'd all be sectioned by the time the cab crawled its way over here.

Then it got worse, Valantina Valentine unexpectedly burst into the kitchen, yelling out rapid Spanish at a million miles per hour, her eyes laced with fire and her jaw set ready for a fight. Adrianna Jasmine felt terrified!

"Drink?" she gestured hopefully.

Valantina was not in the mood, and Adrianna Jasmine's hope was dashed as the wild Latina slapped the glass out of the witch's hand, smashing it onto the shiny tiles below.

The noise in the kitchen became deafening, what with all the blubbering, hiccupping and rapid foreign tongue.

Adrianna Jasmine stared helplessly on at the possessed and crazed group, they wanted answers. Where were they? Who were they? Why, why, why were they here?

It proceeded to get worse. In addition to the throng, Poppy Pilchard, Kiki Reece Kookie and Raul Crook - who had taken it upon himself to sing Any Dream Will Do, at top belt - turned up and joined in with the chaos.

Adrianna Jasmine thought her head was going to explode and for a moment pressed her hands to ears in order for her to block out the din and think. The only comfort to this awful moment was that Freddie Von Zerger was still sipping his drink and appeared to be calm. He actually looked bored.

"Freddie, FREDDIE!" Adrianna Jasmine screamed. "Why don't you go out and circulate, I hear there are some top model scouts out there, you never know, it might be your lucky night!" Freddie acknowledged Adrianna Jasmine's suggestion for a split second, looked down at his almost finished drink, shrugged his shoulders nonchalantly and then announced his departure.

"Later, losers," he scoffed and walked out with all the coolness of a rock star.

Adrianna Jasmine heaved a sigh of relief, one down, she thought, eight more to go. She placed her hands over her ears and shut her eyes tight.

"Hey! What the hell is going on in here?" Sarah had burst into the room looking somewhat exasperated. "I can hear you all on the first floor, you're totally ruining the effects of the burlesque water ballet performance by the British National Synchronized Swimming Team. Can you all please lower your voices. Her request was in vain. Raul was still singing at the top of his vocal chords, Valantina Valentine was demonically still raging in her hot Latin tongue, setting off tinnitus and spitting a little saliva every now and then. The Perez twins sobbed feverishly into each other's arms like frightened four-year-olds. Kiki Reece Kookie was standing by the sink, freakishly flashing the edge of a knife with a disturbingly psychotic look in her eye and Poppy Pilchard's large breasts were giggling about like two jellies on a plate. Sarah drank the situation in for a moment.

"Ok, this is bad!" she concluded. "What's happened to the spell wearing off gradually?"

And to make matters worse, she found Adrianna Jasmine standing in the middle of the throng with her eyes shut and hands clapped tightly over her ears, trying to find a happy place!

Sarah shot over to her friend and vigorously tried to shake her back into reality.

"What the hell is going on?" Sarah yelled.

Adrianna Jasmine looked as if she was losing it. She appeared to be in complete shock, which in all due respect was highly likely as her spells never went wrong and therefore she was not primed to handle such a situation.

Sarah wondered if she should slap the girl across the face in order to snap her out of it; the noise was becoming deafening.

"Adrianna Jasmine…ADRIANNA JASMINE!!!" bellowed Sarah once more, "you need to get a grip! What *is* going on? Is it the spell?

Adrianna Jasmine peered through her fingers, and nodded.

Now Sarah felt confused. Why was the spell turning against them? Adrianna Jasmine had done everything right, chanted the correct words and appeased the threefold law before drugging the crew. So, why the catastrophe? She took in a large gulp of air and wracked her brains. Then, the penny dropped.

Of course! denounced Sarah, *that man she was talking to half the night...he distracted her. She forgot about the staff and that she needed to cast a returning spell to gently bring them back to their normal state. That's why they're all going loopy*! But why would she forget...oh my Goddess! Sarah then came to the conclusion that either Adrianna Jasmine's faux pas was the result of falling in love, or the wrath of the threefold law because she *has* fallen in love and therefore personally gained from her use of magic tonight, resulting in out of control chaos as a punishment, she went for the latter. How rotten.

Sarah put her hands onto Adrianna Jasmine's shoulders and stared deeply into her friend's multi-coloured eyes.

"Jazzy, listen to me," said her friend sternly, "I think you're being punished by the threefold law."

Adrianna Jasmine stared at her friend, wide-eyed and confused.

"Me, why me?" she asked, like a fretful child, never had she felt so vulnerable. "I didn't want *anything* from tonight." Goddess, she wanted her mum. "As always I cast my spells with the purist of hearts and the want of nothing but health and happiness for those around me, so why am I being punished?"

"Because, my dear girl," Sarah explained, "*you* have personally gained from tonight, that's why!"

Adrianna Jasmine stared at her friend, her face scrunched up with perplexity.

"Excuse me, I don't mean to interrupt your little pep talk," came an angry voice, "but I demand to know why my feet are red raw, why I stink of garlic and why I am in the company of a sad stage school nut job, singing a bad rendition of Joseph and his 'I don't give a rats arse' amazing coloured coat!"

Kiki Reece Kookie had approached the two witches, still embracing her shining steel knife.

"I am a child of the theatre and don't need to be subjected to this appalling version of an Andrew Lloyd Webber classic."

"Hey, I heard that!" Raul was now making his way over to the queen of drama queens like a demented penguin.

"I sing Joseph just fine, thank you very much!" Kiki snorted like a pig.

"I'll be the judge of that!" she snapped. "Your voice reminds me of one of the X factor audition rejects."

Raul looked as though he had been slapped in the face.

"How dare you, I'll have you know I'm classically twained."

"What by, Jonathon Woss?" mocked the vicious Kooky, wow she was spiteful.

Sarah had just about had enough.

"Kiki!" Sarah shouted, "the answer is simple. You worked your socks off tonight, you served up a storm, you poured drinks, plated vegetables, handed out chocolate treats on glass trays and basically worked! Is that so much to comprehend?"

Kiki thought hard for a few moments and then screamed out an earth shattering, "YES!"

Sarah glared at Kiki, before turning her attentions back to Adrianna Jasmine. She placed her hands affectionately onto Adrianna Jasmine's shoulders. "Honey, listen to me, the staff are in shock, it's like they've come out of a four hour coma, they are dazed and confused. I need you to perform a calming spell to help soothe them, can you do that for me?" Adrianna Jasmine looked up at her friend, still looking lost and bewildered.

"Why is it *my* fault," asked Adrianna Jasmine like a little girl scolded for a crime she did not commit, "it's not fair."

Sarah heaved a sigh. Goddess, the racket was becoming intolerable.

"Because," she tried to explain again, "*you* have personally gained from tonight, albeit without you knowing or desiring it."

Adrianna Jasmine shook her head in defiance. "No, I haven't, I haven't gained anything or wished for anything from tonight, except perhaps that they would all bloody shut up!"

"Oh, wake up girl and smell the caramel Macchiato," shot Sarah sharply, "of course you've gained from tonight. You've been head-hunted by a top food magazine and let's face it, I think your *spells* might have had something to do with that *and* it looks very likely that you've met your future husband and possibly the father to your child!"

Adrianna Jasmine stood back stunned at her friend's deliberation. It was inconceivable, to think her perfectly planned night was ruined by the prospect of love! Nevertheless, it all made sense: the tummy upset, the Mystic Odessa's prediction. It was all in the stars. But not Adrianna Jasmine's stars, not now, not ever. She was angry, very angry and to think the threefold law had punished her for it! The cheek. Like she even needed love! That was it. Adrianna Jasmine was ready for battle.

Sarah, who was still in grip of Adrianna Jasmine's shoulders, stared deep into her friend's eyes and witnessed a shift, her eyes went from abandoned, aimless and hapless, to determined, decisive and furious. "Thank, Goddess," breathed Sarah with a sigh of relief, "you're back! Perhaps we're now saved, go…go and sort this all out!"

Once snapped out of her trance, Adrianna Jasmine sprang into action. She was still angry with herself, due to the little hiccup of falling for her yummy stranger with the gorgeous brown eyes, gentlemanly mannerisms, good sense of humour, obviously doing rather well for himself…

"FOCUS!" she yelled to herself, "you're doing it again, learn child, learn! This is why you forgot to keep an eye on your staff and why you're in this mess."

With that she clapped her hands together sharply and quickly made her way over to her "first aid kit."

She retrieved a bottle labelled "calming potion," a handful of mixed herbs and a white candle. The witch worked like lightning. She chucked all the ingredients into a saucepan and heated to create a smoke. Now she needed the crazed crew to infuse their minds with calming and relaxing wafts of herby smoke.

The witch lit the little white candle and focused deeply on the flame. After a few minutes of intense staring, Adrianna Jasmine blew out the candle which resulted in her eyes turning to a frightening shade of black. She was in the zone and her spell was ripe to perform.

She walked towards the throng, muttering under her breath over and over again, against the growing hubbub and desperation of the Serve up a Storm crew.

By the power of earth, dark emotions wither.
By the power of water, dark emotions be cleansed.
By the power of air, dark emotions diminish.
By the power of fire, dark emotions burn.

After the tenth time, Adrianna Jasmine sensed the power surging through her body like electricity, she was ready. Her arms shot up high above her head and she began to chant

Oh misery, anxiety, trauma and fear.
I banish thee with courage and might.
Darkness dissolves brightness shine through.
Leave now dark emotions release this plight.

With that, the lights in the house began to flicker, then complete power failure. Chaos erupted upstairs as Pigwell's house became dark as night. People stepped on each other's toes, the water ballet team nearly drowned, drinks were spilt down tops, Lexi homed in on Taylor's bum, silly screams erupted from girls vocal chords and lovers took full advantage of the unexpected black out!

"For God's sake, someone get some candles please," yelled the disgruntled Pigwell, who had unexpectedly stumbled into the kitchen. "Jesus, what's that awful smell?" Adrianna Jasmine glanced over to the stove towards her potion. As she expected the potion had boiled away and the saucepan was now merrily burning to a crisp, hence producing the nasty aroma.

Adrianna Jasmine let her arms down, as they were still dramatically positioned above her head and shot towards the burnt pan. She removed the pan, from the heat and jumped back in alarm, as she felt the presence of a body near to her.

It was Sarah.

"Goddess, you made me jump!" breathed Adrianna Jasmine, her heart booming.

"Yes, well your eyes will make people jump, let's hope they clear up before the lights turn on again.'

Adrianna Jasmine was confused.

"How can you see my eyes, its pitch black?"

"I can't," whispered Sarah, "but I saw them after you inhaled the potion, they were pretty dark, Jazzy, you looked creepy."

"It's nothing you've not seen before," snapped Adrianna Jasmine.

"Not in that shade of psychotic black!"

"Oh shut up, Sarah," snapped Adrianna Jasmine, she was *not* in the mood, "help me find candles, please!"

"No need," replied Sarah smugly, "I've got a better idea."

With an air of satisfaction to her face, Sarah began to chant her own little spell,

"Spirits of light I conjure thee, create light and make them see, by the powers of one two three, so let it be, let vision be free!"

Immediately the lights came on and Charley Fresco's music began to lazily whirr back into existence.

"Eeek," Shrieked Sarah, "put some sun glasses on, will you, you look like a deranged psycho who's just escaped from a Victorian loony bin."

"Thanks," said Adrianna Jasmine sarcastically and positioned her hands over her black eyes and whispered, "return to me"

She then revealed her eyes and viciously stared at her friend

"OK, you'll do," said Sarah sardonically. Adrianna Jasmine rolled her eyes then proceeded to return her thoughts back to a few moments ago; what was she doing? Oh yes, she had just performed a high intensity calming spell, rescued a pot from burning to cinders, the pot however would sadly never cook another meal, turned her black, crazed eyes back to normal and now…? Now she needed to pick up some pieces.

Team Serve up a Storm was pretty much sedated and therefore much easier to handle. The calming spell had actually worked! Gone were the screams and bad energy, lightness and peace prevailed. The group still, however, looked a bit dazed and confused and, of course, their poor, blistered feet still throbbed. Nevertheless, they were mentally comfortable. The spell had zapped away their pulsating anger, quashed the sheer taste for violence and melted away unpleasant, ferocious thoughts.

"OK, all back on track," breathed Adrianna Jasmine, but alas her satisfaction did not last for long.

As she scanned the room, she noticed that Pigwell was still in the kitchen, but for some reason, curled up on the kitchen table fast asleep. Panic once again wafted over Adrianna Jasmine like a black smoke.

"Please let it be too much drink," she begged. Then her heart leaped, "Oh no!!!" She cried out, her hands scrunched up into fists of fury and shot out of the kitchen towards the lift as spritely as a leopard.

"Please, please no!" She prayed as the lift ascended to the fifth floor.

But alas, as the lift doors opened it was as she feared. The whole party had magically transformed from a thriving, buzzing swinging party, to a mellow sleepy Zen Den.

"I've done the whole party!"

She wanted to curl up into a ball and disappear, or shape shift into Jupiter 10! The witch had not only zonked Serve up a Storm but, to her horror, the entire party!

She shook her head, beaten and despondent, "I should just give up now; what a disaster!"

The witch wandered around aimlessly, witnessing the mess she had created. People were literally falling asleep where they stood, or curling up like cats on chairs, unable to fight the overwhelming urge to sleep.

"Why oh why, Adrianna Jasmine?" she questioned herself solemnly, "how could you have done this?" The music was still thumping out and the models, which were walking about on stilts, began to fall to the floor like tumbling towers.

She wandered around, assessing the damage.

"What a mess, what a mess!"

She kept repeating to herself over and over again, then, as if discovering a beautiful rose blooming in the desert, she saw him.

Taylor was slumped on the floor, drunkenly spooning in the remnants of a fruits of the forest crème brûlée, smiling like a love-sick teen. Lexi Howler's head - she had passed out - was nestled into his crotch. Luckily, he didn't seem to notice that she was dribbling on him.

Adrianna Jasmine took a deep breath, wandered over to the food critique and gently kneeled down in front of him.

"Taylor...?" she whispered gently, "are you alright?"

Taylor, in his disoriented state, looked up to find Adriana Jasmine's beautiful face an angel's breath from his very own.

"Hey...it's you!" he said, clearly happy to see her, "I wondered where you'd gone; I thought you'd left me, listen...can I tell you something?"

The witch smiled gently and nodded, she felt as though her heart were melting. His eyes looked disturbingly tired and he tried desperately to stay awake just so he could spend a few more precious moments with the magical woman. He reached up and placed his fingertips tenderly onto Adrianna Jasmine's hot cheeks. Her skin felt like satin beneath his fingers. The witch took his hand into hers and peered into his eyes. She nodded.

"Yes," she whispered, "you can tell me anything."

Still not taking his eye away from Adriana Jasmine, Taylor clumsily threw the crème brûlée onto the floor and pushed Lexi off his crotch. She landed on the floor with a bump. He took a deep breath before mustering the last remnants of his energy, so that he may speak.

"I think... think..." he tried desperately to finish his sentence as the urge to sleep swept over him like a dark fog, "that I'm falling...in love...with...you..." He smiled once more at the witch, and then his eyes closed and finally, he surrendered to a deep, deep sleep.

"What you do comes back to you threefold."
The threefold Law

Chapter 9
The New Forest, Thirty Years Ago

Four witches and a baby lamb trudged deep into The New Forest, Hampshire. It was 4.30pm and night was drawing in, thick and fast. Frosty leaves and twigs crunched under their feet and their breath danced on the chilled air.

"This is the place," the eldest of the witches announced, "this is where it shall be."

Silently the witches came to a stop and removed their heavy knapsacks from their weary backs.

"Unpack quickly," urged eldest witch, "soon it will be pitch black and we won't be able to see."

Heeding the eldest's warning, the witches proceeded to gather into a circle and unpacked their wares. Each witch carried the same tools; a single slab of granite, 30cm in width and length, a thick candle, each one in a different colour, a knife, and a representative of the four sacred elements, earth, water, wind and fire. The eldest of the witches tied the baby lamb around the trunk of the tree and the youngest of the witches placed a plastic container, with air holes punched into the lid, tentatively on the ground. Each witch laid their slab of granite onto the forest floor, and then placed their magic tools on top of the cold, smooth stone. Once everything was in place, the cackle sat on the icy ground, patiently waiting for the witching hour of midnight.

The moon was full and ripe and projected a reddish ring of light, often known as "blood on the moon." The sky was completely cloudless and stars twinkled like ice against the jet black. It would be seven hours before the witches could begin their ritual. As the forest plunged into an eerie darkness, minutes dragged by like hours and still the witches sat silently, only the sound of their teeth chattering from the cold broke the quietness of the place.

"It is time," announced the eldest, "the witching hour is almost upon us, let us do our duty."

"Thank the Goddess," thought the rest of the cackle silently, they were cold and tired and the forest was not the most welcoming of places on an icy winter's night. The witches each lit their candle, and then proceeded to take their stand. They linked hands and the eldest began to chant. Her language was unusual, perhaps hailing from a dark ancient time; even if you didn't understand the words she spoke, you could certainly feel them. They were dark and dangerous and sent shivers down the spine. Fifteen minutes into the chant, the eldest witch's eyes had transformed from a watery grey, to a deathly shade of black, the element earth was filling her very core. Once the eldest was ripe, the chant was passed clockwise around the circle. Each witch underwent the same process, the ancient chanting, the black eyes and the surge of energy on loan from their sacred element. It was intense and disturbing; even if one understood it the act would evoke nothing but fear.

Once all the witches had completed their chant, the eldest witch advanced towards the wretched lamb, which had fallen asleep at the tree trunk. She carried it over to the circle, took out her knife and slit the sleeping lamb's throat. She ripped open its chest, tore out its near beating heart and crushed it in her wrinkly hands. The second witch in the circle took out a photograph and, using her knife, violently slashed it to pieces then spat with venom onto the shredded mess. The third witch removed a piece of hair, tied with a black ribbon and burnt it on the flame from her candle. Then it was the youngest of cackle's turn. She bent down and cautiously removed the lid from the box. Placing a thick glove onto her right hand she removed an adder and without remorse, cut its head off with her knife. She then discarded the body and burnt the head in the flame of her candle. After the sickening ritual, the witches held hands and began to chant once again.

They chanted deep into the hours of the morning, not stopping once for food, drink, or toilet. Instead opting to go hungry and thirsty, even to soil their clothes rather than break the circle.

Then, at six thirty, the birds burst into song. The night was over and the witches collapsed from exhaustion onto the forest floor

Carolina Plum's Easy Happy Home Spell

Buy a new broom for yourself and cast out your old stuffy one. Now sweep, sweep, sweep away using your new broom to sweep, sweep, sweep away any old negative energy that maybe lingering about. Buy a fresh Basil plant and leave to flourish on the window-sill to attract joy into your home.

Chapter 10
Drift Away

It was Sunday morning and Adrianna Jasmine was back at her flat, snuggled under her duvet and hiding from the world. Jupiter 10 was nestled up and snoring contently at the bottom of her bed, exhausted from his nightly shenanigans of catching mice and slinking about amongst the shadows.

Adrianna Jasmine, too, was exhausted from *her* shenanigans! The witch hadn't returned home from the party until 5.45am and was mentally frazzled. She had been so distraught over the safety and wellbeing of the sleeping party-goers, that she couldn't bring herself to go home until safe in the knowledge that everyone in Pigwell's house was protected and out of harm's way.

The witch had spent half the night removing everything from trip hazards, to covering up shivering bodies with blankets and coats. She covered up exposed bottoms, placed pillows under heads and even removed the sleeping dancers from the tall champagne glasses with tricky levitation spells. Well, they could have drowned!

Charley Fresco also had to be removed from the high DJ tower, for fear of him tumbling to his death and that took absolutely ages due to the witch stupidly forgetting to stock up on feathers in her first aid kit. Adrianna Jasmine eventually found some by snipping off the end of a pillow with a pair of nail scissors, before sifting through a mass of white allergy-enhancing goose feathers. She located the biggest one she could find (a pitiful inch in length), then laid four white candles in a circle beneath the scaffold DJ tower. She lit them one by one, starting from the east working around sun-wise, and then entered the circle. She sat comfortably facing her object of levitation, holding the feather gently in her left, less dominant hand and began to chant the following…

In the light they see the colors of day;
In the darkness they are blinded by black.
In the world they walk on earth and stone.
In fire their flesh will but burn,

*In water their body is a washed and cleansed,
In air their body shall take flight.*

After chanting three times, the witch called upon her spirit guide, the Goddess, cleared her mind, gently opened her hand, and focused on the feather resting gently on her palm.

She then focused on the feather becoming Charley and that he were as light and soft as the little feather in her hand, so light that he could float with ease, just like the feather, to the ground.

It didn't work. Charley would only lift a pitiful two inches from the platform before floating straight back down with a mild bump. She was becoming exasperated with frustration, which in turn made the spell even more difficult to perform. You see, to allow a spell like this to work, Adrianna Jasmine was essentially required to keep her mind clear, pure and light, otherwise she didn't stand a chance.

Now in normal circumstances the spell would have worked straight away, due to the aid of a large, vibrant coloured Peacock feather, that laid on her alter at home, not the white puny feather she was forced to work with.

As a result, the poor witch had to focus and concentrate so much harder than usual; she actually gave herself a nose bleed from the strain.

In the end Adrianna Jasmine turned for additional help from Sarah, who was as clear headed as Britney Spears at the infamous VMA awards. The calming spell had unfortunately affected her friend, too, although due to Sarah being a witch, her resilience was much stronger than mere mortals. But at least she was awake, albeit drowsy and less alert than her usual self. However, with Sarah now too performing the spell, it doubled its power and Charley eventually floated safely to the ground.

Then it was the irksome task of covering up the shivering champagne glass dancers with towels and performing warming spells, in order to deter hyperthermia, even death! It was never-ending, what with one trip hazard after another, health and safety issue after health and safety issue. Even when she did eventually make it back to her home, the poor witch was up for a further hour chanting away at her altar trying to rectify the horrors of the night. She had to pray for the wellness of the entire Serve up a Storm crew and cast protection spells for everyone who had accidentally passed out at the party. It was close to six before she managed to snuggle under her marshmallow of a duvet.

That morning she dreamed about Taylor. He was trying to find her in a green maze on a very cold icy morning. He was shouting for her to call out, but she wouldn't and kept running away from him. She was enjoying the chase but deep down secretly wishing for him to find her. He never found her and Adrianna Jasmine woke up at 10am, disappointed that he didn't.

"Ouch. My poor head," Sarah had entered Adrianna Jasmine's bedroom, her hair strewn all over her makeup-smudged face, she looked like she'd been chased through The New Forest.

"I feel terrible," she grumbled, "and it's entirely your fault!"

She flung back the duvet and slipped in beside Adrianna Jasmine. Adrianna Jasmine produced a fake, loud snore: she was not in the mood.

"Shut up, Sarah," grumbled Adrianna Jasmine, "go put the kettle on."

Sarah was indifferent.

"Not bloody likely, not after the hell you put me through last night. The *least* you can do is make *me* a cuppa."

Adrianna Jasmine held on tight to her duvet, she had no intention of moving, even though she was quite parched and a cup of tea would certainly go down a treat. However, after ten minutes, Adrianna Jasmine succumbed, climbed out of her snuggle mountain of a bed and made two mugs of tea. She even popped two cupcakes that she had reserved, on to the tray for good measure.

"Ooh, lovely," cooed Sarah, as her friend entered with the tray.

Adrianna Jasmine wasn't feeling too bad, considering, just a bit dazed but comforted in the knowledge that it was now broad daylight and that the guests were most probably peacefully waking up from their slumber. Her magic had seen to that!

The witch set the tray down on her bedside table and passed the mug of tea, along with a cake, over to her friend. They both sat in bed watching the Sex in the City film, perfect for cheering up two depressed witches.

They both giggled and ooh'd and aah'd at the fab clothes, and compared each other to the characters. Sarah thought Adrianna Jasmine was more like Charlotte, the straight laced, sophisticated optimist who saw good in everyone, but defiantly embraced her naughty side. Whilst Adrianna Jasmine thought Sarah was like Samantha, a man eater! They both agreed with their decisions and continued watching the film.

It was well into lunch time when the film finished and Sarah decided to freshen up before going home. She was not working at the coffee shop today as she knew she would be useless, but was content in the thought that the work experience boy was busy holding the fort with her delightful parents.

"What fun they must be having!" She quipped sarcastically, then sighed and huffed and puffed as she removed herself from the bed.

"Why do you have to go if you're not working?" inquired her friend. "What have you got to do on a Sunday?!"

Sarah thought for a moment, she was actually free today and had nothing planned.

"Stay here," suggested Adrianna Jasmine, "have a bath, we'll order Chinese tonight, do face masks and watch more chick flicks, and it'll be fun!"

Sarah considered the tempting offer for a few moments.

"OK, why not," she smiled, "that does sound like fun. I'll have to rinse my knickers out though, they tend to decompose after 48 hours." Adrianna Jasmine winced.

"Fine, just do what you have to do in regards to your personal hygiene," she said, revolted at her friend's comment. "Just leave them on the towel rail to dry when you're done." She would have offered a pair of her own but she wasn't keen on sharing her smalls with anyone and knew that Sarah would never give them back. "I'll run you a nice bath, too," offered Adrianna Jasmine, "with some Citrus Bang-Bang Boom. That'll freshen you right up. I'll even light some nice candles and pour you a cranberry juice, which you can sip all warm and cozy whilst reading this month's Cosmos!"

Cosmos was the witches' version of Cosmopolitan and was only available to witching folk. It kept hip and happening witches in the know with spells, fashion, places to go for a witching fun holiday, advice columns, recipes, horoscopes (that were actually accurate), gossip about the world's rich and famous witches/warlocks, and the piece de resistance: a complimentary Tallulah Toffee product sample.

"Ooooooh that sounds positively darling," cooed Sarah as she stretched her body lazily from under the duvet.

"OK, I'll do it now," said Adrianna Jasmine full of beans, then she leapt up with the energy of a Springer Spaniel and began the joyful task of pampering her chum.

As she ran the bath for Sarah, Adrianna Jasmine decided she too would enjoy a magical bath shortly after, especially after the night she had endured, it had been enough to send any witch to the Priory. Once the bath was drawn, candles lit and juice poured, Adrianna Jasmine left Sarah alone to sink into her bath. During this time, the witch decided to take the opportunity to have a little tidy up. She enjoyed cleaning as she found the experience therapeutic and used the opportunity to perform a clearing spell. Clearing spells were very simple. You brought yourself a new broom and swept out unwanted negative energy - it is sometimes stored in one's home - out of the door and out of your life.

After forty five minutes, Sarah emerged from her bath, glowing with health. Colour was back in her face, nasty make up removed and her hair was swept up in a towel.

"Gosh that was fabulous," she gushed full vim, "I must say your bathroom is heavenly, Adrianna Jasmine, and, of course, your stock of Toffee products enhances the luxury." Adrianna Jasmine smiled at her friend.

"Pleased you enjoyed it. Right, off to have mine now, make yourself comfy and see you in half an hour or so."

Sarah nodded, plonked herself down on the settee and switched on the TV. She felt good now, no headache and totally refreshed. She had bathed in Citrus Bang-Bang Boom, used Tallulah Toffee shampoo (Tahiti Lime) to wash her lovely red hair and treated herself to a Jelly Palm Hair Mask, which is proven to mend split ends and allow the hair to stay clean and smelling of wild strawberries for a week! She smelt like a fruit salad.

Adrianna Jasmine did not use Citrus Bang-Bang Boom for her bath today, instead she opted for Float Away Holiday, a sumptuous smelling bath gel created from Burdening Plum, Brazil Cherry, Indian Fig and Chinese Jujube. The gel, once combined with water, gently teleports the lucky soaker in mind, not in body, to a pink sanded beach in the Caribbean, complete with crystal blue waters. The bather can momentarily relax and unwind in paradise, without actually leaving the house. It was Tallulah Toffee's most critically acclaimed triumph and to cap it all off, the bather walks out of the bathroom with a slight tan to the skin. (A sprinkling of pink sand is often discovered in the bottom of the bath tub too. Genius!)

After settling down into her deep, luxurious bath, Adrianna Jasmine drifted far, far away to a country of eternal sunshine and exotic fruit. She was on a beach, wearing a chocolate brown bikini, accompanied with a white shell necklace, anklet and bracelets. Her hair was rich and free, flowing down her back and a red exotic a flower sat prettily on the side of her head. She was completely relaxed, tranquil, and content. The sun was warm on her face and she was drinking coconut milk from the shell. Her skin was lightly tanned and exuded radiance and health. She felt wonderful, not a care in the world. Her breath was easy, her muscles warm and pliable, life could not be more perfect. Or could it?

She turned her head towards her right shoulder and there, sitting beside her in blue and white board shorts, was an addition to paradise. A warm, bronzed body was sitting next to Adrianna Jasmine, so close that skin was touching skin. There they sat, gazing out towards the sea, content and relaxed in one another's company. As they continued to gaze towards the azure blue, Adrianna Jasmine found herself snuggling deep into the man's strong embrace, breathing in his luscious scent of coconuts, sea air and Chanel Allure for men! She felt protected, safe and the happiest she had felt in ages. Could this be the result of the love of a good man? Adrianna Jasmine wasn't sure, she was just relishing in the moment, this glorious moment of love, beauty and warmth.

The sun began to set and the sky was washed with fine looking colours: gentle pinks, vibrant scarlett, rich gold, soothing purples and azure blues. The sea, mill pond still, reflected these luscious colours, transforming the magnificent water into a liquid rainbow. *Could a scene be any more beautiful?* Then her body began to chill ever so slightly, the sun began to disappear and blackness softly overpowered the coloured delight. Adrianna Jasmine was back in her bathroom. The water had cooled, gradually drifting her back into reality.

She opened her eyes, stretched lazily and smiled to herself. "What a lovely trip," she told herself quietly, then began to wash her hair.

After rinsing off the remnants of her imaginary holiday and Tallulah Toffee's Tangle Taming conditioner, Adrianna Jasmine dried herself off with a nice rough towel, great for exfoliating the skin and wrapped her hair up in a smaller towel. Once dried, she smothered her body in Angel Kiss Body Lotion, which smelt of lemon grass, honey and orange blossom, and massaged her face with Tick Tock Stop the Clock, moisturizing cream, which did exactly what it said on the packet. All witches who used this exclusive creamy dream to their thirst quenched, appreciative faces, would never crack a wrinkle, endure a laughter line, experience puffy eyes or droopy jowls! Can you imagine if Joan Rivers could get hold of it? Alas, there would be no such luck: Toffee products, including Tick Tock Stop the Clock, are not available to the non-witching world. Therefore non-witching cosmetic companies will continue their search for the latest beauty treatment in a tube, an anti-wrinkle cream that actually works and of course, clever ways to make cosmetically challenged folk fork out their cash. Will they ever get even close to the ability of Toffee products?

Adrianna Jasmine, feeling totally revived, padded out of her bathroom. In her wake, a plume of gorgeous aromas followed.

"Bless Toffee products," she praised appreciatively, even she was overjoyed by the cocktail of joyful scents.

She entered the living room where she found Sarah snuggled up watching re-runs of The Good Life.

"Ah, there you are," Sarah teased, "and where have *you been* missus? I thought you'd left the country or something. I nearly called the coast guard at one point, why on earth were you so long?"

Adrianna Jasmine smiled, and stretched lazily before assembling herself on the couch next to her friend. Jupiter 10 jumped effortlessly with the grace of a prima ballerina, onto his mistress's lap and settled down for more cat nap.

"Well... I suppose I did leave the country!" Adrianna Jasmine said with a smug little chuckle.

Now anyone else, who had just heard this remark, would have thought Adrianna Jasmine was nothing short of stark staring raving bonkers, but not Sarah, she knew exactly what Adrianna Jasmine was driving at.

"Don't tell me," Sarah asked, her jaw almost hitting the floor, "you've only gone and brought Toffee's latest and greatest product of the century...Float Away Holiday?!"

Adrianna Jasmine nodded and waited for it. "WHY DIDN'T YOU TELL MEEEEE?!" screamed Sarah, clearly displeased.

Adrianna Jasmine laughed.

"Because I wanted to try it first," said Adrianna Jasmine flatly, "I bought it! Honestly! Besides, you can have a go next time."

Sarah pouted and looked sulky; she had been dying to try out the stuff since she read about it in last month's Cosmos.

"Oh, come on. Cheer up," said Adrianna Jasmine as she patted her friend on the knee. "Hey, at least your 'spellover' has gone (witching term for hangover). Only Citrus Bang-Bang Boom has the power to do that; escapism wouldn't have stood a chance."

Sarah pouted and folded her arms like a six year old.

"Anyway, so what was it like, then, is it as fantastic as they say?"

Adrianna Jasmine set the scene.

"I was on a beach, a beautiful beach with pink sand, sipping fresh coconut juice. You know, from the shell?" Sarah nodded.

Cow! she thought

"And I was so happy, really happy, just staring out into the crystal blue waters, the sun on my face, the smell of the fruit and ocean, the warmth and protected feeling from Tay..." Adrianna Jasmine sat up sharp and slapped her hand across her mouth.

"What did you nearly say...?" asked Sarah, her jaw once again almost hitting the floor, "you said Tay..."

Adrianna Jasmine was indifferent.

"No I didn't!"

"Oh yes you jolly well did!" stated Sarah firmly. "Go on, finish what you were about to say...Taaaaaaay...."

Sarah looked as though she were winding up a great invisible clock. "Come on! Finish it!" Adrianna Jasmine's hand was still covering her mouth, her eyes stretched wide like saucers.

"Oh my Goddess," she eventually whispered, "he was there, he was with me, right on the beach with his arm around me, watching a bloody sunset!" Her face then darkened. "What the hell was he doing in my virtual holiday?"

Sarah was clearing loving it.

"Honey," she said soothingly, albeit with a hint of satisfaction in her voice, "you wanted him there!"

"I most certainly did not!" snapped Adrianna Jasmine. "All I wanted was a relaxing magical bath, *on my own,* in order to escape from last night's escapades. Goddess, Sarah," she continued clearly exasperated, "*he* was the main reason why last night was so stressful, and why I needed so desperately to escape! Why on this Goddess green earth would I want him at my sunset? WHY? WHY? WHY?"

In frustration, Adrianna Jasmine was thumping her fists on the settee, she needed a holiday!

Sarah shook her head in disbelief.

"Oh, wake up, Adrianna Jasmine, again! It's time for a few home truths. *You* wanted him."

Adrianna Jasmine opened her mouth in astonishment, but Sarah simply waved her hand dismissively and continued.

"Deep down, Adrianna Jasmine," explained Sarah with all the drama of a Shakespearean actress, "beneath all that resistance to love, all that respect for your craft and all your fear that love will render you powerless, you really like that chap you met last night and Tallulah Toffee's happy holiday spell simply coaxed it out of you. Tallulah, it seems, simply honed in on your inner desires."

"But... but I don't like him," Adrianna Jasmine tried pathetically. "I don't, I swear, I have no feelings for him, for Goddess sake, I only met him last night!"

Adrianna Jasmine felt panic wash over her, her hands were a little sweaty and she felt as if the room were closing in on her.

"Oh, you swear, do you?" asked Sarah a little darkly.

Adrianna Jasmine nodded with assurance.

"Yep!" she said, "I swear I don't love Taylor Jameson!"

"Really?" said Sarah, unconvinced. She didn't believe her friend for a moment. "OK then, let's prove it!"

Adrianna Jasmine scoffed.

"*I* don't have to prove anything, I know my heart."

"Precisely!" said Sarah, "that's the point I'm trying to make."

Sarah then rose from the couch and made her way to Adrianna Jasmine's bedroom, only to return moments later with her friend's Book of Shadows. The Book of Shadows was the bible of spells. It was 150 years old, filled with spells from witches past and present and was Adrianna Jasmine's pride and joy. She respected this book more than she respected the threefold law.

Adrianna Jasmine appeared a little nervous as her friend loomed over her with the impressive book. The Book of Shadows was so powerful that one could practically feel the magic crackling out from the bound, gold leaf pages.

"Err...what're you doing Sarah?" Adrianna Jasmine asked nervously. "Why've you brought in my spell book?"

"Swear on it!" demanded Sarah firmly.

Adrianna Jasmine's eyes were now as large as Habitat dinner plates.

"I beg your pardon," gasped Adrianna Jasmine a little taken aback, "I'm not swearing on anything. Put it back and stop messing about, I'm not in the mood."

Sarah stood her ground, she had a devious twinkle to her eye, her jaw was set and her erect frame looked positively giantess against the curled up little Adrianna Jasmine.

"I don't want to," whined the little witch; she looked as though she were about to start sucking her thumb.

"Come now, Adrianna Jasmine," teased Sarah, "play the game! It's simple, if you really don't like this Taylor food critic, then it shouldn't be a problem. All you have to do is place your hand onto The Book of Shadows and say 'I swear on the book of shadows I do not like Taylor Jameson.' Then I'll pop the book back on your altar and we can finish watch television. Simple!"

Adrianna Jasmine sat up with a steely glint of determination in her eye.

"OK, smart ass, I'll do it. Give me the book."

Sarah handed her friend the book then crossed her arms as she waited to see what her friend would do. Surely her friend wouldn't swear on the book and lie. Still, it would be an interesting few minutes.

Adrianna Jasmine stared down at the book; her heart was beating fast and her palms were still sweaty with nerves. She fondled the front cover, which was bound in thick brown leather, strong and cool on her fingers. She could feel the power of the spells penetrating her very soul. She adored the book and respected it as much as Princess Dianna respected Mother Theresa.

She shut her eyes and tried to say the words that she so desperately wanted to hear.

Go on, say it, she urged herself. *Say you don't like Taylor. Say it!*

But she couldn't. She couldn't because it was a lie, her heart knew it and the book knew it, too. Page 210, Truth Spell, was shining out like a luminous glow stick at a rave, preventing the witch from saying an untruth.

Adrianna Jasmine opened her eyes and looked defeated; she passed the book back to Sarah and shook her head.

"I don't want to," she whispered, then started to giggle.

Sarah, who accepted the book, excitedly stared down at her friend.

"Ah ha, I knew it," she announced triumphantly, "you *do* fancy old foodie, ha ha. Wow!" She cocked her head to one side, "Adrianna Jasmine: I never thought I'd see the day."

"And you won't see the day, Sarah," exclaimed Adrianna Jasmine angrily, "because there won't be a day!"

"Yeah right, whatever," said Sarah plonking herself back down onto the couch, "I see the sparkle in your eyes. You like this chap!"

Adrianna Jasmine sighed.

"I only met him last night, Sarah. For all you know, I may never see him again, and to be honest, it wouldn't bother me in the slightest if I didn't."

Sarah laughed.

"Yeah say that with your hands on the Book of Shadows!'

"Ahhhhhh," wailed Adrianna Jasmine as she clutched at the sides of her hair in frustration, she had had enough of this game. "That's it!" she snapped; leapt off the couch and snatched the book from her friend. "Book of Shadows, go home," she commanded and with that, the book softly floated away out of the living room, back into Adrianna Jasmine's bedroom, and landed gently on the prayer altar.

"Spoil sport," whined Sarah, completely unfazed by the fact that a book had just flown out of the room.

Across town in Canary Wharf, that same Sunday afternoon, Taylor Jameson was woken by his telephone ringing. He was a little confused, as the night before had seemed weird and surreal.

"Hello!" he croaked, once he located the phone under his pillow.

"Afternoon, Taylor, my old bean. How was the party?" It was the voice of Archie Soames, his boss at Fantastico Banquetto, he sounded like Bob Hoskins. Taylor was even more confused.

"Afternoon?" he asked, his voice etched in bewilderment; then he saw the time on his bedside clock, 2.15pm!

"Oh, God," he wailed as he clapped his hand across his forehead and sunk back onto his pillow, "I can't believe it's quarter past two! Ugh, my head feels like a fat lady and her mate are sitting on it."

"That bad, huh?" his boss chuckled. "Well, serves you right, what with all that access to fine wine, rich food and fat women. You'd think you'd know better by now, Taylor my boy!"

Taylor just nodded down the phone. *Who knows?* He was feeling most confused. He could remember *her*, the beautiful little brunette he adored talking to and…the food, oh the food! He could honestly say he had never eaten anything quite so delicious in his life, it had been like culinary intercourse, never had food had such an orgasmic impact on him.

"Anyway," boomed Archie's voice, "I'm intrigued to know more about this incredible night you've just had. Honestly, by the way you went on in your text, anyone would think you'd just had a watch-a-ma-call-it… you know, an apparition!"

Now Taylor was confused again.

"Err... what text was that Archie?" asked Taylor, not sure if he was still awake or asleep.

"Come on now, Taylor!" Archie's voice was getting even louder. "Last night, you sent me a text, which I might add has left me and the missus absolutely intrigued! It's more exciting than an East Enders cliff hanger!"

Taylor scratched his head, "I don't remember sending you a text."

"Well, I bloody well do, it woke me up, and it was about 1am. I know, I know, not late in your book, but it most certainly is for me and the missus." Luckily for Taylor, Archie was laughing, Taylor however, was still confused. "So," Archie carried on excitedly, "who *is* she then, this food goddess, this sensual beauty with her perfect crème brûlée's? She sounds absolutely gorgeous."

At first Taylor drew a blank, but after a few moments, remnants of the night before began to play out like an old glamorous black and white movie. He remembered that girl, that beautiful girl he had spoken to, the one with the captivating mysterious eyes, one brown, one blue, her flawless skin and the whole reason behind the exquisite food he had tasted. He then remembered he asked her if she would be interested in appearing in the December issue of Fantastico Banquetto, she was interested and handed him her business card, then that awful Lexi Howler thrusting herself over him and spoiling the fun. Then the beautiful brunette vision of loveliness disappearing; the lights going out; feeling sleepy, oh so sleepy; texting, blurred vision, pressing send; needing to sit down; falling into an uncontrollable sleep; seeing her again (was that a dream?); waking up and discovering Lexi Howler dribbling into his crotch. *Ugh*! He exited the Pigwell property at about 10am, dazed and confused, but in love? He remembered collapsing into his bed, falling asleep, dreaming about her and being woken by the maddening telephone and speaking to boss. Oops, he was on the phone to him right now!

"Ok!" Taylor announced and jubilantly leapt out of bed, "I know what happened, but that actually isn't important right now…"

"It isn't?" cut in Archie, sounding a little disappointed.

"No," stated Taylor, "the important thing is, *I've found her.*"

"Yeah!" Archie sounded excited, "her, who?"

Taylor didn't mince his words as he leapt about with gusto.

"Only the most exciting thing to come out of a kitchen since Nigella, Gordon, Delia and Jamie all rolled into one; the sexiest thing since Jessica Rabbit; the most fascinating figure since Marilyn Monroe. Archie, I present you with the celebrity chef of the millennium, the face will launch a thousand magazines. I give you, Adrianna Jasmine, The Magic of Food!"

"Is that a recipe or a person?" asked Archie teasing, "Adrianna Jasmine hey? That's a pretty name, pretty by name, pretty by nature, hey?"

Taylor smiled with utter delight down the phone.

"You bet she's amazing, Archie. Absolutely amazing."

"So what's the plan, then, Taylor my boy, what do you propose we do with this absolutely *amazing* girl?"

Taylor took a deep breath.

"I'm thinking about using her for the December edition for the magazine." Archie nodded down the phone.

"Well, that could be good."

"Oh, more than good," added Taylor, "it's going to be phenomenal."

"Wow, phenomenal, hey?'"

"Archie…!" Taylor warned teasingly.

"I'm sorry, I'm sorry, go on!" apologized Archie with a throaty chuckle.

Taylor hurried excitedly on.

"Well, not only do I think we should give this girl a feature in the magazine, but I'm thinking a full seven page spread and, here's the best part... the front cover!"

"COVER!" yelled Archie, "now I think that's a bit extreme, Taylor my boy. After all, it's *the* Christmas edition, I thought we were going for more of a well know celebrity chef for the cover, like Gary Rhodes or something. You know, to use their *fame* to sell the magazine!"

"Archie," said Taylor with determination in his voice, "I have a good feeling about this, no I have a *great* feeling about this. I know she will sell your magazine."

"Oh, why's that?" asked Archie curiously.

"Because of her beauty, her eyes, oh Archie, when the readers peer into those eyes of hers staring so seductively and mysteriously back at them, I promise they'll want nothing but to buy. Plus, she's an absolutely exquisite chef, a perfect combination. We can use this opportunity to promote her, propel her into celebrity chef stardom, but bigger than any of them and it'll be *us* that gave her her big break! Come on, Archie. It's perfect! Let's do it, what do you say?'

Archie was silent for a moment as he weighed up the consequences.

"Okay, Taylor, my boy," he finally answered. "It's your baby."

Taylor was ecstatic.

"Yes!" he punched into the air, "you won't be disappointed."

Archie grunted down the phone, "Just make sure I'm not. Oh, and by the way, you're off to Chutney Mary's tonight at 7pm, we're running an article about their new menu, *also* in the December's edition. Get down there and get tasting, full report tomorrow morning, and Taylor...?"

"Yep," asked Taylor full of glee.

"What happened to Luca?"

Taylor went blank for a moment, and then let out a shriek.

"Oh my God, I forgot about him!"

Paranormal Pizza

6 oz sifted plain white flour
1 tsp salt
1tsp caster sugar
1 tsp dried yeast
1 tbsp olive oil
4 fl oz warm water
One fat clove of garlic, crushed
8 sun-dried tomatoes, chopped

Combine flour, salt, sugar and yeast together into ball, then make a well in the centre and add the oil, followed by the water. Mix everything together, then add the garlic and sun dried tomatoes. Remove from the bowl and begin to knead the dough on a floured board. Roll into a ball once more and place into a clean bowl, cover with a clean tea towel and leave to rise for a couple of hours in a warm dry place. Once raised, roll out your dough onto a floured baking tray, decorate with tomato sauce and anything you desire, then bake at 180C for ten to twelve minutes.

Chapter 11
Halloween Holiday Plans

The girls spent the rest of the day watching girly films, making cakes for the coffee shop and chatting about the elusive Taylor Jameson.

Sarah still stuck firm to her belief that the Mystic Odessa's prediction was true and that love, marriage, honeymoon, conception and babies were most definitely on the cards. Adrianna Jasmine strongly disagreed. She appreciated that the first part of the prediction had come true, they had certainly met, and yes, there was no denying the chemistry, but to fall in love, marry, and horror of horrors: babies! At least destiny was in one's own hands and could be changed!

It was 3pm on a wet and windy October day and the girls were looking forward to finishing their baking, ordering their Chinese and collapsing onto the couch, when then the phone rang. Adrianna Jasmine knew instinctively who it was.

"Hello, mummy," Adrianna Jasmine puffed down the phone, she felt exhausted already.

"Darling, it *is* mummy, you clever girl, you always know! Oh, you never cease to amaze. How is my domestic goddess of a daughter doing today?"

"OK, thanks," Adrianna Jasmine answered lifelessly, "Sarah and I are just baking cakes for the shop tomorrow, watching films and chatting. You know, the usual stuff!"

"Oh, that sounds nice, monkey pants," Sicily tinkled, "say hello to that lovely child for me, will you?"

Adrianna Jasmine nodded down the phone.

"Anyway, pumpkin pip, what I really want to know is *how* did it go last night?"

Adrianna Jasmine felt herself get all hot and flustered. *Goddess, what was she meant to say?* "Oh, you know, fine mother, apart from the fact I drugged my staff into zombie slaves, triggered a massive power cut and accidentally propelled the whole party into the land of nod, which included the likes of famous sporting personalities, pop stars' kids, TV personalities, glamour models and

119

well known early morning TV presenters." There was absolutely no way on this Goddess's green earth she could tell her mother any of it, she'd have a field day. Moreover, her mother would probably arrange for her to go away on some magic awareness course or something.

"You know what, mum," said Adrianna Jasmine nonchalantly, "it was a bit boring, actually. Sarah and I were stuck in the kitchen all night, working like *dogs*!"

"Like dogs, darling?" echoed Sicily

"Uh huh," Adrianna Jasmine confirmed, "it was really not on, and we left about midnight, literally scuttled through the back door… like mice!"

"Like *mice*, darling?" Sicily was finding it all rather amusing.

"Yes," stated Adrianna Jasmine, "it was a miracle that I was actually able leave out a few business cards here and there, you know, just in case someone actually *did* like my cooking and fancied hiring me! Therefore, sorry, mother, there's nothing more to report."

Sicily was trying to hide the suspicious sarcasm in her voice.

"Really, darling? That's odd, because I popped into the coffee shop this morning with daddy, you know, for our Sunday morning coffee and cake?"

"Uh huh," Adrianna Jasmine answered weakly, a sudden sense of dread rising up from her toes.

"And I got chatting to Sarah's mother!"

Adrianna Jasmine felt her body get all hot again.

"Oh right…!" she squeaked.

"Yes, darling and Sarah's mother told me that Sarah had called her on the telephone at 4am, waking up the entire household, complaining that she had been drugged and forced to do magic! Apparently the girl sounded absolutely frantic and kept mentioning your name, darling, and that you were in desperate need of a tailor! Did you split your skirt or something? You know, if you just carried a needle and cotton around with you, there'd be no need for a tailor, you could do it yourself! Self-sufficiency, mop chop, that's the ticket!"

Adrianna Jasmine laughed nervously down the phone.

"Yes...a needle and cotton, err...I'll remember that for next time, how stupid of me... oh, so, err... she phoned, did she? Ha ha! Err... how very bizarre!"

"What on earth the poor girl was dribbling on about is anyone's guess!" chuckled Sicily, "but to actually *feel* like she had to call her *mother*, darling. Oh, she must have been in a right old state!"

Again Adrianna Jasmine laughed nervously. She recalled only too well snatching the phone off her confused, magic-intoxicated friend, as she prattled on to Blaire about their misuse of magic and the state they had gotten themselves into - well, that Adrianna Jasmine had gotten them into. What else was she meant to do, allow Sarah to tell her mother all about the night's ghastly escapades? Absolutely not! So she snatched the phone away and shamefully made up some story about her daughter drinking too much champagne, saying she was severely drunk and about to pass out.

"Well, um...yes, she was a bit of a mess, anyway..." said Adrianna Jasmine desperate to change the subject, "not that I actually saw much of the party, what with being hauled up in a hot kitchen all night, but you were right, mother, you would have looked absolutely splendid in one of those champagne glasses. Those girls had nothing on you, I could have just pictured you lolloping about in a sapphire blue bikini, amongst all that...glitter, and, err... bubbles."

Adrianna Jasmine cast her mind back to the night before, where she'd painstakingly rescued the dancers from drowning in cold water, bubbles and glitter. Her mother tinkled a girlish giggle.

"Of course I would have, darling, I know only too well how to work a champagne glass and by all accounts, your friend there knows how to drink one dry."

Sicily chuckled and Adrianna Jasmine winced, she couldn't let people think Sarah was a drunk! Still, at this moment in time, truth was not an option. Her mother would only criticize her daughter's ability in regards to practicing safe magic; not to mention the shame! The young witch clumsily changed the subject again.

"Anyway, mother, what's happening Halloween, then? Are we still all going down to the New Forest?" (On All Hallows Eve, Adrianna Jasmine, Sicily, Sicily's sister, Kristobella who Adrianna

Jasmine adored, cousin Clementine Poppleapple, Carolina Plum, Bella Bell and the latest addition to the girlie group, Sarah, all flock down to the traditional New Forest village of Burley.)

"Darling, it's all booked," Sicily sang, sounding more like an editor from Vogue than a mummy. "We're all staying at the Burley Manor hotel. I booked it the moment we returned from last year's visit."

This made Adrianna Jasmine happy: she loved the hotel that was brimming with tradition and history. She adored the baronial-style entrance; the roaring log fires that warmed her tootsies after a bracing broomstick flight high above the forest trees; the beautiful surroundings and the fry up in the morning wasn't bad, either.

"Yippee," yelled Adrianna Jasmine in delight, "oh, I can't wait, it's just what I need!"

"Oh, I know exactly how you feel," said Sicily dramatically, "I can't wait, either. It's all too thrilling: the spells, the atmosphere and of course watching my little girl flying on Whiz (Adrianna Jasmine's broomstick), just sends shivers down my spine. You know, sweetheart…" Sicily's tone became serious, "you could have been a champion."

Adrianna Jasmine nodded down the phone.

"I know, mother, I know," sighed Adrianna Jasmine, her voice dripping with sarcasm, "but unfortunately there isn't much call these days for national broomstick flying champions. You know, due to us witches not being *supposed* to actually exist outside of fairy tales. So, who would I tell, mother, who would I show? The world is not ready for a twenty-six-year-old woman to be zooming about on a broomstick, you know that!"

"Stop being facetious," snapped her mother, "mummy knows that tone in your voice and believe me it doesn't suit you. Anyway, I'll speak to you again soon, now I must *fly*! Byyeee, darling," and with that she was gone, like a puff of smoke.

Adrianna Jasmine clicked off her phone and stared down into nothing for a few moments. She inhaled a few deep breaths, taking care to keep her shoulders completely still, thus creating a much deeper and more effective breathing technique. After various inhales and exhales, Adrianna Jasmine felt calm again. Goddess, her mother always felt like hard work after a telephone conversation. She then returned her attention to the kitchen to finish the cakes with Sarah.

"Shall we add that fantastic little Summer Sunshine spell to the cakes, Adrianna Jasmine?" suggested Sarah cheerily. "You know, so we can treat the poor Brits to a bit of winter warmth?"

Summer Sunshine was a wonderful and joyous spell, which allowed the lucky customer to experience the joys of summer during the cold, miserable winter months. Adrianna Jasmine agreed wholeheartedly and set about gathering the appropriate ingredients. "Yes, let's do it," she announced happily.

When everything was gathered up, Adrianna Jasmine popped a small purple saucepan onto the stove and began to add the ingredients whilst chanting words as the key ingredients were added.

One red chilli for heat and spice;
Milk from coconut, evoke paradise.
Jamaican rum to make you merry,
Sweetness and joy from a wild strawberry.

A pinch of sand, salt from the sea
Breeze from ocean, strong and free.
Carotene from a carrot, gold from a mine,
Skin now bronzed, shimmer and shine.

Once all the ingredients were added, Adrianna Jasmine sucked up the weird bright, yellow, liquid into a pipette. She added a teeny tiny droplet to each cake (you only needed a miniscule drop, otherwise not only would people taste the potion, which was actually quite revolting, people would also experience severe cases of heatstroke, sunburn, drunken stupor and severe dehydration). Luckily, Adrianna Jasmine was an expert on potion quantities (except from the Pigwell party poop), so the customers would only experience bliss!

Cheerful Chocolate Cup Cakes
7oz self raising flour
1oz cocoa powder
8oz unsalted softened butter
8oz caster sugar
4 large eggs
Minstrels

Combine everything in a bowl and mix with an electric hand whisk until smooth. Divide mixture into cupcake cases and bake at 180 for twenty minutes, but check a few minutes before to see if they are firm. Allow to cool, and decorate with butter icing and Minstrels

Chapter 12
Beep, Beep

It was approaching 5pm and six sumptuous cakes laid neatly in a row, topped with luxurious frosting, apart from the fruit cake: they truly had outdone themselves.

"There!" announced Adrianna Jasmine as she placed her hands proudly onto her hips, "all done. Right, lets hit the couch, watch a chick flick, ponder over our Chinese takeout menu, and ooh, what about a nice chilled glass of Prosecco?"

"That sounds like the best idea of the century, my dear," answered Sarah enthusiastically, "I'll go pop the DVD player on, whilst you pop the Italian fizz."

Adrianna Jasmine reached into her fridge and retrieved her bottle of icy cold Prosecco; she grabbed a couple of champagne flutes from the cupboard, switched off the kitchen light and joined Sarah in the living room.

"Hmm... charming, Jupiter," said the witch as she entered the living room, the little black cat was spread-eagled on the mat, licking himself clean. He didn't seem to care that ladies were present. "You really are an uncouth contortionist of a cat, aren't you?"

"Wish I could do that," said Sarah flatly, who was staring blankly towards the cat, "I'd never leave the bloody house!"

Adrianna Jasmine twisted her face up in disgust at her friend's comment, "that's revolting, Sarah. Anyway, you'd be lucky with *your* flexibility!"

"And what do you mean by that?" enquired Sarah, a little stung by the comment.

"Well, you can't even perform a down-facing dog at yoga class, let alone attempt what he's doing!"

It was true, Sarah was stiff as a brick. Still, one could dream.

Adrianna Jasmine poured the Italian fizz into the glasses, and then sat down next to Sarah and the pair of them settled in front of the TV to watch, *You've Got Mail*. It was one of their old time favorites, featuring Meg Ryan and Tom Hanks. As the titles ran, the pair pondered over their Chinese takeout menus. The girls both decided to stick to their usual tried and tested choice of sweet and sour prawns with vegetable fried rice for Adrianna Jasmine and hot beef curry with egg fried rice for Sarah, accompanied with a bag of prawn crackers and crispy seaweed to share.

The girls decided to call Wong's Wanton and order the food for 7pm, as it was still too early to eat dinner and if they couldn't wait that long, there was a packet of salt-and-vinegar Hula Hoops in the cupboard to tide them over. Sarah phoned the take away shop and placed their order, then promptly settled herself back down to enjoy the movie.

"Beep, Beep, Beep, Beep."

"Is that your phone or mine?" inquired Sarah, not taking her eyes off the screen.

Adrianna Jasmine heaved a sigh: she would have to move from her cozy position. "It's mine," she sighed and made her way over to the dark walnut coffee table where her phone had been discarded amongst copies of Cosmos, candles and a bowl of sugared almonds. She glanced down at the number that had been responsible for interrupting their film. The number was unrecognized; she wondered who it could be.

She opened her message box and her heart leapt into her mouth. "Oh my Goddess," she cried out in shock, "it's him!"

Sarah knew immediately who "him" was.

"Ooh, what's he say?" she asked excitedly, clapping her hands. Adrianna Jasmine read out the message.

'It was fun meeting you at the party last night and your food was exquisite. Am not sure what exactly happened though, but everyone like me seemed to have fallen asleep. Woke up a bit confused, maybe too much alcohol! Anyway if you can remember conversation about magazine spread, am still interested, hope you are!!! please call ASAP, as I would like you to be in Xmas special, I am able to hold photo shoot with you on Nov 7 Taylor x

"Let me see that," demanded Sarah whipping the phone away from her friend. "Wow, a photo shoot, Adrianna Jasmine, you're going to be famous! How glamorous, how exciting and oh, look," she added, "he's even sent you a kiss. Goddess, he must be keen!"

Adrianna Jasmine rolled her eyes and sighed.

"Sarah, I'm hardly going to be famous and that," she poked sharply towards the kiss, "doesn't mean anything. It's just, you know, something that people do after a text, like I do and you do. Anyway, this is a business text; I actually find it impertinent and unprofessional that he dared to finish his message with a *kiss* symbol. I hardly know him!"

Sarah laughed at her ridiculous friend, "well *he* obviously thought there had been a connection professionally and personally! What's wrong with killing two birds with one stone?"

"Hey?" enquired Adrianna Jasmine confused. "What are you twittering on about?"

"Come on, Adrianna Jasmine, catch up. Not only will he attain a killer spread for the magazine, but he snares a sexy little minx to take out on a date, to boot!"

Adrianna Jasmine was defiant. "Well, he'll get the article, but nothing else, I can assure you of that!"

Sarah shook her head in mock disbelief. Goddess, Adrianna Jasmine really was *petrified* of falling in love. She decided, however, not to push her, if their love was meant to be, it would happen whether it was invited or not. Adrianna Jasmine, as powerful as she was, could not triumph the supremacy of love's power. However, Sarah was curious enough to ask if Adrianna Jasmine would reply to the text. Adrianna Jasmine agreed to reply, but opted for a simple, yet informal response *without* a kiss. Well, she didn't want Taylor to receive the wrong impression, now did she?

Thank you for text, not sure why you fell asleep but am sorry that you did! Am most interested in Magazine article, am free on that day AJ

Sarah looked disappointed as Adrianna Jasmine read out her bland text: "What, not even a little flirting?"

Adrianna Jasmine answered with a sharp, "No!" and left it at that. She wanted to enjoy the film!

Moments later the mobile beeped again, it was Taylor. Sarah laughed, "Wow! He *is* keen!"

Adrianna Jasmine sighed deeply, opened up the message and read it aloud so her friend could hear.

'Gr8!!! Meet at the Conran shop, Marylebone at ten am, as we will be using one of their kitchen displays for your photo shoot. Bring a selection of clothes suitable for an Xmas photo shoot (dressy and casual) Makeup artist and hair will be on hand. I would like to interview you before shoot when would that be possible?

"What, no kiss!" snorted Adrianna Jasmine.

"Why? You disappointed?"

Adrianna Jasmine shot daggers back at her friend, "Still, the Conran shop seems like fun, plus hair and makeup. Oh, Jazzy, you'll be a star for the day. Goddess, I'm so jealous!" Sarah was leaping about in excitement, "you'll have to buy something new to wear! I'm thinking casual sweet red jumper with jeans to portray your natural, humble and sweet side, or maybe a black, glittery, sexy little number that says 'Hello, I am sexier than Nigella!'"

Adrianna Jasmine said nothing; she was replying to the text.

That all seems fine, I'm free Mon 3rd Nov, where would you like to meet for interview? AJ

Sarah excitedly enquired as to what Adrianna Jasmine had written back and then commented on how boring and short the reply was.

"Honestly, you're no fun," she said as the excitement drained out of her pores.

"Beep, Beep, Beep, Beep," the excitement was once again thrust upon her.

"What's he say?" asked Sarah hurriedly as she jumped onto the settee next to Adrianna Jasmine, nearly bouncing the witch high into the air.

"Oh, Sarah, be careful!"

"Sorry, honey. But it's all too thrilling. Come on, read it out!"

'Let's meet at Hotel'78' Buckingham Palace Road on Nov 3rd at one O clock on the Menzine. We can do lunch, see you there?'

The reply was too much for Sarah to handle, she nearly passed out.

"Shut up," Sarah barely whispered, "Hotel 78 is only the most exquisitely beautiful boutique hotel in London and *you're* going there for lunch? I am so, so jealous, but so, so whole-heartedly excited for you." Sarah then dramatically took it upon herself to place Adrianna Jasmine's hand into her own, whilst staring deeply into her eyes. "Text him, Adrianna Jasmine, text him back and agree to meet him, this is Hotel 78, for Goddess sake. If you don't end up marrying this guy, at least do yourself the honour of experiencing a light luncheon at one of the most gorgeous hotels on the planet with him!"

Sarah's curls were bouncing about wildly on her head. Adrianna Jasmine patted Sarah's hands gently. "Calm down, Sarah," she soothed, trying not to laugh. "If it makes you happy, then of course I'll go, in fact, I'll do it for you!" Sarah closed her eyes in relief, and then advised her text back agreeing to the meeting.

'ok free 3/11 whr wld u like 2 meet 4 interview? X'
Send.

"AHHHH, OH MY GODDESS,' yelled Adrianna Jasmine in horror, Sarah nearly fell off the sofa. "I've only gone and sent him a bloody kiss!" Sarah's eyes were stretched to their utmost limit (imagine wider than a Pizza Hut's large stuffed crust). "What did you do that for?" Adrianna Jasmine shook her head, she was flabbergasted.

"I don't know," she spluttered, "habit?"

Sarah shook her head defiantly. "Hardly, Jazzy, what with you smooching with him on the beach, frolicking amongst coconuts and gazing out into the sunset like you're in some 1940s romantic romp. This just proves you like Taylor Jameson, the handsome and frightfully posh food critic."

Sarah, who looked positively triumphant, then poked Adrianna Jasmine playfully on the arm. Adrianna Jasmine looked positively horrified; even *she* had to admit her ever-growing interest in the man was becoming increasingly difficult to suppress. Goddess, this love stuff was powerful!

'Place a sprig of lavender under your pillow at night time, it will help you sleep.'
(Bella Bell)

Chapter 13
Deep Space Sleep

Adrianna Jasmine and Sarah had eaten their Chinese and were on film number two, City of Angels, and Taylor *still* hadn't replied to her text. Adrianna Jasmine was convinced that the lack of reply was down to the accidental kiss; that she'd frightened him off.

"Goddess!" a cold dread washed over her, "he probably thinks I'm a stalker, or like that character, Kathy 'I'm your number one fan' Bates, from that sick film, *Misery*. He's probably halfway across Mexico by now. That stupid kiss," she cursed herself, "that stupid, stupid kiss! A cross, an X, a symbol that means NOTHING! No, No," she cried out loud, "I am most certainly not your number one fan!"

Sarah looked over to her friend, her face perplexed. "What *are* you talking about, you weirdo? Who aren't you a fan of...? Madonna? Dancing on Ice? Satan...?"

Adrianna Jasmine immediately felt embarrassed. "Oh, was I speaking out loud?" Sarah nodded. "Err..., no one special," she couldn't let on that she was thinking about the elusive Taylor, "I was just... err... thinking actually...yeah, about the Devil! Ooh, she's a real cow, that one!"

Sarah looked on at her friend as if she were quite mad. "The Devil, you were *really* thinking about the Devil?"

Adrianna Jasmine nodded, "Yes, I most certainly was."

Sarah looked unconvinced, "Why?"

"Well...I was just thinking about what a nasty piece of work she is and how some witches worship her, like they're her *number one fan* or something, isn't it silly?" Sarah raised her right eyebrow as Adrianna Jasmine continued babbling on. "She's nothing more than a sly old fox really, very tricky, not worth the bother. Oh no, you wouldn't want to conjure her up on a wet Sunday afternoon, make no mistake of that! Actually, I believe my great, great, great grandmother met her, you know?"

Sarah's face was deadpan, "Really?"

"Yes!" confirmed Adrianna Jasmine, "it was at a séance in some old castle in Romania. Apparently the Devil tricked them into believing that she was one of the circle's dead husbands: bet they got a hell of a shock when *she* turned up! So, err...yes, that's that then..."

Silence trailed for a few moments. "Good," Sarah finally said, she felt as if she were having an out of body experience, "well, I'm glad we sorted that out," and patted her friend on her leg. "Nutter," she muttered under her breath, "she's definitely, definitely turning into her mother."

It was nearly 3am; Adrianna Jasmine was in bed but couldn't sleep, she was totally frustrated about the fact that Taylor had not yet replied. Sarah had advised that perhaps he, too, didn't want to come across as a stalker and therefore politely left her alone. Adrianna Jasmine however, was still adamant that her kiss scared him away, even though he had sent *her* a kiss in the first place. Oh, she was exceptionally frustrated and even toyed with the idea of appearing in his thoughts and convincing him to text her back. Luckily, she came to her senses and dismissed the idea. Goddess, was she really *that* desperate?

After too much tossing and too much turning, the witch opted for another, less dramatic option that would help her to soothe her nerves and forget about the incommodious Taylor. So she decided to treat herself to a little of *Dr Goombah's Heavenly Sleep Away Spray in Lavender and Peace Rose* on her pillow, to help send a fidgety witch to sleep.

She switched on her night light, gently padded over to her altar and found Dr Goombah's miracle spray placed next to an assortment of semi-precious stones. Once located, she tip-toed over to her bed, sat down and sprayed a gentle mist of delicate golden sparkles onto her pillow. She then read the little spell from the back of the bottle, to evoke the magic.

Take me on a journey where I can sleep,
Drifting through galaxies weightless and free.
Let me touch the stars and moon,
Help me sleep now dear potion I surrender to thee.

The sparkles lingered on the pillow, glistening prettily in the darkness for a few moments. Adrianna Jasmine switched off her night light, popped the bottle onto her bedside table, snuggled under the duvet and laid her heavy head down onto the twinkling pillow!

She luxuriated in the luscious aromas from the wild lavender and peace rose, which instantly soothed and calmed her body from head to toe. She then gazed up towards the ceiling and smiled, for the ceiling was temporally no longer a mere ceiling, but a multi-coloured, yet tranquil spectacle of the wonders of deep space.

Adrianna Jasmine breathed a deep, satisfying sigh as she surrendered to Dr Goombah's sleep aid. She gazed up at silver stars, colourful planets and golden moons. To add to the sheer delight, harmonious, melodic textures of untarnished choir-like voices, wafted through the air like sensual spirits, as vibrant clouds of whirling space dust and winking stars distracted one from fretting about their problems and bothersome food critics! She felt free; she had released all muscle tension, released her mind of any pending distressing thoughts and was simply living in the moment.

Then, just when one would believe that that was miraculous enough, Adrianna Jasmine's body became lighter than air and her room slowly began to disappear, she was now in deep, deep space. Her body was completely suspended, floating freely amongst the moon and the stars, weightless and content. She drifted peacefully from planet to planet, star to star, observing the beautiful colours, enjoying the gentle swaying from the cosmic ride, which, in turn, evoked an overwhelming sense of drowsiness and then much anticipated, blissful sleep.

Adrianna Jasmine's radio-alarm clock kicked into life at six am and the cheeky voice of Lula Hula filled the room. Lula Hula was a DJ for radio broomstick and was a favorite amongst the witching stock. She played great music, held debates, ran entertaining competitions and always had interesting guests on the show, such as potion expert Audrey Lipinski, who offered tips and healthy advice on how to get the best out of your liquid spells and, of course, Warlock Heller, the famous black witch hunter, who, over the years, shared many a story on how he apprehended bad witches with his wand.

Adrianna Jasmine peeled her eyes open and peered out of her covers at the clock. "Yuck, 5.00am," she groaned and painfully slid out of bed and into the day ahead.

The coffee shop was holding a big open day on All Hallows Eve for children, which included spooky story telling for the little ones, face painting, simple spell lessons, tarot card readings, a magician and apple bobbing. The kids would also receive a soft beverage and a cookie as an additional treat, and all for a fiver! Moreover, whilst their children safely played, fresh cups of Brazilian coffee and homemade apple cider were on hand for the adult's pleasure, as well as freshly baked chocolate cakes, hot cinnamon buns and dreamy homemade flavoured breads, which were also available to adults.

The witch slipped on her warm, towelling bathrobe and made her way into the kitchen to make tea and toast. Then she made her way to the bathroom and undertook her morning ablutions. Once completed, the witch retuned back to her kitchen and made a strong coffee, sliced the toast into triangles, smothered butter and strawberry jam onto them and placed the toast onto a plate and transferred everything onto a tray, all ready to be taken in to Sarah.

Adrianna Jasmine balanced the tray on one hand and knocked sharply on Sarah's door. There was no answer, so Adrianna Jasmine went in and found Sarah splayed out on the bed, with a pillow half covering her face, most of the covers on the floor and snoring like a drunken pirate.

"Morning, oh stunning one," Adrianna Jasmine teased. "Come on, wake up!" Sarah groaned from under her pillow; she expressed her hatred for the mornings and said that it was too early to even contemplate getting up. She did, however, perk up when her sleepy eyes focused on her breakfast brought to her in bed.

"Ooh, thanks, honey bun, yummy coffee and toast!"

"You're welcome. I'll just pop GMTV on, for you."

After such a blissfully deep sleep, Adrianna Jasmine fancied an invigorating and refreshing shower with Citrus Bang-Bang Boom to liven her up to the max. Once the shower was hot, Adrianna Jasmine removed her robe, black silk slip nighty and took her place under the soothing jets. She squeezed her favorite product onto a puff and began to massage the delicious gold-coloured gel onto her slim body. Immediately her skin began to tingle and glow with health, she felt positively radiant, luminous and dazzling.

After a few glorious minutes, Adrianna Jasmine stepped out of her shower, dried herself with a nice rough towel and made her way into the kitchen. Moments later, Sarah entered the kitchen in order to refill her cup and to pinch an additional slice of toast. She bustled around the kitchen, much livelier then when Adrianna Jasmine had disturbed her from her slumber and appeared to be in fine spirits.

"You want toast?" Sarah enquired; Adrianna Jasmine shook her head and said that her yoghurt had been satisfactory. Sarah nodded then informed her friend that she was off to have a shower.

"Hurry up, then" said Adrianna Jasmine glancing over at the clock, "I want to leave in fifteen minutes to beat the traffic."

"Really!" exclaimed Sarah, that's not much time at all." Adrianna Jasmine shook her head in agreement, "no it isn't, so you'll have to get a wiggle on, or you'll be tubing it into work!"

"Damn it," cursed Sarah, "Ok, I'll be ready in fifteen minutes," she announced dramatically and with that she leapt up and made her way into the bathroom. Seconds later Adrianna Jasmine could hear the shower jets and decided that it was about time she, too, was getting ready. She opted for a baggy pair of chocolate brown Abercrombie jogging pants teamed with an orange, fitted, soft wool sweater. She twisted her rich brown hair into a loose knot and placed a pair of delicate diamante studs on her ears. She moisturized with Tallulah Toffees Daylight Savings Cream, which activated with sunlight and deactivated when the sun set. It promised to keep one's skin dewy and supple throughout the day and provided the epidermis with a protected layer against UVA/UVB. The cream would also disallow spots to appear by zapping the yellow pustules before they even contemplated bursting onto the scene. It was such a shame that brides-to-be couldn't get their hot little hands on this stuff, but like mentioned before, Toffee products are only available to witches.

Adrianna Jasmine slipped her socked feet into a pair of UGGS and sprayed *Honey Dew Dream Perfume* over her head, picked up her little brown velvet sling bag and shouted at Sarah, who had now completed her shower and was trying to dress. Due to being totally disorganized that morning, Sarah felt under pressure to be ready within the five minute deadline. It was impossible, she thought, and her stress levels began to rise. To top it off she had showered in Citrus Bang-Bang Boom shower gel, which only enhanced her now ever increasing and somewhat disturbing adrenalin that was pumping furiously about her body.

"Use it, Sarah," she advised herself in the manor of top athlete psyching themself up just before a race, "use the adrenalin to quicken your step, speedily slip on knickers and slap hair back into a casual ponytail-type thing." Her hands were shaking and for some reason her teeth were chattering as if she were in the middle of the North Sea.

"Goddess," she puffed, "why on earth anyone would voluntarily take cocaine is beyond me, especially if all it's going to do is make you feel like you're standing on a giant vibrator, without the pleasure, and render your inability to apply mascara."

Poor Sarah. She was quivering like a terrified puppy. However, like the trooper she was, she was ready in the allotted five minutes, looking perhaps a little beleaguered and slightly mad due to her blotched cheeks and a twitching left eye. She clumsily made her way towards the front door where Adrianna Jasmine was waiting impatiently.

"All showered and ready, Jazzy," she said breathlessly. Adrianna Jasmine simply eyed her friend suspiciously, "really? You don't look as though you've showered: your skin is silvery and slimy, and look, you're dripping with sweat, what's up with you?"

Sarah shrugged her shoulders, she was grinding her teeth and her eyes looked as though they were about to pop out from her head. "I have showered Jazzy, I even showered in Citrus Bang-Bang Boom."

"Oh no, you didn't!" implored Adrianna Jasmine, "Sarah, you know you shouldn't use Citrus Bang- Bang Boom twice in the space of twelve hours, it's too much for the body to take. Goddess, girl, people will think you're on speed or something."

Sarah, who was hopping from one foot to the other because she was unable to stand still, tried to explain that she wasn't actually aware of the rule; however, she found it to be impossible to talk due to her lips trembling so much. Adrianna Jasmine sighed deeply and retreated back into her kitchen, "and the morning started off so well," she muttered under her breath. She reached into one of her top cupboards and located a packet of Unflustered Floss. Unflustered Floss is just like candyfloss that we have at the fair, although this candyfloss is rather special and is in a bite sized piece, wrapped in a red and yellow packet. It does look like candyfloss; however it's bright purple, opposed to its more commonly known colour of pale pink, and tastes exactly the same. Unflustered Floss is best consumed when one is experiencing high levels of stress and anxiety - as it has the ability to calm a troubled body or mind into the realms of utter tranquility - apparently consumers have compared the calming effects of Unflustered Floss to spending six months at a Yoga retreat with Mr Iyengar, chanting on hand woven mats, saluting the sun, eating nothing but home grown vegetables and totally skipping out those 99 pence frozen microwave meals. She rooted around and found the box that she was looking for; a small cardboard box with, luckily, one last Ulustered Floss. The witch shook the box and to her amazement, discovered that there was only one packet left.

"Where did they all go?" she pondered, slightly puzzled, "Goddess, I couldn't have eaten all of them...could I?" Maybe she wasn't as in control as she liked to think she was, if she'd consumed a whole packet of unflustered floss. When did she purchase the packet from Dr Goombah's website?

"Goddess," she contemplated in slight shock, "only last month. Wow. I've eaten a whole pack of unflustered floss in less than a month!" She shuddered a little and made a mental note not to buy any more Unflustered Floss, it would be cold turkey from now on. Thank Goddess there were only ten per pack, or she would wind up so laid back she'd actually fall down.

Adrianna Jasmine tore the little packet open, placed the wispy piece of purple floss in the palm of her hand and made her way back to Sarah, now performing grapevines up and down the corridor and adding two jumping jacks on the end.

"Ok, Jane Fonda, let's just take a moment to be still whilst I pop this into your mouth." Goddess, she was being difficult. Adrianna Jasmine had to be careful as every time she tried to lay the floss on Sarah's serpent-like flickering tongue, she feared for her fingers being nibbled off by the overzealous, chattering teeth. After a few painful attempts, Adrianna Jasmine administered the floss into Sarah's quivering mouth and watched as the purple wisp dissolved delicately on Sarah's hot, wet tongue. A few moments later, Sarah's contorted face began to soften, her rapid breath regulated to calm and her hurried heart rate leisurely fell to a more appropriate beat. She stood still for a few moments trying to gather her thoughts, feeling extremely discombobulated. Why was her body all wet, hadn't she just had a shower?

Adrianna Jasmine informed her that she had had a shower but had not dried herself properly due to rushing. Goddess, she wasn't going to tell her that it was sweat! They'd never be on time!

"Huh," said Sarah, not quite with it. Adrianna Jasmine smiled sweetly and began to lift up her cakes.

"Here, grab this one, Sarah," Adrianna Jasmine gestured towards a crate loaded with cakes, a couple of packs of unsalted butter, cocoa powder and icing sugar. Sarah floated towards her friend, she was feeling pretty relaxed, chilled and only too pleased to help out her dear, dear friend.

The witches stepped outside of Adrianna Jasmines front door before being triple locked and bolted, then made their way to the lift.

Once inside they pressed for the garage and waited patiently for the lift to reach its destination. The doors slid open and the two witches made their way to Adrianna Jasmine's pale blue catering van. The garage was full of cars, as most people were probably still having their breakfast, it was quiet and echoed.

"Right, off we go," Adrianna Jasmine announced, when, "beep, beep, beep, beep." At first the witch thought nothing of it, but then as she reached into her bag to open up her message she began to remember. She remembered everything! Taylor, Taylor, Taylor! Then, to add fuel to the fire, her tummy immediately knotted up again.

"This is ridiculous!" she thought furiously. "Get a grip, for Goddess sake." She glanced over at Sarah, who was happily humming the theme tune from *Out of Africa*, looking dopey and trouble-free. *Cow*! thought Adrianna Jasmine enviously, *how come she gets to be all stress free, and I'm literally about to have a breakdown, it's payback for the other night, that's what it is, curse the threefold law. Curse it to hell! And she's eaten all my floss*! Goddess, she could do with a fix of that herself right now.

She decided to read the text from Taylor, the exasperating food critic, and mind monger. But she was put off by Sarah's irritating humming and obscene smile.

"Sarah! Can you stop bloody singing for a few moments and listen. Look, he's texted."

"Ooh, far out," Sarah whimsically replied.

"Pah," said Adrianna Jasmine agitated.

'Yep it's a date! Look forward to seeing you too, mind you if fancy meeting up before, for a coffee, I'd really enjoy it, take care Taylor!'

At first Adrianna Jasmine was filled with joy. "He hadn't fogged me off!" she cried happily, "he doesn't think I'm a psychopathic stalker *and* he made the first move! Yes!" she said punching the air, then her face fell. "Hang on, how come it took him such a long bloody long time to contact me? I don't like that, it's as if he's playing games. Oh, I can't be bothered with a man like that!"

Sarah, in her dopey state, who'd actually been listening to Adrianna Jasmine's ranting, made a suggestion, "Why don't you see when the message was sent!" she was sounding more like Jim Morrison by the minute. Adrianna Jasmine scrunched up her face.

"Well, he obviously sent it now because here it is, look!"

Sarah shook her head sill with her hippy-happy smile. "Sometimes they *don't* get sent, Adrianna Jasmine, even if you press the send button, it's one of those mysteries of life, I'm afraid. Go on," she urged, "check it."

Adrianna Jasmine scrolled down to the message details and low and behold, he had sent it last night. It just hadn't been retrieved until that very morning.

"Curse that damn network," groaned Adrianna Jasmine, "why didn't it send?" Sarah, who was still resigning the magic mushroom look, rested her fist under her chin and contemplated why the message had been blocked.

"Hmmm," she mused, "it could have been the network, of course, but perhaps it was something more powerful than modern day technology."

Adrianna Jasmine looked slightly confused.

"What do mean, like the weather or something? It was miserable yesterday…maybe the rain…?" She looked back towards Sarah for recognition.

"No, it wasn't the weather that blocked that message," Sarah proclaimed with all the wisdom of a guru, "but you!"

"Me!" Adrianna Jasmine scoffed, "I did nothing of the sort!"

"Oh yes you did, little witch," stated Sarah dreamily, "your subconscious cast a little spell. Now," she mumbled to herself thoughtfully, "was it the heart or the head that created the blockage?"

"What are you prattling on about, Sarah? What blockage? I haven't got bowel problems, you know!" Sarah tinkled a laugh and continued to explain in her soothing yoga voice.

"You were very torn last night in regards to your feelings towards Taylor. Deep down, you really like this sexy gentleman that you met and your little heart was going pitter patter with delicious excitement, and why not? It's only natural! So your heart was happily embracing the situation." She paused for breath before continuing on with her theory. "Now, your *head* was telling you something very different. It was telling you to get a grip, stop being so foolish and most importantly, that witchcraft comes before, dare I say the word... love! Therefore, your brain somehow subconsciously cast some kind of blocking spell, thus resulting in a blocked signal."

Adrianna Jasmine sucked in a lungful of air, she had a feeling Sarah's theory was correct, but if she had subconsciously cast a spell, that was worrying. After all, she was an adult witch and adult witches grow out of that. It was a bit like growing out of wetting the bed, you just learnt to control it!

"Great," she said' sarcastically, "I'm reverting back to childhood now, can it get much worse?"

Sarah, once again, tinkled with laughter.

"Oh, you are funny, Jazzy. Of course not, although, I'd be careful in regards to your thoughts about this Taylor chap; make sure you're true to your feelings, otherwise your deepest, darkest secrets and desires could rise to the surface with extreme consequences."

"I know," Adrianna Jasmine sighed. "That's why I never say anything like, 'I wish you were dead' because knowing my luck, my wish could quite possibly come true."

'An ye harm non, do as ye will'

Chapter 14
Chloe with Two Dots

As the witches battled through the London traffic, Adrianna Jasmine thought long and hard about her accidental spell. It worried her that her mind had cast a spell without her knowledge and thanked the Goddess that she had only blocked a phone signal and *not* accidentally harmed Taylor. She shuddered at the thought; the poor unfortunate food critic could have endured all sorts of nasty experiences due to her deepest, darkest desires. She would need to try and calm down and keep her thoughts pure in regards to Taylor Jameson: she didn't want him accidentally snapping a tibia in half now, would she?

The witch drifted her thoughts back to a time when she was a mere seven years old, when unfortunately an incident similar to this had first occurred. The little witch was back in Junior One at her Catholic junior school, St Catherine the Great. Her hair was dark brown and tied in loose pigtails, and she wore her uniform of a red and grey tartan tunic over a white shirt and grey tights. Her skin was like porcelain, speckled with a few freckles and her personality quiet and observant, yet approachable and helpful towards her fellow students.

Amongst her fellow students was a girl called Chloe, who spelt her name with two dots above the 'o' and 'e'. She was an extremely nasty character and made many of the children's lives in Junior One very unhappy. She can remember Chloe with the two dots adorning long strawberry blonde hair, which was the girl's pride and joy, and she constantly flicked it about like a shampoo model, simply to demonstrate its lustres.

Chloe with two dots was the only strawberry blonde in the class, apart from Ashley O Hara, but she was a dirty blonde and therefore didn't stand a chance. Chloe with two dots believed herself to be like one of the Disney princesses and regarded everyone surrounding her as servants, ugly step sisters or wicked witches! The latter belief used to make Adrianna Jasmine smile, although the constant reminding about her two dots and the fact that it was the French version of the name, grated the young witch ever so slightly. Well, I suppose back in those days, having two dots above your name was classed as unusual. Nowadays, due to kids being called absurd names such as Panther, Miami, Princess and Tinkerbelle, the dots wouldn't be quite so taboo.

Adrianna Jasmine was not so keen on Chloe with two dots, not because she was envious of the blondness, but because the girl was spiteful, rude, arrogant and the leader of a gang of equally brat-like girls. Chloe with two dots also came from a pretty wealthy family and her mother, Monique, had dabbled in a spot or two of modelling and starred in a Christmas Pantomime every year. Monique's quest for hierarchy, the ability to look down on everyone at the school gate and her scary competitiveness on school sports day, resulted in the childrens' parents disliking Monique as well as her daughter. Her father, Ceri, owned a chain of risqué underwear shops which were, in Sicily's opinion, "simply common, darling," but seemed at the time to be popular with the public and so the family were doing rather well. Anyway, Chloe with two dots had been quite unbearable when they all returned back to school, after the summer holidays. For some reason, the six weeks off had not been a cooling off period for the golden child, it had simply made her even more infuriating. The name taunting became unbearable for those who had to wear glasses; the kids with speech impediments didn't stand a chance. And you can only imagine the psychological damage the tubby kid went through. Despite everything, if she couldn't find anything to pick on with an unfortunate classmate, the child's parents were in the firing line.

"Your mummy's fat," she would say to Louise O' Hare. To be fair, Louise O' Hare's mother was as big as house, but still it was pretty mean. And, "your dad doesn't love you, Michael Strong, he lives in a home for crazy people." Nasty!

The taunts, however, never bothered little Adrianna Jasmine, as she was a strong little girl, and evil simply bounced off her. But one day, Chloe with two dots overstepped the line and the little witch became angry.

Her mother, Sicily, had picked her up from school on a warm September afternoon, graced in a beautiful red summer dress that had fitted her body like a second skin and billowed out into a long feminine skirt cascading down towards her matching red, high-heeled sandals. She looked beautiful, just like a film star, what with her ample bust, tiny waist, shiny, perfect hair and glowing beautiful face. She was everyone's perfect vision of a mother, soft and warm for a child to hug, and sexy and sultry for a man to lust over. Everyone was admiring her and Adrianna Jasmine swelled with pride when she saw how gorgeous her mother looked. Sicily had enthusiastically hugged and kissed her daughter when she ran up to her and Adrianna Jasmine's friends all came over to say hello and gawp at the goddess in red. The next day, Chloe with two dots and her cling-on friends, had been overheard calling Adrianna Jasmine's mother nasty names, some names Adrianna Jasmine had never heard before and it made her angry.

Sticks and stones may break my bones, she thought clenching her fists during art and craft, *but I do not like words that insult my mother*!

Able to control her anger with deep breathing and concentrating on her work (she was colouring in a picture of a tropical fish), but wasn't quite so able to control her thoughts, and before long a spell had formed in her head.

Be careful oh one with the blonde wavy hair,
Your comments are neither true, nor are they fair.
Your tongue is spiteful, your words sharp and cruel
With your eyes that sparkle like an evil jewel.
Learn this lesson and learn it well
Or your life will turn into a living hell.
All your remarks that cause so much pain,
Will now turn on you, the one who is vain.
A lesson I think to make you realise
That it is you in this room that is loathed and despised.
The possession that you believe makes you unique,

Will now turn against you and make you a freak!
And worst of all it will not be returned,
Until I believe that privilege has been earned.
Now you will learn what it is like to be sad
And it's only because you've been so bad.

As soon as the spell entered her head, poor Adrianna Jasmine's little face was crumpled up with woe and she tried so desperately to dissolve the words that were flooding into her mind like toxic water, for yes, she hated Chloe with two dots, but she had no right to cast a spell on her. But it was useless and before she knew what was happening, the spell had been cast and Chloe with two dots was in for a nasty shock.

The next day, Adrianna Jasmine arrived at school and everything seemed relatively normal. Chris Swanson was sitting next to Terry O'Thomas and Pearl Grey and Tanya Lamont were talking intensely about their Barbie and Cindy dolls. Other children chatted amongst themselves about the TV programmes they had watched on Children's ITV the day before; they seemed to love Dungeons and Dragons and Rod And Emu, until the teacher, Miss Staples, rapped on her desk and asked for everyone to be silent for her to take the register. As she worked through the list the children answered, "Present" when their names were called, but Chloe with two dots did not.

Playground gossip concluded that Chloe with two dots had been unwell in the night and therefore was away from school. Adrianna Jasmine's heart skipped a beat when she found out and panic began to rise up through her body like a raging fever.

Oh Goddess, what have I done? she thought. *What's happened to Chloe with two dots?*

For days she kept her fear to herself and was very quiet at home. Her mother noticed the change in her daughter, as her little girl's loss of appetite was apparent and she seemed to be nervous and unable to relax. Her mother asked her a few times what was wrong, although Adrianna Jasmine would simply reply, "Nothing" and bury her head in a book, or relocate to her bedroom. Sicily decided not to push her daughter into answering, for she knew that when her little girl was good and ready, she would open up and talk. Then it happened. Adrianna Jasmine came home one day after school and burst into floods of tears and buried her face into her mother's warm embrace; she could no longer hold the secret.

She had heard that the very next morning after accidently casting the spell, Chloe with two dots lifted her head off the pillow but her strawberry blonde hair remained on the pillow. Chloe with two dots was now completely bald!

Adrianna Jasmine wailed into her mother's arms, partly because she felt so terrible about what she had done and partly because she was now sure she was no longer a white witch but an evil black witch who cast evil spells.

As she sobbed and sobbed, her mother soothed her daughter and hugged her tightly. She rocked the little Adrianna Jasmine back and forth for ages until no more tears could be cried and a hiccup-type noise - due to Adrianna Jasmine becoming so worked up - replaced the sobbing. When Sicily took Adrianna Jasmine's delicate face into her hands, she felt sadness and pride towards her daughter. Sadness because of what her daughter had been through over the past couple of weeks, (the little girl was practically skin and bone) and pride because of how very powerful her daughter was.

"Oh, turnip top, no more tears," Sicily advised through a warm smile. "You mustn't blame yourself. After all, you are a very powerful witch and unfortunately you aren't quite able to control your wonderful powers yet. But you will, and then you will be even greater. And as for casting a spell to protect mummy's honour: well, I am deeply, deeply grateful my little pumpkin. But you must understand," and with this Sicily's voice went one shade darker than mahogany, "mummy can most certainly look after herself!"

She peered into her daughter's eyes and Adrianna Jasmine found herself, for the first time in weeks, smiling, then more tears came.

"What's wrong, pumpkin? Is the thought of that girl without any hair upsetting you?" Adrianna Jasmine nodded feebly. Sicily sighed, "well it's a good job that you are upset my sweet, otherwise your intentions would certainly be dark and I must admit, I would be a little worried about what I've got for a daughter!" Sicily joked, "but as it happens, I have a wonderful, beautiful daughter. Although, you have looked better darling than you do right now, but let's not dwell on that. Your guilt just proves your innocence, so, apple popsicle, you are a white witch through and through."

Adrianna Jasmine nodded with a little more conviction, but then deflated again when she realised she had no idea how to reverse the spell. Unfortunately the spell that had been cast was extremely powerful and was not able to be reversed, not even Sicily could put her powers to helpful use.

"I'm afraid," Sicily explained, "that this spell will finish when it truly believes it's time to finish." Adrianna Jasmine looked confused and asked why.

"You have accidentally cast a *lesson learning spell* on your school companion, darling, and until she actively learns her lesson about the things she's done in the past, I'm afraid her hair will not return." Sicily and her little daughter heaved a sigh.

"It's useless then," said Adrianna Jasmine shaking a heavy head, "she has no idea about how nasty she is, so she'll be bald forever."

Sicily went over to the stove to boil some milk, to make a sweet hot chocolate for them both.

"Oh, she will, darling," sang Sicily, "albeit in a rather over dramatic way, as hair loss is rather a harsh punishment, darling. But everything happens for a reason and this unfortunate event *will* make that girl a better person and as soon as it does, her hair will grow back, good as new."

They both drank their hot chocolate and sat snuggled up on the couch for a while as Sicily sang Adrianna Jasmine a soothing lullaby. Before long, the little witch could hardly keep her eyes open and was escorted to bed, where she slept dreamlessly through the night and woke up, eye-puffiness free and feeling much more positive, thanks to her mother's enchanting little lullaby.

When Chloe with two dots returned to school, wearing a pink bandana to hide her baldness, she was much quieter, stayed close to a few loyal friends from the clique, whose mummys were adamant that they must support their unfortunate chum, and never once hurled abuse towards the fat kid. She would wince when her friends made fun of other children and scolded them for being mean. It appeared Chloe with two dots was changing; she was beginning to see the light.

This was all thanks to a bunch of new friends she had been introduced to during this difficult time. Her new friends were children who were undergoing treatment for leukaemia/cancer or had suffered severe alopecia and as a result had sadly lost their hair.

After a few meetings with these brave children, Chloe with two dots saw the light and she no longer felt it was right to be spiteful to those who were different or had to endure physical hardships. No longer would she spray Tinkerbelle perfume at the smelly kid at the back of the class, or laugh at the fat kid in his/her PE shorts. She had changed; it was cool to be nice and after a while hanging with her new crew, just as Sicily predicted, Chloe with two dots' hair began to grow back.

Adrianna Jasmine found out years later that Chloe with two dots was married to a doctor, is a mother to a little blonde girl and works as a physiotherapist in an NHS hospital, helping to rehabilitate shattered bodies.

An easy do it yourself cooling mask for a sunburnt face
1 tbsp natural yogurt, room temperature
1 tsp runny honey
Mix everything together gently, then apply to the face and leave for fifteen minutes, wash off with cool water.

'You shouldn't go burning your face in the sun, anyway. Look at me, I'm as pale as pasteurised milk, but you won't catch me looking like Ribena girl'
(Sarah 2008)

Chapter 15
Red Bull and too Much Sun

"Thank Goddess," cried an exasperated Blaire when she spotted the two witches entering the kitchen. Her horn-rimmed glasses had steamed up and her greying red curls appeared somewhat flat and limp, "You're here! We hardly have any cakes left and your father was just about to run over to the convenient store and buy a load of muffins!"

Adrianna Jasmine winced.

"Yuck! Pre-packed readymade cakes from a generic food chain group: revolting, sacrilege!"

"Did you bring everything that was ordered?" asked Blaire, with a slight edge of desperation to her voice, Adrianna Jasmine smiled and nodded.

"I'll display them now," said Adrianna Jasmine with a warm smile, "it's all under control."

Blaire nodded her head, "Good girl," then returned her attention to making a large, triple, hot chocolate chip, marshmallow dream, topped with fresh cream and chocolate chips.   Adrianna Jasmine hurried to work and set about unpacking her cakes, after which she began expertly sprinkling *merry* on top of each delicious looking ensemble. Once sprinkled, the two witches worked hurriedly and whisked the cakes from the kitchen, straight behind the glass-protective counter.

"Good, that's all done," announced Adrianna Jasmine as she rolled up her sleeves, "now, onto the Halloween treats for tomorrow."

"Good idea," said Sarah. "Right, I'm off to help out with the heaving, pulsating throng outside."

"Have fun!" smiled Adrianna Jasmine. Sarah rolled her eyes and seconds later she was gone.

Adrianna Jasmine began to lay out her ingredients, she was feeling good, there was nothing like Halloween baking to enliven the spirits. As the morning rolled on, the witch whizzed up a batch of homemade chocolate biscuits shaped liked spiders and witches;

whipped up cupcakes topped with bright red butter icing that was meant to look like blood and decorated with green jelly worms; toffee apples, sprinkled with hundreds and thousands; fresh pumpkin and apple soup, a perfect winter warmer; marshmallow witches; green slime, which was basically mashed up lime jelly decorated with gummy worms; caramel & pecan pumpkin pie and devils crunch (a delicious munchtastic collision of flour, porridge oats, brown sugar, desiccated coconut, cocoa powder, butter, milk chocolate and hundreds and thousands). After a couple of hours of hard baking, Adrianna Jasmine had finished and as a reward, decided to treat herself to a grande mochaccino.

She flopped herself down on one of the coffee shops' squashy old leather armchairs, read a discarded copy of The Mirror and enjoyed her frothy treat. She allotted herself a quick twenty-minute break before returning back to the grind stone, as there still was plenty of work to do. The witch had been booked to cater for a child/adults Halloween party for an important client. The client in question was a forty year-old woman named Emmalina Lucci, a beautiful and voluptuous painter and ex model, who lived in an equally beautiful and voluptuous house. Adrianna Jasmine was secretly excited about this contract, as she was actually an admirer of this fine lady and enjoyed her art. (Yes, there was actually a celebrity that Adrianna Jasmine admired.) She was one of those women you simply couldn't help but admire and was so stunning, one assumed that angels must have put her together.

Emmalina stood a statuesque 5ft 9 in height, adorned long raven hair, big brown eyes, a tiny nose, the most sensuous lips ever created and a perfect oval-shaped face. She was talented and had founded her own art company 'Pastiche Designs". She was intelligent, strong, spoke four European languages and was well-humoured. Adrianna Jasmine had excitedly won the contract due to Emmalina learning about Adrianna Jasmine's cooking talents from, yet another satisfied customer. What's more, Emmalina actually called her personally. So Adrianna Jasmine, ever the trouper, was now preparing to cater for the delectable Goddess, by laying on one fabulous spread. There was only one hitch: the party was being held on the day the cackle was off to Burley.

"Piece of cake," she encouraged herself, "I'll make all the party food today, store it and deliver it over to the Lucci residence tomorrow afternoon; set up what I can, drop off the van, jump on the tube, then catch the train down to New Milton. It'll be a piece of pecan pie!"

She smiled happily to herself and began to think about the menu she had planned for Emmalina Lucci's party.

'Kids Menu'
Mini Homemade organic Cheese and Ham bagels
Homemade organic Sausage Rolls
Savoury Mini Scones
Dips and Crudities
Milk Shakes and Frappuccinos made with Fresh Fruit
Millionaires' Shortbread
Gory Cup Cakes
Naturally Pink Pop Corn
Nut free Rocky Road
Chocolate Witch and Spider Biscuits
Marshmallow Witches
Slime Jelly with Gummy Worms

'Adults Menu'
Dead man's fingers, Crudities and Dips
Organic Mini Spicy Burgers
Home Made Mini Hawaiian and Pepperoni Pizzas
Pumpkin and Apple Soup

Fish Pie

Saffron and Potato Mash

Wild Mushroom Risotto Cake

Spooky Tuna and Green Pesto Pasta

Homemade Foccacia

A Medley of Seasonal Salad Vegetables

Lasagne

Alcoholic Vampire Blood Punch

Belgian Chocolate Mousse

Chocolate and Amaretto Flan

Banoffee Pie

As Adrianna Jasmine drained the last of her coffee, she recalled that she had not yet answered Taylor's pesky text. Not wishing to be deemed rude, she decided to answerer his text politely, yet to the point.

'Would have enjoyed to have met for a coffee, but unfortunately I'm away with the girls over Halloween, take care AJ ☺

Adrianna Jasmine was pleased she had opted for a smiley face this time and not the customary kiss, and even allowed a little smile to appear across *her* pretty face. However, her smile was soon replaced with a frown, Taylor replied quicker than Road Runner.

"Why did he have to respond so bloody quickly?" she fumed, irritated at his keenness. She read the message and promised herself she wouldn't answer it unless it was highly necessary. No problem, have fun and I'll look forward to our meeting T☺.

"Pesky copycat, does he not have a mind of his own? I send a smiley face; he sends a smiley face…"

She snapped the mobile shut, stood up huffing and puffing and began to clear her table. She was not going to reply, silly man!

Muttering under her breath, so she could remind herself not to accidentally set Taylor on fire with her mind or something, she was about to take leave and return to her work, when a bizarre conversation between a couple of young men stopped the witch dead in her tracks. Intrigued, she discretely listened in.

"Wow, I'm telling you, mate," said one of the chirpy chaps, as if he were on a day trip to Amsterdam, "I can see the air! It's amazing, so colourful." "That's great man," answered his pal enthusiastically, "but you should sooo be giving yourself a pat on the back right now, due to your infectious enthusiasm for life."

Adrianna Jasmine turned her nose up in disgust, "disgraceful," she thought, "they're obviously on something they shouldn't be, I have a good mind to start putting up drug awareness posters in here. Goddess, what is the world coming to? This is a respectable place!"

"Thanks, man," answered the first chap with a dozy smile on his face, "I will," and playfully patted himself on his own shoulder. The men chuckled and glided out of the coffee shop.

Adrianna Jasmine shook her head. *Unbelievable, it's not even 9.30am, what a state to be in!* She clicked her tongue disapprovingly as she observed the men's behaviour; however more and more bizarre conversations began to float passed her like wisps of dreamy pink air.

"Wow, I feel like I've just licked a hallucinogenic mushroom and my feet are being tickled at the same time," came one voice giggling and gurgling like a baby. "I feel like I've just had a Pina Colada, a *large* bag of pickled onion monster munch and four cans of red bull!" came another. "I'm full of adrenaline, crank me up, crank me up!" Hey, you ever wonder why Red Bull is called Red bull is called red bull it's kinda orange, don't you think?"

"Wow, that's sooooo true, but think about this one: could eating ice-cubes substitute for drinking water?"

Intrigued, Adrianna Jasmine silently listened in on more bizarre conversations, she had never heard such claptrap. What had evoked such strange conversations? *Ahhhhh!* A piercing cry from behind the witch's shoulder caused her to very nearly jump out of her skin. A thirty-something man was screaming at the top of his voice.

"How infuriating," he wailed twisted in torment, "why is it so difficult to open a packet of Weetabix?" He appeared to be absolutely distraught and the veins in his head looked fit to burst. Although, the peculiar thing was, he didn't even have a packet of Weetabix anywhere near him.

"Never mind that," barked a frantic looking woman, "I feel really sick and my face! It feels so hot, blow on me, blow on me!!!"

Adrianna Jasmine felt her blood pressure dangerously rise as panic overwhelmed her body. Why was everyone around her acting like they were drunk, sick or crazy?

"I'm telling you mum," nagged a grumpy teen, "I feel like I've had too much sun!"

"Don't be ridiculous, Oscar," screeched the flustered mother, "it's raining outside! Mind you, your face has gone a rather peculiar shade of beetroot!"

Adrianna Jasmine stared across at the boy's face; it appeared to look nothing short of radioactive.

"Goddess," breathed the witch in shock, "the cakes!" and raced towards the counter. With her heart in her mouth, she tumble-rolled under the serving hatch with the ability of a nubile gymnast, and pounced towards the cakes and treats. Without prior warning to her colleagues, the witch began to frantically snatch up the goodies, even finding a spare second and extra pair of hands to grab a hunk of chocolate cake from a customer's plate."

"Hey!" cried the disgruntled customer, "what're you doing? Give it back!" Adrianna Jasmine ignored him.

"Oh, Goddess," said the witch panicking "oh no, oh no! What have I done!" "Adrianna Jasmine!" cried out Blair in shock, "what on earth are you doing? Stop it. Give that chocolate cake back to the customer, this instance."

Adriana Jasmine shook her head defiantly and marched straight into the kitchen. Flabbergasted at Adrianna Jasmine's remarkable behaviour, Blaire followed suit.

"I'll ask you again," warned Blaire, as she burst in through the door, "why have you stolen that customer's cake, and all the other's, for that matter?" She added, looking around.

Blaire looked furious; she was waiting for an explanation, and fast.

"Blaire," said Adriana Jasmine seriously, "we have a problem."

Blaire raised her eyebrow, "What do you *mean* a problem?"

Adrianna Jasmine flushed scarlet and clumsily began to explain her plight, "Look... err," she fumbled, "I may have err... put too much of the, err...you know the *stuff* into them!"

At first, Blaire's expression was nothing but confused, as she tried to understand what the flustered witch was struggling to say, then it hit her and a surging rise of terror stirred in her toes.

"Oh my Goddess," she cried, you've overdosed the customers with stuff... magic!"

Adrianna Jasmine nodded shamefully; Blair buried her head in her hands.

"How bad do you think it is?" Blaire's mouth was dry with shock and fear.

"Bad!" said Adrianna Jasmine brutally, "please bring all the cakes back in here now, it's a code red!"

Blair's eyes had popped out onto stalks; a code red, no less, What was a code red? "But, but, we've sold half of them already! What'll we do, oh my Goddess, we've poisoned half of London! We'll all be sent to Holloway!"

"Well, go and get what's left of them, then," shouted Adrianna Jasmine, clutching at her hair, "before the other bloody half are poisoned, too!" She was losing what was left of her sanity, it was all becoming too much.

Blair tried to calm herself down by encouraging herself to pant like a dog, a bit like how women are encouraged to breathe when in labour, and made her way back into the coffee shop. She slid the cabinet door open and, as inconspicuously as she could, removed the coffee cake and the lemon drizzle cake.

"Hey!" yelled Sarah, "I need that!" and pointed sharply at the lemon drizzle as her mother whisked it away with the speed of light. Unperturbed, Blaire ignored her daughter and whispered, "code red, code red," like some Russian spy, and shot towards the kitchen door. Sarah looked on in bewilderment, "code red?" The customers began to complain.

"Oi," they chorused simultaneously, "what're you doing with those cakes?"

"That's exactly what I want to know," said Sarah and chased her mother into the kitchen.

As Sarah burst angrily through the door, she was immediately taken aback by the chaos before her again! Cakes were strewn all over the place, flower and sugar had exploded all over the floor and a somewhat disturbed Adrianna Jasmine was pacing like a deranged tiger and chewing her fingernails down to bloody stumps.

"What the hell is going on," Sarah demanded, her eyes flicking back and forth as she tried to make sense of it all, "Adrianna Jasmine, what's the matter with you? You look loopy and why have you stolen our cakes?"

Adrianna Jasmine continued nervously pacing up and down and with nothing to chew on anymore, settled for twisting her fingers into knots. She took in a deep gulp of air.

"I think, no I *know* I've made a terrible, terrible mistake."

"What do you mean you think you've made a terrible mistake?" asked Sarah dubiously, "why? What've you done now?" Adrianna Jasmine winced and tried to explain.

"What did we put in the sponges last night?" she asked without looking up. With a shrug Sarah answered, *Summer Sunshine!* Adrianna Jasmine felt as if her blood had turned to ice.

"Oh no!" she groaned and dropped to her knees in despair, "oh Goddess, I was hoping you weren't going to say that." Sarah looked on in utter bewilderment, what was going on? "Oh Goddess, yes, Summer Sunshine, how stupid of me," wailed Adrianna Jasmine to herself over and over again, "you idiot, Adrianna Jasmine. Idiot, idiot, idiot!" Blaire and Sarah looked over to one another, Blaire shrugged her shoulders. "What else did I add to the cakes this morning?" asked Adrianna Jasmine, who for some reason was now covering her eyes with her hands. Sarah shrugged her shoulders as she cast her mind back.

"Err… it was merry, I think, yes, merry," she confirmed, Adrianna Jasmine didn't answer, instead, opted to simply repeatedly bang her head onto the floor.

"And why is this problem?" piped up Blaire, "and stop that, you'll give yourself concussion. What's so terrible about mixing summer sunshine and merry to a few sponges? I say we take those cakes out again NOW!"

Blaire turned around, picked up the lemon drizzle and began to march stubbornly towards the coffee shop. Adrianna Jasmine looked up and caught site of Blaire marching with the defiance of Napoleon, cake in arms, towards her customers and screamed out an ear shattering, "NO!" Immediately the microwave behind her blew into a thousand pieces, resulting in screams of shock, Blaire dropping the lemon drizzle cake onto the floor and the room filling with the foul stench of burnt plastic.

"It'll be fatal," Adrianna Jasmine shrieked, her eyes dancing madly, "I've made a terrible mistake!"

With that, she charged towards the remaining cakes and proceeded like a wild, crazed lunatic to throw them on the floor. Bits of sponge and icing exploded everywhere, even hitting Sarah's poor father Jude, who had simply entered the kitchen to see what all the noise was about. He took one look around, and then decided to retreat back behind the counter. *Witches*, he thought and rolled his eyes. He had wised-up over the years so as to not get involved with matters of women and their witchcraft.

"Adrianna Jasmine!" cried out Sarah and Blaire simultaneously, "what *are* you doing?" Never had they seen the calm, cool Adrianna Jasmine act so out of control.

"You don't understand," cried the witch, her legs splattered in frosting and sticky lemon, "you can't mix merry and summer shine together, it's one of the most deadly cocktails you could ever create, they'll all be dropping like flies!" There was silence for a few moments as the information hit home.

"So…you're telling me," edged Blaire, "that you added *two* magic ingredients that should never be mixed to my customers' cakes without even realising!" Steam was practically screaming from her ears. Adrianna Jasmine nodded sheepishly. "Oh my Goddess," whispered Blaire filled with horror, "we'll all go to prison, we'll be exposed and paraded through the streets just like in the 16th century, there'll be vegetables hurled towards us from every direction, cauliflowers will be launched like missiles at our heads and carrots stuck up …"

"Enough!" shouted Sarah sharply, "no one is going to be exposed, let's all just calm down, Adrianna Jasmine, what are we dealing with here?"

Adrianna Jasmine, who had once again resumed to the psychotic pacing again, explained to her two fellow witches that the people who ate the cakes would be experiencing the effects of severe alcohol poisoning combined with the effects of an unhealthy amount of sun exposure.

"Oh great, so sunstroke directly from hell!" spat Blaire, "what's going on with you, Adrianna Jasmine? You're meant to be a professional potions producer, what's making you act so doolally?"

Adrianna Jasmine looked as if she were about to burst into hot raging tears.

"Love!" she screamed with venom, "bloody love!" and with that, she broke down and began to sob. "I'm so, so sorry," she wailed. "This should never have happened."

Sarah rolled her eyes unsympathetically; no way was she going to let Adrianna Jasmine off for this one, not after Pigwell's party nightmare! She rolled up her sleeves and was ready to unleash a good piece of her mind when she was cut to the quick, by Blaire.

"Leave it, Sarah," said Blaire as she placed her arm across her daughter's path and made her way over to the crumpled Adrianna Jasmine. She had felt a pang of pity towards the hapless heap. Perhaps because she, too, could empathise with the difficulties that love could often bring to a young witch. Yes, she knew only too well. She took Adrianna Jasmine warmly into her arms.

"Oh, sweetie," soothed Blaire kindly, Adrianna Jasmine looked so tiny and lost, "it'll be alright, you're a good witch, you can reverse this, you just need a little…focus. That's all."

Through sobs Adrianna Jasmine mustered a weak nod, "I'll fix it, I promise." She was snotting and sobbing onto Blaire's T shirt.

"I know you will," Blaire gently encouraged as she tried to ignore the hot watery stuff pouring from Adrianna Jasmine's nose. "You're a brilliant witch, but sweetheart, you need to pull yourself together, as we've got a bit of a crisis on our hands!"

Adrianna Jasmine nodded again and peeped out from Blaire's hug like a mole coming out of hibernation on the first day of spring. "OK," she said feebly, "I'll try."

"Right, that's the spirit," encouraged Blaire similar to that of a cheerleading coach, "the last thing we want are people drunkenly falling into the Thames, and killing themselves!" She laughed nervously.

"No," Adrianna Jasmine squeaked, "we don't."

"Too right!" piped up Blaire, "and to make matters worse, people are starving out there, they need feeding, and they need *you*, Adrianna Jasmine, and your magic. Your wonderful magic that spreads light on a gloomy day, or softens even the hardest of hearts, makes cheese on toast taste like fillet steak, so come on, let's apply our war paint and get to work."

Adrianna Jasmine nodded her tear-stained face, Blaire's words of encouragement seemed to pull her out of her slump a little.

"Ok," she said quietly, still looking vulnerable and meek, "start off by using all the Halloween biscuits, pies and other food that I've prepared for tomorrow's festivities and use them for today."

"Great idea!" announced Blaire, "Sarah, get to work." Sarah huffed and puffed then began to plate up the treats. She wasn't too sure how Adrianna Jasmine's blood muffins and green slime would go down with customers, but hey, it was better than fresh air.

"Now what about the...err...other little problem sweetheart?" Blaire trod carefully, Goddess, she didn't want to send her over the edge again.

"I'll also create a protection spell for all the people who have eaten those cakes," said Adrianna Jasmine still sounding teary, "Goddess, I don't want anyone falling into the river on my account."

"Great!" encouraged Blaire, "go get them, kiddo," and she patted Adrianna Jasmine on the back, before racing out of the kitchen.

As expected, the customers were not overly convinced with the tray of blood thirsty cupcakes and spider biscuits: their sceptical faces said it all.

"Ha ha, we thought we'd get into the spirit of Halloween a little early," chirped Blaire, "don't be put off by their spooky exterior, they taste simply divine! Here, try a slice of our famous pumpkin pie! It'll knock your socks off!"

Once all the cakes were out, Adrianna Jasmine set to work on casting a protection spell for those who had been poisoned.

"Here I go again," she sighed solemnly to herself and began to rummage through her first aid kit. She pulled out three red leaves, to be laid out in a triangle shape, a white candle that needed to be placed directly in the triangle's centre and chrysanthemum oil. She placed a few drops of the oil onto each leaf, lit the candle and chanted the following lines three times:

Protect those souls; I not know who they are
But they left this place they shouldn't be far.
Shield them from darkness, bathe them in light;
Stop these dear souls drowning in plight.

Adrianna Jasmine then extinguished the candle and wrapped everything up in a clean white cloth, before tucking the bundle away safely in a storage cupboard. It would only be removed when the remnants of inebriation spell had worn off.

"Well, that's that," she sighed and went on with the rest of her day, although not before a strong cup of coffee to refuel her very existence. As she popped the kettle on, Sarah came back into the kitchen.

"I hope one of those is for me," her friend asked with a smile. Adrianna Jasmine smiled back, grateful that her friend didn't want to perform a binding spell on her to prevent her from performing anymore mischievous magic.

"Come on, you," coaxed Sarah and reached out towards her friend so she could give her a hug. Gratefully Adrianna Jasmine accepted her friend's offer of affection.

"Oh, Jazzy," said Sarah, through a heavy sigh, "it's been a rough day today for you, hasn't it?" Adrianna Jasmine nodded whilst trying to hold back fresh tears. "Mind you, I'm also to blame."

Adrianna Jasmine pulled away from Sarah's hug and screwed up her face. "Don't be ridiculous, Sarah, how could it have been your fault as well, it was all me, me, me!"

"No," argued Sarah gently, "*I* also forgot we added the Summer Sunshine, I should have reminded you this morning when I saw you sprinkling this and that to your cakes, I just didn't think!"

Adrianna Jasmine appreciated the fact that Sarah was offering to ease some of the blame from her shoulders, but alas her efforts were in vain.

"Goddess," sighed the witch, "I messed up big time, didn't I?"

Sarah chuckled, "a bit I guess, you nutcase!"

Then Adrianna Jasmine, too, found the funny side, "Good Goddess," she said suddenly laughing out loud, "I don't do things by halves, do I? Let's see, night before last, I sent nearly 200 people off into the land of nod and transported you off to La-La Land. Oh goddess, you were so funny. Then I overdosed you with Citrus Bang-Bang Boom, shoved Unflustered Floss down your throat and turned you into a new-age hippy! Nearly gave you and your mother a heart attack and poisoned half of London. Not bad, huh? What else could I possibly do to top all that?" It was too much; the two witches were in fits of hysterics.

"Oh Goddess!" cried Sarah with laughter, "witches hats off, you really did outdo yourself during these last two days, Adrianna Jasmine."

"I KNOW!" cried out Adrianna Jasmine, the witches were virtually on their knees as they found the funny side to Adrianna Jasmine's magical blunders.

"Oh, my abs are killing me from all this laughter," winced Sarah, "you should have seen yourself head-banging the floor: you looked deranged!"

Adrianna Jasmine was in fits of hysterics and barely able to get her words out, "Oh, and did you see your father's face when he came in to see what all the noise was about. Oh, it was a picture, ha, ha."

"Oh Goddess," wailed Sarah, "my tummy muscles are killing me from all this laughter, who needs to perform hundreds of sit ups to achieve rock hard abs when laughing is far more effective?"

"I know," agreed Adrianna Jasmine, as her abs, too, were going for the burn. Unfortunately they soon cooled when reality hit home for the witch. "Bloody hell," she puffed breathless and exhausted, "I've got a hell of a lot of work to do!"

Magical Strawberries

'For an instant summer twist, why not squeeze some fresh lime juice and sprinkle caster sugar over some wild strawberries, the taste is truly magical'
(Adrianna Jasmine, 2008)

Chapter 16
Le Pamplemousse Magnifique

Grateful to be outside and away from the hubbub of the mornings trials and tribulations, the grotty wet and miserable weather failed to add to Adrianna Jasmine's misery. She simply tucked herself deeper into her Mac, which seemed to cloak her from the world, and made her way out onto Neal's Street. Soon enough she was at the entrance to the Market at Nine Elms Lane and was at immediate access to the fruit and vegetables. She wandered about amongst the hundreds of different varieties, embracing all the vibrant colours, smells and sounds from the lively place. She adored the market and almost forgot the real reason she was there. She could have quite happily wandered amongst the vastness and magic of the place, just pottering about, drinking in the atmosphere and forgetting about cooking.

"Focus, Adrianna Jasmine," she scolded herself, "you've got too much work to do, there's no time to act like a tourist today."

She sprang into action and made her way over to her favourite fruit and vegetable stall, Le Pamplemousse Magnifique, where husband and wife Cerise and Maxence, who had moved over from Paris some thirty years ago, were busy at work selling their perfect produce. In Adrianna Jasmine's eyes Le Pamplemousse Magnifique was the most proficient fruit and vegetable stall in the whole market place. There was no fruit they didn't sell and nothing was too exotic to import. Their produce always tasted fresh and flavoursome, not like the giant tasteless strawberries one can purchase at any time of the year from a generic supermarket.

"Ah, allo, Adrianna Jasmine," welcomed Cerise when she saw Adrianna Jasmine walking over to the stall, "how are you? It's so good to see you!"

Still feeling glum, Adrianna Jasmine shrugged her shoulders heavily, "Oh, you know, OK."

"Oh dear, that's not good," remarked Cerise, "we can't 'ave you miserable. Here, eat this, it will 'elp you feel more perky!" Cerise threw a lovely Nashi apple or Asian pear as it's more commonly known, at the witch. Adrianna Jasmine caught the fruit, produced a watery smile of gratitude and then bit deeply into its yellow-brown skin.

"Mmmmm," said Adrianna Jasmine as the fruits sweetness tingled her taste buds, "that's lovely."

Cerise produced a smile of satisfaction. "They're magnifique, no? Go on, eat, enjoy. I'll call Maxence over to sort out your order. Is it a big one, by the way?"

Adrianna Jasmine nodded, "Actually, I'm not sure if I can carry everything on my own. I stupidly forgot to bring the van, isn't that silly?"

Cerise looked puzzled and furrowed her brow, "You forgot your van? Oh dear. I didn't think you looked like yourself today, young Jasmine flower, you seem on another planet. Fancy forgetting your van, a purse, yes! But your van! That is...odd."

Adrianna Jasmine shrugged her shoulders. Goddess, if she only knew what she'd truly been through these past two days, she wouldn't think it so strange. Cerise handed back some change to a customer who had just brought a tub of blackberries.

"Let me call Sylvain," Sylvain was Cerise's 18 year old wayward son, "He's somewhere around the place, he may be able to help you carry your load."

"Oh no," Adrianna Jasmine flapped, "I couldn't put him out."

Cerise simply waved her hand in dismissal and called her son on his mobile. After a few minutes of rapid French, Cerise informed Adrianna Jasmine that Sylvain *would* be on his way and able to help carry her stuff back to the coffee shop.

"Oh, you shouldn't have," said Adrianna Jasmine feeling a little guilty. He was probably in the middle of something really fun and now probably utterly miserable because he's been told to run a boring errand for his mother.

Cerise simply laughed, "Don't you feel guilty now," she soothed, "that boy has it far too easy if you ask me and his father agrees," she glanced over at Maxence who was selling a lovely bunch of bananas to a little old lady. "Honestly, Adrianna Jasmine, he does," her voice shrieking a little at thought of her son's idle behaviour. "I know, I know he's a very clever boy and I'm sure he will become a brilliant lawyer or surgeon one day, but who's putting him through his studies, I ask? Us! You want a bag, my love?" A woman in a green coat had brought four blood oranges and nodded a firm "Yes." Cerise then threw them into a brown paper bag, handed the oranges over and continued ranting on about her errant son. "It's a nightmare tying get him to work, he won't even do a Saturday job. Not even with us, yet he lives at home, has his food all taken care of, no rent!" Adrianna Jasmine gasped, "I know! And when he goes off to university, who'll be footing the bill?"

"Err… you?" suggested Adrianna Jasmine.

"You bet it'll be me, £8.75, my love."

Adrianna Jasmine pondered for a moment before she spoke.

"You know, you could always sit him down and say, 'You know what, this is how it's going be,' then set down your terms and conditions and if he doesn't comply, well stop cooking for him and padlock the fridge, remove his TV from his bedroom, stereo, Nintendo etc, inform him that his electricity has been cut off. Cease to do any of his washing, don't worry about him trying to use the washing machine himself, he won't be able to work it, nonetheless, hide the washing powder! Issue a curfew, no friends allowed, no pets, not even a goldfish, I'm sorry but you must be firm, Cerise, and basically make him understand that unless you are a royal prince, you must work to live and that its time he got the hang of it!" *Wow!* thought Adrianna Jasmine *that felt good!*

Cerise stared at Adrianna Jasmine deep in thought, "I take it you're talking about Sylvain?" Maxence had just walked over to the two women; his voice appeared weary, "because that sounded like music to my ears."

"Well, err…it was just a thought," fumbled Adriana Jasmine, suddenly feeling a little impertinent. "Hey, he's your son. Ha ha. Who am I to say. Hell, I'm not a parent, no sir!"

"No, but you're absolutely right Adrianna Jasmine," Cerise had broken her silence, "No, you *are*, it's definitely food for thought, but it's just doing it, I don't know if I could starve my own son!"

"I could!" Maxence grumbled, which made Adrianna Jasmine giggle, "anyway, my lovely, what can I get you, as my wife has not yet had the decency to serve you, too busy chewing your ear off," he teased.

Cerise rolled her eyes at her husband, "Pah," she said and busied herself serving a small group of Japanese tourists. Smiling, Adrianna Jasmine asked for a crate of strawberries and twenty bananas, twenty mini pumpkins, ten punnets of raspberries, fifty golden delicious apples, 2 kilos of floury potatoes and 24 medium free range eggs, three tubs of cherry tomatoes, one large cucumber and readily chopped fresh pineapple. Maxence raised his eyebrow.

"You were going to carry all this by yourself?" Adrianna Jasmine just shrugged. She was definitely losing it! Moreover, the shopping didn't stop at Le Pamplemousse Magnifique. She had forgotten to order the fresh tuna from New Covent Garden delivery services, so a trip to the fish market beckoned. In addition there was chocolate, flour, butter, and amaretto…the list went on! Adrianna Jasmine was now looking totally crestfallen. *What's wrong with you?* she thought through a defeated sigh, *you never forget ingredients or mode of transport.* She then enquired if Maxence's son would be available to perhaps help load up the van when he arrived, as she decided the only possible solution was to go back, pick it up and bring it back to the market.

"Please, could you keep all this stuff for me until I return?" she asked, "I'll try not to be too long."

"You go ahead, ma petite," Maxence said kindly, "I'll tell you what, why don't you finish your shopping *now,* that way you can leave *all* your shopping here with me! And then you can just run in and load it all up, no more shopping headaches. Also," he added with a cheeky grin and a wink, "I think I'll still send the boy down to the coffee shop, perhaps with the crate of strawberries and raspberries, ha ha," he chortled. "Between you and I, he could do with the exercise! That'll teach him for being so damn lazy," then with a hint of playfulness he asked, "Is it still raining?" Adrianna Jasmine smiled and told him that it was drizzly and miserable out. "Ha ha," he chuckled again, "That'll teach him to mess with papa!"

Twenty minutes after her conversation with Maxence, Adrianna Jasmine had bought exactly what she needed, which included: one gigantic block of dark chocolate and one block of milk chocolate from Chocolate Rain, flour from the bakers, amaretto from the liqueur shop and tuna steaks from the fishmongers. She left her shopping with the folk at Le Pamplemousse Magnifique and hurriedly made her way back to the coffee shop. With any luck she would be back within forty-five minutes and cooking in the kitchen within the next hour and a half. She had much work to do and in all honesty, she was worried about just how much she had been set back.

Boo and hiss, she thought with frustration and began to walk faster. She kept her head down to shelter herself from the rain and was doing well dodging the maddening crowd until...

"Ooops, I'm so sorry!" She had bumped into a tall, handsome man, who was holding hands with a girl wrapped in a stunning purple rain coat, fabulous knee-high suede leather boots and holding a turquoise umbrella. After the initial bump and a few courteous apologies, the girl erupted into a huge grin, her face was simply glowing.

"Well, hello there!" said the girl in purple, "you're that wonderful caterer from the other night, The Magic of Food!"

At the mention of The Magic of Food, the handsome hunk suddenly clicked into life, "Oh yes, its Adrianna Jasmine, how could we ever forget you! It's great to see you again."

Then the penny dropped and Adrianna Jasmine immediately realised who she was talking to.

"Oh Hannah, Antonio...sorry," she corrected herself, "Angelo! How great it is to see you both again!"

Angelo reached forward towards Adrianna Jasmine and planted a kiss on each of her pink cheeks. "So how are you?" he inquired warmly, "I heard great compliments about your food all through the evening." Adrianna Jasmine smiled humbly at the comment. "I tell you, everyone was very impressed."

Adrianna Jasmine giggled. "Why thank you, but I must say your immaculate waiting skills had something to do with the success of the evening. I don't think the food would have tasted half as good if it hadn't been for you and your expertise. Why, you make waiting look as if it is some kind of art."

"Where I come from," said Angelo with a proud smile, "in Madrid, it *is* an art, we do not become a waiter to forward a career in acting, and in my country being a true waiter is a very respectful job!" Then he added, "if you ever need a waiter, Adrianna Jasmine, just let me know, OK?! You and I, we'll make the perfect team." Adrianna Jasmine nodded thoughtfully clearly interested in the proposal.

"You know what, that's a good idea."

"And I'll do your PR and marketing for you both!" suggested Hannah enthusiastically through her Colgate smile. "We'll be the next best thing on the catering circuit. No one else will stand a chance!" She then reached over to embrace Adrianna Jasmine with the warmest of hugs.

Wow! thought Adrianna Jasmine, as the warmth radiated through Hannah and into her bloodstream, *that's almost on par with Carolina Plum, such a different energy from the nasty, stuck up, Hannah of old."*

Hannah was still beaming with a smile and Angelo had a wonderful look of contentment on his face. Adrianna Jasmine shifted her eyes from Hannah to Angelo.

"So, err..." she hedged playfully, "I guess you two had fun at the party?" The pair both smiled and looked happily at one another, "I'm pleased for you," said Adrianna Jasmine sincerely, "Good for you. It's nice when two people deservingly get together."

"Thank you," said Hannah graciously, "but I must say, for some reason we think if it weren't for you, we just have this niggling feeling that Angelo and I wouldn't be together." Angelo nodded seriously in agreement. Adrianna Jasmine stayed calm and dismissed the suggestion with a wave of the hand.

"Oh, it was just coincidence. You see, I hired out Angelo's company, you were there already and..."

"No!" Hannah broke in with a smile, "we both *feel* it was you." Adrianna Jasmine gulped, had they seen her spike the food? "You're like some wonderful charm, Adrianna Jasmine, you are very special person, we both feel it. Gosh, we're so pleased to have bumped into you, and we were just saying how much we would like to see you again and as if by magic…here you are." Adrianna Jasmine chuckled nervously. "Who are you?" asked Hannah, her eye brows pulled together as she stared at the witch in total wonderment.

"Hmmm," contemplated the witch, "well, I guess I'm the Magic of Food!" and a big cheesy grin broke out across her face. They all giggled and after a few more pleasantries and promises to keep in touch, the trio kissed each other goodbye.

"Ah, how lovely," reflected Adrianna Jasmine. "Well, at least I did *something* right over the last couple of days. I'm not completely useless after all." And for the first time since her ghastly morning, she actually felt a little more cheerful.

Adrianna Jasmine made her way into the coffee shop and walked straight through. The Mystic Odessa, who was sitting alone reading some cards, caught her eye and beckoned the witch over.

"I can't," urged the witch, "I'm in a rush," and flew into the back kitchen, trying desperately to avoid eye contact with Sarah, and everyone else for that matter. She then went straight out the back door and into her van, turned the ignition and backed out onto the road, eager to make her return to the market. After a thirty minute drive, she turned into Elms lane and parked up. She then made her way back to Le Pamplemousse Magnifique. As promised, Maxence had looked after all her purchases and even helped Adrianna Jasmine load up her van.

"And don't forget that your strawberries and raspberries have been personally delivered by a young, handsome Frenchman," said Maxence with a chuckle. Adrianna Jasmine laughed.

"Oh dear," she said, "poor Sylvain won't be best pleased, but thank you so much for today."

Maxence leant over and kissed Adrianna Jasmine on both of her cheeks, "that's my pleasure, ma petite. Well, au revoir Adrianna Jasmine, see you soon, hey?"

"See you soon, Maxence and thanks again!"

She climbed into her van, shut the door and pulled the seat belt across her. She sucked in a large gulp of air and for the first time since the mishap in the coffee shop, an overwhelming sense of calm swept through her body,

"At last," "she contemplated, "back in control?" She smiled, turned the ignition and drove back to the coffee shop; she had a lot of work head of her but nonetheless, was now feeling up to the challenge.

A Serenity Bath
Shut the doors and window, take the phone off the hook, play your favourite chill-out CD and light some tea candles. Run yourself a nice warm bath and add the following essential oils to the water.

**2 drops Lavender
2 drops Bergamot
2 drops Cedar wood**

'Always test aromatherapy oils before you use them, Adrianna Jasmine doesn't want you coming out in boils now, does she?!'
(Sicily, 2008)

Chapter 17
Sang the Bells of Saint Clementine

Subsequent to Adrianna Jasmine returning from Convent Garden, the witch had worked herself into frenzied twirl. She had ploughed through Emmalina's party menu, remade all the cakes for the coffee shop, plus all the Halloween treats. It had taken her hours late into the night to complete her mission and by 11.00pm she was able to go home. It was nearly midnight, the witching hour, and as she walked into the haven of her home, and she sighed thanks to the Goddess.

"Thank you for bringing this hellish day to an end," she said with a grateful sigh, it had possibly been the most stressful day of her life and to add gloom to her grisly day, Sarah had unexpectedly announced that she would not be attending the Halloween get-together at Burley Manor. Apparently Blaire had been fretting over the possibility that the coffee shop's Halloween party would be overrun with customers and Sarah's extra pair of hands would appease nervous tension. Moreover, due to Adrianna Jasmine's little faux pas earlier that day, Blaire apparently felt more at ease if Sarah were present, in case any other magical mishaps occurred, like the spider cookies suddenly bursting into life and scuttling into people's hair, or the apples in the bobbing bowl unexpectedly exploding like bombs.

Adrianna Jasmine had desperately tried to convince Sarah that there would be no more magical mishaps as the cakes had been sprinkled with the teeniest bit of merry and nothing else! Nonetheless Sarah was not swayed; she apologised profusely and promised to take the disappointed Adrianna Jasmine out to San Lorenzo for a yummy pasta lunch as a gesture of goodwill. "OK," Adrianna Jasmine had grumbled with utter disappointment – that was after an hour of trying to persuade her friend to not cancel out on her girlcation and she finally admitted defeat.

As Adrianna Jasmine opened the door to her flat, she was immediately greeted by Jupiter 10. The silky cat entwined his body around her ankles and meowed with affection, he had missed his mistress today. The witch picked up the silky cat, cuddled him into her arms and collapsed in the living room. Jupiter 10 nestled into his mistress's embrace and began to purr. She closed her eyes and surrendered to the soothing sounds the little cat was creating. *Oh, bliss*, she thought, *at last: peace*. And she began to hum a soothing song. The song was called Rose Garden and was rather special. Once the words, or notes, were released from one's lips, the beautiful smell of fresh cut roses would waft through the air, comforting the senses and exuding tranquillity in its wake. The witch continued to hum, snuggled into the luxurious sent of peace roses on a hot summer's day, with Jupiter ten expertly harmonising his purrs with her voice, when…

Ring- Ring, Ring- Ring.

"Oh no!" she wailed in frustration, "just when I'm starting to relax, I know, it's you, mother, I know it is!" With that, Jupiter 10 jumped off his mistress's lap, taking his warmth with him and the sweet smell of roses to boot. Oh, why can't you allow me a moment's peace, you silly old witch. "Hello mother!" said Adrianna Jasmine with a strained chirpiness to her voice.

"Hello, darling," boomed the theatrical voice of Sicily, "how on earth did you know it was me, I didn't even say hello!"

Adrianna Jasmine shrugged, "I'm psychic, mother."

"Well, I know that, hot pocket, but you still never cease to amaze me with all your talents." Adrianna Jasmine rolled her eyes in despair. "Anyway, mummy just called to ask you about your arrangements for tomorrow. Are you and Sarah travelling down with us? Because if you are, Kristobella will pick you girls up with Clementine and myself."

'Stop, pause, may I introduce you to Clementine Poppleapple!'

Kristobella and Sicily's mother, Lilliana Poppleapple, had a brother called Elwood. Elwood, too, possessed supernatural abilities and practiced his craft frequently. When he was 22, he met and fell in love with a lovely witch from the Flash-Blossom Coven named Gilder Rose and as a result, gave birth to a boy who they named Columbus.

Columbus grew into a brilliant Warlock and took great pleasure in healing physically broken bodies with his gift. However, due to his dedication in regards to protecting his magical heritage, he decided to mix his supernatural healing powers with that of a more mainstream method and decided to study medicine at Oxford. There he met an attractive and very tall German girl, named Claudine, who was also studying medicine. They became inseparable, and after graduating with honours, the pair decided to marry. Two years later Clementine was born and all seemed perfect until the little girl hit six months. In the beginning, Claudine thought nothing of it, just coincidence. But why did the lights always flicker when the little baby cried? Or, why would she find the child giggling to herself in the middle of the night, as if someone were in the nursery playfully tickling her tummy and playing peek-a-boo? It was all very strange, and even her medically brilliant mind couldn't conjure up any reasonable, scientifically proficient reasons why somewhat supernatural occurrences were commonly materializing. Then one day it became all too extraordinary, too much for Claudine's clever and rational mind to handle. Well, how would *you* feel if you found your baby girl levitating above the covers of her crib, cooing away without a care in the world. Claudine felt terrified, screamed, subsequently fainted, came round, and then got straight on the phone to a catholic priest to perform an exorcism. But how can you exorcise a demon that isn't there? Feeling dreadful, Columbus had no choice; he had to tell his now unstable and terrified wife the truth. Unfortunately, Claudine did not accept the news too well and a few days later, she left Columbus and took baby Clementine back home to Germany, to live with her parents and away from witchcraft! Poor Columbus begged Claudine to stay, but it was in vain. Claudine was adamant that she wanted to leave. So he let them go, for he knew one day they would return. Besides, he could visit his little girl in her dreams every night and he was confident that her true calling would bring her home to him one day. Over the years, Claudine tried and tried to curb Clementine's magical abilities, but it was no use: the little witch's power was too strong to contain. What made matters worse was the fact that Clementine had no one to guide her, or teach her how to control her magical powers. So unfortunately, television sets were often accidentally blown up when a temper tantrum raged through her body, or an unfortunate school chum went down with measles if they were mean to her. So when Clementine was nine, Claudine called her estranged husband and begged him to take her back to England. She couldn't handle the trauma anymore.

Columbus refused, it was either the pair of them together again as a family, or nothing at all. For days she deliberated, should she stay or should she go? What kind of a life would she have once she had surrendered to the coven? How would she feel, could life be…normal? On the flip side, Columbus had told her that once Clementine was around elder witches, she would be taught how to control her magical abilities, so no more exploding TV sets: it would save a fortune! So they tried again. To this day, Claudine still has reservations about her daughter being a witch and will not allow any form of witchcraft in the house. She is also adamant that her daughter lead as much a normal life as possible, goes to the cinema with normal friends, takes her studies seriously and has non-magical hobbies. But alas, Clementine's true calling is too strong and even though she has made her mother proud by studying psychology at University, her magic always triumphs. Probably due to her German roots, at the age of 22, Clementine now stands a statuesque 5ft 9. Her skin is the colour of caramel and she wears her white blonde hair in a cool pixie crop. She is nothing short of stunning to look at; she's very sexy, likes to party and downs the occasional B52. She speaks her mind, is clever and takes her mother's dislike to her craft with a pinch of salt. She adores being a witch, although has been known to experiment, much to her coven's dislike, with the dark stuff.

Action!

Adrianna Jasmine sighed with disappointment, "Sarah isn't coming anymore," she said, her voice monotone, "and I'm working until two, so I'll be making my own way down."

"Oh, that's a shame, darling," said Sicily her voice slightly suspicious, "Sarah always comes with us, what's happened?"

Adrianna Jasmine bit her lip. "Oh, she's needed at the coffee shop," she tried to say matter-of-factly, "so… anyway it doesn't matter, we'll still have a good time and I must say, I'm really looking forward to the break."

"You *are,* darling?" asked Sicily detecting the weariness in her daughter's voice, "why's that? Tell me, my little chocolate drop."

"Oh, I don't know, mum," mumbled Adrianna Jasmine, "I've just been busy, I fancy escaping for a night, that's all. You know, get out of London."

"Mummy understands completely, darling. We'll have a wonderful, magical time and you'll soon feel on top of the world again." Sicily then let out a little squeal of delight, "Oh, I bet you can't wait to get out there on Whiz, a good flight above the tree tops will sort you right out, you just wait and see."

Adrianna Jasmine smiled at the thought of taking flight with her faithful broomstick, Whiz, and Jupiter 10, nestled deeply into his bristly twigs.

"I know, I can't wait," sighed Adrianna Jasmine dreamily.

"I bet you can't, darling," answered Sicily excitedly. "Anyway, how are you travelling down?"

"I'll catch the train from Waterloo to New Milton; then taxi to the hotel."

"Don't be ridiculous, darling," said Sicily. "Kristobella will pick you up from the station, no need for a silly taxi."

"OK," agreed Adrianna Jasmine, "that would be nice if she could."

"Course she can, darling and we'll all travel home together, how's that?"

"Perfect." *That'll be a laugh*, Adrianna Jasmine thought sarcastically, her mother and Kristobella clashed terribly at times, and with Clementine taking great pleasure in stirring the poop, the journey would be nothing but one big nightmare. She would have to remember to take some Unflustered Floss, and then remembered she hadn't any left. Prozac?

"I should be there about five," informed Adrianna Jasmine, "just in time for tea, if all goes to plan with Emmalina Lucci's party."

With the mention of Emmalina Lucci's name, Sicily's ears pricked.

"What *the* Emmalina Lucci, kitten mittens? The model/actress/artist?"

Adrianna Jasmine nodded down the phone. "Yep, the very same."

"Well, well, I must say, tea cake with strawberry jam and clotted cream, I am impressed. My Goddess, you are doing well, aren't you? Why, only a few weeks ago you were simply rustling up two bit cakes down at the coffee shop and now look at you, catering for A list celebrities! Oh, mummy's very proud. Still, you must tell me all about it tomorrow."

"I will," promised Adrianna Jasmine with a tired sigh, "but for now, mum, sorry to be rude, but I'm exhausted. I need a bath and bed."

"Say no more, darling, say no more. To be honest, my programme's just about to start and I don't want to miss it. It's that fly on wall series about the life of that couple, you know the one with the big breasts and the little Greek guy!" Adrianna Jasmine had to think for a moment then realised what programme her mother was on about.

"I think he's Cypriot, mum," said Adrianna Jasmine.

"*Is* he, darling?" said Sicily sounding a little confused, "oh well, my bloomer, but I do love it. I know its oeber fromage and car crash telly but I find it very comical and a deserved change from my usual heavy, classical and intellectual programmes, like Tess of the D'urbervilles, Poirot, Panorama and anything Greek and tragic, really. Car crash telly tends to treat the brain to a well-deserved holiday, and then it's all re-charged and raring to go once more." *What a load of piffle*, thought Adrianna Jasmine; she knew full well that her mother would choose Absolutely Fabulous over Jane Eyre any day of the week. However, due to Sicily's quest to be a thespian, her daughter knew that she would never admit to such a heinous crime. "Oh well, my perfect pomegranate, I must fly and see you tomorrow. Take care." With that, Sicily hung up the phone and dashed towards the television set to watch her programme.

With a gentle sigh Adrianna Jasmine placed her phone back onto its cradle, picked Jupiter 10 back up and carried him into the kitchen so she could pop him onto the kitchen window sill and release him out into the mysteries of the night. He meowed his thanks before expertly jumping onto an adjacent branch from a tree just outside the window and then he was gone.

"Have fun," encouraged Adrianna Jasmine, then she shut the window and ran herself a bath infused with enchanted herbs and secret oils.

'Do unto others as you would have them do unto you'

Chapter 18
30 years earlier, Australia

The sky was a strong, vibrant blue and the golden sun shone with power and might onto the sugar-white sand below. The sea was warm and clear, it sparkled and glistened, reflecting the sun's kiss. Waves gently lapped against bare feet on the shore, bathers swam freely in the warm waters and sun worshippers snuggled deep onto their towels, smothering their bronzed bodies in rich coconut oil.

Lifeguards sat high on their towers, slathered in industrial strength sun protection, peering out to sea with one eye and ogling the talent with the other. Families enjoyed their pre-packed luncheons of sandwiches and bananas, whilst young teens either played Frisbee, or had their noses buried deep into a good book. The beach was truly one of Goddesses playgrounds, life was bliss and nothing could spoil the holiday makers' sun-nourished world.

It was 3pm when it happened, the disturbance of peace and goodwill. First there came a scream and then a gathering of people, all intrigued why a piercing scream had shattered their idyllic world. The lifeguards raced from their towers, running at full pelt towards the commotion, filled with adrenaline and kicking into leadership mode. But all the training in the world couldn't have prepared them for the sight before them.

On the sand, washed up and discarded like a rag, was the body of a woman. At a glance, she was not young, but then again, it was hard to tell, what with her skin a ghastly shade of silvery blue, her body bloated, almost fit to burst. Her hair was long, matted; she was missing chunks of flesh from her scalp. A woman screamed in distress at the horrific sight; then came the putrid smell of vomit as onlookers, who were not hardened to such a disturbing sight, threw up onto the sand.

"What happened to her?" whispered a spectator, sickened by the image of the body. Fellow onlookers shook their heads in disbelief, "and are those slash marks on her body?"

Whispers and groans came from the crowd, a woman ran off to be sick.

"God, what did *that* to her?" a man in a pair of green speedos enquired.

At first there was no answer, but then a lifeguard answered the question "Box jelly" he said. The lifeguard was only about twenty, blonde and lean, he looked as if he was about to be sick. "Yes, box jellyfish," the lifeguard confirmed. "Otherwise known as Portuguese man of war, highly unpleasant, a sting from one tentacle is enough to kill a child and by the look of it, she swam into a swarm of them!"

More sounds of vomiting filled the air and mothers ran to the sea to remove their children from the deadly waters.

"It's like someone's taken a white hot cat o' nine tails to her and flogged every square inch of her body," said green speedos, mesmerised by the horror that laid before him. There wasn't one part of the woman's body free from the shocking marks.

"Crikey, it must have been excruciating," said the blonde lifeguard as he gazed glumly at the body. He looked up at his colleague, who appeared to be somewhat pale and sweaty, and told him to go and call for the ambulance. The pale colleague nodded and went off to inform the authorities and probably to be sick himself.

Still kneeling down besides the unfortunate woman, covering his nose to protect him from the stench of the woman's decaying flesh blended with the smell of muscles and fish, the lifeguard began to ask everyone to clear the area and to stay out of the sea. Portuguese man of war were not often found in these parts, but for some reason they had drifted into these waters and the proof was lying right in front of them.

The now forlorn holiday-makers sombrely made their way back to their designated spots and began to pack up their wares, their holiday spirit broken. The ambulance arrived fifteen minutes later; the body was covered up and carried away on a stretcher. All that remained were a few crabs scuttling about and rummaging for bits of flesh for their supper.

The beach, thriving with life only moments before, had now become desolate. Gone were the portable radios, books and sandwiches; gone was the laughter of teenagers and the sounds of splashing feet, all that was left now was an eerie silence and a woman standing roughly 100 yards from the dreaded spot. She was young stunningly beautiful and wearing a dark brown bathing suit and a giant, floppy straw hat. Her face was expressionless, her breathing calm.

Mochaccino Cup Cakes

2 tbsp instant coffee powder
3 oz butter
3oz caster sugar
1tbsp runny honey
7fl oz water
8oz plain flour
1 large beaten egg
3tbsp milk
1tsp bicarbonate soda
2tbs cocoa powder
Whipped cream

Pre heat oven gas mark 4, pop the water, honey, sugar, butter, coffee powder into a bowl. Heat everything up and gently stir until sugar has disappeared. Bring to the boil, simmer for five minutes, then pour into a bowl and allow to cool. When cool sift in the flour and cocoa. Dissolve the bicarbonate of soda into the milk, then add to the mixture with the egg and beat until smooth. Spoon the mixture into cupcake cases and bake between fifteen and twenty minutes. When the cupcakes are cool, whip up some fresh cram and spoon on top. Dust with cocoa powder.

Chapter 19
Bobo, Yoyo and Coco

As Adrianna Jasmine pulled up to Emmalina's gate, she was simply fizzing with excitement at the prospect of meeting *and* working for a personal heroine. She slowed her van down to a gentle stop, unwound the window and pressed the buzzer on the intercom.

"Hello?" inquired the sultry Italian voice from inside the little holes.

"Hi, it's Adrianna Jasmine, the caterer!"

Seconds later, the large iron gates parted dramatically and Adrianna Jasmine, utterly spell-bound, drove into the stunning grounds.

As she pulled up to the beautiful house, which was surrounded by a moat - no less - Emmalina herself was standing like a Roman Goddess on a small bridge by the front door. She was accompanied by three very handsome, yet virtually identical looking, men. Adrianna Jasmine guessed that they were waiters. Emmalina walked over the bridge and welcomed the witch with warmth and gusto.

"Ciao, Adrianna Jasmine, come stai?" she asked brightly

Blushing, Adrianna Jasmine smiled shyly, she actually felt quite flustered, it was the one and only Emmalina Lucci!

"Bene grazie," she answered with a shy smile.

Impressed with the fact that Adrianna Jasmine spoke Italian, the actress burst into a smile and hugged the witch like an old chum.

"Oh molto bene, very good," praised Emmalina cheerfully and gestured the witch to step over the bridge and through front door.

Emmalina was wearing a high-waisted, fitted, black leather pencil skirt, teamed with a beautiful aubergine silk shirt, tucked in at the waist. She wore a stunning pair of black killer-heeled, Jimmy Choo shoes, and her black hair, which she wore centre parted, hung like rich velvet down to the bottom of her back. On Emmalina's slim wrist was a beautiful platinum Cartier watch and on her wedding finger, the most gargantuan diamond Adrianna Jasmine had ever seen. In fact, if you were really observant, you would have noticed that the diamond was actually a delicate shade of pink. .

"Come," she gestured to her three cardboard cut-outs as she walked Adrianna Jasmine through her impressive front door, "help this luv-ah-lee-lay-dee bring her fay-moose, moreish morsels into the kitchen, no?" As if trained at some sort of Emmalina Lucci boot camp, the waiters jumped to attention and began to unload the van.

Once inside the vast hall, Adrianna Jasmine couldn't help but stop and gawp at the sheer magnificence of Emmalina Lucci's incredible home. She felt as if she had stepped back in time and had accidentally walked into the home of a 17th century Italian prince. Beneath her feet were custom designed Travertine floor tiles, that felt heated, and as she looked up there was a jewel toned oil painted frescos, executed in 15th century Renaissance style that covered the entire ceiling.

Gosh, thought the witch, *oh, to live in a house like this*!

With her customary welcoming smile, Emmalina ushered the utterly bedazzled witch towards the lift which was masked by a heavy, rich, plum velvet curtain. They stepped inside and moments later Adrianna Jasmine walked into a magnificent kitchen. Firstly, the room was huge and the walls were the shade of burnt orange, just like her little kitchen at home! There was a giant work island in the centre that housed two ovens, a grill, eight cooking hobs and what was that? A pizza oven?

"I've died and gone to heaven," sighed Adrianna Jasmine, Emmalina smiled again.

"You like?" she asked. Adrianna Jasmine nodded silently. "Well, enjoy it, my love, it's your office for the next few hours," said Emmalina with a tinkling laugh.

Emmalina excitedly began to show Adrianna Jasmine where everything was, like the state-of-the-art-fridge-freezer, steam oven, ice machine, and the sub-zero under counter refrigerator drawers. Adrianna Jasmine felt as if she were in a dream, trying desperately to process the information. It was all too much, what with the side-by side-sub-zero under the counter refrigerator drawers and her most admired heroin of all times under the same roof! Then a phone rang.

"Will you excuse me?" said Emmalina politely and she went off to take her call, leaving Adrianna Jasmine alone with some much-needed quiet space.

She wandered about the kitchen on her own, drinking in all the features such as the antique chandelier dangling from the ceiling and the old antique table where Adrianna Jasmine discovered rough sketches that Emmalina had obviously been working on, an October copy of Italian Vogue, with Emmalina's beautiful face gracing the front cover, French Vogue, Harpers and Queen, and a copy of Fantastico Banquetto! Adrianna Jasmine smiled when she saw the magazine.

"How magical," she thought happily, "Emmalina reads the same food magazine as I do." Smiling at the thought that they had another thing in common, she reached over to pick up the magazine, and then her jaw dropped to the floor. The face on the front cover had momentarily knocked the wind out of her. "Hey… I know that face!" she said pulling her eye brows together, "Oh, my Goddess," her bust was heaving like an actress's when trussed in some abnormally tight corset, swooning during a love scene in some turn of the century romp, "It's you!" She was all flustered.

Taylor Jameson's familiar and annoyingly handsome visage was staring directly back at her. Adrianna Jasmine's stomach did a triple-back-summersault with pike. Yes, it was him, alright, Taylor Jameson, holding a giant glass of ruby red wine and smiling playfully into the lens.

Shaking a little, Adrianna Jasmine read the front cover. *'Fantastico Banquetto's Taylor Jameson samples London's top ten restaurants'*

She flipped quickly to the appropriate pages, so she could absorb more information and hopefully locate more pictures of him. The magazine didn't disappoint and soon she was lusting over four or five scrumptious photos of the mouth-watering Taylor.

"Oh, darling!" Adrianna Jasmine nearly jumped out of her skin; it was Emmalina returning from her phone call. "Take eet, take eet. I've read it, I justa lova Fantastico Banquetto, don't you?"

Feeling rather like she was on the outside peering in, Adrianna Jasmine just managed to nod her head. "Oh…yes," she smiled, struggling to gain control of her thumping heart, "it's the best food magazine out there and err, I, err..." She began to laugh nervously, "well this chap is very good, too, very honest with his... err... criticism." She pointed at Taylor's font cover picture. "In fact," she said as if she were letting Emmalina in on some huge secret, "I sort of know him."

"Ooh, you do?" purred Emmalina intrigued, "lucky you. Oh yes, he is very handsome, no? In fact," she said glancing down at the picture once more, then flicking her eyes back to Adrianna Jasmine's darling face, "you two would make a lovely-looking couple, don't you think?"

Adrianna Jasmine blushed scarlet. "Oh, err... ha, ha! Oh, well... I suppose he *is* rather handsome. But I barely even know him." She waved her hand dismissively.

"Well, get to know him," encouraged Emmalina with her usual gusto, "I see chemistry there, darling. It's practically crackling through the paper." Emmalina tinkled a laugh that sounded more like Angels ringing handmade Swarovski crystal mini bells. "I'm teasing... sort of." She laughed again, "no, take the magazine, darling," she said more seriously. "I've read it, plus..." she winked playfully, "you can swoon, swoon and swoon over his picture." She giggled again then in a puff of expensive smelling perfume, was gone leaving Adrianna Jasmine alone in the kitchen.

With a smile and a sigh, Adrianna Jasmine popped the magazine down and made a mental note to remember it before she left: well, it would be good reading material for her train journey later on. She then began to unpack her amaretto flan and chocolate mousse, the lasagnes and fish pies, saffron mash, salads, the goujons, crudities with dips and spooky sandwiches into the fridge. Luckily, Emmalina had plenty of space in the oeber-cool black Smeg, something which lead Adrianna Jasmine to believe that the woman ate out a lot. *Oh, what a life she must lead*, contemplated the witch dreamily. Ten minutes later, a waft of perfume tickled Adrianna Jasmine's senses again, the lovely Emmalina was back in the room once more.

"Can I helpa you with anything, sweetie?" inquired Emmalina. She was so vibrant and warm, you couldn't help but fall in love with her. Adrianna Jasmine pondered for a moment.

"Err, well... I really need to think about setting up the buffet table in the next few minutes, so perhaps you could show me where you're holding the party?"

"Sure. Follow me," said Emmalina, beaming a huge grin and she lead Adrianna Jasmine into the dining room. They made their way back into the lift and made their ascent to the hallway. The lift doors slid open and Adrianna Jasmine trotted off behind the model. "Here we are," sang Emmalina as she opened an impressive set of heavy oak doors. Adrianna Jasmine stepped forward and stood, stuck to the spot, utterly taken aback by the beauty of the room. "This is the dining room," explained Emmalina, "we'll be eating in here."

As Adrianna Jasmine stepped through the doors, once again all she could bring herself to do was nod silently. It was too breathtaking for words. It seemed to remind the witch of a lavish medieval court. Crimson velvet curtains hung lavishly from the oversize French windows, where copious amounts of winter sunlight poured in and onto the back and white floor tiles, making them shine to a gleam. The furniture was made from heavy wood and the hand carved dining table was enormous, perfect for a medieval banquet. Adrianna Jasmine began to imagine what it must be like to eat supper in a room such as this, sat like a queen on one of the high-backed antique chairs, gazing out towards the Italian inspired garden that would put Tivoli to shame.

"It's perfect," she managed to almost whisper, "it's going to be a wonderful party."

"Of course it is, Bella," said Emmalina matter-of-factly, "you're doing the catering!" Adrianna Jasmine smiled shyly, "thank you for this opportunity, Emmalina," she said sincerely, "I won't let you down."

"Oh, don't be silly Picalina. Besides, I like to present up- and- coming young talented people with the opportunity to further their lives, it makes the evening so much more personal, don't you think? Now what do you need to do?" Overcome with gratitude, Adrianna Jasmine explained that she would need to start thinking about decorating the room. "You needa some elpa?" asked Emmalina all businesslike, and before Adrianna Jasmine could answer, Emmalina clapped her hands together and called out three extraordinary names.

"Bobo, Yoyo, Coco. Come in here and elpa Adrianna Jasmine."

The three men who had helped Adrianna Jasmine when she first arrived, appeared moments later in perfect unison and obediently awaited instructions. They were all dark haired, dark skinned and chiselled to perfection, as if Michelangelo had carved their bodies himself. They didn't talk, they hardly breathed for that matter, and they stood with the discipline of the Royal Guard. Adrianna Jasmine said nothing, she was still in shock. *How had the boys magically appeared from nowhere?* In addition, they were ridiculously handsome.

"Just give them your instructions;" said Emmalina playfully, "they're very well trained!" She tinkled her famous laugh once more, "go on," she encouraged, "give them some instructions, they won't bite."

"Right!" said Adrianna Jasmine, feeling slightly foolish, "well, um, if you could start by please bringing all the non-edible things in here such as the cauldron, plate warmer, mirrored trays, black tablecloth, candles and decorations, that would be really helpful. Oh, and a pen!" she added. The boys nodded simultaneously and with that, disappeared. Emmalina smiled proudly and clapped her hands together excitedly.

"Oh they are wonderful, no? Such good boys. Completely fuss free and so very dedicated to me. Every time I hold a party they're just a Godsend, in fact they *are* a Godsend, full stop. Their talents don't just end serving party food, either. Why, Bobo is a fantastic cook and housekeeper, Yoyo is a wonderful gardener and takes care of the pool and house maintenance and Coco is a wonderful nanny, very helpful with my little girl's homework and a very talented masseuse!" She turned proudly towards the trio who were busily carrying in Adrianna Jasmine wares, "they're also experts in the art of mixed martial arts, you know, like Bruce Lee? They make wonderful bodyguards; yes I adore my little Lucci

Botts!" Adrianna Jasmine was stunned: how did Emmalina manage to hire such a trio of delights? Witchcraft?

"Oh, it's so very exciting," gushed Emmalina, "my gosh look ata all this!" Emmalina was referring to the cauldron and black plates, hired from Sparkling China, decorative spiders, wafting ghosts and whatever else the trio had lugged in from Adrianna Jasmine's van. "It's going to be a magnificent party, my child and friends will lova it, but now iffa you will excuse me, I have some things I need to do, so you carry on and if you need anything Bobo, Yoyo and Coco will be more than happy to elp!" With that, she turned on her heel, swishing her long hair like black fire, before disappearing into a cloud of expensive perfume. Adrianna Jasmine shook her head in disbelief, what an extraordinary woman Emmalina was.

Thirty minutes later, Emmalina's dining room was transformed from her stylish medieval décor to Count Dracula's grandiose lair! With all due respect to the witch's decorative skills, it looked amazing. The black tablecloths hung dramatically over the banquet table, sprinkled with diamantes, silver stars and moons. Dark, blood-red roses from Covent Garden market were placed decoratively into stylish vases, tall and erect, and spiders and ghosts hung from the ceiling with spooky effects. The cauldron sat proudly as a centre- piece on the banquet table, later to be filled with Sangria. Mini pumpkins that had been personally carved out by the witch were peppered about, ready to be lit up with tea lights.

As a special touch, Adrianna Jasmine had ordered purple napkins with spells written on them: simple healing spells, protection spells, banishment of nightmares and safe travelling. They were harmless but, of course, very real and if performed with lightness in the heart, the spell would actually work!

"Not bad," commented Adrianna Jasmine to herself as she stood back to admire her work, "not bad at all." She then retired to the kitchen and began to make a start on her scrumptious, homemade mini pizzas. She kneaded out the dough, expertly twirled it about on her fist, before throwing the elasticised mass into the air like a pro. She loved doing this, as not many people could! After the pizzas were beautifully made and ready for the oven, Adrianna Jasmine set about placing numerous post-it notes on food containers and the table in the dining room, with instructions for Bobo, Yoyo and Coco. She then called in the trio, so she could go through every detail with them; she wanted the night to be perfect for Emmalina.

The trio concentrated as Adrianna Jasmine explained the process of the evening: where items were to be placed, how to wiz up the milkshakes and how long the pies needed to be cooked. She was reasonably satisfied that the information was processed correctly by the trio, but just to make triple sure she went over to her first aid box. She took out an incense stick that smelt of cinnamon, the most unsuspicious smell for a kitchen, and a candle. She put some water into a cup for cleansing, some salt into a dish to represent earth, a cupcake onto a plate to represent an offering to the Goddess and a bit of her soup into a separate bowl (to represent ale, well the soup had cider in it!), and she was ready to begin her spell.

"Encouraged by the air," she then lit the candle, *"brightened by flame. With water I cleanse,"* she speckled water about her. *"Reinforced with earth,"* she sprinkled salt about and finally held her hands over the centre of her offerings and whispered, *"Spirits of the North may you bless Bobo, Yoyo and Coco with the powers of earth. Help them perform their best and not their worst! Spirits of the South, powers of fire, may you bless Bobo, Yoyo and Coco with courage and passion. Help them serve up this feast in a perfect fashion. Spirits of the East, powers of air, bless Bobo, Yoyo and coco with clarity and vision in the hope that this evening is run with precision. Spirits of the West, powers of water, bless Bobo, Yoyo and Coco with love and dreams, in the hope that this feast is more than it seems. Blessed be!*

Unfortunately, due to the nature of the spell, she was not able to blow out the candle as it would snuff out the spell, so she had to patiently wait until the candle extinguished itself naturally. Luckily it was only the size of a birthday cake candle so Adrianna Jasmine didn't have too long to wait. Ten minutes later the candle had died and she set to making her departure and running through every final detail in her head. *Had she missed anything out*?

The food was spiked with the *correct* sprinkles, harmony and merry, the table was looking fabulous, post-its out and, of course,

Bobo, Yoyo and Coco were covered. Adrianna Jasmine decided that her work here was done, so she picked up her car keys and not forgetting her precious magazine, made her way up to the hall once more and called out to Emmalina.

"I'm in here, Bella Bambina, in the living room."

Adrianna Jasmine followed Emmalina's voice and found the glamorous goddess seated at her black grand piano, bathed in a magical blue light that was projected from a translucent blue window directly above her head. She was already wearing her Halloween costume. Well Adrianna Jasmine hoped she was wearing a costume - she was trussed out in a rather raunchy all-in-one leopard print catsuit that appeared to have been killed and skinned with her own bare hands.

"Oh my!" complimented Adrianna Jasmine, as she stepped into large airy room strewn with comfortable velvet sofas and overstuffed chairs, "you look sensational!"

"Oh, you lika my costume?" asked Emmalina as she stood up from the piano feeling the curves of her bottom with a slinky hand.

Adrianna Jasmine nodded. "I think you look amazing," she said whilst discreetly glancing around the room at the sumptuous cushions, candelabra and grand, yet stylish, chandeliers, "and may I just say, it's been an absolute pleasure meeting you."

"Oh, thank you, Bella," said Emmalina placing her right hand onto her heart, "you're too sweet, and thank you for all your hard work and 'ere izza your cheque."

Emmalina handed the witch a crisp white cheque made out for £500 and a piece of card about the size of an A4 sheet of paper.

"What's this?" asked Adrianna Jasmine.

"Oh, it's just a little something I whipped up," explained Emmalina matter-of-factly. "When I see something beautiful, I simply have to paint it. That way it's kept forever and never dies."

Adrianna Jasmine turned the sheet over and gasped, for the thing of beauty was Adrianna Jasmine herself. "I don't believe it!" gasped the witch, "it's me!" It was a signed portrait of Adrianna Jasmine. Emmalina had somehow, in a matter of minutes, painted her face using swirls of rich colours and textures that captured the mystery of Adrianna Jasmine's multi-coloured eyes and her very essence to perfection. It was signed, *'To my little Adrianna Jasmine from your friend Emmalina Lucci.'* "I don't know what to say," said Adrianna Jasmine, she felt close to tears of joy, "thank you so much, I'll treasure it always."

Emmalina reached over to hug the witch, thanked her for all her hard work and bid her a fond farewell.

Outside in her van Adrianna Jasmine felt as if she'd been in a dream. *Wow, what an afternoon!* she thought proudly, *who would have expected that! What an honour!*

Still beaming a smile, she turned on her ignition and made her way out through the long drive, past the gates, onto the roads of London and towards the witching hour. *What a difference a day makes*, she contemplated.

> *'Do you know, that if you're thinking about someone, really, really thinking about someone, take comfort in thought that they are thinking about you at that exact same time!'*
> (Kristobella Poppleapple-Mariposa, 2008)

Chapter 20
Thinking of you, thinking of me!

Adrianna Jasmine snuggled down into her seat. She was on the three thirty train to New Milton and was feeling relaxed, warm and comfortable. The witch had driven back to her home, parked her van, picked up her overnight case and popped Jupiter 10 into his carry cage. (Of course Jupiter 10 was coming with her, who else would sit on the back of her broomstick on Halloween night?) Her broom had already been sent on before her. Last night when Adrianna Jasmine let out her cat, she also released Whiz into the night sky. You see Whiz was a very intelligent broom and could fly himself anywhere in the world unaccompanied. He was the equivalent to a highly trained homing pigeon, or satellite navigation system. He had been instructed to fly without stopping until he reached the Burley Manor, then to hide himself somewhere in the hotel grounds. He would then, at an appropriate time, fly up to Adrianna Jasmine's window and tap gently on the glass in order for her to let him in. Whiz already knew her room number. (Just in case you're wondering)

Adrianna Jasmine was enjoying a grande hot chocolate that she had bought from one of the convenient take-away coffee shops at Waterloo, and treated herself to a couple of yummy donuts. As the train sped off into the already looming twilight, Adrianna Jasmine gently traced her finger around the picture of Taylor Jameson. She caught herself smiling, and then shook her head vigorously to shake out the girlish crush from her brain. With a fluttering heart, she opened the magazine so she could read the article about him. She read every word, every comment he spoke and devoured each sentence with such heartiness, she honestly believed she would never feel hungry again.

"Is it wrong" she whispered to herself, "to feel these powerful emotions for a man I have only just met? I'm a witch and love, especially with a non-Wiccan, doesn't always end happily." She sighed. "What's going on with you, Adrianna Jasmine, what's going on?"

She peered out of the window at the rushing trees and brightening moon. Her heart filled with excitement. *Halloween*, she thought passionately, *my time, my night, my magical night.* How she longed to jump onto Whiz that very second and take flight above the trees; to be in her all-in-one leather flying suit, lined with fleece to keep her warm, and accompanied with a fitted hood to protect her ears from the biting wind. "Soon," she soothed herself, "soon."

Meanwhile, over in Canary Wharf, Taylor Jameson was at his desk still writing his review for Lexi Howler's new restaurant. It was even more problematic now that Taylor's thoughts were infested with Adrianna Jasmine. It was all he could think about: the beautiful, dark haired, mysterious, lovely creature with the captivatingly, charismatic multi-coloured eyes. He had been totally bewitched and his work was suffering as a result of his infatuation. Usually his sentences flowed like silk and witty quips skipped about on his page with more punch than Ricky Hatton. But not today. Today, Taylor's thoughts were overshadowed by thoughts of Adrianna Jasmine. He longed for a photograph of her, something to ease his craving, to ease the ebb, so to speak, and then he had a thought. *Of course, the World Wide Web*! He clicked hurriedly onto Google and typed in: "Magic of Food." After scrolling through a load of useless sites about antioxidants and their magical properties, Taylor finally found her.

He breathed deeply, his heart thumping wildly in his chest as the anticipation stirred within him. The home page was on a purple background with twinkling stars. Frank Sinatra sang out "Witchcraft" in his smooth, distinctive voice. There was a witch's hat on the left-hand top corner of the page and a cauldron that was bubbling merrily on the bottom left. A quick welcome was smack in the middle, along with a brief description about the company and links across the top.

"Quirky," thought Taylor, impressed, and clicked on her profile. A few moments later, a head and shoulders picture of

Adrianna Jasmine appeared with a brief description about her business. At once Taylor beamed a smile when he saw her lovely face appear. She looked beautiful, really happy and full of life. She seemed to be staring deep into his eyes, and appeared to know exactly what he was thinking. "Ridiculous," he snorted, "it's just a photo." But then he looked closer, "those eyes," he whispered, "those magical eyes. What have they done to me?!"

He continued to read her profile, research for the interview! Then he clicked onto all of her links: menu suggestions, contact and policies. After he had devoured all the information over and over again, he clicked back to her picture in order to stare, once more, at her lovely face. He reached out and traced his fingers around her photo, wishing desperately that he was touching her for real, not a computer screen. Little did he know that Adrianna Jasmine was delicately stroking a picture of Taylor Jameson at the exact same time and wishing the exact same thing!

"Adrianna Jasmine...sweetheart!" Kristobella opened out her arms and threw them around her niece, "how are you, my gorgeous girl? And Jupiter 10!" She exclaimed with delight, "Oh, how lovely."

Adrianna Jasmine hugged her aunt back and breathed in the scent of Kritobella's Tallulah Toffees signature Elegant Grace Perfume. She was wearing a tailored wool priest's coat, with a mandarin styled collar and a corseted style cinch at the rear. She finished off the look by sweeping her blonde hair loosely under a cool black trilby hat.

"Great," replied Adrianna Jasmine, "all the better for seeing you, though!"

"Ah, that's nice, sweetheart. Come on, tell me everything you've been up to in the last month, it's just you and me for the next twenty minutes and we need to catch up!"

Kristobella had picked Adrianna Jasmine up in her top-of-the-range, very high and very luxurious white Range Rover.

"Hey, this is nice," remarked Adrianna Jasmine approvingly as she hoisted herself up onto the passenger seat, "mum said you'd bought one."

"Well," replied her aunt, "business has been good to me, my darling, people simply love my shop! Even this ghastly credit crunch hasn't, touch wood, damaged my business, if anything it's enhanced it. People do like to treat themselves when they're feeling blue and for some reason my clothes seem to have this *magical* ability to literally lift one's dampened mood." She winked at Adrianna Jasmine, who smiled back at her aunt knowingly. "Young girls and women alike are still going out buying designer clothes and expensive makeup, having facials and waxing their upper lip. Goddess knows how they can afford to do it, they probably live on baked beans or something! Still, touch wood, my shop is flooded everyday with women and men purchasing beautiful pieces of Dior, Chanel, Gucci shoes, Lu Lu Guinness handbags and other knick knacks that I've purchased from glamorous fashion shows! So, I decided to treat myself with a new car!"

Adrianna Jasmine was smiling at her aunt; she was so effortlessly chic, and a very shrewd business woman, at that. She looked similar to Sicily, but Kristobella for some reason was blonde, slightly taller and not so over the top as her sister. She definitely possessed a wicked sense of humour like Sicily, but somehow was more discreet about it. Sicily was a little too over opinionated at times and therefore lacked discretion.

"Anyway, my angel, tell me all about you, mummy tells me you've been highly successful lately?"

Adrianna Jasmine shrugged humbly, "I've been doing OK. I've been working very hard and I guess it's been paying off... I'm going to be in a magazine in December!"

Kristobella smiled brightly, filled with excitement at the prospect of her niece in a magazine. "You are? That's wonderful, poppet. Tell me all about it!"

Adrianna Jasmine snuggled into the seat and told her aunt all about her exploits over the past couple of days, the contract with Pigwell, the nervous tummy, the menu, Chrystal Rose, the crème brûlée, even sending an entire party to sleep, and the reason! At the mention of Taylor Jameson, Kritobella's intrigue increased.

"Ah, so that's what that glow about you is. I knew there was something different from the moment I met you off that train!"

Adrianna Jasmine screwed up her nose, shook her head and giggled.

"That's not true, Aunty Kristobella. I'm still the same witch; I'm just excited that I'm going to be in a magazine, that's all. You know, it's new and different, plus who knows where it could take me in my career!" Then Adrianna Jasmine paused thoughtfully, her voice became a little subdued. "I'm just a bit askew at the moment."

Kristobella was confused, "Askew? What do mean, askew?"

Adrianna Jasmine sighed, "Well, um... even though work is going well, my magic...," she trailed off due to feeling tired of it all.

"Go on," her aunt coaxed gently, "It's been...well a bit off and it's frustrating and...well, I'm just not used to my magic spiralling out of control. I don't like it!"

"Oh, I see," said Kristobella raising her left eyebrow, "hmmm," she pondered, "looks like this Taylor chap is a bit more under your skin than you would like to admit, my darling."

Adrianna Jasmine shook her head, although without much conviction, "No he's not..." she tried weakly before turning to peer out of the window. It was pitch black now, but somehow she knew she was out of London. The air was fresh and clean and the world seemed quiet. The shadows from the passing trees excited her. They were dark and mysterious, perfect for hiding secrets and shielding magic from the outside world. This was her territory, the forest.

"Adrianna Jasmine," Kristobella gently shook her niece from her thoughts, "it's nothing to be ashamed or frightened of, for that matter."

"Huh?" said Adrianna Jasmine; she was a million miles away. "What's not to be ashamed of?"

"Succumbing to your feelings about this young man." Adrianna Jasmine tried to find the words to revoke her aunt's comments, but no words would come out. "It's OK, my darling," Kristobella soothed, "love is not the be all and end all of one's magic, I can promise you that, you've just got to realise that the love flood-gate has been opened for you and its water is now gushing through uncontrollably. But I promise you, once the water has settled, *you* will settle and your magic as a result will settle. However, until then it's all rapids and waterfalls, I'm afraid!"

Adrianna Jasmine heaved a dramatic sigh, "so I'm stuck with it, then, that's it. I'm screwed, I might as well not perform any magic until my feelings for him wear off!" Then a hot fear rose through her body, *Goddess*, she thought, *I hope I didn't fry Bobo, Yoyo and Coco's brains any more than they already are tonight with that bloody spell I cast, I felt so confident earlier, now I feel all paranoid.*

Kristobella tinkled a laugh, "Of course you can perform magic."

Adrianna Jasmine shook her head firmly.

"No, I can't. It keeps going wrong and it keeps going wrong because I'm distracted. Even when I'm not thinking about him, I'm distracted! I'm even a bit worried about a couple of minor spells I did earlier on today, I wish I hadn't bloody done them now, oh, I feel all unsettled."

Kristobella looked kindly towards her niece, "Well, I think it's rather beautiful, Adrianna Jasmine."

"Beautiful!" cried the young witch with utter revolution, "I sent nearly two hundred people to sleep and drugged almost the entire coffee shop in the last few days, all down to this… love thing. It's ghastly, whatever is happening to me is not beautiful, it's a goddess damn curse!"

Kristobella smiled and shook her head. "Love, my sweet, is not a curse, but a beautiful gift. Once you've embraced the power of love and truly succumbed to its wonder, all your negative feelings towards love will seem utterly ridiculous and you will never feel so happy. In fact you will never understand how you survived without it!"

Adrianna Jasmine was silent for a moment, she wasn't wholly convinced. "But can I still perform magic, though?"

Kristobella smiled once more, "Adrianna Jasmine you could perform magic on the moon if you wanted to because, like love, your magic will always find a way.'"

Over at the coffee shop, Sarah had been working flat out all day. Not only had there been a huge rush from the moment the front door was opened, what with customers demanding pumpkin cookies, blood lust cupcakes and frothy coffees, but as soon as school was out, the kids turned up in droves, all dressed up for Halloween. White wispy ghosts, adorable witches and ghoulish vampires excitedly hurried about the coffee shop, racing from one activity to another. If they weren't apple bobbing, the children were playing the chocolate game, and spookily-themed pass the parcel. However, it was the story corner which proved to be the most popular attraction. The Mystic Odessa had been reassigned to children's story hour, where she sat like a medieval queen, perched on a wooden chair, reciting spooky tales about ghosts and witches. The children were extremely well-behaved and they sat and listened intently to the fascinatingly strange woman with the entrancing eyes and exotic accent. It was almost as if they'd been hypnotised.

Sarah whizzed about offering Adrianna Jasmine's witch-shaped cookies and Devil's crunch, accompanied with creamy glasses of milk to the grateful children, they really were very well-behaved, Sarah smiled knowingly to herself. *Good old Adrianna Jasmine*, she thought fondly. However, at the thought of her friend, she couldn't help but feel a pang of sadness. She imagined the girls all travelling down to Burley together, laughing, joking, performing magic tricks.

I should be there, she thought sadly, *instead of being surrounded by mini people dressed up in ASDA skeleton costumes and Tesco witches outfits*! Sarah sighed and glanced over at the clock, it was four o'clock. Goddess, she was shattered. *Oh well, only another three hours to go, then home and a bowl of pumpkin soup, telly and bed. Happy Halloween*!

Green Slime and Worms

Buy two packets of green jelly and make according to instructions. Once set, put the jelly into a bowl and mush it all up. Add some jelly worms or creepy crawly sweets and stir into the jelly mix; it looks gross but it's wickedly tasty!
(Adrianna Jasmine, 2008)

Chapter 21
Halloween Night

The white Range Rover pulled into the village of Burley and the two women immediately felt a mixture excitement and nostalgia. All the quaint little restaurants and pub were warmly lit up with jack-o'-lanterns and candles, their flames dancing in the dark like wild spirits. Tourists and locals wondered about the village dressed in Halloween costume, popping in and out of the souvenir shops and simply losing themselves in the atmosphere and occasion.

"What better place to spend Halloween," commented Adrianna Jasmine, "even for non-witches. I bet they feel it, you know."

"Feel what?" enquired Kristobella with an interested smile.

"The magic," whispered Adrianna Jasmine, "even non-energy sensitive mere mortals could feel the crackles of power and wonder that Halloween creates in a place like this, they truly are experiencing Halloween here."

The Range Rover continued through the village, turned right and went over a cattle-grid, creating a vibration that went right through you. Moments later they were on the hotel grounds and pulling up to the hotel. It was pitch black and the thought of the surrounding forest sent shudders of excitement through Adrianna Jasmine's spine. The forest could be a scary place as who knew what terror may lie amongst the tree trunks, earth and toadstools.

Moments later, the two witches were clambering out of the car and carrying their overnight bags to reception. Jupiter 10, who had been a dream traveller, was escorted through in his little cat carrier, snoozing lazily with his little paws poking out through the cage.

The pair walked in through the main entrance and were greeted excitedly by the rest of the cackle. Clementine Poppleapple threw her arms around Adrianna Jasmine and merrily announced they were to be "roomies." She had grown her pixie poppet hair style into a white blonde bob; she looked like a model from a shampoo advert. Sicily, who was impatiently waiting behind Clementine, kissed her daughter on both cheeks with a theatrical and over-the-top, "Hello, darling!" Her black bob was shiny and sharp, like Catherine Zeta Jones's in Chicago.

Bella Bell hugged her excitedly around the neck; her grey hair tied back in a French pleat, and informed Adrianna Jasmine that she was looking as beautiful as ever. Then, at last, the moment Adrianna Jasmine had been waiting for, since what had appeared to have been an age, the hug from Carolina Plum.

"Hello, my beautiful girl," greeted Carolina like a regal Goddess and took Adrianna Jasmine into her arms. The young witch closed her eyes and breathed in the scent of Carolina's exquisite perfume and immediately began to feel the healing effects from the magical embrace. When Carolina gently let go of Adrianna Jasmine and looked deep into her eyes, she could instantly tell that the young witch had successfully reaped the magical rewards from her hug. For Adrianna Jasmine had adopted that gaze one receives during time spent on a relaxing holiday to the Maldives.

A few moments after her magical hug, Adrianna Jasmine was able to compose herself once more and checked herself in. As she signed her name with her signatory signature and received a key for her bedroom, the witch began to take stock. She soon noticed that her cackle was not the only cackle of witches on the premises. You see, a witch can always tell a witch from the crowd. Perhaps it's their scent, or their aura. Either way, there's no escaping it: a witch simply knows her own kind. A witch can even tell if a witch is white or black magic orientated, if it's the latter a white witch would probably steer well clear of the black witch, in order to escape possible locked horns.

Luckily Adrianna Jasmine didn't seem to sense any dark magic on the premises, not that a black witch would stand a chance against Adrianna Jasmine's magically formidable crew. There was more power amongst these six women than the whole of Las Vegas times two! However, if there were more than one black witch, let's just say would be an interesting meet.

"Come, darlings, let's get you two settled in," announced Sicily, "why don't you have a nice shower, Adrianna Jasmine and get into your evening wear. Dinner is a seven thirty, so you've got an hour to wash and brush up. Ooh, and I love your boots, darling. Are they Gucci?"

Adrianna Jasmine shook her head. "Like I could afford Gucci, mother. Stop acting as if you're Kathy Hilton, they're Karen Millen, actually."

"I might have guessed," said Sicily. "I love the way they go over the knee, darling, very sexy, very pretty woman!" Adrianna Jasmine wasn't sure if her mother was complimenting her on how nice she looked, or if she'd just been compared to a prostitute. Either way she decided to keep her mouth shut, she was still feeling good from her hug, no need to spoil it. The cackle were all on the same floor, with Kristobella and Sicily sharing, Carolina and Bella in together and, of course, Adrianna Jasmine and Clementine sharing their room.

"What fun, darlings," said Sicily excitedly, "I'll knock you all up in one hour, TTFN!"

As the door shut fast, Clementine immediately began to chatter enthusiastically to Adrianna Jasmine, explaining all about the magic shenanigans that she had been up to since the two had last met. From the sound of things, Clementine was steadily becoming a gifted witch, although Adrianna Jasmine couldn't help but feel a little concerned that Clementine was dangerously crossing the line between white and dark magic. Clementine had excitedly described how she made a dead wasp come back to life after finding it dead on a windowsill in her flat. Clementine described to her cousin how she actually brought the wasp back to life with a spell she had found in an old trunk of her father's.

"It was very interesting: when I brought the wasp back, it was no longer yellow in colour, more like a tarnished grey and resembled a wasp version of Dawn of the Dead. It moved and buzzed just like a regular wasp, but looked very creepy." She then explained that in order to send it back to the underworld once more, the creature had to be beheaded.

Adrianna Jasmine, who was not impressed at all, gulped. "Be careful, Clementine," she urged, "we don't interfere with death, it's not what we do and you know that!" Clementine rolled her eyes.

"Come on, it was only a wasp, nothing major!"

"Yes, well," Adrianna Jasmine cautioned, "a wasp today, a cat tomorrow, then a sheep, a horse, then a human. Once something has crossed over, Clementine, it can never come back, you know that!"

"Yeah, yeah," jeered Clementine, "I'd never go that far, I just wanted to see if I could do it, that's all. It's a pretty big thing, you know. I thought you'd be impressed!" Adrianna Jasmine played it carefully.

"I know it is," she tried to sound supportive, "it's a very big skill indeed to bring back something that has crossed over to the Summer Lands, but you must never resort to the black craft, sweetie. No matter how tempting it is, especially dabbling in resurrection." Adrianna Jasmine couldn't help shudder as she said the word "resurrection" and decided to change the subject. "So what else have you done, then?"

"I gave someone the measles the other day," answered Clementine happily, Adrianna Jasmine closed her eyes in despair; "I just pointed my finger at her and said 'you deserve the measles!' And guess what: she went down with it three hours later!"

"Shame on you," said Adrianna Jasmine disapprovingly; screw the diplomacy, "you're telling me you actually gave an innocent the measles?" Clementine nodded proudly. "Don't tell me;" said Adrianna Jasmine through a deep sigh, "she gave you a funny look at university!"

Clementine gave her cousin a look mixed with shock and admiration. "Yeah, how'd you guess that!"

Adrianna Jasmine just shook her head and shrugged her shoulders.

"I don't know, but don't be surprised if you wake up sometime soon with an inflamed abscess under your wisdom tooth."

Clementine looked stunned, then she realised what Adrianna Jasmine was driving at.

"Ah, I seeeee. You think that the threefold law will come back to bite me on the butt?" she said folding her arms.

"That's exactly what I mean," stated Adrianna Jasmine firmly, "you'd better be careful, girl. It's all very well experimenting, but be respectful!"

"Come on!" challenged Clementine. "Like you've never brought anything back from the dead!"

Adrianna Jasmine couldn't deny it.

"You know full well you brought a dead butterfly back to life when you were about twelve?"

"Yes I did," confirmed Adrianna Jasmine calmly, "but I was so disgusted by the gruesome outcome, you will recall, that I vowed never to go there again. Besides, two days later my pet Clown fish Angel croaked it. You see: threefold law. Be careful, little witch, you're messing with powers that are not in your league."

"Yet!" boasted Clementine, then she saw Adrianna Jasmine's face turn to thunder and backed down immediately. "OK, OK, I'm joking. Come on, let's get changed for dinner."

Hmmm, thought Adrianna Jasmine suspiciously, *I don't believe your cute little face for one minute.*

After the girls had showered, they changed into their evening wear. Clementine went for the demonic ballerina look and put on a short cherry red, netted tutu, accompanied with a red and black tartan vest top. Victorian fetish-style, vertical stripe stockings with lace tops, punk scene laced tartan boots that were stacked on a mind blowing 9cm platform sole. She wore black lace gloves, smoky black eye shadow over her eye lids and bright red lippy. Strangely enough, she looked extremely sexy but totally unapproachable. Adrianna Jasmine opted for a similar, although more demure, look of a black stretch velvet bodice with a low rounded waistline, attached to a long dark red ballerina style net skirt. The skirt was slashed on the right hand side, so that when she walked, her beautiful leg was visible for all to ogle. She wore fine, black mesh honeycomb patterned tights, high-heeled, black leather, Neo Edwardian boots and a dark red lace gloves on her hands. She wore her hair down, long and wavy and painted her eyes similar to that of Clementine's, all dark and dramatic, she teamed this with dark redlip stick. Whiz, who had successfully found his way and made his presence known by tapping on the window, had arrived just in time to be part of Adrianna Jasmine's completed look!

The girls admired one another's party frocks and came to the conclusion that their outfits were pretty darn fantastic.

"Shame we're here with all the old cronies and not in some cool bar in London right now," sulked Clementine, who seemed to think that their sexiness was wasted in a hotel in the middle of the New Forest. "Think of the men who would be dropping at our feet right now: footballers, millionaires, professional comedians. I mean, look at us, we look drop dead gorgeous!"

Adrianna Jasmine couldn't help but laugh, they did look stunning, even if they were dressed rather whacky.

"Come on, you," she said playfully to Clementine, "there'll be other chances, let's go and meet the others."

The girls made their way downstairs to the bar to a sea of startled looks from other guests. Not because they looked strange or weird but because they simply looked so beautiful. What with Clementine looking all blonde, sexy and fun next to the dark, mysterious Adrianna Jasmine with her ravishing right leg!

"Oh, look at you two, darlings," cried out Sicily, who was sitting on a stool at the bar buying a large jug of Halloween Sangria for the cackle. "You two look wonderful. Why, Clementine you look like a mad fairy and Adrianna Jasmine, you look like you're the lead singer in a vampire rock band. Shame you can't sing. Oh, it's too delicious. Here, have a glass of Halloween Sangria!"

The witches accepted their beverages and returned the flattering compliments back to Sicily who was wearing a black and cream, pin striped, tailored Victorian-style jacket, coupled with an extravagant long black bustle skirt and black top hat!

"Thank you, darlings," she said as if she were accepting an Oscar, "you're too kind."

With that, Bella Bell, Carolina Plumb and Kristobella joined the cackle. They all squealed with excitement when they caught sight of one another.

"Ooh, look at you two," said Kristobella as she caught sight of Clementine and Adrianna Jasmine. "Oh, to be young!"

"You don't look so bad yourself," commented Clementine, "love that dress!"

Kristobella was wearing a beautiful dark grey Victorian-style satin bustier and train skirt with an embroidered black lace overlay, with sequins and jet black beading, she looked wonderful.

Adrianna Jasmine handed Carolina Plumb a glass of Halloween Sangria.

"Thank you, my precious," she said as she accepted her drink; she, too, looked a picture of Halloween, devilish delight. She was wearing a beautiful, deep purple, satin corset, with black lace trim, that somehow kept her enormous bust from spilling out all over the table. She teamed her outfit with a dramatic yet romantic, black, full, wispy, chiffon skirt, adorned with pretty, gothic, black roses and ribbons stitched onto the girly festoon hem. She wore a theatrical purple velvet choker and black, short, fingerless leather gloves on her perfectly manicured hands. To Adrianna Jasmine, Carolina Plumb looked how every witch should look: sumptuous, sexy, powerful, yet warm and loving, all rolled into one. She then turned her attention to the sweet and almost shy, Bella Bell, who was smiling happily at the cackle.

"Wow, you look great, Bella," complimented Adrianna Jasmine enthusiastically. She always liked to encourage Bella Bell, as Bella was a very giving witch and never really spent much time on herself. She let her grey hair get the better of her, wore glasses, no makeup and dismissed Tallulah Toffee products! Bella, who was dressed in a rather nice, crushed dark green velvet Morticia Adams style dress, teamed with a matching velvet witches hat, black stockings and black leather hob-nailed boots, blushed and dismissed the comment with an embarrassed wave of the hand.

"Oh, you're too kind, Adrianna Jasmine," she said through nervous giggles, "but may I just say how beautiful my Adrianna Jasmine looks tonight, and how brilliant and sexy Clementine looks!" The girls laughed.

"What, in this old thing?" said Clementine playfully, even Clementine's acid tongue sweetened at times when it came to Bella, she was so nice. The witches finished their Halloween Sangria, then realised it was just after seven thirty and so it was time for their Halloween meal.

"Come, darlings," announced Sicily with aplomb, "let us feast!" She sounded as if she were leading the witches to a royal banquet.

The witches all stood up laughing and chatting, Bella Bell felt a little tipsy already and Carolina Plum had a distinctive pinkness to her cheek.

"Goddess," said Adrianna Jasmine rolling her eyes, "they're tipsy already!"

The witches were escorted to their table by a young waiter called Thomas, who couldn't help but stare in amazement at the cackle as they walked confidently to their reserved place. He wasn't used to escorting such a quirky and attractive group of women to their table, and was in a fluster by the time the witches sat down. It must have been difficult for the poor chap to keep a straight face, what with Carolina's bursting-out boobs; Sicily's striped get up and over-the-top hat; Kristobella's sexy blonde locks; Bella's *unusual* style; Clementine's tutu and Adrianna Jasmine's leg! Still, he managed to politely ask once the ladies were seated, "What can I get you to drink?" before turning around, clumsily crashing into a fellow waiter and falling into a heap on the floor. Carolina Plum leapt up to assist the hapless chap back onto his feet.

"Oh, thank you," he mumbled, dazed and confused, as he was being helped up, "how clumsy of me." At first he seemed to be nothing short of embarrassed - well, the whole restaurant was staring at him – but after a few moments of simply holding onto Carolina's hands, he immediately began to feel better. He even managed a smile.

"OK now?" asked Carolina smiling beautifully, "you had quite a fall there."

Thomas smiled and nodded. "Thanks," he said shyly, "let me get you your drink." A few moments later, Thomas returned with new-found confidence and a jug of Halloween Sangria before faultlessly taking their order. The witches smiled knowingly at one another, Carolina Plum had come to the rescue again!

All witches opted for pumpkin soup for starter, roast beef and Yorkshire pudding, except Clementine who had taken it upon herself to become a vegetarian, even though she frequently decapitated wasps, and chose vegetable cannelloni, followed by the velvet chocolate torte.

As the witches waited for their food, they took it upon themselves to glance discreetly about the room. The restaurant was filled with real witches and faux witches; all dressed in the spirit of Halloween, there definitely was some power in the hotel tonight. No one seemed to be of the black magic variety and the atmosphere was cheerful and highly spirited. They didn't recognise anyone that they knew, for sometimes they would bump into a witch or two from another coven, but not this evening. However, glancing around the room once more, Sicily just so happened to come across a witch who appeared to be highly familiar, but from where, she wasn't quite sure. She was a witch, approximately her age, dressed in a black Victoriana dress with a high lacy black collar, sitting with about nine companions. She couldn't quite put her finger on it, but she felt as if she knew her from somewhere and immediately got the distinct impression that she didn't like her.

"Maybe I went to school with her?" Sicily suggested to herself and knitted her eyebrows together as she tried to think who she was. It was irritating her immensely. *Perhaps Bella might know*, she considered and discreetly kicked Bella in the shin to grab her attention. "Hey, Bella. Do you know who that witch is, the one on the large table with the high necklace collar? She looks strikingly familiar, darling. Any guesses as to who she may be?"

Thanks to the Sangria, Bella, who was now seeing quadruple, drunkenly turned towards the witch in question. Her eyes squinted together as she struggled to focus.

"I've never seen any of those witches before in my life!" she slurred, before deciding that it would probably be a good idea to drink some water before she keeled over. *Goddess, I've only drunk two glasses*! she thought in horror.

"Great use you are!" snorted Sicily, "I'll figure it out myself." She could detect no black magic oozing from the witch and her aura, for some reason, was undetectable. *Odd*, she thought, *everyone possesses an aura*. Sicily then shut out the clanging and chattering noises from around the dining room, in order to surrender to a deep state of concentration. She wanted to know why this woman made her feel so uncomfortable. The noise in the dining room became absolutely silent and the guests and staff slowly began to fade from sight. Moments later, two soft spotlights appeared from out of nowhere and shone upon Sicily and the strange witch, as if they were acting on a stage. The strange witch's dark eyes flashed towards Sicily's, sending icy chills down her spine; she began to feel wintry and disillusioned. Nonetheless, Sicily stuck fast to her remembrance spell for three minutes, before finally concluding that she had never met the stranger before in her life. But her face, oh, her face... it reminded her of someone, someone not very pleasant. It was uncanny; the menacing icy chill returned once more, this time with a vengeance.

"Surely," she breathed in disbelief, "surely it can't be Gunnora Pan."

The arrival of the soup and Clementine shamelessly flirting with Thomas, soon shook Sicily out of her trance. "Ah, splendid!" she announced. "The soup's here!"

The witches slurped through their soup, devoured their beef and glorified in their chocolate desserts.

"Mmmmm," declared Clementine after the meal, "that was like culinary intercourse."

"Darling, please," grimaced Sicily, "must you lower the tone? Couldn't you say something like, 'ooh, that was delicious, that was just like culinary *merry making* in my mouth'?"

Clementine scoffed and the others began to laugh. "Shut up," snapped Sicily to Kristobella, who was nearly snorting chocolate Torte out of her nose from laughing.

"Well, what a bloody stupid thing to say."

The others were crying with laughter. Sicily went to defend herself, but instead opted for a slurp of Sangria, they were on their third jug!

After the meal, the cackle decided to retire to the lounge area for coffee and mints, then hit the dance floor at the Halloween disco for a bit of a boogie woogie. The disco went on until midnight and the cackle had a great time doing the Time Warp, Monster Mash and re-enacting the moves from Thriller. Clementine took over the whole floor with her steamy moves, where she gyrated and squatted down, opening and closing her knees seductively and trying to look like a lap dancer. Bella Bell, who was pretty drunk by now, was in her own little world and became very energetic when Ghost Busters hit the decks. Carolina and Kristobella danced together and Sicily was trying to vogue. Adrianna Jasmine was thoroughly enjoying herself, laughing and dancing with her family and friends, looking beautiful and care free. In fact, she was enjoying herself so much, that she didn't even notice the pair of dark eyes watching her intently from the shadows.

At midnight, the Halloween disco came to an end and guests stumbled drunkenly back to their rooms. *At last*, thought the cackle, *let the Witching hour begin*
.

*

Adrianna Jasmine entered her mother's suite, now wearing her leather all- in-one flying outfit. She found the cackle chatting merrily amongst themselves. Clementine, however, was sat with her striped legs dangling over the arm of a chair, texting a friend. Sicily and Kristobella were sprawled out on the bed, giggling like naughty schoolgirls who were drunk on their mother's sherry, and Carolina Plum and Bella Bell were in the middle of creating some kind of spell that prevented sound escaping from their room. It was a highly useful trick as it helped to keep their magic a secret from the public, their husbands and unwelcome witching folk.

"Oh good, you're here, darling," sang a slightly tipsy Sicily, "now we can commence forthwith the exchanging of the offerings."

Excitement stirred amongst the witches; Clementine swivelled off her chair, threw her mobile onto the bed and plonked herself down on the carpet. Kristobella set about lighting the Jack o lanterns, which she had personally carved scary faces into, and Sicily dimmed the lights in order to set the mood and ambiance. Bella Bell and Carolina Plum wrapped up their spell, gathered up their gifts, then popped themselves down onto the carpet joining Clementine. Clementine lit four candles to represent the four corners with her trusty lighter, made from real silver, and inscribed with a Celtic knott. She turned on her iPod, which immediately began to play music similar to the sounds of spirits dancing freely in the afterlife.

Once the witches had gathered up their gifts, they all sat down in a circle, simply fizzing with anticipation.

"Right, who's going first?" enquired Sicily. "Who'll get the ball rolling? Carolina?"

Carolina shrugged and agreed to hand out her gifts first. She then reached into her goody bag and presented each and every one with her Halloween offering. The witches received a beautifully wrapped gift that was in the shape of a thick stick.

"Oh, Carolina!" giggled Sicily, "Since when did Ann Summers start investing in magic tools!"

"Mum!" snorted Adrianna Jasmine, disturbed by her mother's rude joke. "Really!"

Carolina giggled. "Open it up," she encouraged happily, "I promise you it's just as pleasurable!" The cackle broke off the silver ribbons and tore off the pale green tissue paper.

"Just as I suspected," announced Bella Bell triumphantly, "a candle."

"But not just *any* candle," said Carolina. "These are very special candles." The witches oohed and aahed, teasing Carolina.

"Ha ha," laughed Carolina, "very funny girls. Anyway, you will be shocked to know that these are *magic* candles." She continued on excitedly. "You must light your candle when you are absolutely sure you wish to light it, it must be lit on the night of a full moon in your own company and in a room that is totally silent and dark, or the spell won't work. Then clear your mind, sit quietly, stare deeply into the flame and think of a time in your life that you would simply adore to revisit. Perhaps, for example, a Christmas morning when you were five, your first kiss, or even a happy conversation with someone who has passed over to the Summerland's. Nonetheless, choose wisely because you only get one chance, once the candle has been lit it can never be re-lit. Now, here's the magic part." Carolina paused dramatically for effect. "When you think about your memory, you will relive it, as if you are really there! You feel it, taste it, and smell it. Oh, it's wonderful; you will really experience something very special. I did it once and I relived an afternoon with my mother. I was twelve and we were at home, just her and I, in the house and …" Carolina trailed off; she looked as if she were trying to hold back tears. "Oh, it's silly," she smiled bravely and fought off her emotions, but her fellow cackle could see that she had become upset. "It was wonderful," she whispered through a choked-up voice, wet eyes, yet smiling lips.

Kristobella, who was sitting next to her, reached out and squeezed Carolina's hand, "I know," she said. "I think I'd feel the same if I saw our mother again." Sicily nodded, their mother had been dead five years now, and they both missed her very much.

"Well," announced Clementine clapping her hands together sharply. "Thank you very much, Carolina for your fab gift. But let's keep this party pumping, time for mine now!" The women shook themselves out of their emotional plummet and thanks to Clementine's abrupt jolt, re-entered the world of Halloween fun! "OK," said Clementine excitedly and began handing out her gifts, singing at the top of her voice, murdering That Old Black Magic. Their presents were wrapped in black wrapping paper and tied with a blood red ribbon; very Clementine, they all thought. Although what could it possibly be? Last year they had all received a dried-out dead bat, which understandably hadn't gone down well.

"Oh, wow," announced Adrianna Jasmine, who was the first to unwrap the gift. "It's a CD! What's on it, though? The cover's blank!" Clementine rolled her eyes.

"Of course its blank," she said, a little irritated. "You have to put your favourite song on it!"

"Oh, right. Like, downloading a song from the computer?" Asked Adrianna Jasmine, a little confused.

"Sort of," said Clementine, "but it would be a bit tight if I'd just brought you all a blank disk from Tesco and said 'there you go have a riot!' Even I'm not that heartless! Anyway," she continued on with the speed of a bullet, "you put the CD into a CD player and think of a recording artist that you absolutely adore and basically they'll appear in front of you, dead or alive." The witches all gasped, shocked at Clementine's brilliant gift, it was most certainly an improvement from last year's offering. "And what's more," Clementine added, full of aplomb, "they will perform for you, your very own personal concert."

The witches' mouths hung open in shock; they couldn't quite believe Clementine had pulled this one off.

"You're kidding me, darling," said Sicily, totally flabbergasted. "You mean, I could actually meet Frank Sinatra, it truly could happen? Does he know he'll be in my living room next Friday night at 11pm sharp? How will he feel? Will he be like a hologram or human, what if he's totally freaked out, darling, what if he starts running about the house like a crazed loon?"

"I don't know!" exclaimed Clementine crossly. "I don't know the rules. All I know is that Amy Winehouse will be at *my* beck and call this Saturday. Come over if you want, it'll be a blast.'

"Oh, I do like her," Bella Bell chipped in, "her voice reminds me of old sixties soul divas, like Aretha and Dusty, although it's a shame her face looks as though it should be on a leaflet raising awareness for abused animals."

The witches totally agreed, thanked Clementine for her extraordinary gift, then shouted out "next!"

"Well, I think I'll go next!" piped up Bella Bell and handed out slim shaped boxes to everyone. "Although, I'm afraid it's not quite as thoughtful as Carolina's or as *wild* as Clementine's, but I do hope you all like it."

The witches all smiled and said that they were all sure that the gift would be wonderful and that it was the thought that counted. Moments later, they were tearing off the paper.

"Oh, it's a pen!" announced Clementine, her tone ever so slightly edging towards facetious.

"Well, yes," fumbled Bella, slightly ruffled by the rudeness in Clementine's voice. "But it's not just any old pen, my dear: it's rather special!" Bella continued, determined to explain the importance of her pen and quash Clementine's impolite opinions about her gift. "When you use this pen," she explained, "your handwriting will no longer be scratchy or spiky or messy or unreadable, but as beautiful as a top calligraphist. Your handwriting will be so exquisite, so amazing, that everyone will be asking you to write out their party invites. Adrianna Jasmine, you could use your pen to write your menus, or Kristobella, the labels for your shop, either way it'll most certainly come in handy for something!"

"Well, I think it's absolutely charming," declared Sicily smiling, "what an amazing idea!"

"Really?" said Bella Bell, surprised, yet happy, that her friends had appreciated her gift. "Oh, I'm so pleased you all like it."

"Yes, we do," Sicily enthusiastically confirmed, "and Clementine could use it so her university tutors could actually read her handwriting!" she added sarcastically. Clementine shot daggers at her eldest cousin. Oh, if looks could kill.

"OK, well I guess I'll go for it now," announced Kristobella, who was sensing rising hostility between her sister and Clementine and decided to quickly hand out her presents to appease the mood. Clementine and Adrianna Jasmine immediately became excited when they recognised the chic red and pink striped bags used at Kristobella's shop. Clementine practically snatched the bag from Kristobella, then apologised when she saw the outraged look in Kristobella's eyes.

"Sorry," she giggled nervously, "I'm just excited!" Kristobella raised her eye brow. *That girl is incorrigible,* she thought to herself as she continued handing out the bags. There were oohs and ahhhs, giggles and wows coming from the cackle when they reached into the bag and each dug out a pair of designer jeans.

Bella giggled, "Oh my Goddess," she said, "I haven't worn a pair of jeans since the late 70's. I'll never get into those!"

Kristobella shook her head and just smiled. "Oh yes you will," she said firmly, "all of you will. You see these jeans are rather special, even if they look too small or too big, they will fit you, even if they look too short or too long they will fit you. Even if you're a size eight today and a size fourteen tomorrow, they will fit you! They will always fit you and work with whatever shoes you want to wear, whatever top, whatever the occasion, trust me, these jeans will not let you down!" Excitement stirred amongst the cackle.

"Well, in that case," announced Bella Bell with a new found confidence. "I'll give them a whirl!" The cackle applauded her with a cheer and moments later she had removed herself from the circle and returned looking svelte and hip, modelling her new jeans.

"Wow!" was the reaction from the girls as Bella turned around like Twiggy in a fashion shoot. They were so impressed that very soon, all followed suit and changed into their new jeans, too.

"My goddess," marvelled Sicily when she saw her bottom in the mirror, sculpted like two firm nectarines in denim. "Not bad for 49!" Kristobella scoffed.

"What, your jean size or your age?" Sicily poked her tongue out cheekily at her sister, rubbed her bottom and smoothed down her tummy. Clementine was prancing about in front of everyone, looking like she should be a model for Guess or something. Carolina Plum had somehow morphed into a sexy Marilyn Monroe look-alike, and Adrianna Jasmine just looked downright perfect, as the jeans made her bottom and thighs look like a Latin Ballroom champion's. "Well, I guess you all love them, then?" said Kristobella giggling.

"Oh yes," replied the witches passionately, "thank you so much!"

"Good, well let's all settle down again then," Kristobella suggested, "we've still got Sicily's and Adrianna Jasmine's to open yet!"

The witches all tore themselves away from the mirrors and from admiring each other's new look, in order to plonk themselves back down in their circle. They were hyped up and full of anticipation as to what could possibly be next. The gifts seemed to get more and more charming.

"OK, darlings," said Sicily, "these ones are from me!" Sicily began to hand out exquisitely wrapped presents to the witches. "I have a feeling you're all going to enjoy this," she said with a wry smile. "I think you'll find it most entertaining." The witches were each handed an unwrapped DVD.

"What's this, all your greatest dance hits since 1963?" teased Kristobella. "Unfortunately it isn't," shot back Sicily unfazed by the mock, "but almost as entertaining as watching an hour and half of moi in feathers and high heels, tripping the light fantastic in gay Paris!" Kristobella just managed to stifle a laugh. "Anyway, this DVD is rather similar to Clementine's CD. However *you* have the chance to be the star, darling." The witches looked interested. "All you have to do is pop that DVD into a DVD player thingy, announce the title of your favourite film, followed by the name of the character you wouldn't mind playing..."

"What, like Mary Poppins?" broke in Bella Bell.

"Or Mrs Smith, opposite Brad," offered Clementine.

"Or Ginger Rogers dancing romantically with Fred Astaire in a film where life was pleasant and naturally magical," enthused Kristobella.

"Err... yes," said Sicily. "Anyway, after a few minutes you will find yourself in that actual *film*, it's like literally stepping into the television screen. However, you won't hear the director shout 'cut,' no-one will fluff their lines and there won't be any cameras or clapperboards. Then once the film is finished, you'll find yourself back in your living, filled with the most amazing memories from your unique experience. You can even record it, if you have one of those double-decker DVD recorder thingies." The witches were dumbfounded.

"Oh-my-Goddess," breathed Clementine, "this is amazing. I don't know what film to choose, though, there are so many I'd be perfect in!"

"Hmmm," said Sicily dryly, "anyway, be careful with what you choose, otherwise you could end up experiencing something nasty. I wouldn't recommend being one of the victims in Saw, or Kate Winslet in Titanic, brrr too cold! But of course, darlings, it's your film experience. Whatever floats your boat, I suppose."

The witches nodded thoughtfully. "Oh, I know my film," said Carolina excitedly. "I want to experience the life of Lorali Lee, played by Marilyn Monroe in Gentlemen Prefer Blondes. Just imagine all those wonderful numbers I could perform, the amazing costumes I'd get to wear, and to dance next to Jane Russell!'

"Yes, and you'd probably be a darn sight nicer to work next to, darling," added Sicily. "I heard Monroe was very difficult! Anyway," she said surly "*I* want to play Scarlet O' Hara; I could always see myself playing her."

"Is that wise?" asked Carolina Plum, "she goes through an awful lot of stress and it's a very long film."

"I know," said Sicily with a dramatic sigh, "but I was born for that part. I can handle it, and oh, Clark Gable, darling. The period costumes, Mammy; the chance to perform my perfect southern belle accent, and to experience history, oh it'll be breath-taking."

"Well, for me," said Kristobella, "due to the iconic clothes..." Kristobella winked at Adrianna Jasmine, Adrianna Jasmine smiled back knowingly. "It's Holly Golightly and Breakfast at Tiffany's!" The witches all marvelled at her choice and tried to come up with more suggestions for one another.

"Well, you've got plenty of time but what's the bet Clementine chooses Pretty Woman?!" spat Sicily.

Clementine turned up her nose. "Nah, I'm thinking more on the lines of a Bond Girl, or perhaps Laura Croft, or an assassin, maybe! You know something a *young* person could handle; I'll have to have a think."

Sicily's face darkened dangerously, she looked ready to hex. Clementine remained nonchalant.

"OK, everyone. Well, I guess it's my turn to take centre stage," broke in Adrianna Jasmine swiftly. Goddess, she could do without magical warfare tonight! "Who wants another present?"

The cackle became silent, with Sicily and Clementine glowering at each other from across the circle. Adrianna Jasmine reached into a large Tupperware box and produced what appeared to be giant round circles. They were wrapped up in bright orange tissue paper tied with a yellow ribbon.

"Oh, wow! A giant cookie," exclaimed Bella.

"Ah, but not just any giant cookie," clarified Adrianna Jasmine with a mischievous giggle "Not only are they the most deliciously chewy, yet crumbling double chocolate chip, brownie cookies that you have ever tasted, but each one is special unto you." The witches looked intrigued. "For example," said Adrianna Jasmine, "mum, when you take a single bite out of your cookie, not only will your taste buds dance in delight, but you will soon discover that you can speak fluent Russian!"

"You're joking, darling," said Sicily sounding slightly sceptical. "Are you sure? My Goddess, I've always wanted to learn Russian, such a dark and mysterious language, rather like me!" Adrianna Jasmine rolled her eyes.

"Of course, mother. But after you've swallowed your bite, be sure to read the spell that's on your little name card, otherwise the spell won't work. Also, let me just explain something else: one nibble of the cookie will allow the spell to work for up to one hour, a small bite, four hours and a hearty bite, up to eight hours. The cookie will stay fresh for up to a week, although keep it in a jar and it's freezer friendly; just defrost it before you eat it. So maybe break it up into pieces?"

"Well, I'm going to have a go at mine right now," announced Sicily then proceeded to nibble on a corner of the cookie like a mouse. She swallowed, commenting on how delicious it was, then began to read out her spell.

Moscow is known as the city of vice,
Sometimes naughty sometimes nice.
Swans glide gracefully upon a lake,
Best vodka in the world they do but make.
Dolls that shrink, dancing by flames,
Hot summers, cold winters; exotic names.
Russian is now my native tongue,
New words to learn, old songs to be sung.

Sicily then began to speak and to her utter amazement she began to converse in one of the most complex languages in the world; pronunciation perfect.

"Oh my Goddess," she gasped and stood up in order to show off her knew skill with more pizzazz. "I speak Russian!"

She began waving her arms about, as if she were acting in some great Russian stage production, as rustic Russian words tumbled from her lips, with vim, vigour and verve. "Здравствулте! Моя грива пунш Сицилии Mariposa прямолинейный и здравствулте! Я всего времени, я люблю этап, я обожаю этап и я живу для того чтобы станцевать, станцевать, станцевать!" Basically she said, "Hello, my name is Sicily Mariposa Forthright Punch, I am the greatest actress of all time. I love the stage, I adore the stage and I live to dance, dance, dance!"

"Oh, so invigorating, darlings," she said in English. "Я чувствую настолько живым, настолько мощным, и настолько сексуальный!" (I feel so alive, so powerful, so sexy!)

"Ok, well moving on," said Adrianna Jasmine swiftly, "you just carry on, mum." Sicily nodded, her eyes alive with passion. "Aunty Kristobella, read your spell; see if you can guess what is!"

Kristobella happily opened up her little card. "Oh?" she said, "this sounds interesting."

The sound is known to make angels weep
Or children to fall softly to sleep.
Shivers of pleasure down my spine,
Clear as crystal, delicious as wine.
Defining moments, memories are made,
The sound is often played and played.
Sing like a bird, evoke sheer delight,
Your notes will soar high as a kite.

"Hmmm," pondered Kristobella and took a small nibble from the yummy cookie. Everyone was silent as they waited for Kristobella's spell to take form.

"Well?" asked Carolina Plum. "What do you feel?"

Kristobella said nothing for a moment, and then announced that she had this massive urge to sing. "I don't know why but I feel I could sing absolutely anything!"

Sicily burst out laughing, "go on," she said mockingly. "Do something easy like, O Mio Bambino Caro." Kristobella looked at her sister, shrugged her shoulders then stood up and began to sing a pitch perfect rendition of O Mio Bambino Caro, literally knocking Sicily off her Russian perch and into a ditch.

"Oh my Goddess," breathed Bella Bell clapping exuberantly, "that was so serene, so brilliant. Look, it's brought tears to my eyes." Even Sicily was humbled, jealous, but humbled.

"My Goddess," said Kristobella, taken aback. "I didn't know I had it in me, I feel quite emotional!"

"We've all got it in us," explained Adrianna Jasmine. "It just takes a little boost to squeeze it out of us!"

"Well squeeze it out of me!" said Clementine and proceeded to read out her spell card.

Softer than an angel's kiss,
Light and free, utter bliss,
Ascend then float, spiral and soar,
Defy the gravitational law.
Become so light, touch a star;
See the distance from afar.
Oh this fantasy is such a desire,
It's my chance to ascend higher and higher.

Clementine took a small bite from the cookie, and then popped it down on top of the discarded paper. She sat still, waiting and waiting for something to happen, yet nothing did.

"Err... what's meant to happen, because whatever it is, I'm not feeling it. I'm not belting out La Traviata or twittering on in Chinese, so, sorry AJ, but you failed, sweetie, nothing's happening!" The cackle was trying desperately not to laugh and to keep straight faces, for something was happening to Clementine. It wasn't until she went to pick up her cookie again that she realised she was no longer sitting on the floor, but hovering about five feet above the carpet.

"Ahhhh," she shrieked, "I'm floating! I'm actually floating! Whoa, this feels strange. I didn't even notice. Will I go higher?"

Adrianna Jasmine said that she would, but only up to about ten feet above the ground and the more cookie she ate the longer she would levitate, she would probably be in the air for about an hour, due to the small bite she took. "Oooooh, this is heaven," said Clementine, who was now laying flat out on her back, hands under her head as if she were stretched out on a comfortable bed. "I could get used to this. I think I'll just stay here while the rest of you open your cookie cards." The witches, of course, didn't seem to mind that Clementine was hovering above them like a UFO, so they continued.

"Go on, Bella," urged Adrianna Jasmine, "open yours!"

Bella smiled and a wave of anticipation swept over her, *"what does it saaaaaay?"* sang Kristobella in style of Katherine

Jenkins, which in turn made everyone laugh. Bella cleared her throat and began to read out her card.

What are they thinking, what words would they speak,
To hear sentences opposed to a bark or a squeak.
What are their views on politics and life?
Wish they could say when they're experiencing strife.
How bizarre, how strange to sit and talk
Or listen to the views from a spider or stork.
So open my ears and open my eyes,
This spell will be a bell of a surprise!

"Surely not?" contemplated Bella, "is it what I'm thinking it is?"

"Well take a bite and find out for yourself," coaxed Adrianna Jasmine.

Bella bit off a small amount of cookie and sat quietly for a while.

"I wish you lot would hurry up," came a strange voice. "I'm desperate to get a bit of night air!"

"Who said that?" asked Bella, looking behind her and over her shoulders, "who wants fresh air?" The witches all looked slightly confused.

"Fresh air, Bella, what do you mean darling?" asked Sicily, "We could open a window, I suppose."

The voice piped up again, "Yes, so Clementine could float out!"

Bella stood up and began to look around the room, it was making her feel uneasy. Plus, it was a man's voice and considering that everyone in the room was a woman… "Now who said that?" Bella said sharply. "Come on, show yourself!"

"I say, steady on, old bean, OK, OK, I give up, chill out, take a pill, lighten up, it was me OK. Don't shoot your wand!"

Bella's eyes were out on stalks, it couldn't be! "Jupiter 10, is that you?"

"Well it's not Toto the dog, but yes it is I."

Clementine, who was drifting about like a helium balloon, tried to breast stroke herself back over to the group. "You can talk to Jupiter 10?" she asked, "wow, that's creepy, what's he saying?"

"Ugh, Clementine is about as appealing as an American trying to act in an English accent," Jupiter 10 said lazily, "apart from when Gwyneth did it, of course. That was pure genius."

"Err," Bella fumbled, "he just said that he's having a marvellous time."

"Yeah?" said Clementine, "ask him something else and tell us what he says!"

"Err..." Bella was feeling a little awkward from the attention, "Jupiter 10, what's your favourite meal?"

"Chicken liver!" said Jupiter 10 without hesitation, "Chicken liver!" translated Bella Bell with a smile.

"Yuck," proclaimed Clementine, "that's disgusting; I don't know how anyone could stomach that filth."

"No one's asking your opinion," Jupiter 10 spat back, "you butterscotch bed hopper!" He was sounding more like a female dog than a male cat, by the minute!"

"Ha Ha," Bella forced out a false laugh, "he just said that he understands it's err... well... err, a required taste!"

Adrianna Jasmine raised her right eyebrow, *I bet he did*, she thought for she knew exactly what Jupiter 10 was really like, it was highly amusing. "Well let's not keep Carolina from opening up her cookie any longer;" said Adrianna Jasmine, "you're the last I believe Carolina?"

"I believe so," said Carolina and opened up the final card. "Oh my!" she said.

The spirit strong, the passion deep,
The music so haunting eyes do weep.
The rise of the sun at the glorious dawn.
What's that I see but a Leprechaun,
Sparkling Emerald, lucky are they.
Feet in unison astonishing display,
Black hair, blue eyes, beautiful face,
I stand in line to dance at my place.

"OK...?" said Carolina, "I'm not sure but, if Michael Flatley walks through that door I'm not responsible for my actions!" She took a small bite, and waited for the cookie to work its magic. Suddenly she began to feel a prominent heat rise up through her toes and into her feet. "Ooh, I feel all inspired to trip the light fantastic in the manner of an Irish jig," she cooed.

Moments later the haunting music of River Dance, from where no one was sure, began to play and immediately Carolina Plum was up and jigging about to the soft shoe! She leapt and whooped, whirled and preened. Her feet were in perfect unison, her posture erect and strong.

"Bravo," they all cried as she leapt about like a professional Irish dancer, she truly was the Lady of the dance. When she completed her River Dance, she bowed gracefully and then burst into an encore while everyone cheered. They soon, however, learnt to stop cheering, as it provoked Carolina into performing one encore too many and by the time she approached her fifth, the novelty had worn off.

"Well, I must say ladies, you have *all* outdone yourselves this year!" announced Kristobella. "Thank you everyone for your marvellous gifts." She then took it upon herself to subsequently explode into the highest most pitch perfect *ahhhhhhhhh* that anyone had ever heard.

"Goddess," said Jupiter 10 sarcastically, "she actually makes Charlotte Church sound like a puffed-out old steam train."

Sicily continued babbling on in Russian, tap, tap, hop, prance, spring and shuffle, went Carolina.

"Ugh, I feel sick," moaned Clementine.

"Nessun Dormaaaaaa," sang Kristobella.

"No, no I totally disagree with you Jupiter 10," argued Bella Bell with the cat, "men *do* refer to women as motor cars, because once she's clapped out, she's simply traded in for a new, shinier, younger model."

Time to get out of here, thought Adrianna Jasmine as the circus was becoming a little too overwhelming. She whipped up

225

whiz and made her escape towards the coolness and calmness of the night sky. It was time for her to take flight.

<u>Black Velvet Halloween Cocktail</u>
1 ½ Shots of good quality vodka
1 ½ shots Kailua
A dash of lemon juice
Lemon slices
Black liquorice sticks

Using a cocktail shaker, shake the entire ingredients together.
Crush some ice and put it into a tumbler.
Pour the liquid over the ice.
Garnish with a black liquorice stick and a slice of lemon

Sexy, dark and smooth, oh that's rather like me!
(Sicily, 2008)

Chapter 22
Black Velvet Night

Halloween is about the only time of year when a person can carry a broomstick and wear a witch's outfit without anyone so much as battering an eyelid. Adrianna Jasmine had casually walked from her mother's room and into the main reception area without so much as a glance from the other guests. (However when a sexy girl is wearing a black, slinky, leather catsuit, holding a long bristly broomstick in one hand and a cat in the other, non-witching folk will tend to stare whether its Halloween or not!) She walked casually through the main reception area towards the hotel's front door, ignoring the admiring looks from the male staff. She was too full of adrenaline to care.

"Soon," she said to herself with a knowing smile, "soon you will be at one with the night."

She stepped through the front door and walked briskly towards the surrounding forest, her step quickening with every beat of her heart. On and on the witch walked, until she was quite sure that she was no longer visible to the hotel. Satisfied that she was now lost in the shadows of the night, Adrianna Jasmine began to run. She ran gathering speed towards the dark mysterious trees of The New Forest, faster and faster, clutching Whiz with her right hand, holding Jupiter 10 in her left. Her breathing began to increase and her heart pounded with exhilaration as she made her dash towards her ascent.

"This is it," she said to her faithful broom and with one fell swoop, she tucked Whiz in between her legs, thrust Jupiter 10 into the broom's bristles, shouted "up," and whoosh, the broom began its ascent towards the stars. As the broom climbed higher and higher towards the sky, Adrianna Jasmine sucked in a large gulp of air, relief overwhelming her body: at last she felt free. She threw her head back and closed her eyes as the night air kissed her face.

"Thank you, Goddess!" she cried into the atmosphere, "thank you for making me a witch, woo-hoo!" She laughed with joviality, she felt so alive and invigorated; then she realised something important.

"Ooops," she said, putting her hand to her mouth, "almost forgot." She realised that amongst her excitement she had forgotten to check if Jupiter 10 had experienced a safe take off, so she peered behind her left shoulder to make sure he had not splattered onto the forest floor. As it was, the little black cat was fine; busy trying to make himself comfortable amongst the brooms' twigs. She smiled happily at her cat, "Good boy, Jupiter 10," she said proudly, then returned her eye straight ahead.

Sooner than later the broom was higher than the trees and clear from dangerous branches that had so often been the reason behind a nasty accident. So safe in knowledge that rogue branches would not be decapitating Adrianna Jasmine tonight, Whiz sped up like a Ferrari.

"Oh!" said the witch, "you wanna play?" The broom sped up even more, resulting in Adrianna Jasmine yelling out in sheer delight; she was thoroughly enjoying herself. The wind swept past, it was cold, but she didn't care, her body was hot with exhilaration and passion for the night. The witch was free, free from the hubbub of her life, her spells, her slip ups, the chaos of her mother's hotel room and of course, Taylor! She travelled with Whiz for miles, who entertained his mistress with impressive manoeuvres such as the Big Dipper, Loop the Loop and Tornado Twists. The moves were great fun, but very dangerous and Adrianna Jasmine needed to wrap her legs and body tightly around the broomstick to stay on, she looked like a Swiss Roll. Then after about an hour of thrill-seeking flight the broom stick slowed himself down to a gentle stop. There it stayed for a few moments, hovering just above the trees, with Adrianna Jasmine slowly catching her breath. It was dark and the trees made it impossible to see the ground. It frightened her a little and she appreciated the safety of the sky, no one could harm her up here!

As Adrianna Jasmine adjusted her body to side-saddle, she sat quietly and began to think.

"Oh, Blast," she thought, slightly aggravated at herself, "I have one moment of stillness, and you pop into my head." She was of course thinking about Taylor. *Why?* she thought, *why are you in my mind? I know you're handsome, successful and appear to come from a good family, but that's no reason for you to distract me from my perfect life. It's all because you're fascinated with me, I can sense it! That's why you're ruining my life; you haunt my dreams at night, bombard my thoughts during the day and upset my magic. Not because I like you! So I tell you this, Mr Jameson, even though I admit I find you deadly attractive and your bottom looks as appetising as two freshly picked mangos, your love is uninvited and I will fight it all the way to Saturn if I have to*! Then she paused for a few moments and sighed deeply. "But," she whispered, "Do I *want* to fight it?" Then, to the witch's amazement, her thoughts were broken, without warning, Whiz began to ascend towards the stars, climbing higher and higher, almost lifting the witch from her broom. She looked up to the moon above and began to laugh, for Adrianna Jasmine knew exactly what was coming. It was Whiz's speciality, "The Drop of Death." In order to prepare herself for the up and coming moments, she sensibly repositioned her body from side-saddle to the more secure straddle stance, that way she had a chance to stay alive! Whiz was like some crazed, rocket fuelled elevator, he just continued to climb, heading straight towards orbit. The speed was ferocious and even Jupiter 10 had to dig his little paws deeper into Whiz's bristling twigs to prevent him from plummeting to his 5th death.

Whiz still continued on, "he's actually gone higher than last year!" cried out Adrianna Jasmine to herself, "surely he can't go any higher than this. When's he going to stop?"

Still Whiz continued to climb, without redemption, without remorse, without sense! Then just when the witch thought she was going to die the broom simply stopped in mid-air, then proceeded to plummet like an out of control meteor heading straight for earth. The wind was tearing passed Adrianna Jasmine's face, she screamed with fear and thrill as the broom tumbled faster and faster towards the forest bed, spinning like a frenzied Catherine Wheel. She clung on for dear life, her knuckles white and her inner thighs burning from the continuous isometric contraction, which probably saved her very life! Her eyes were squeezed tight and due to the sheer speed, the witch found it hard to breath. Then whoosh!!! Whiz expertly swooped back up towards the stars, missing the tops of the trees by centimetres.

"Ahhhhh," yelled out the witch not knowing whether to laugh or be sick, "you, blast... ahhhhh." Whiz took it upon himself to speed up like a rocket once more, zooming through the night, filling his mistress with utter exhilaration, ducking and diving, loop the looping, swishing and whooshing, it was the ride of a lifetime. He continued on like this for another hour, until sheer exhaustion made the witch beg the broom to come to some sort of climax! Moments later, Whiz slowed down to a steady pace, with Adrianna Jasmine slumped, exhausted, over the rampant handle.

"Oh, Goddess!" she said, barely able to breathe. "That was amazing!" Whiz playfully bucked up and down to say "thank you" for his mistress's approval.

"Please, no more!" begged the witch as Whiz bucked and bumped, "I can't take it. You've worn me out: my inner thighs are on fire!"

Then at last Burley Manor came into view and the broom carefully started his descent towards the ground, it had been one hell of a ride.

'Where there is great love, there are always miracles'
(Willa Cather)

Chapter 23
A Mother's Concern

The witches woke up to a cold, grizzly day. The icy rain beat down on the windows and the grey clouds blanketed the sky with misery and doom. However, the weather didn't dampen the spirits of the cackle! They'd had a wonderful evening and were still full of festive cheer. They all met up for breakfast at 8.30am, where they feasted and drank plenty of tea and coffee, and ate toast to appease their rumbling tummies. They ate and drank until they were all quite full, then packed up their belongings in order to return to the hectic rat race known as London. Bella Bell and Carolina Plum were travelling home together, and Sicily, Adrianna Jasmine, Clementine and Jupiter 10, were all packed in Kristobella's white Range Rover. So once the cackle had returned their keys to reception, they bid their farewell and went on their merry ways. Adrianna Jasmine sat up front with her aunt, whilst Sicily and Clementine chose to sit at the back. The four witches chatted cheerfully about their fantastic night, the crazy dancing, the food and, of course, their wonderful gifts! However, for once, Sicily was quiet.

"What's up with you?" enquired Clementine in her usual straightforward manor.

"Oh, just thinking, darling," said Sicily somewhat distracted, "I can't seem to get that witch out of my mind, she's really infuriating me."

"What witch?" asked Adrianna Jasmine whose ears had just pricked up, she had no idea what her mother was on about.

"Oh nothing, darling, it's just one of those times when you think you look at a complete stranger and they remind you of someone... you agree, don't you Kristobella?"

Kristobella nodded, "yes," she replied, "her face was highly distinctive and yet for the life of me, I can't think who she is." Sicily was silent.

"Perhaps you went to school with her," suggested Clementine "was she about your age?" Sicily shrugged her shoulders. "Well, it's hard to compare her age to me, darling because, of course, I don't look my age, I look far younger." Clementine rolled her eyes. "No, seriously," said Sicily, "looking at her from a realistic point of view, I guess she looked how a *typical* fifty-something-year-old woman is supposed to look. She was obviously not bothered about her appearance, doesn't watch her figure and appears to opt for double cheese pizza rather than the odd session of yoga!" Now it was Kristobella's turn to roll her eyes.

"Shut up, Sicily," she said to her sister, which resulted in a few minutes of sibling bicker.

Two hours of driving and two hours of Sicily reciting Oscar Wilde, singing Frank Sinatra songs and stating her opinion about everything from American politics to Posh Spice, they were back in London and outside Sicily's house in Hammersmith.

"Well, goodbye, darlings, it's been fun," sang Sicily as she blew a barrage of kisses to everyone as if she were at the Oscars. "I'll call you later, byeee!"

Kristobella sighed in relief. "Peace at last, she doesn't half go on, what batteries does that woman use?" The girls giggled at the comment, Sicily was exhausting, even Clementine's energy had died a death after ten minutes tying to compete with her and she had opted for the escape of sleep. She was hung over, anyway, from too much Sangria.

"Right," said Kristobella, "let's get you back to Covent Garden, then Clementine off to Tottenham."

The traffic in central London was rubbish as always and therefore it took an additional hour to arrive outside the coffee shop. Adrianna Jasmine exited the car, kissed her aunt, waved goodbye and promised to visit the shop before the photo shoot so she could borrow some glamorous dresses. She waved goodbye to Clementine, who had just ungainly clambered over from the back into the front seat, before skipping into Princess Sarah's Magic and Coffee Shop, a brand new witch.

As soon as she walked in, Adrianna Jasmine was greeted with a massive hug from Sarah. The two witches embraced warmly and Adrianna Jasmine took the opportunity to present Sarah with a bag of gifts that were from the cackle. Sarah squealed in delight.

"They're fabulous," said Adrianna Jasmine genuinely, "you'll enjoy them so much."

Sarah looked all excited, "thanks. Come on, let's go into the kitchen, I'll make you a hot cocoa and you can make the cakes!" Adrianna Jasmine chuckled

"Don't tell me you've run out?"

"You could say that," said Sarah, "the cakes went down a storm yesterday; I've got about ten business cards to give to you from parents who want you to cater for their kids' birthdays and dinner parties!"

Adrianna Jasmine was impressed. "So it was a success, then?"

"Was it ever!" confirmed Sarah with enthusiasm, "so much so that the local newspaper popped in to see what all the fuss was about and look: we're on page six." Sarah thrust the paper at her friend, "look, read it, it's very positive!"

Adrianna Jasmine read the paper and was pleasantly surprised, her name had been mentioned in a highly positive light as the "enchanting" caterer and that the coffee shop's party had been the most magical Halloween party in town!

"This is great," gushed Adrianna Jasmine excitedly, "it advertises you, it advertises my food and it's all *free* advertising!"

The two witches high-fived one another then caught up with all the gossip – well, the two hadn't spoken for 24 hours!

That evening, prior to baking up a frenzy, talking until she was hoarse and tubing it through the madness of London's underground, Adrianna Jasmine and Jupiter 10 finally made it through the front door to their cosy flat. She kicked off her shoes and went straight to the fridge to retrieve some milk to make herself a cup of hot cocoa.

She then opened a can of chicken liver cat food for Jupiter 10, which he immediately devoured.

"Bet you're hungry, little chap," said Adrianna Jasmine as she watched her cat guzzle up his meal, "what with all that flying last night!" Then, when he was fit to burst, she popped him onto the window sill so he could take his evening's constitutional. "Night, night," she whispered before she watched the slinky, black, velvety cat disappear into the shadows of the night.

It was chilly out so Adrianna Jasmine lit her fire and snuggled up on the couch. She'd just made it in time to watch Strictly Come Dancing, the wonderful glitzy show where professional dancers coach celebrity non-dancers how to trip the light fantastic in ballroom and Latin. Adrianna Jasmine oohed and aahed at the beautiful costumes and wished that one day she, too, could trip the light fantastic in such extraordinary gowns. How beautiful she would look. Once the show was over, Adrianna Jasmine flicked over to find something else to entertain her, then the phone rang. A little annoyed that her peace was disrupted, she begrudgingly answered the phone.

"Hello darling!" *Oh Goddess,* she thought, "It's me your mother!" *Well who the bloody hell else would it be,* thought the witch. "I thought I'd wait until Strictly was over, because I knew you'd be watching it, jelly bean, it was good, wasn't it? Oh, I adore Vincent, darling. I think you should become a famous chef, then you could go on there and dance with the Italian dynamo, you'd be perfecto! Then again, maybe I should become famous as I wouldn't mind him packing my cannelloni, if you know what I mean! Ha ha."

Adrianna Jasmine rolled her eyes in despair, only her mother would come up with something as vulgar as that!

"Yes, mother!" said Adrianna Jasmine with tiredness to her voice, "maybe one day, anyway, what's up?"

"Well," said Sicily keenly, "I just realised who that woman was!"

Adrianna Jasmine was confused.

"Woman? What woman?"

"Oh, darling, you know... *thee* woman!" Adrianna Jasmine drew a blank. "You know, the one who Kristobella and I were talking about in the car."

Adrianna Jasmine cast her mind back to the journey home and faintly recalled a conversation between Sicily and Kristobella recognising some woman, or something along that line, at the hotel.

"I think so, yes," said Adrianna Jasmine, "what about her?" Was it really worth her mother phoning her up on a Saturday night?

"Well, darling its rather exciting. You see, I thought I'd recognised her firstly at dinner and couldn't put a name to her face, but oh, I desperately needed to find out why her face was haunting me so; it was killing me. Then when you and Clementine were dancing about like something out of a Burlesque peep show, mummy noticed something very peculiar."

"What was that, then, mother?" asked Adrianna Jasmine nonchalantly, flicking through the channels. Goddess, wasn't there anything worth watching?

"Well," continued Sicily, "I caught her staring at you, staring at you as if she were trying to look into your very soul," said her mother with all the drama of Meryl Streep. "Honestly, I thought she'd give herself piles, darling. She was staring at you that hard."

Adrianna Jasmine clicked her tongue. "So what if she was staring, it happens you know, from time to time, people do stare!"

Sicily chuckled down the phone. "Darling, I know people have often been caught eyeing you up, but this was different, her stare was evil and it was headed directly towards my little button mushroom. Besides, it looked...well, menacing."

"Mum," said Adrianna Jasmine, trying to sound diplomatic, "you know as well I do that there were no black witches in that hotel last night, she probably just had some kind of woman's issue with me or perhaps Clementine, which, let's face it, isn't unusual when it comes to that girl."

"No, darling," said Sicily firmly, "I hear what you're saying about Clementine, but it was all about you! So as soon as I saw the apple of my eye in danger, I kept a watchful, yet very discreet, eye on her." Still not entirely sure what all the fuss was about, Adrianna Jasmine told her mother that she had probably been worrying over nothing, but nonetheless thanked her mother for her concern. "That's okay, Lemony Snickets," she said appreciatively, "because thanks to my instinct, I may have just saved your life!"

Adrianna Jasmine rolled her eyes in despair. "Mother, you're sooo dramatic. I hardly think my life was in mortal danger!"

"Well, darling," said Sicily, "the plot thickens. When I got home today, I cast a little memory regression spell on myself, because she was really infuriating me, darling, and guess what? I found out who she was!"

"Drum roll, please," joked Adrianna Jasmine; Sicily ignored her. "She's only none other than Richenda Pan, darling. The daughter of Gunnora Pan!"

At the mention of Gunnora's name, Adrianna Jasmine immediately felt cold.

Immediately, Adrianna Jasmine's voice became serious "You're joking."

"Yes, Gunnora Pan," her mother confirmed once more, "the most evil witch to come out of modern London, the witch who was stung by jelly fish and died horribly in order to prevent the murdering psychopath from killing innocents with her magic."

"Hang on," said Adrianna Jasmine suddenly feeling confused, "why was Richenda glaring at me, then?! What have I done?"

"Err ... not sure," fumbled Sicily, "oh darling, it's probably nothing," she added with a little chuckle. "But just to be extra safe, especially due to her coming from the despicable Pan family, mummy has sorted it all out, ok?"

"Err...sorted what out?" asked her daughter a little worried. Goddess, what was her mother up to now!

"Not much, gummy bear," said Sicily whimsically. "I just cast a little protection spell around you, that's all. She won't be able come within a hundred and fifty yards of you!"

"I'm sure you didn't have to go that far, mother. I think that's being a little neurotic!"

"Nonsense!" said Sicily firmly, "you can never be too careful!"

Hmmm, Adrianna Jasmine thought unconvinced, "anyway what type of protection spell did you cast around me?"

"Oh, nothing too potent, my little megabit it's just the one where the intruder experiences a fatal heart attack when they enter the no-go zone."

"Ah, well that's all... MOTHER!" Cried Adrianna Jasmine in horror, "you can't do that!" Honestly, this was becoming ridiculous.

"I can, darling, and I have," said Sicily stubbornly digging in her heels. "I tell you, I will not have you threatened." Adrianna Jasmine paused for a moment, she needed to think.

"OK," she said trying to sound rational, "is this really necessary, I mean, a heart attack! Can't you give her an electric shock or something, instead?"

"Don't be ridiculous, olive oil," said Sicily, as if her daughter were quite mad. "That would never warn her off, no, no, a heart attack should do it, anyway her heart will restart as soon as she's back within *her* territory."

"That's if she's not dead beforehand," yelled Adrianna Jasmine.

"Well, I'll guess she'll just have to die then!" shouted Sicily fiercely, before slamming down the phone with a sharp bang.

Utterly dumbstruck, Adrianna Jasmine stared down at the receiver: she was in shock. Never had she witnessed her mother so angry and she had never, ever hung up on her, what was going on? Perhaps she *was* in danger and her mother was simply carrying out her motherly duty of protecting her daughter? Adrianna Jasmine clicked off her phone and went into the kitchen, she decided to pour herself a glass of whiskey to calm her nerves, her pre-ordered Unflustered Floss wouldn't arrive for a few more days and whisky was a good alternative. She sipped the golden liquid and closed her eyes as the heat trickled down her body. She took a few more hearty gulps and returned back to the living room, where she tried to explore the possibilities as to why her mother had behaved so out of character. Little did Adrianna Jasmine know, back over in Hammersmith, Sicily was pacing up and down her corridor locked in thought, her face was whiter than snow.

'Top tip for a first date, remember your date is not a therapist, and therefore please spare him/her the details about your previous relationships, that's so dull!'
(Clementine Poppleapple, 2008)

Chapter 24
The Grand Meet

Adrianna Jasmine spent most of Sunday trying to convince her mother to appease the protection spell that she had cast upon Richenda. She simply couldn't allow Richenda to suffer heart failure, no matter how threatening her mother believed her to be. So in the end, the mother and daughter came to a strained compromise. Sicily agreed to change the gruesome outcome of cardiac arrest, to acute nausea. Apparently Richenda would be submitted to "waves of sickness" if she stood too close to her beloved daughter, and the closer she stood, the more fierce the sickness. It still wasn't quite what Adrianna Jasmine had in mind, but it was better than death.

That night, Adrianna Jasmine was home alone again. She enjoyed her little moments when she was able to watch her favourite channels, work on menu plans and look up recipes on the net. She was also excited about the next day, for she would be meeting up with Taylor Jameson at Hotel 78 which would hopefully lead to a well-deserved boost in her career. She was happy with her work, but baking for the coffee shop was not her life-long ambition, and even though she earned good money when she catered for a party, it wasn't regular work. Some weeks she was flush and her bank account was full, other weeks she struggled and felt poor. Luckily, she had no mortgage to pay, but bills were going up and up, petrol wasn't cheap anymore and she still had to buy her ingredients.

"Oh well," she sighed, "maybe Taylor would offer me something fabulous!" She sat back and dreamed about becoming a famous TV chef, cooking for the nation and projecting her feel good magic through the television screens and into the homes of millions of people. The nation would be happy once more and the dark depressing days of credit crunch Britain would be appeased; all thanks to this delightful woman cooking cupcakes and lasagne in their very own living rooms. At 2.30am she tucked herself into bed and fell asleep within five minutes of her head softening into the fluffy pillow. She slept soundly and dreamt that Jupiter 10 could talk and was hosting a cooking show, wearing a white chef's hat and promoting liver. He sounded like Terry Thomas. I say, steady on!

At 5.30am Adrianna Jasmine's radio turned on and the witch woke up giggling. Tula Hoopla, the witching worlds morning radio DJ, was reading out a joke, *"why is brunette considered evil? Well when have you ever seen a blonde witch?"* Adrianna Jasmine chuckled, "hmm, clearly you haven't met Clementine Poppleapple."

She leapt out of bed and straight into her shower. She had a busy morning ahead. So she showered quickly, cleaned her teeth, popped on her Abercrombie and Fitch tracksuit and a little moisturiser to her face, guzzled down half a pint of milk and shoved a banana hungrily into her mouth. Her outfit, which she had picked out for her meeting with Taylor, was hanging up prêt e porter, in a protective suit bag on the back of her bedroom door. She had chosen an Italian black, stretch wool, tailored, pinstripe high-waisted skirt, with button hole detailed waistband, with a sexy yet subtle front split. She had teamed the skirt with a raspberry red, viscose knit, top with sweetheart neckline which would show off her delightful curves and teeny waist. For her feet, black stiletto, stretch suede and patent leather knee-high boots and for warmth, her dramatic floor-length, black leather, single-breasted coat.

Somehow she managed to carry her outfit in one fail swoop, out the door and into her trusty van. As she placed everything down onto the seat beside her, she heaved a sigh of relief: at last she had the freedom of her arms once more.

The traffic at 6.00am wasn't too bad and she drove without anxiety towards Covent Garden. It was still dark and most people would still be in bed, but not Adrianna Jasmine, she loved being up early and she loved being up late at night, much more exciting! At 6.45am she parked her van and walked into the kitchen. Blaire was already there and welcomed Adrianna Jasmine warmly: it seemed all had been forgiven in regards to the spell fiasco a few days ago!

"Hello, Adrianna Jasmine. How are you, my love?"

"Good thanks," answered the young witch chirpily, "got my interview with that magazine today, so I'm rather excited!"

"Oh yes, of course," enthused Blaire, "yes, yes Sarah told me all about it, it's wonderful!"

Adrianna Jasmine smiled, "well hopefully," she said modestly, "and I'm going to mention this place, of course."

Blaire beamed a grateful smile, "oh, Adrianna Jasmine you truly are goddess sent, aren't you? Why don't I bring you in a nice cup of cocoa and a muesli bar?"

"Mmmmm… scrumptious," said the young witch and with that, Blaire turned on her heels and went off to fetch her employee of the month the breakfast treats.

As the morning rolled on, Adrianna Jasmine baked and iced her cakes, creamed and caramelised, kneaded and folded, whipped and whisked. She had created a sumptuous batch of chocolate sponge giant cupcakes, filled with a lip-smacking toffee sauce, sprinkled with a caramel crunch. In addition, Mini Baby 4 inch Cheesecakes in five different flavours: Blackberry Swirl, New York Vanilla, Amaretto, Zesty Lemon and Mint Madness. She had also conjured up Spicy Orange Chocolate, Cranberry Wrap Cake, Giant Cake Balls coated with a crisp white chocolate coating, Millionaire Shortbread, a moist Fruit Cake, Rocky Road and her all-time favourite, Banana Malteser cake.

By twelve thirty she was done! Although there wasn't much evidence that she had made such delectable delights, for as soon as the cakes were cool enough to be decorated, Blaire and Sarah whipped them out onto the shop floor faster than a shooting star. However, they never seemed to run out; for some reason Adrianna Jasmine would always make just the right amount for the day's trade. How she managed it, well that's anyone's guess!

"Right. I'm done for the day," announced Adrianna Jasmine to herself and made her way into the little changing area adjacent to the kitchen. She slipped on her outfit, applied her makeup, pulled up her boots, brushed her lovely thick hair and spritzed herself with Tallulah Toffee's Sultry Shadow perfume. She put on her fabulous coat, wrapped her soft scarf around her neck and picked up her bag and keys.

"Hey!" called out a familiar voice, it was Sarah, "quickly," she said whilst running towards her. "I just wanted to say good luck! The coffee shop is booming out there, I've had to sneak away, do you know how hard it is to get away from my mother?!" Adrianna Jasmine smiled knowingly.

"I know it's chocker today, maybe it was the write up?!"

Sarah nodded in agreement, "I think it has something to do with it, yes!"

"Well, anyway, I'm off. Thanks for the luck!" Sarah embraced her friend warmly.

"Go knock 'em dead, kiddo. You'll be great!" then she looked serious for a moment.

"What's' up?" asked Adrianna Jasmine with slight concern in her voice.

"I know you're in a rush, honey," said Sarah, "but before you go off, I rather think it's a good idea if you just, ever so quickly, pop over to see the Mystic Odessa, she's been desperate to catch you!"

Adrianna Jasmine shook her head. "No way, there's no time."

"I think it's important. Please, for me!"

Adrianna Jasmine sighed, "Oh, very well, then," she said grumpily, "but if I miss my meeting, I won't be happy."

"You won't! Just go!" said Sarah almost frog marching her friend out of the kitchen.

They found the Mystic Odessa gazing dramatically into her crystal ball, her raven hair loose and wild.

"Sit down, Adrianna Jasmine," she said without even looking up, "I understand you're feeling somewhat rushed, but it's for the best that you have decided to take this opportunity to speak with me."

She looked up; her eyes were serious and staring deeply at the witch. She then resumed to peering once again into her crystal ball. She said nothing for a few moments which frustrated Adrianna

Jasmine who was tapping her foot impatiently. *Will she ever come on?*

Then The Mystic Odessa began to speak.

"Yes, it's all about time, time and timing, taking the left path opposed to the right, perhaps taking a step back before commencing with a step forward."

What are you twittering on about, thought the witch, *why do they always have to speak in bloody riddles?*

"Gut instincts," Odessa continued, raising her voice slightly, "or changing one's mind, will you be decisive or indecisive? As a Taurus and ruled by Venus, the Goddess of love, believe it or not," Odessa winked at Adriana Jasmine knowingly, "you are stable, conservative, and home-loving. You rarely become frazzled or upset and your personality will almost never lose course. You are aware of your own strength and can handle any situations with dignity."

Goddess, fumed Adrianna Jasmine, *if I wanted my bloody horoscope read out, I'd of brought Now Magazine.* "But push her too far," The Mystic Odessa boomed "and she can turn into a raging bull: impossible to calm."

Adrianna Jasmine sat there nodding her head, "yep, that's me alright," as she glanced down at her watch. The Mystic Odessa didn't even look up and told the impatient witch that staring at her watch wouldn't make a blind bit of difference, it would be wise to stay and listen for a few more minutes. Adrianna Jasmine sighed and slouched back into her chair whilst Odessa rattled on.

"An important life-changing decision is to be made today, perhaps by you responding to a decision a stranger has made or a decision that you have made due to a decision of a total stranger." Adrianna Jasmine felt her brain twist as it tried to make sense of the ridiculous sentence; she was not in the mood.

"Oh Goddess, get me out of here!" muttered Adrianna Jasmine under her breath.

"Just a few more seconds," informed Odessa. "OK, here we go!"

The next few moments were a bit of a blur, one moment Adrianna Jasmine was close to having a tantrum, the next she was locked in an intense stare-off with the Mystic Odessa. Neither blinked nor lost eye contact, neither sneezed nor giggled, they simply remained frozen in stillness. The noise from the coffee shop seemed to cease, along with the light and customers. Was she dreaming, fitting? Adrianna Jasmine wasn't sure, but like all dreams and hopefully most fits, they do come to an end. On this particular occasion, the journey came to end when the Mystic Odessa softened her intense stare and prompted blinking from the witch. She then shooed off Adrianna Jasmine as if she were some annoying child with chocolate smeared around her mouth.

Feeling dazed, Adrianna Jasmine picked up her bag and floated towards the tube station. She felt as if she was in some virtual reality game, and the natural noise of the city seemed somewhat quieter to her than normal. However, she was soon snapped out of her delirium when she noticed masses of people being turned away from entering the tube station. "What's going on?" she could hear people ask. "What's happening, why has the tube been closed off?" She soon discovered that not ten minutes ago a train had crashed into another train due to the driver experiencing a heart attack, resulting in death, destruction and twisting metal. Adrianna Jasmine's blood ran cold, and the colour of her skin turned to a deathly shade of alabaster: she was in shock. Her thoughts went back to her annoying meeting with Odessa, "My Goddess," she whispered, "she held me back, she held me back to stop me getting on that train. If I'd just left a few minutes earlier..." Adrianna Jasmine's cool exterior had been rattled, what with the daughter of an old psychopathic nutcase after her and now narrowly missing a potential death train, she was very rattled indeed.

"If I'd left ten minutes earlier," she contemplated, "what if, what if. That's why Odessa wanted to talk to me, it was to stall me, I knew what she was saying didn't make any sense. Riddles indeed, it was all a smokescreen!"

She walked in a daze amongst the chaos towards the curb and hailed for a taxi. "Err, Hotel 78," she managed to say as she stumbled into the black cab.

"No worries, love," said the cabbie, who was a forty-something-year-old Chinese cockney called Ding Bang. "But I warn ya, it could take a while, me love what with the tubes in strife."

"That's OK," Adrianna Jasmine whispered, her eyes still hadn't blinked since her ordeal, "I'll just send a text to let someone know I may be a bit late!"

Forty-five minutes and nearly thirty quid later, Adrianna Jasmine pulled up outside the beautiful hotel. She was still a little cloudy, but Ding Bang had been good company during the trip and had even offered her half of his Twix for the sugar rush.

"You take care, my love," advised Ding Bang after the pair exchanged money.

"Thanks, Ding Bang. See you soon."

She stepped out of the cab and walked towards the front entrance where she was greeted by a well-groomed doorman who gallantly opened the door for her.

"Thank you," she said politely and the doorman granted her a modest bow. When she looked up at the beautiful boutique hotel, her excitement had slowly overtaken her shock and she began to feel more like the Adrianna Jasmine who had woken up that morning. As she made her way into the lobby, the witch was immediately hit by the eminent pleasant and appealing atmosphere of a hotel that had simply captured an old 1920s, Agatha Christie novel. She walked on black and white floor tiles that complimented the dark wooden panelling and open fire places. She dreamed of sinking into the relaxing soft leather chairs, running her fingers over the exquisite cool marbles and lavish fabrics. She continued to journey through the black and white wonderland and towards reception, where she was greeted warmly by a smart, sophisticated female receptionist.

"Good afternoon and welcome to Hotel 78, how may I help you?" Adrianna Jasmine smiled back at the woman with, what she guessed to be, a Swedish accent and informed the lady that she was meeting a Mr Jameson for a business lunch. "Ah yes," said the receptionist, "he's been expecting you. Mr Jameson is up on the Mezzanine level, if you just go over to the lift and press Mezzanine level, you will be taken straight up there."

Adrianna Jasmine bid her thanks and went over to call the lift. Moments later she was inside and smoothly being taken up to meet Mr Jameson. As she stepped out of lift into the private lounge, she immediately found Taylor seated at a table reading a newspaper and sipping a small glass of red wine. She walked towards him, her tummy was twisted into excited knots, and she couldn't help but smile.

As he sensed someone approaching, Taylor looked up. When he realised it was his lunch date with the girl who had simply captivated his heart, he stood up. He took her warmly by the hand, then drew her in towards him so he was able to kiss her softly on both cheeks. Adrianna Jasmine closed her eyes and breathed in his intoxicating aftershave.

Oh to bury my head in your throbbing chest, she thought wildly. Little did she know that Mr Jameson was thinking the very same thing! Taylor stepped back to reveal an enormous smile across his face.

"So glad you made it, Adrianna Jasmine. Here, take a seat and we'll order your drink, I bet you could do with one!"

"Thanks," she said appreciatively and quickly explained, as the waiter took her dramatic leather coat from her shoulders, how she nearly took the tube and if she hadn't been delayed by a friend, the consequences could have been disastrous. As her coat was being removed, Taylor discreetly scanned her body. Her outfit hugged every heavenly curve and smooth line; he couldn't help but admire and lust. She sat down and casually flicked her hair sexily over her shoulders causing the chocolate brown waves to cascade over her ample breasts like melted Lindt chocolate, sumptuously poured over vanilla cream and fresh raspberries.

"What can I get you to drink?" he asked. Adrianna Jasmine decided that she would join him with a glass of red, so he ordered a bottle of Mascarello Barolo, Monprivato, 2000. As they waited for their wine, Taylor started the conversation off with formal pleasantries such as complimenting the witch on how lovely she looked, and made enquiries in regards to her work. Adrianna Jasmine answered the questions simply and told him that her life was all about making cakes and treats for the coffee shop and catering for the odd private soiree. As Taylor listened intently to every word the witch had to say, the waiter appeared and expertly opened the wine; he poured a small measure into Taylor's glass for him to taste test.

"Very good," said Taylor, nodding his head in approval. The waiter continued to pour the ruby red liquid into the clean, crisp glasses. After a few moments of allowing the wine to breathe, Adrianna Jasmine took a well-deserved sip. She closed her eyes as the subtle, velvety liquid kissed her lips, massaged her tongue and trickled down her throat.

"Hmm," she said, "I taste a smoky and floral flavour that possesses scale and depth, which brings out the maturity and breadth of the fruit." She licked her lips, "You have excellent taste!"

Taylor was impressed, "a wine connoisseur as well as an excellent cook, is there no ends to your talents?"

Adrianna smiled in delight, she was enjoying this! After careful consideration, the pair ordered their meal. Taylor opted for Foie Gras terrine with French bean & truffle salad, followed by Lamb steak with mashed potatoes and an almond and mint pesto. Adrianna Jasmine, who was highly impressed with the exquisite choice, decided on scallops with cauliflower purée and Madeira sauce, followed by a filleted sea bass, pan-fried in butter, served with a hot salmon mousse and accompanied by a warm lemon and prawn, butter sauce.

"I'm in a fishy mood today," she shrugged.

Taylor smiled then realised something ghastly. "Oops, we should have ordered white, then." Not wishing to spoil Adrianna Jasmine's fish, he called the waiter over and ordered a glass of crisp white wine to compliment her fishy luncheon. As they ate and drank, the pair chatted merrily, happy and comfortable in one another's company. It was an extremely pleasant luncheon although, if truth be told, it seemed to appear more like a first date as opposed to a business meeting.

When their plates were removed, the pair decided to skip pudding and retire to the stylish club-style lounge for coffee and liquors by the fire. As they snuggled down on the cosy couch and stared happily into the roaring flames, it felt more natural to interlock fingers and nestle into one another's sexy nubile bodies than talk shop. Adrianna Jasmine actually felt quite light-headed from the wine, and was becoming slightly flirtatious towards the handsome food critic. Nonetheless, they soldiered on.

Taylor flipped open his note pad and asked Adrianna Jasmine how she had wound up in the catering business. Due to Adriana Jasmine feeling slightly tipsy from the wine and sweet Amaretto, she answered the questions freely and unabashed, staring deeply into Taylor's eyes. He was captivated and appeared to be literally falling into her, as if under a spell. She spoke without losing eye contact, which resulted in poor Taylor, twisting in ecstasy and agony.

Oh God, I want to kiss you, he thought. *It's too much.*

"I trained at college for two years," said the witch nonchalantly, "then I went to the Leith's School of Food and Wine, where I studied for a further year in an *intensive*," she said the word "intensive" as provocatively as she could, "course in classic and creative cookery."

"Intensive?" Taylor licked his lips.

"Intensive," confirmed Adrianna Jasmine before swallowing. All she needed now was to be dangling a cherry teasingly on her tongue. Taylor was a mess! She went on sounding more and more like a sex-siren-come-soft-porn-star by the minute.

"I've also embarked on numerous day courses at Padstow seafood schools, courses at the Wilton cake decorating school and spent one hot sticky month in the hills of Tuscany, learning to cook authentic Italian cuisine."

Taylor was ready to burst. "I adore Italian food," he breathed.

"You do?" She smiled as if she'd just been hand delivered from Venus, "maybe I'll cook for you sometime, just like a real Italian woman."

"A real Italian?" Taylor was becoming more overwhelmed by the second.

"Oh yes," said Adrianna Jasmine, "you do know that Italy is in my blood?"

"Why?" asked Taylor with all intensity of a stock market trader waiting painstakingly for his fate.

"My Grandpa was Italian," she shrugged playfully. "I am a natural mixture of passion, and domestic Goddess."

"That you are!" stated Taylor, mesmerised. He wasn't going to argue, "carry on... say anything, I don't care, it's all fantastic."

Adrianna Jasmine kept the eye contact and smiled wickedly, she was like a cat toying with a mouse.

"I've been on sushi, Indian and Chinese cookery courses and attended various master classes with Marco Pierre White, Rick Stein, Ferran Adrià's, and Delia Smith. My inspirations are; Alain Ducasse and Ferran Adrià's because, in my eyes, they are the best chefs in the world; Jane Asher because I love her cakes, Emmalina Lucci because, bar my mother, is the most beautiful woman on the planet; Audrey Hepburn, because of her effortless style, and the internet, it never fails you when you need a good recipe." They continued on and on with Adrianna Jasmine telling him everything from her favourite colour, to her favourite film, food, wine, her ambition to own her own coffee and cake shop and even where she would love to go on holiday next year.

It was late afternoon and the couple were still talking, Adrianna Jasmine had even managed to turn the conversation around, in order to discover more about him. She had learnt that Taylor was an avid fan of sport and the gym, which enabled him to maintain his good physique and health. He confessed he enjoyed playing rugby with the boys on Sunday mornings, and that he nearly played professional if it hadn't been for a nasty fall resulting in the end of his career. He also enjoyed weight training, the odd circuit class and of course, good food and wine. In addition, he had discovered that the lovely Adrianna Jasmine had managed to maintain her dream figure by attending Ashtanga Yoga classes, Salsa once a week and running on Hampstead Heath whenever she had a free moment. She didn't mention that broomstick riding kept her inner thighs in great shape; he would only have thought she were off her head with red wine and liquors if she had, though.

It was becoming late and as much as Taylor would have been happy to stay in the comfy lounge, he asked her if she wanted to go anywhere else and if she had any plans. She shrugged her shoulders as she deliberated.

"I want to go somewhere and have some fun!"

Taylor smiled and sat back into his chair beaming at this petite and beautifully put together creature.

"OK," he said with a twinkle in his eye, "what do you have in mind?"

Clementine Poppleapple's Sangria, seriously over 18's!
One big bowl!
1 litre of your favourite red wine
4 tablespoons sugar
2 shot glasses of white Martini Rossi
2 shot glasses Cognac
1 shot glass of Cointreau
1 bottle of lemonade
4 fresh lemons sliced
4 fresh orange sliced
Add a tray of ice cubes to the mix, then get a whopping great spoon and stir it well
This particular recipe will serve around 8 or 9 glasses

'I'd drink this one slowly, party people, because it could very well blow your head off!'
(Clementine Poppleapple, 2008)

Chapter 25
Living La Vida Loca

It was 6pm and the pair had clumsily made their way out into the freshness of the night. They walked arm in arm, laughing and joking towards Victoria tube station, stopping briefly for a packet of Wrigley's spearmint gum. They chatted and sat close together on the tube until they reached Covent Garden, where Adrianna Jasmine then leapt up, took charge and steered Taylor expectedly towards their first stop of the evening: The Gardening Pub!

"What do you fancy to drink?" asked the witch with a cheeky grin

"Err... a pint of bitter please," replied Taylor. When the barman came over, Adrianna Jasmine cheerfully asked for a pint of bitter and a whiskey and coke for her. She paid the bill and the two of them made their way over to a table. They plonked themselves down and drank their drinks, giggled and gossiped. They sat closely together, canoodling like two lustful teenagers; in fact, they appeared to be so hot for one another they looked as if they could revive the dead! They drank a few more rounds in the Garden Pub, before Adrianna Jasmine dragged Taylor off to the Punch and Judy for another and then another and another.

"OK, you're the boss," Taylor saluted playfully. "Lead me to the Punch and Judy." Adrianna Jasmine stood up, put her black leather coat on wrapped her scarf around her neck. When she'd finished buttoning up, she stood and stared at Taylor who was smiling up at her admiringly.

"I must say, Adrianna Jasmine and I hope you don't mind, but you look so sexy in that coat, you remind me of that woman from Allo Allo!"

Adrianna Jasmine began to giggle like a piglet, "Who? The one in bed with the trumpet?"

"No!" exclaimed Taylor, "the German one, Helga!"

"Huh," said Adrianna Jasmine mischievously, "yes, and who knows, there could very well be a kinky surprise underneath." She moved an inch closer towards his thumping heart, "like stockings and suspenders," she whispered seductively.

Taylor swallowed hard, he was picturing Adrianna Jasmine in black lacy underwear, stockings and suspenders.

"Come on," he said, "I need a drink, badly!" and proceeded to lead Adrianna Jasmine outside. As they stepped out of the door, the cold hit them both like a bullet and Adrianna Jasmine found herself snuggling up into the safety of Taylor's arms. *At last*, the pair thought simultaneously, *body contact*! They walked quickly with Adrianna Jasmine shivering and chattering nonstop about this, that and everything, and with Taylor simply listening and losing himself in the scent of her luscious, thick as treacle hair.

"OK we're here!" announced Adrianna Jasmine, "I feel a shot coming on." Her extreme likeness for drink tonight was even shocking *her*, but hell, when in Rome. *I'm celebrating my life, I'm celebrating being alive*!

She pulled him into the third pub of the night, the Frog and Spawn, where the two continued to drink, flirt and laugh. Adrianna Jasmine had Taylor in fits of laughter, she was very funny, so different from the reserved persona that she usually adopted; her mother would have been so proud! She told Taylor about her mother and her family, being careful not to mention their special talents. She did impressions of her mother's voice, described her cousin, Clementine Poppleapple, and the fact her father tinkled on the piano for a living!

"I'd love to meet them," he enthused.

Adrianna Jasmine smiled, "Well I'm sure you will one day. Come on, drink up. We're off to our final destination!"

Ten minutes later they were in the authentic Cuban night club and eatery, Vino 2 Mojito. Taylor could hear live music and vigorous drum beats from inside the club which immediately vibrated through his body, this was going to be interesting!

Adrianna Jasmine led Taylor to the front of the queue and, thanks to her mother being a regular at the club and a friend of the brawly bouncer Leonardo, who was at student Sicily's drama school, they walked straight in!

"Well, at least she's good for something," mused Adrianna Jasmine. Leonardo ushered them to a table near the band. Taylor was impressed.

"You hungry?" yelled Adrianna Jasmine over the band, Taylor nodded frantically. It had been hours since their exquisite meal at Hotel 78 and with all the booze and flirty behaviour, their tummies grumbled greedily. A waiter soon sashayed over and planted a kiss on Adrianna Jasmine's flushed cheek.

"Hey, beautiful!" said the waiter happily with a smile. "It's great to see you, you look hot." Adrianna Jasmine playfully battered her eye lids and giggled.

"Thanks, you don't look too much of a piñata yourself, Carlos. Make sure you dance with me later, ok? Oh, and get Estella to whip this one into shape, too!"

Carlos raised his eyebrows, "You think he'll be able to handle Estella? She's wild!" Taylor had no idea what they were talking about, but seemed pretty interested in Estella. By the sound of it she was either a Latin lady boy, or a saucy minx who wouldn't look out of place on Strictly Come Dancing. "Anyway beautiful, what can I get you two to drink?" before Taylor could blink, Adrianna Jasmine yelled out, "Two mojitos!"

"No problemo," said Carlos, "you want food?"

"Yeah, just bring us a platter for two, that'll be great, Carlos."

"OK, coming right up." He disappeared into a cloud of music, lights and people.

Two mojitos arrived fast and furiously and were consumed dangerously quickly, resulting in Adrianna Jasmine suggesting that they try every flavour in the house. Taylor simply surrendered and said he'd try a strawberry one next, what the hell, if he was going to die of alcohol poisoning, he might as well do it with a bang. The platter arrived as their second batch of Mojitos made their grand entrance and the pair tucked into patatas bravas, breaded calamaris, muscles, lemon chicken, olives, chicken paella, chorizo in red wine, hot almond, dates wrapped in bacon and fresh bread and salad. The pair licked and smacked their lips as they tucked greedily into the scrumptious feast. They looked like any other couple in love, comfortable and totally ravenous. Once the platter was devoured, the pair opted for their third Mojito, an orange flavoured one this time, before hitting the dance floor. They were both stark staring raving plastered and it was a miracle that they could stand, but nonetheless the uplifting Cuban music somehow guided their feet and swayed their hips. Adrianna Jasmine was a fantastic dancer, she moved with a natural grace and rhythm to the music, her perfect bottom swishing to and fro to the beat of the bongos. Then Carlos jumped in and soon the pair were fired-up in a partnership of flamenco and passion. Taylor watched admiringly, even though his partner had been temporarily snatched from him, he could have watched her all night. However, unexpectedly, a black-haired beauty with rich, chocolate brown skin and a body to die for, grabbed his hands and pulled him onto the dance floor.

"Hola, I'm Estella!" she shouted and began to lead Taylor into sexy a Salsa. Surprisingly, Taylor was rather good, in fact, very good!

"You sly old fox!" thought Adrianna Jasmine; she yelled over, "hey, you never said that you could dance!" Taylor threw his head back and laughed, he had never had so much fun.

"Hey, I needed to keep something as a surprise. You know everything from my date of birth to my mother's maiden name." Adrianna Jasmine laughed and turned her attention towards Carlos; she loved every moment and felt a dance-off coming on.

The next thing, a large group had surrounded the two couples and the crowd were cheering for their favourite pair. The two girls tried to out-flick their hips, and the two boys attempted to out-strut one another. If Carlos wasn't flinging Adrianna Jasmine up into the air, Taylor was throwing Estella into the splits! It was one hell of a sight, the crowed were cheering, the bongos were booming and bottoms were giggling. Oh too be young and full of fire! Then the two girls went head to head, causing every man in the place to yell with ecstasy as they watched the sassy pair dance together in a mixture of competitiveness and admiration for one another's beauty. Estella reached over to Adrianna Jasmine and began to dance closely to her, gyrating her hips sensually into the witch's. The dancing became sexually charged and Estella seemed to be leading the witch into succumbing to her dark side. Their lips became close at times, tantalising the crowd, but just leaving enough for the imagination. It was hypnotic; the girls certainly knew how to work their magic! Then Taylor jumped in and swept Adrianna Jasmine off her feet, leaving Estella in the capable hands of Carlos. The pairs continued dancing into a frenzy, setting the floor on fire with every hot step, twirling and whirling, kicking and twisting, until the band reached a crescendo and the dance floor erupted into rapturous applause. The foursome lapped up the attention, laughing and clapping one another admiringly. Estella and Adrianna Jasmine, who were actually good friends, gave each other a joyful hug. They often caused a stir when they danced together and tonight was no exception. After their unique performance, the couple left the dance floor and Taylor and Adrianna Jasmine sat back down again. They were wet from sweat, yet both had never felt so sexy and alive. Adrianna Jasmine looked wild and beautiful, and Taylor hot and muscular under his white shirt. They were breathing deeply, staring intensely into one another's eyes; suddenly they could no longer hear the music, only their beating hearts. They moved closer towards one another, electricity crackling between their lips, how they longed for their bodies to finally interlock…

Hey, you two, these are on the house. Thanks for the show," It was Carlos with another two Mojitos, blackcurrant flavour this time.

"Ooh, lush," cooed the witch, who by now was seeing quadruple and dived towards the straw, missed and got the straw stuck up her nose! Taylor, who couldn't believe out of all the moments he'd been here, now he was interrupted by a blackcurrant Mojito, just shook his head and laughed to himself.

God, I love this girl, he thought.

'Burning sage is the perfect way to purify the home from any evil spirits and unhealthy energies that may have rudely entered without being invited.'
(Bella Bell, 2008)

Chapter 26
Sparkle without Smoke

The pair exited the club in a fit of giggles and chatter, then stumbled into a black cab with Adrianna Jasmine nearly head-butting the window.

"Where to?" asked the taxi driver, a little concerned by the drunken pair.

"Take Adrianna Jasmine home to Islington please," he handed the cabbie some cash, then slid out of the car and peered through the window at his drunken lush. She was laughing and singing, "It's all so Quiet," Bjork, which made Taylor chuckle.

"Night, you!" she said, winding down the window, Adrianna Jasmine was staring deep into his eyes. *Oh those eyes!* thought Taylor, losing himself once more into them, *they're hypnotic.* Adrianna Jasmine then cupped his face into her hands.

"Night, my darling food critic, thank you for a fabulous day," and with that she planted the softest, lighter than a whisper, kiss onto his lips, which made the star-struck Taylor fill with the most overwhelming sense of pleasure he had ever experienced, Adrianna Jasmine smiled sweetly. "Just a little something Carolina Plum taught me!" she smiled before sliding back into her seat. "Upper Street, please driver," and with that she was driven off into the night. Bemused at who or what a Carolina Plum was, Taylor simply stared at the back of the cab, a dopey look over his face.

Twenty minutes later Adrianna Jasmine was home, she had paid the cabbie and managed to shut the door without slamming it too hard. She placed her key into the front door and fumbled around until the key fitted and was able to turn. She let herself in and collapsed onto the floor, laughing and saying "shhhh" to herself over and over again. She decided not to take the lift, as the thought travelling up in a box would make her feel sick and dizzy, so she opted to crawl up the stairs giggling like a baby.

Once at her door she attempted to stand, however, she kept sliding back down again and again, until it got to the point where even *she* got fed up. In the end a very determined witch hoisted herself up the door and pushed her key into the lock, twisted and turned the key and *viola* she was in. "Ah," she sighed closing her eyes, "made it," then she switched on the light, adjusted her eyes to the brightness of the hall then, "ahhhhhhhhhhhhh," she screamed in shock, for standing beneath her feet was a snake hissing wildly, eyes dancing like evil fire. Adrianna Jasmine tried desperately to focus, was it the alcohol, or was there really a snake in her flat. She desperately tried to sober up. *Think Adrianna Jasmine, think!* Her heart was beating fast.

"What the hell are you?" she slurred, then it began to speak to her in a hissing, sly voice.

> Sparkle without smoke, give up hope
> A life of doom, ulpa and rope.
> Cotton, bones, sand and snake,
> Death will be my merry make.
> Broken mirror, a fallen broom,
> Meat with no bone, point at moon.
> Step on a crack,
> Break your mother's back.
> Bad luck to you and all you love,
> Death is near…

"*ARRISE WHITE DOVE!*" yelled out Adrianna Jasmine in a frantic voice and moments later a white dove appeared from nowhere, causing the snake to coil up in fear. Adrianna Jasmine eased her way around the snake, trying to stay alert, her vision was blurred; her mind was fighting to overcome the alcohol. The snake hissed as it sensed that its prey was on the move, which caused the witch to scream in fright. She briefly shut her eyes trying to breathe.

"Think," Adrianna Jasmine, she pleaded with herself again, then with that she remembered what to do, she made a frenzied scramble to the fridge where she lunged for the litre bottle of milk. She frantically twisted the lid off the bottle and just as the snake looked ready to strike, Adrianna Jasmine screamed and poured the entire content of the milk over the evil serpent. Adrianna Jasmine stood back and watched in horror as the snake writhed and wriggled in agony, screaming and hissing in pain. Adrianna Jasmine's eyes were like saucers and her mouth was dry as she witnessed the snake melting like plastic in a fire, reduced to goo before completely disappearing, leaving nothing but a puddle of white milk in its wake. Adrianna Jasmine was breathing heavily, her heart still pounding.

"What just happened?" she said aloud. "What the hell was a bad omen doing in my home?"

She stumbled towards her telephone and punched in the numbers for her mother's house. Luckily Sicily and not her father answered the phone, it would have been a bit difficult to explain to her father that a rampant serpent had been thrust into her home and tried to kill her! Sicily, even though it was three o'clock in the morning, answered the phone with her usual energy and aplomb.

"Mum, can sew come snover," slurred the witch, "I need you, real badly."

"Darling?' said Sicily a little concerned about her daughter's speech, "what's going on, its 3 am?"

"A sna-sna snake, mum, a snake in my home, hissing, slithering, speaking!" "What!" cried Sicily as she jumped out of bed.

Henry Forthright Punch, stirred from his slumber, "is everything aright, Sis?" Sicily just kissed her husband on the forehead, "it's just the daughter," Sicily soothed, "she's a bit unwell, nothing to worry about, go back to sleep," and with that Henry Forthright Punch fell back into the pillow and into a deep sleep.

Satisfied that her husband had arrived back in the land of nod, she continued with her phone call. "What do you mean, it spoke, Adrianna Jasmine?"

259

"It spoke," yelled Adrianna Jasmine, "it spoke, OK? Can you please scum over here?" Adrianna Jasmine's head was spinning; she felt sick.

"OK, darling. Mummy's on her way. Just make a circle of salt and sit in the middle of it until I get to you, OK?"

Adrianna Jasmine nodded down the phone and then hung up. She made her way back into the kitchen, careful not to slip on the spilt milk. She reached into a cupboard and located a large box of sea salt. She tensely made her way into her bedroom and poured the salt onto the floor, making a white circle from the granules. She took her little bell from her altar, which was used to ward off evil spirits and bad omens as they hated the sharp, pure clarity of the bell's chimes, and her knife! Then she placed herself into the centre of the circle. She rocked back and forth like a frightened child, chanting auspicious words out loud like, "sandal", "fresh green grass," "unbroken mirror," "conch shell," "honey," "flower" and "fruit."

She wasn't sure how long it took for her mother to arrive, but the witch almost wept with joy as she heard the key in the lock.

"Darling? Where are you?" Sicily found her daughter sitting pitifully in a circle of salt, a deathly shade of white, and green around the gills. It nearly broke her heart

"Ok, chocolate sponge, mummy's here now, there's nothing to fear." She bent down to hug her child and then helped her up from the circle of salt.

Swaying as she stood, Adrianna Jasmine felt as if she were going to be sick and scrambled to the bathroom, where, for the next hour, she had her head down the toilet, puking for England. As Adrianna Jasmine was retching and spewing, Sicily took it upon herself to "clean" the flat. She firstly opened the front door and began to sweep out any negative energy with a broom. Then she set light to a large bundle of sage until it began to smoulder, she blew out the orange embers in order to let off a fragrant smoke and, working anti clockwise, proceeded to walk around the flat, waving the sage and chanting.

"Spirits of the watch tower, guard my child tonight, she shall not be harmed. Spirits of the watch tower guard this home tonight, it shall not be harmed. Spirits of the watch tower banish all evil, all shall not be harmed."

After Sicily was satisfied that she had thoroughly smoked out the evil presence, she offered bread as thanks to the household guardians. Unfortunately Adrianna Jasmine only had garlic bread left over in the freezer, but it was better than nothing. She lit a cinnamon incense stick; then made her way into the bathroom to find her daughter's head still hanging over the toilet bowl.

"Oh to be young," she sighed. "Where did you go tonight, then? I take it your interview was, how I should say...entertaining!" Adrianna Jasmine raised her head from the toilet bowl, a little smile curled from the corners of her mouth.

"It was fab-you-lous!" then she flopped back towards the toilet bowel, hitting her cheek on the lid. "OUCH," she moaned.

Sicily sighed, "Stay there, you *also* need to be cleansed, young lady," and she began to draw a bath.

Adrianna Jasmine nodded. "Oh yes, I think I do, but mum, I did have a lovely night tonight, shame that horrible snake went and spoilt it."

Sicily thought her heart was going to break again.

"Yes, well you did very well, my lolly pop, considering you're sloshed, but the nasty snake has all gone now and when you're in your bath, you can tell me all about your day." Adrianna Jasmine stuck her thumb up in approval and then shot her head down the toilet in order to throw up for the last time that night.

As Adrianna Jasmine's head was lolloping by the toilet bowl, Sicily set to casting a circle in the bathroom by calling the four elements, earth, wind, water and fire, and lit a lavender candle. She sprinkled dried lavender into the bath and popped a camomile tea bag into the water: Adrianna Jasmine was out of fresh camomile flowers, so she had to improvise. Sicily then added some dried rosemary and a big squirt of jiff lemon into the mix, improvisation was once again called for, of course, there were no fresh lemons.

"Call yourself a witch, my girl, or caterer, for that matter?" said Sicily with mock disapproval, before gently undressing her and delicately placing her daughter into the warm soothing water. "Now sit back and relax, Adrianna Jasmine," advised her mother, "and take three deep breaths." Adrianna Jasmine sucked in three lungfuls of air. After her deep breaths, she opened her eyes and felt more like her old self. She was alert, lucid and the double vision had now blended back into one.

"Hello!" said her mother with a wry smile, "welcome back to the realm." Adrianna Jasmine nodded at her mother.

"Hello!" she said, hers eyes set like stone. "Right, now who the hell broke into my home?"

'Not all of us can afford a designer wardrobe, but there is one thing that will help us stand out from the crowd and that's our scent. Treat yourselves to a mysterious and desirable perfume and allow your unique fragrance to trail behind the masses and linger in their minds forever.'
(Kristobella Poppleapple, 2008)

Chapter 27
High Fashion and Plastic Food

Adrianna Jasmine woke to the sound of someone rustling about in her wardrobe: it was her mother seeking out some ensemble to wear for work.

"Morning, pom puff," said Sicily full of beans, "sorry to raid your closet, but I need something to wear for work, darling, it's too much of a nuisance to go all the way home to change."

Adrianna Jasmine waved her hand dismissively as she slowly peeled herself up from under the duvet; her brain was swimming about inside her painful skull. She would be requiring a Citrus Bang-Bang Boom shower today. Tempted to stay in bed, Adrianna Jasmine made her way tentatively to the bathroom and ran her shower.

"Ooh, that hits the spot," said the witch as the warm jets massaged her aching body and the lemon fragrance livened up her senses; ten minutes later she was the witch she once was.

"Oh, that's better!" said Sicily approvingly when she saw her daughter wrapped up in fluffy bath robe and head towel. "Now you look like Adrianna Jasmine and not some drunken floozy!" She tinkled a laugh and Adrianna Jasmine poked her tongue out as she began to towel dry her hair.

"Hope you don't mind, pear drop," said Sicily who was now dressed to impress in a pair of pinstriped trousers, red fitted cashmere V-neck, red ankle boots and a fake Gucci scarf, "but mummy is very appreciative that you let her borrow your clothes. I'll pop them all back to you washed and neatly pressed sometime during the week, ok?"

Adrianna Jasmine, not really caring, shrugged her shoulders. "Whatever, mother."

"And don't worry about that nasty little witch," Sicily added casually. "I've seen to it but I'm afraid she will die the next time she tries something like that, darling. So don't be surprised if there's a sudden death in the near future."

Adrianna Jasmine shook her head in disbelief at her mother.

"Goddess," she said to Sicily, "you're like a schizophrenic, you are! One minute you're like Tinkerbelle on poppers and the next the princess of darkness!"

"Well, at least with my two personalities, darling, I'll never be lonely. Byeee!" She departed in a cloud of Tallulah Toffee's Bella Frutti perfume and shot off towards the tube.

Adrianna Jasmine spent her morning at the coffee shop making apple crumble, white chocolate mousse cake, rich chocolate brownies and rose petal cupcakes. The rose petal cupcakes were truly delicious, as the cake mix was actually made with essence of rose oil and decorated with sugar-coated rose petals. She chatted with Sarah and brought her friend up to date with all the drama. Sarah was pleased that her friend was succumbing to the power of love, but concerned about the snake and, more to the point, that Sicily was ready to kill!

After her cakes were cooled, iced, decorated and displayed, Adrianna Jasmine caught a tube over to South Kensington to collect the dresses that Kristobella had personally picked out for her to wear at the photo shoot. Whilst in the shop, Adrianna Jasmine tried on various exquisite pieces. Her favourite, as she twirled about, was the beautiful dark, dark blue, floor-length, halter neck gown, which cascaded into several layers of chiffon. It was adorned with a fabulous chiffon gypsy-esque sash that swept around her bottom and tied loosely at the front. She was ready for the pages of Fantastico Banquetto.

That evening Adrianna Jasmine opted for a quiet night, a pre-made salad from Marks and Sparks and a rose cupcake for her supper. She had heard from Taylor via text, which thrilled her immensely, and giggled when he explained just how rough he had been that day and that he still felt terrible. Apparently he, too, had thrown up frequently, missed work the next day and woke up at 2pm to a string of voicemails from an angry boss. Luckily, he didn't get into too much trouble.

Tula Hoopla woke Adrianna Jasmine up at 6am with a silly joke: "What do you call a pirate without an eye?"

"I don't know," said Adrianna Jasmine as she rolled over towards the radio, "Prate!"

"Ha ha," giggled the witch and jumped out of bed, she was excited and happy this morning. She felt good, it was the day of her photo shoot and she would see Taylor again! She ran herself a nice bath and poured some Tallulah Toffee's Float Away Holiday into the hot water, in order to create that just come back from holiday, sun kissed glow. As she luxuriated in the hot water, she soon found herself frolicking on a pink sandy beach, adorning a white teeny bikini, sipping a refreshing Mojito with Taylor. They were in absolute paradise and life was perfect. As the water began to cool, she gently drifted back to reality, then smiled as she looked down at her body. Her skin was now kissed by the sun and glowed with radiance. She followed her tanning session with a thorough facial cleanse using Tallulah Toffee's Subterranean Cooling Bianca Mud, followed by a Zeal and Peel exfoliation mask.

"Yes," she mused, "the makeup artist would adore working on such perfect silky skin today." Then she massaged a splodge of It'll be Alright on the Night shampoo into her hair, followed by a dollop of Banana Dream and Brazil Nut Thick Shake Conditioner, to create a bit more bounce to the ounce. She rinsed away any soapy residue, set about shaving her legs and underarms, rinsed off again, then proceeded to dry and dress.

Half an hour later she was dressed casually in skinny jeans, warm boots, casual sweater, scarf and warm coat and as it was a special day, Adrianna Jasmine decided to treat herself to a cab. Well, she wasn't going to catch a tube, darling, she was a star for the day! It was great fun as she pulled up outside the Conran Shop, she was greeted by the dashing Taylor who immediately took her into his arms and hugged her tightly, resulting in an instant swoon from the witch. He then proceeded to whisk her onto a bustling set, filled with lights, cameras and plenty of action. At once the director, Todd, came over to greet her with a vigorous hand shake and bucketfuls of energy. He was about forty and struggled to pronounce his r's.

"Ad-wee-anna Jasmine," he gweeted her warmly, "how good it is to meet you. Let me in-twow-deuce you to the hair and makeup artists."

Immediately her hairdresser Aluino, an uproarious thirty-something-year-old from Tenerife, came bounding towards her.

"Ooh, look at those locks," he purred when he met the witch. "Ooh, let me get my fingers entwined around every follicle." Aluino reached out and began to stroke and play with Adrianna Jasmine's mane, he looked deep into her eyes, "ooh I could do some damage," he breathed dramatically; Adrianna Jasmine looked terrified! He began to giggle and squeezed her arm with assurance, "you're fabulous, sweetie, fabulous. Oh, I can't wait to work my magic. Mind you, not that we'll need much of it with *your* hair! What *do* you use on it, it's so thick and shiny, I want to twirl it around on a fork like spaghetti and eat it."

Before Adrianna Jasmine could answer, Taylor whisked her away towards the makeup chair, driving their way through a surge of colourful people ranging from lighting technicians, PA's, assistants and the set designer, Greta. Greta was an attractive middle-aged, blonde Bohemian from former East Germany.

Adrianna Jasmine plonked herself onto the makeup chair, feeling delirious and dizzy amongst the chaos as, Pepper, the makeup artist from Manchester, who was on loan from "Oi" cosmetics, greeted her warmly by the hand. She was dressed in black boot cut jeans, with a black fitted T shirt and heavy red DM boots. She wore outrageous cherry red lipstick, mad, bright orange and yellow eye shadows and her hair was short, spiky and pink! She also seemed to be heavily into piercing and tattoos. She had a diamond stud on the right side of her nose, a hoop pierced through her eyebrow and a tongue piercing. Adrianna Jasmine also counted at least eight silver studs on her left ear, and a mammoth nine on her right! Still, for some reason, she wore it well and would have probably looked weird without it.

"Well, hello there, beautiful. Aren't you the one with plump lips, sexy eyes, gorgeous smile and to-die-for skin?"

Adrianna Jasmine smiled bashfully.

"I couldn't agree more," said Taylor admiringly. Adrianna Jasmine blushed. She suddenly felt very overwhelmed and girlishly buried her head into Taylor's chest. He placed a deep kiss on the side of her forehead. "OK, champagne, I think!" he said enthusiastically and went to find a glass of bubbly for the star. He returned with a cold glass of Veuve Clicquot and handed it to the grateful witch. She smiled, took a healthy gulp and closed her eyes as the warmth and pleasure from the bubbles kissed the insides of her body.

"OK, what you wearing, sweetie?" inquired Pepper. Already feeling a gentle buzz from her gulp of champers, Adrianna Jasmine told Pepper that she was going to wear her dark blue dress. "Blue hey?" said Pepper, "right, let's get creative with the blue pots!" She wasn't sure exactly what Pepper was doing, but Adrianna Jasmine found that she trusted this girl implicitly; she had the feeling that Pepper was going to make her look sensational.

As Adrianna Jasmine looked up, Pepper began to apply smoky black eye liner to her lower eye line and Aluino, armed with a pair of pink GHD's, expertly twirled and twisted Adrianna Jasmine's hair around the flat irons.

"Oh, fabulous darling," cooed the hairdresser, as strands of Adrianna Jasmine's hair fell into alluring, bouncy curls. "You look like Susanna Hoffs from the Bangles, you know, walk like an Egyptian?"

He then began to take small stiff steps forwards and backwards mimicking the sand dance. The witch began to giggle.

Thirty minutes later Adrianna Jasmine was standing fully dressed in her screen goddess gown, and beautiful bouncing curls tumbling down her back. She stood a respectful model height thanks to her skyscraper Karen Millen's and she certainly would have given a model a run for her money.

Taylor, who was talking to Todd and sipping a coffee, stopped mid-sentence when he caught sight of the lovely creature standing a few feet away from him. She really did possess a magical quality. He smiled admiringly at her and felt his heart swell with pride. She was his discovery, his protégé, perhaps his love? He wanted nothing more than to bundle her up in bubble wrapping and keep her out of harm's way, and other men!

Adrianna Jasmine was whisked over to one of the display kitchens that had been decorated with colourful cupcakes, a giant strawberry tart, lattice topped apple pie, chocolate swirled cheese cake, triple layered chocolate cake, fruits of the forest mille-feuille, blackberry, strawberry and orange fruit pastry, a tray of strawberries dipped in white chocolate, and mini doughnuts dipped in pink icing and sprinkled with hundreds and thousands.

"Mmmmm," said Adrianna Jasmine hungrily as she reached out to touch the glistening strawberries towered on top of the crumbly flan, "this all looks delicious." "No!" came a piercing cry from afar, "don't touch the food!"

Adrianna Jasmine froze in fear. With the speed and grace of an Olympic diver, Greta hurled herself towards Adrianna Jasmine. In shock, Adrianna Jasmine slapped her arms down to the sides of her thighs. She wanted to cry!

"I'm sorry," she grovelled through wide, innocent eyes. "I won't touch your display again."

Breathlessly, with a heaving chest, Greta shook her head.

"No, no you don't understand. I'm not vorried if you touch the display, but you must not eat it, the food, you see, is *highly* inedible. I thought you vere going to eat it!"

Stunned, Adrianna Jasmine just shook her head, "No, no, I wasn't going to eat it," she fibbed. "I just, err, wanted to err…" she trailed off.

"Look, smell!" said Greta as she trussed the strawberry tart towards Adrianna Jasmine's unrepentant nose. Immediately the witch was hit by the smell of nail polish, hairspray and was that formaldehyde? "It's to keep the food looking fresh and photogenic for the cameras, even food needs a touch up here and there!" Adrianna Jasmine gulped and looked closer at the food, the berries were all made out of plastic, the chocolate cake's icing smelt of varnish and the cream inside the mille-feuille looked unmistakably similar to that of shaving cream. "You might have been killed," expressed Greta neurotically, "there's more toxic substances in this food than a nuclear bomb!"

"Oh, OK!" nodded Adrianna Jasmine like a scolded six year old, "I'll look, but I won't touch."

"Good girl," said Greta with an abrupt pat on Adrianna Jasmine's shoulder, then she hurried off to boss her terrified PA about.

Adrianna Jasmine took a deep breath before the photographer, Fela (pronounced Fay la), who was approximately 4ft 11 inches tall, began to give direction.

"Alright, gorgeous, I want a full length shot of you in that dress, come and stand by the side of the counter, that way I'll get you and the food." Adrianna Jasmine shuffled nervously towards where Fela was directing her to stand. *Goddess,* she thought, *I wish I knew what I was doing.*

"Ok, now smile to me, oh yes, loving it, more with the eyes, give me food, passion, give me treacle tart, and give me chocolate mousse!" Adrianna Jasmine began to laugh and with that she started to relax and enjoy her moment of stardom. "Perfect, beautiful, hand on right hip, lift your chin up, now stand side on, arch your back, stick your bum out a bit, yes, fantastic, let's have a sultry look now, let's give Nigella a run for her crab cakes! Give me a chocolate fountain; give me red hot jalapeño chillies, give me whipped cream and sprinkled nuts, oh yes! Give me lashings of vanilla custard and the best piece of beef on the market."   Strangely, Adrianna Jasmine found herself becoming quite turned on by all this reference to food, how sad was she! Still, the thought of runny honey drizzling over wild strawberries, or the sound of a big German sausage sizzling in a pan could be classed as highly erotic to some. She began to find the inner confidence to pose for the camera. "Fabulous, ok, I think the desserts shots are done, now onto cocktails, GRETA! Get out the Cosmopolitans!"

In a whirl of excitement, Adrianna Jasmine was whisked off by Pepper, Aluino and wardrobe, thrust behind a screen and changed into her red cocktail dress, another stunning ensemble picked out by

Kristobella. She came out from behind the screen to a chorus of oohs and aahs from Pepper and Aluino.

"Wow," complimented Pepper, "that's looks amazing." And she hurried her over to the makeup chair, so she could wipe away the electric blue from her eyes and replace it with a smoky charcoal. As Pepper then applied we- looking red lipstick to Adrianna Jasmine's juicy lips, Aluino re-tousled her hair.

"Greta!" yelled Todd, "get all this dessert and pudding crap out of here, now! Bring me Mojitos, electric blue liquids in tall glasses with cherries and umbrella's, Cosmopolitans, Singapore Slings and trendy-looking drinks that wouldn't look out of place in a posh Soho bar!"

Greta and other members of the photo shoot team all hurried to clear the area and replaced the plastic deserts with luscious, lip-smacking cocktails. Greta caught Adrianna Jasmine eying the cocktails up. "Don't even think about it!" she warned, "they're made with watered down paint and windowlene!"

Adrianna Jasmine promised not even to take a sniff, before being bustled over to pose with a pink cocktail in a tall glass, decorated with an umbrella and black straws.

"Now," enthused Fela, "give me sophistication in a New York piano bar, give me 1940's Hollywood, show me Ava Gardner, show me Havana, actually, show me a bit of leg." Adrianna Jasmine, who was propped up on a stool, turned her body to the side, crossed her right leg over her left and allowed her dress to ride up ever so slightly, just to keep the readers hungry for more. "Baby, you're smoking like a rasher of bacon, keep it coming, yes, yes, yes!" Adrianna Jasmine was in fits of giggles, and in the end she had to be removed from the stool for fear that she would fall off. "Ok, I want a hot chocolate with lashings of whipped cream; I want chocolate sprinkles, flakes and tall, large decorative mugs. I want Irish coffees, liquors, brandy and Amaretto, flaming Sambuca with the coffee beans and all the trimmings, come on, people, bring it to me now, now, now."

Feeling like a princess, Adrianna Jasmine was once again whisked away in order to change for her next shot. Her look this time was casual and comfortable, as she was dressed in baby blue sweat pants, teamed with a clean, white fitted T shirt.

Aluino expertly swept her hair up loosely, allowing tendrils of curls to fall effortlessly down the sides of her face and neck. Pepper wiped off the heavy makeup and went for a pretty, neutral look with soft pink lips. She was placed onto a large squashy sofa, where she sat cosily, pretending to drink a large creamy hot chocolate with marshmallow and chocolate bobbing about on top. In fact, it was very strong coffee, topped with shaving foam and mini marshmallows that had been colourfully enhanced with pink nail varnish.

Taylor watched her intensely, not missing a heartbeat. Out of all the outfits he liked this one the most. She looked so natural, cute and pretty. Oh, to run over to her, whisk her away and lock her up in a luxury hotel room for the week, only using the phone to order room service. *Mmmmm, that's not such a bad idea!* he thought smiling to himself.

"Fabulous, darling," gushed Fela, "that one was easy, now go and change into something that cries out 'I can cook and still look like a sex siren.' I'm thinking the talents of Delia Smith but with the looks of Cindy Crawford. Go. Go. Go!!!"

Adrianna Jasmine presented Fela with a firm nod as she was rapidly whisked away to change into her final ensemble. She opted for a black and white satin 1950s style dress, black high heeled shoes and red pinny over the top. Her hair was swept up in an elegant beehive, set off with a pair of drop diamond earrings. Her makeup consisted of liquid eyeliner, matte red lips and false eyelashes,

"Ooh, you're a young Liz Taylor, aren't you?" gushed Aluino. "Ooh, I'd kill for those hips." Looking every inch the hour glass sex siren, Adrianna Jasmine sauntered over to the set for her fourth and final shoot of the day. She was ready for her close up.

"Hold it!" shouted Todd, the crew all became silent. "You know what would be really fun?" The crew all looked at him with baited breath, "if Adrianna Jasmine had a husband! You know to add a bit of fun to the shoot!"

There was stirring and chatter amongst the cast and crew, then nods of excited approval, "Yes, that's what we need," said Fela, "the perfect husband for the perfect housewife." He thought for a few moments, "I've got it!" he announced snapping his fingers. "Taylor, get your butt over here now, it's all too perfect! The food critic of Fantastic Banquetto playing the part of the husband to the up-and-coming, sexy young chef. It's fantastic, it's quirky, it's fun; you're doing it!" And without argument, Taylor was thrust over to Pepper, who immediately began to smear foundation and blusher over his bewildered face. A red Polo neck sweater was thrust over his head and Aluino began to gel and style his hair.

"Oh, it's Paul Newman to complement our Liz Taylor, Taylor," said Aluino. "Oh, I've been dying get my hands on your follicles all day!" Taylor looked horrified, Aluino began to chuckle. "No seriously, darling," said Aluino, "it'll be like watching Cat on a Hot tin roof in 3D with you two!"

Taylor wanted to speak but nothing came out, how he wound up being a model for the day, he couldn't quite comprehend. The only consolation was that soon he would be close enough to Adrianna Jasmine to breathe in her intoxicating scent. And breathe in he did! The pair gazed into one another's eyes over a flaming Christmas pudding, laughed adoringly at one another as they carved a mock Christmas turkey and giggled as they pulled one another's crackers. They literally melted into one another's souls as Taylor stood behind Adrianna Jasmine and wrapped his strong arms around her tiny waste. The two gazed full of Christmas joy at the camera.

"Oh, fabulous," cried out Fela, "you're both like a pair of sizzling sausages and sexier than a raspberry pavlova. Taylor, you're like a piece of thick beefsteak and Adrianna Jasmine you're the delicate all-butter puff pastry, enveloped around his hunk of manliness." The pair were in fits, where did he come up with all this? "Oh, Adrianna Jasmine, you're whipping his cream and Taylor you're basting her turkey with hot, thick, salty gravy. Oh, yessss!" Then finally, after nearly four hours of long arduous posing, Fela shouted out the immortal words that everyone was dying to hear: "That's a wrap!" Everyone cheered and clapped with joy. "Thanks for doing that," said Fela genuinely, "I think the readers will love it, what with you being Fantastico Banquetto's most well-known feature writer; it shows you're a good sport and totally up for a laugh, plus," he winked playfully, "the ladies will love you!" Taylor raised his eyebrows.

"You don't think they'll see it as a bit corny?" Fela looked shocked at the comment.

"No way," he firmly stated, "when you see these photos, you'll think they're anything but corny, its high fashion with food, darling, all the way, you'll see!!!"

Taylor chuckled, "I'll take your word for it," then turned towards Adrianna Jasmine, busily handing out her business cards to Pepper and Aluino.

"Please come into the coffee shop some time and please stay in touch!" urged the witch, she had grown extremely fond of the pair and was desperate to treat them to one of her cakes and a large cup of cappuccino. With frantic nods the pair agreed that they would meet up again; they were already looking forward to it!

"Adrianna Jasmine!" she looked over to see Taylor smiling. She excused herself from Pepper and Aluino and walked over to him. "You hungry?" he asked her. Adrianna Jasmine thought for a moment then realised her tummy was actually on the verge of eating itself, and nodded.

"Grab your things," said Taylor, "how does a late lunch at Hotel 78 sound?"

Two witches meet in a hospital, one is a patient.

Witch 1: Oh, thank you so much for coming, the nurse said they called you.

Witch 2: I came straight away, are you alright?

Witch 1: Yes. I'm okay now, although I did have a rather funny turn, I must say. One moment I was wandering around Covent Garden as fresh as a daisy, the next I'm on my hands and knees in Neal's Yard.

Witch 2: Why were you on your hands and knees?

Witch1: I came over all sick, it was awful, and I've never experienced sickness like it. I think my body just shut down, it couldn't handle the enormity of it.

Witch 2; Oh my Goddess that sounds terrible!

Witch 1: It was! I must have lost a gallon of water in sweat, you could have wrung my clothes out. It was disgusting: the room spun like a waltzer and the floor appeared to be made of jelly!

Witch 2: Jelly?

Witch 1: Yes, the floor felt all wobbly. Anyway, the last thing I remember... oh, it's all rather fuzzy, was me on my knees, head buried into my arms and trying to weakly shoo the sales assistance from touching me and a vague memory of the ambulance ride. I thought I was dying.

Witch 2: Sounds strange, Hazel, did you eat anything unfamiliar or out of date within the last few hours, perhaps it was food poisoning?

Witch 1: No, I don't believe I did, but they're doing tests, like checking my blood and urine to find out why I became so sick.

Witch 2: Hmmmm, sounds very suspicious, Hazel. You didn't eat anything unusual, and you say nothing you ate was out of date. I wouldn't be surprised if the tests come back clear.

Witch 1: Oh, why's that?

Witch 2: I've been thinking, that's why. I don't personally believe the reason you were sick is physical or viral.

Witch 1: You think I just had a funny turn, then, do you? Well I don't think I did! You just think of the last time you felt really, really sick, then times it by fifty and I bet you it wouldn't even come close to how I felt!

Witch 2: Calm yourself, Hazel, I'm not having a go at you, all I'm saying is that your sickness might have been caused by something far more serious.

Witch 1: What are you insinuating?

Witch 2: Well, I personally believe you were cursed, to me it sounds rather like a witch has done this to you, Hazel, and a powerful one at that.

Witch 1: …you're not thinking?

Witch 2: Yes, I am, come to think about it, where were you again?

Witch 1: Covent Garden!

Witch 2: Exactly! And who works in that tacky coffee shop baking her prize cakes?

Witch 1: The daughter!

Witch 2: Yes, the daughter! She's been circled with some kind of protection spell, and unbeknown to you, you invaded her territory and paid the sticky price.

Witch 1: But why did I pay for it, you're the one who's setting the wheels in motion, I'm just your lackey...as always, and now I've ended up injured. Anyway, what a rotten, cheap, nasty, trick to pull!

Witch 2: Hmmmm, it is. It's been done many a time to ward off enemies, although I have to say marvellously executed, but you are absolutely right, this little... venture *is* all my doing really, yet Poppleapples's spell hexed you too. Very clever.

Witch 1: scoffs

Witch 2: You may scoff, my dear Hazel but think yourself lucky, it could've been far worse, you mark my words.

Witch 1: Lucky! I thought I was going to die.

Witch 2: And in all fairness, I'm surprised you didn't!

Witch 1: What's that supposed to mean?

Witch 2: Well, you're lucky you were only cursed with overwhelming feelings of sickness and nothing more sinister! If there's anything I know about the Poppleapple cackle, is that they don't muck about, they can be vicious, believe me, I know!

Witch1: Oh my, this is getting rather frightening, should we perhaps lie low for a while, at least until it all blows over a bit? Why are you laughing, you look deranged.

Witch 2: Oh it's all too perfect, I couldn't have hoped for more.

Witch1: Stop laughing. (Pause) Why's that?

Witch 2: Oh, wake up, dear cousin. I know you've been ill, but really! It means that the cackle fears for the daughter's safety and in order to keep her safe, they're protecting her with spells and curses.

Witch1: So?

Witch 2: Ugh! Don't you see....Goddess! It means that *Sicily* believes that her daughter is in danger; she is putting all her energy into keeping her daughter safe! Therefore Sicily is unaware that darkness is afoot, she's ripe for the picking, the old bitch is vulnerable!

Witch 1: Oh, I see, ha, ha. Ooh… it's delicious!

'A great way to keep a relative reflection of all those things that have happened in your life is to keep a journal or diary.'
(Doreen Clement)

Chapter 28
Magical Months, The diary of Adrianna Jasmine Poppleapple, Mariposa Forthright-Punch

November 08

After my photo shoot, the delicious Taylor whisked me off to none other but hotel 78! Oh it was bliss. He treated me to a truly magical time. We tucked into sandwiches, cakes and champagne in the hotel's lounge then, well... OK, yes, we stayed overnight in one of the beautiful rooms. Hey! The weather outside was rotten; it only made perfect sense to stay sheltered from the rain! Anyway, the moment the bedroom door was shut, I'm not ashamed to say, we lunged towards one another, feeding our sexual hunger. Oh I still get shivers just thinking about it! Our lips frantically pressed against one another's, hot and alive. And with rapidly beating hearts we kissed and kissed, tongues meeting, massaging and pelvises thrusting. Entangled in a swarm of arms and legs, we began to tear off each other's clothes, right before Taylor pushed me onto the bed which made me to gasp in delight at his power.

He ran his hands all over my skin and licked every square inch of my body with his tongue. Thank goddess I had de-fuzzed that morning! We explored one another's bodies for hours, using hands and fingers, evoking a mixture of pain and pleasure. I don't believe I have ever experienced a higher state of ecstasy in my life, not even using magic. Then, after five hours of nonstop sexual bliss, we collapsed into one another's arms and lay quietly until a hot bath, room service and a movie, beckoned. It had been a perfect night and, I am not embarrassed to say, I play the memory from it over and over again like a record in my mind.

December 08

The December issue of Fantastico Banquetto had been a great success and subsequently my life has been filled with nothing but colour, joy and fantastic work opportunities. The readers had apparently been nothing but "charmed" by me. They had adored my recipes and of course loved Taylor's surprise appearance. The whole shoot had somehow brought a much needed touch of glamour and fun to the public during the miserable credit crunch Christmas. It's all rather thrilling, I must say. The public are calling Taylor and I the new Fanny and Johnnie, except with more attractive names, and as a result, I've been signed up for a 12 month deal with the magazine! Hurrah!!! So this month I was called back to pose for the Health Kick January! I was photographed in fitness gear surrounded by hearty vegetable soups, smoothies and healthy meal ideas. I also got the chance to work with Pepper and Aluino again: those two are truly artists!

December (continued)

Oh I love Christmas! It's been the best ever, what with my new work lined up and, of course, Taylor, my lovely Taylor, my lovely, scrumdeliumptious Taylor. Anyway, due to Emmalina Lucci singing my praises to her exclusive friends about the Halloween party I catered for, I ended up catering a party for an actress-friend of hers. It went down a storm and I spiked the mulled wine with my latest magic sprinkle: Christmas Morning Excitement, designed to take you back to when you were a kid on Christmas morning. Oh, it was tremendous fun, the laughter from the guests was truly infectious, and I can honestly say they had a perfect time. Oh, and I got to see Angelo di Angelo again, as I hired him for the party and guess what: he's only getting married next spring to Hannah! I can't believe it, I'm so happy for them and they've asked me, oh Goddess I'm so excited, to do their wedding cake! Must get cracking with ideas, ASAP!

I also met Taylor's parents this month. I cooked them a sumptuous feast for their thirtieth wedding anniversary at their beautiful apartment in Waterloo, overlooking the Thames. It was so romantic, just the two of them, with Taylor playing waiter for the evening. Although I think he's better at critiquing food than serving it! He made a hell of a mess with the spicy butternut squash soup. His parents, Austin and Patty are lovely. They are typical middle class English, well, his father is. Austin is a retired barrister; Oxford trained and sounds a cross between Winston Churchill and Colin Firth! He favours rugby to football and refers to footballers as fairies in pretty shorts and rugby boys as hardy men who aren't afraid of blood. Patty, his mum, originally from Romford in Essex, is from a working class family but was accepted into a grammar school. She's tall and skinny, with dark auburn hair. They both met in court during a trial, Austin working on the defence and Patty as the courtroom typist; it was love at first sight! However, Patty is now a successful author of three published books: *Love At the Witness Box, The Stubborn Juror* and *Death Penalty*. Hmmmm... I wonder how she will fair with my mother?

Oh, and (joy) I got to meet old Lexi Howler again! Taylor and I were invited to the Oyster Pearl on Christmas Eve for a rather splendid party. Apparently the Howl had caught wind that Taylor was all loved-up with me and demanded that we attend, probably so she could check me out! I caught her eying me up and down in that way women do, especially whilst I was shimmying on the dance floor. Oh well, she'll get over it, but I must say we did have a fantastic night, especially when some girl projectile vomited electric blue puke over Lexi Howler's back. Oh it was horrible! She must have been drinking some cocktail. The girl was shortly asked to exit the building.

Ah Christmas 08; Winter Wonderland in London's Hyde park; going to see Mama Mia, the musical; the New Year's Eve party at Taylor's flat in Shepherds Bush. If my life was a cake, I'd eat it: it's so delicious!

January 09

I made my debut on This Morning so I could advertise the magazine and their recipes. I took to the set and whizzed up a frenzy of berry smoothies, vegetable soups and charmed the pants off the nation with my delectable smile, mysterious eyes and enchanting presence. Well that's what the papers said the next day! The viewers had adored me; never once had a figure on the television screen brought so much sun shine to a living room, even during a gloomy January morning.

Into the bargain, Taylor and I are truly head over heels, madly and frantically in love. How do I know? Well, he told me silly!!! It was at dinner in San Lorenzo over a bowl of spaghetti, very lady and the tramp, and he just came out with it. I can honestly say I have never felt so complete. I am truly astounded at just how powerful love actually is and out of respect for love, I've brought a beautiful picture of the Venus di Milo and placed it with affection on the wall above my altar. Love is now truly worshipped!

Speaking of love, the February feature for the magazine is all about Valentine's Day: Taylor and I were whisked off to the O'Sullivan Castle in Scotland for the photo shoot. We were flown first class, treated to a hearty breakfast on arrival, and then Pepper set to work on my makeup. Aluino, who is a right old pansy when it comes to the cold and spent half the morning huddled over the GHD's to warm his hands, performed his magic on my hair. Oh, and I must tell you about my dresses! Kristobella truly outdid herself this time. She lent me an emerald green, Versace, floor-length chiffon dress, a purple Jason Woo, made from shimmering sequins, with plunging neck line and a Grecian style dark red dress by young designer called DEE-DEE Sugar Cane. She's trying to make her way into the fashion world, so hopefully the magazine will help kick start her career.

Taylor, who looked even more handsome than Sean Connery as 007, wore an elegant tuxedo; oh, he looked intoxicating and it took all my strength not to have ripped his clothes off there and then in a frenzied passion. We were photographed enjoying romantic meals for two, with recipes included, in the castle's dining and drawing rooms. It was a bit cheesy as we gazed adoringly into one another's eyes whilst enjoying creamy, sticky deserts and glasses of fine champagne. But we did have a romp! However, due to this love stuff being so wonderful, I feel it is my duty to spread a little of it to the masses. So, although against my principles, I cast a teensy wincey love spell at the bottom of page 96. Oh, don't be like that! It's not a proper love spell! I convinced the editor to include a small love poem, just below the strawberry seduction picture, which would then be read by the reader, and love in all its many splendid forms would find its way into the reader's hearts. However, and I strongly add, this would not include making a person fall in love with someone against their will, I'm not incompetent, you know! This spell is much more beautiful and subtle.

February 09

The magazine wanted to celebrate Mother's Day, so they asked my mother if she would be interested in posing for a few pictures with her daughter. Of course, she said yes, wild horses wouldn't have kept her away from an opportunity like that. So we partnered up and posed for the camera whilst cooking fancy colourful cakes and chicken soup in perfect mother and daughter harmony. The collection of photos looked wonderful; I must say my mother is very photogenic. Although she's now even more annoying than ever. Just one little photo shoot and she thinks she's an A list celebrity. Oh, she's very difficult!

Now onto more interesting news: Taylor and I enjoyed our first Valentine's together! It was out of this world. We went to see the show, Flamenco Flamenca. One word: astonishing, and then, of course, where else, but back to Hotel 78. Honestly, it's beginning to feel like a second home, that place! Well it was magical nonetheless and not only was I a treated to a sumptuous four-course meal with champagne, but an overnight stay in one of their suites. I am officially the luckiest girl alive. And, oh, Clementine's got piles, ha ha! Apparently the threefold law wasn't too happy about a little spell she cast on her tutor at uni. The poor man was only doing what tutors normally do when handed a red pen and crap work. So she punished him for it: gave him diarrhoea, I think. Silly Clementine. And Sarah has a new man! He's called Sergio Draganoff, he teaches psychology at some university and is half Portuguese, half Latvian. Exotic mix. He's very mysterious, highly intelligent and what with his dark skin and eEstern European features, looks like a sun worshipping vampire. Sarah says she's transfixed by his wisdom and philosophy on the human psyche. Apparently she knows more about herself than ever before because count Draganoff (my nickname for him), psychoanalyses her constantly and listens to her soul. Deep!

March 09

It's official: the public adored my mother. Great, that's going to make her even more hellish. Apparently they had fallen hook, line, and sinker for her perfectly pretty face, bucketful of charm and motherly tenderness that somehow oozed through the pages of the magazine. Hmmmm... sounds suspicious to me. She'll be the nation's favourite mother next! If they only knew what she was really like. Oh I'm going to have rant now. For goddess sake, don't they know that the woman probably dabbles in black magic, somehow fools the threefold law every time, and that she's as dark as Queen Dracula and probably much scarier! It's infuriating. Anyway, moving on, or I'll self-combust.

"Easter Treats" is theme for Fantastico Banquetto's Easter publication. So I posed in a pretty yellow spring dress in front of a beautiful roast chicken feast, flowery Easter cupcakes, sunflowers and homemade Easter eggs. It was a very bright and vibrant shoot, which I hope will evoke optimistic energy and new beginnings. Well, I know it will because I did it again, I cast another little spell. Oh I know but I can't help myself! It's so miserable out there, what with the credit crunch, plummeting property prices and people more aggressive towards fellow men than ever; that's just in England! My spell will encourage people out of any depressive slumps and catapult them into a much more confident and positive state of mind and health. You wait, it'll be the making of this country!

As for Taylor and I, well, we couldn't' be feeling any more cheery, it would probably be illegal if we did! It's rather exciting, you see, we've both been offered the chance to present our own TV shows. We've been meeting with producers and offered the chance to leap out of the pages of a magazine and into the magical world of television. *The delight of Jasmine* is to be shot in a cottage down in

Devon for the whole month of June. Oh, it's so thrilling! Each episode is to be unique; focusing on a theme of cooking that could easily be replicated in the home. Furthermore, there is to be a book with the series and I'm just delirious with delight. Think of all the magical opportunities this could bring. To think, all those homes and families I'll have access to. It would offer me the chance to correct bad eating habits, encourage scared mums into cooking and entice kids to eat their vegetables, oh, the power! Jamie Oliver will be moved to tears. As for my handsome hunk of a food critic, Taylor has been offered a series called *Michelin Star vs. Mamma's Cooking*. The lucky chap is to be sent to Rome, Paris, Barcelona, Amsterdam, Berlin and Madrid. Sampling some of the finest restaurants in the city, then visiting family-run businesses and homes, where Mamma does the "cooking" and compares tastes. It's genius!!! The only snag is that it would take a good six months to shoot and we won't see one another that much. Although I do have hope. "Oh well," he said to me, "best make sure got your passport up to date!" I've always wanted to travel Europe.

April 09

"Toot, toot, little star," came the exuberant voice of my mother down the phone, "how are you, darling?" I had left a message on my mother's mobile informing her about the exciting news regarding my TV show and now she wants to make a guest appearance on it. Honestly! "By the way, darling," she hedged, "I don't suppose mummy has a chance of appearing with you, not on every episode but, you know, the occasional one or two" The cheek of it! "Because, you see, butter nut squash, I think I did rather well, that photo shoot I took part in, apparently your magazine said it was the most popular month ever!" Like she didn't already know. "And I'd like to try my luck at television, I feel I'm ready to move on from still life to action"

"Hmmmm," I said, "well yes I suppose it would be an idea, I'll run it past the producer."

"Make sure you do, dumpling stew, sales were up 20% when mummy took to the glossy print."

"That's probably because you enchanted the pictures," I told her bluntly, which didn't go down at all well. She fought her corner by saying that magic was not to be blamed and that her own natural beauty, charisma and charm wooed the readers. I tell you!!!

"And let's face it, darling," she went on. "I've still got it. Anyway, I'll pop myself on a diet straight away, ready for my grand entrance into the nation's living rooms. Oh yes. This could be it, darling," she said full of rapture, "this could be the moment I get plucked out of C list obscurity and into the arms of Vincent Simone on Strictly Come Dancing."

"C list celebrity!" I scoffed and reminded her that she actually needed to be *famous* to even be classified as a C lister. But she wasn't having any of it.

"Of course I'm famous," she argued back.

"No you're not!" I told her firmly. Well she needs to be told and I reminded her that all she had done was share a three page spread in a food magazine *and* that if weren't for me she wouldn't even have done that.

"Don't be ridiculous, pom-pom," she irksomely continued, oh she's exasperating, "my talents and bottom surely were to be noticed at some point, in order to catapult me into stardom, it was in the star."

Oh, I give up! Anyway, I told her to keep her diary free for the third week of June, just in case.

"OK!" she said, "mummy will be there. Anyway, my little pot of gold at the end of the rainbow, I am famous, whether you like it or not!"

"No you're not!" I reminded her again. But she fought on like Wellington at Waterloo.

"Yes I am," she said defiantly, "I've got my own Blog and Titter page."

Oh it does make me laugh when the old dabble in modern technology; I'm surprised she can use teletext!

May 09

As summer is just around the corner, Fantastico Banquetto did a whole feature celebrating the splendour of summer, with me dressed up like a 1950s pinup girl. I wore a fabulous red '50s-inspired bathing suit, giant sunglasses and oversize summer hat. I winked and smiled tantalizingly at the camera, and sucked Long Island ice tea through a curly wurly straw with my red lip gloss shining like cherries. I can honestly say it was my favourite shoot so far, I felt just like Dita Von Teese. Moreover, I also took the opportunity to treat my readers to a little summer sunshine for themselves. OK, OK, I did it again, I cast another spell, but it's the last time, I promise! It's just that I feel so sorry for people these days and I wanted to treat them to a little holiday happiness, you know, the feelings you receive when the sun is shining warm on your back. When the sky is blue and you haven't a care in the world. I'm sure it'll be appreciated and well received, so no harm done.

Oh yes! Taylor and I went on our first holiday together where we spent two glorious weeks in Cuba. It was fabulous. We spent three nights in Havana and stayed at the famous Hotel National De Cuba, which was once frequented by the likes of Frank Sinatra, Ava Gardner and the notorious Rat Pack. I could almost sense their spirits still partying in true rat pack style, rock stars these days are amateurs compared to those bad boys. Due to arriving late, we opted for a light supper in the gardens, a couple of Mojitos and fun between the sheets. We slept soundly in our large room, which was overlooking the swimming pool and woke up the next day to a scrumptious breakfast. Later, we jumped onto a horse and carriage and were whisked off to visit Ernest Hemmingway's old haunt. That evening we went to see the world-famous Tropicana show, which was nothing short of spectacular, what with the colourful costumes, energetic dance routines and hundreds of dancers that looked like Naomi Campbell cut-outs. Yes, Havana was fascinating and after three nights, we travelled by coach down to Varadero. We enjoyed ten undisturbed days in a luxurious five-star hotel, swam in the warm waters, walked hand in hand along miles of private, white sandy beaches, drank more Mojitos, rode horses in the surf, snorkelled and ate until we were ready to burst. We spent our evenings snuggled up watching cracking thunder and lightning displays by mother earth and listening to the tropical rain. Taylor also treated me to an afternoon swimming with dolphins, which I adored - apart from when a dolphin went to kiss me on the cheek and ended up head butting me on the nose, no wonder sharks hate them!

June 09

Oh, this was fun: I teamed up with Clementine to pose for the July edition of Fantastico Banquetto. She had been desperate to do a bit of modelling and asked if I could pull a few strings. So I did and when the team met her, well what else can I say, they loved her. Mind you, she would have given the girls from the Playboy mansion a run for their money. Clementine, I hate to admit, is smoking hot! I wouldn't be surprised if she lands a modelling contract after this, especially if they print the photos of her wearing the bright orange bikini and kitten heels. We even tried out a couple of shots with me spraying her with a hose, although I doubt they'll print those, they would probably be too provocative. Well anyway, I'm writing my diary now from North Devon, as I'm filming my series! I'm in a gorgeous five bedroomed cottage on a cliff top, with a huge kitchen backing onto a giant garden. Oh, I could just imagine Taylor and I settling down here one day. I can imagine waking up every morning to a view of the rugged Atlantic and growing my very own herbs in the garden. Sarah is, here, too, Pepper and, of course, Aluino. The only person who is not here is my Taylor, he's in Paris. Although he phoned me at lunch and is unfortunately experiencing a few hiccups. It appears he will be in Paris much longer than the production team had anticipated. They're being held up by some silly, greedy little backstreet restaurant owner.

"He's demanding more money, and a change to the contract," he sighed tiredly down the phone to me, I told him to walk away and find another backstreet restaurant to use, after all, they're in Paris; there must be hundreds of them. But alas, no, Taylor's boss is adamant, he wants that restaurant. Apparently the restaurant is filled with history, as it was open for business during the German occupation; it was believed to be a favourite haunt amongst the German soldiers and generals. However, unbeknown to the Germans, the restaurant's basement was home to one of the most sought after group of French resistance fighters. Ha! Right under the Hun's noses!

"It's' got a history and it's stunning," Taylor told me, "it's very quintessential, yet quaint and the food is to die for. But, like most people, when cash is thrown into the mix, they get greedy." Poor Taylor. I told him that I wished I was there with him to make him feel better.

Strawberry Tumble cottage is a wonderful place. I just adore lunch times where Sarah and I enjoy a feast of ham and cheese crusty rolls followed by delicious Victoria sponge cake. We chat and laugh in the sunshine, with me twittering on about Taylor, and Sarah twittering on about count Draganoff. It's very serious their relationship, you know. She's off to Latvia next month to meet the parents, I advised her to wear a clove of garlic around her neck and to keep a bottle of holy water close by, just in case. Oh, it's very peaceful at the cottage, you can just drown in relaxation until the immortal two words that have been the bane of my life since the day I was born, appeared from out of nowhere, and broke the tranquil bliss.

"Hello, darling!" Yes, it was my mother zooming towards us like Cruella Deville on amphetamines. She planted two lip smacking kisses on poor Sarah's sun flushed cheeks and then proceeded to vigorously pinch and shake my cheeks as if she were shaking meat from the bone. She's so annoying, and to make matters worse, she's only gone and got herself a bloody assistant!

"Let me introduce you to Effie," she announced, "I've pinched her from school, she's my assistant."

Sarah and I both looked up in astonishment as we caught sight of a lanky loser of a girl, with watery blue eyes, limp mousy brown hair and the personality of a drippy tap, standing next to my mother. What on earth did she need an assistant for?

"Goddess, you only pretended to knock up a few cakes whilst wearing a flowery pinny!" I cried.

"Be that as it may, raspberry ripple," she said. "Everyone in the TV business has one and even you've got one." And with that she looked patronisingly at Sarah. I could have screamed.

"Oh, for goddess sake," I yelled, "she's not my assistant."

"Course not, darling," she said with a condescending look. "So when do we start filming? I need to wash and brush up, hair and makeup needs adjusting and then there's the certain little matter of wardrobe and…" This is where it gets really funny!

The silly old witch was under the impression that she was to be filming that very same day. However, as it happened, her *assistant*, Effie, had got the dates mixed up. When she found out, my mother proceeded to turn sharply towards Effie, who at this point was already frantically searching through the giant Filofax, desperately trying to find out if the dates were incorrect. Then, oh I must admit at this point I did feel for her, Effie looked up with utter fear in her eyes and confirmed the mistake.

"Ah!" said my mother calmly, "you're sacked!" We did try to stand up for Effie, but mother was having none of it.

"The girl's meant to be my *PA*, darling," she fought. "She's meant to organise my life, be on the button! She should know if I'm about to break wind before I do. Honestly! No, she's out of here," she said. "Sorry, Effie, but it's a dog eat dog business, the quicker you learn that, the better you'll succeed. I'll see you Monday at college; don't forget your homework!" and with her tail between her legs, Effie skulked off.

Last week in June 09

Shooting turned into nightmare, my mother made sure of that. I was all happy until she ruined it. There I was, merrily smiling at the camera, gently guiding the nation on how to cook, being totally professional and at the end of each episode, casting a little spell. Oh I know, I know, but they're all in a good cause, I promise! I would stare into the camera during the last few minutes of filming and recite a few words that the public would neither hear, nor recall.

Vitamins, onions, garlic and peas:
Eat this my friends and you won't sneeze.
A delicious soup full of wealth,
Pearl of barley, tomatoes and health,

Soften carrots, celery sticks ,
Antioxidants, minerals, magical tricks,
Chesty coughs, nasty sore throats;
Sail far away on honey boats.

Eucalyptus leaves, clear the nose,
Lavender flowers sleep and doze.
Ginger stem to settle rumbles,
Arnica cream to soothe your tumbles.

Viruses, coughs, flu and colds,
Replace with health and marigolds.
Take heed, oh sickness, be gone with thee,
By the power of three, mother earth and me!

That was just a little pick-me-up spell, so the nation would wake up feeling the healthiest they had ever felt in their lives. Although my mother had to go one step further. The moment she joined me on set, the old witch took the opportunity to cast a spell and you won't believe the spell she cast! Oh, she looked every inch the doting mother in her pretty red summer's dress, matching red kitten heels and flowery pinny. In fact, she looked like something from a kid's fairy tale, but oh, appearances can be deceptive. She was horrendous; she continuously disrupted filming, quarrelled with the director and constantly called upon Pepper for touch-ups. She was adamant that she were to filmed from her best side and appropriate angle. It got worse, too. For example, just as the chocolate cake was all mixed up and poured into a cake tin ready for the oven, she'd shout out, "No, no, I'm not happy with my lines!" This would result in a large groan from the crew and additional eggs and flour were brought once again onto the set, so the whole scene could be done again. I was feeling quite emotionally drained, her blood-sucking energy was bleeding my spirits dry. The poor director, who looked close to a breakdown due to sleep deprivation and twisted nerves, pathetically winced as he whimpered "action," to film the chocolate cake scene for the sixth time. Surprisingly though, mother, during the sixth take, was perfect. Not only did she pronounce every syllable with the greatness of Judy Dench, but she seemed to project the kind of aura that separates the feeble from the elite. Mother and daughter were on fire. However, just as I naively began to believe she wasn't that bad, I found out that I was sorely mistaken. She demonically stared towards the camera and proceeded to wonder far from the script. Her eyes penetrated with an intense darkness and her sweet, fairy godmother face dissolved into the wicked stepmother's.

"Mum," I whispered, trying desperately to avoid moving my lips, "what are you doing?" She, of course, ignored me and stared straight at the camera, I noticed, too, that Sarah was looking somewhat perturbed, but couldn't seem to talk. *The bitch*, I thought, *she cast a trance spell on us*. Everyone in the room was drifting off into a dream-like state.

Now listen here and listen well,
With your attitude creating a living hell.
You cover your faces, hidden by dark,
Swimming in neighbourhoods, wild as the shark .

Terrorise the old, young and the weak,
With guns, foul language heightened with drink.
Loiter on corners, gangs fight their space,
Legs shot to pieces, scars on their face.

You fester like mould, double in size,
No respect for others with your bricks and lies.
Understand don't you that you cannot be touched,
After a life has been damaged, killed and crushed.

This is our turf; you're not in our gang.
Move or be shot, knifed, or hang.
The innocent will suffer they have to endure,

As the law protects you well I say no more!

Pedal on bikes, well, you're too poor for a car,
Hoodies your history I have now raised the bar.
Your parents, well yes, sometimes are to blame,
Will now control you with the whip of the cane.

You are hereby banished from corners and bins,
Oh hoodies of Britain you shall pay for your sins.
Your voices shall crack if you dare to shout,
Street corners and parks shall cast you out.

The invisible hand will push you away,
Chew you up, spit you out, now come: let's play!

"And Cut!"

"I've always hated hoodies," mother confessed to me later, no kidding! I was livid. How dare she use my TV programme to cast a spell against the hoodie fraternity, the cheek! I argued with her for about an hour, poor Sarah looked terrified! Mother was beginning to look evil and apparently I possessed a demented look in my eye or something. Poor Sarah, she's very sensitive you know. Then came the grand finale, the speech as to why the spell had been cast. I tell you what she deserved, a BAFTA.

"There are three reasons why the Goddess made it possible for you, dear child, to appear on this television programme," she said. "One is to make you some money, two so I can finally get on Strictly Come Dancing and dance with Vincent Simone, and three, to rid the world of hoodies." And with that, she strutted out the room with all the attitude of an Argentinean tango dancer.

"Personally," said Sarah after mother had vanished, "I blame the parents!" Shocking!!! Oh, and I was meant to fly out to Paris to meet up with my beau; however, due to not finishing the shoot on time it was impossible, bloody old witch!

July 09

Fantastico Banquetto, decided to use my apparent photogenic skills for a wedding feature. The shoot consisted of fancy cupcakes and menu ideas for a wedding on a budget. I was styled in the most exquisite Oscar De La Renta dress, not exactly supporting the budget theme, I must say, but it was on loan from Harrods wedding department. I was surrounded by rouge noir and sugar pink roses and cream church candles, I felt like a princess. Sarah actually cried when she saw me. I also took the opportunity to cast a little spell again. Yes, again! Just a little spell to ward off spots and pimples on the most important day of a girl's life. No girl should have to endure a big, aluminous yellow spot on the end of her nose. So I fixed it.

Oh yes, Clementine is going to be famous. FHM saw her pictures in my magazine and couldn't get her in front of the camera quick enough. She posed in a see-through body suit, spayed with glitter or something and looked like a freaky, yet beautiful creature from another planet. In all fairness, that witch probably is. I enjoyed a good night out with her this month, actually. She invited the cackle over to her flat to enjoy a personal Amy Winehouse concert in her front room. Amy, I must admit, is a genius and very well behaved. Not once did she walk off the stage, forget her lines or guzzle alcohol. Personally, I think the press is nothing but a negative impact on poor Amy! She was nothing short of spectacular.

July 09 continued

I'm engaged!!!

I'm so excited: I need to tell you the whole story right from the beginning. Oh my Goddess. Ok, here goes. I was offered the chance to visit Taylor this month and guess where he was? Glorious Rome! He had been sent to sample food at a wonderful restaurant called Flavia's, just off the Via Veneto, and compare its menu to a smaller restaurant up in the hills behind the city. I arrived in the morning and travelled by taxi to the hotel Regina Baglioni, which was just a stone's throw from the restaurant. The hotel was spectacular and their bar, Brunello's, made the most exquisite cocktails and bar snacks I've ever tasted. The weather was stifling and my Citrus Bang-Bang Boom came in good stead, as it warded off any undesirable odours. After showering and applying my makeup, etc, I changed into a cool and feminine black and white Maxi dress and met Taylor patiently in the hotel's beautiful lounge. My heart nearly skipped a beat when I caught sight of him, he looked so tanned, healthy and dazzling. Ooh, I'm a lucky little witch! We greeted each other passionately, before hitting the streets of Rome. We headed straight to the Piazza Navona, where we sat and enjoyed the most expensive coffee in the world, whilst listening to a male street performer singing Nessun Dorma and other favourites from the operas, he was really good for a street performer. We continued exploring Rome; bought ice cream from the famous Galati parlour, people-watched and strolled through the Villa Borghese. I was in heaven. That night Taylor took me to Flavia's for dinner, he was under the impression that the food there was excellent. It was certainly a Roman feast. I loved it there. Apparently it's the second oldest restaurant in Rome and the walls were adorned with signed pictures of movie stars from Sophie Lauren to Audrey Hepburn. The next day, Taylor and I took a stroll down towards the Vatican City, I wanted to visit St Peter's, however on the way, we noticed a makeshift ice rink that had been erected just beneath the castle of St Angelo, so we decided to have a skate. I didn't really look the part, as I was trussed up in a billowing orange and brown Boho chic dress but I gave it a go. Taylor was astonishingly good; he was zooming about all over the place. I, on the other hand, stuck fast to the barrier, well, it was difficult. After about ten minutes or so, Taylor came skating towards me and, looking back now, he rather pathetically tumbled over beneath my feet. I laughed and told him to get up, but he didn't, he just sat there on the ice looking up at me with this beautiful smile on his face. He reached into his pocket and pulled out a ring box. My heart was beating ten to the dozen at this point; I think I was in shock. He opened the box and revealed the most stunning pink diamond engagement ring. My jaw hit the ice in astonishment; I couldn't quite comprehend what was going on. Then he asked me something I thought I would never hear.

"Adrianna Jasmine Poppleapple Mariposa Forthright-Punch, will you do me the honour of becoming my wife?"

"Yes ," I cried, without a moment's hesitation. "Yes I will!"

August 09

Fantastico Banquetto asked if I would be able to persuade a few members of my circle to join in with my monthly photo shoot as they required a group of lovely ladies to pose for a picnic scene. Of course I had to ask my mother - there would be blood if I overlooked her - along with Sarah, Clementine, who is quite the little starlet at the moment, Kristobella and Carolina Plum. Our outfits were supplied by DEE-DEE Sugar Cane, as she too was becoming a bit of a star and the magazine was keen to exploit her fashions. We all posed on blankets on Hampstead Heath one glorious August day and pretended to tuck into cold spicy chicken wings with potato salad, scones with clotted cream and Dorset apple cake. We sipped homemade lemonade and sparkling pink rose wine. I must say we all looked very elegant, although mother did look a little over the top, what with her straw bonnet and baby blue lace parasol. Ever since she used that enchanted DVD I gave her, where she had the opportunity to become Scarlett O' Hara for the night, she hasn't been quite the sam.! My mother has taken it upon herself to adopt a strong southern belle accent, honestly it's ridiculous. When someone asks, "Where are you from" and she answers, "Hammersmith," with a thick southern twang, people look at her like she's mad! The shoot was a quintessentially English scene that reminded you of the good old days when men bowed and opened doors, and women wore pretty dresses, didn't swear or fall out of taxi flashing their crotches.

Taylor and I are still on cloud nine since the wedding proposal and everyone was so happy for us when they heard our good news. I can't believe everyone, including my mother, cried! Mind you, any excuse for theatrics. His parents are also ecstatic and as an engagement gift, Patty presented me with a beautiful black pearl necklace that had once belonged to Austin's great, great grandmother.

Oh thrilling news! My father had been offered the chance to play in the hit West End show, Chicago! Mother is over the moon, although I believe a little jealous. I know for a fact she always believed she herself would make a great Velma Kelly. Although I must admit, I can see the resemblance between Velma and my mother, what with Velma's sharp temper, seductive power's and killer qualities, it's her to a T!

September 09

To celebrate Halloween, ironically, Fantastico Banquetto asked me to grace the front cover dressed as a witch - it's hilarious! They dressed me up in a beautiful black lace vintage dress, on loan from Kristobella's boutique, and Pepper was a genius with my makeup. She gave me really smoky eyes and red glossy lips. I felt incredibly sexy. Aluino lived up to his usual genius, by styling me in a black, short, sharp 1920s bob; I looked like mother! Scary! The feature included recipes for festive Halloween food and drinks, games and treats. I also decided to use my magical skills, just the once, to cast a little spell. It's a nice spell, actually, and one that I feel most proud of. It evokes consideration towards the animal kingdom and works by encouraging humans to empathise better with their everyday needs be it a pet rabbit, dog or a lion in a zoo. There would be no more torturing cats on barbeques, burning ants with magnifying glasses, or drowning puppies down the loo. The NSPCA will be thrilled!

September has proven to be a busy old month, what with the television series ready to air this week, film premiers, social events, booking The Burley Manor for our annual Halloween bash and of course, booking our wedding! Yes, we have booked it already. It's on Saturday 12th June, 2010 at Hotel 78, well, for sentimental reasons. We will be exchanging our vows before 80 guests in the hotel's stylish art deco 1920s room, before enjoying a sumptuous wedding breakfast in their fabulous black and white ballroom, overlooking their beautiful gardens. For the guest's entertainment, we have decided to hire an Irish folk band that specialises in barn dancing, the lead singer Rick O' Shay, says it's a real hoot. I think the guests will love it, especially Sarah, she loves anything like that and they include professional Irish dancers! Ha! Carolina could show them how it's done! And oh, look at the menu we've chosen, although *I* will personally take care of our wedding cake.

Entrées

Sevruga caviar & sour cream on wholemeal blinis

Cuban Mojitos

Starter

Salad of Scottish Langoustines served with a Coral Jus

Blackberry Noir sorbet

Main

Tournedos en croute, accompanied by Maple Glazed Baby Carrots, aligot and beef jus

Honey roast Scottish salmon fishcakes, served with saffron mash and seasonal organic vegetables

Desserts

Rich chocolate torte drizzled with Blueberry wine coulees,
White chocolate and bitter raspberry Mousse
Black and white cheesecake

Café Bonbon

Wedding Cake

October 2009

"Hello?" said my mother full of theatrical energy and aplomb, even though it was first thing in the morning.
"Mum?" I croaked.
"Darling, is that you? What's the matter with you? You sound dreadful, is everything okay?"
"No, I've got the flu, please come over."
"Don't be ridiculous, darling. Of course you haven't got the flu, if you had the flu you wouldn't be able to lift your head off the pillow. No, no, it's probably just a heavy head cold." *I don't believe this*, I thought. "Mum, I can't lift my eye lids, let alone my head," I said, barely moving my lips.
"Are you sure, darling? Okay, well I suppose mummy to the rescue, I'll be over in a jiffy." Thirty minutes later, my mother was hovering over my bed feeling my forehead. "Goddess, darling you're burning up. I think you've got the flu!" If I had the energy, I would have yelled at her. "Oh well, not to worry mummy's here!"
Soon I could hear her bustlingly about in the kitchen, taps running and the kettle being boiled. Moments later my mother entered the bedroom carrying a small cup of steaming liquid.
"Here we are, darling, try to sit up with mummy so you can drink this," I moaned and squirmed into my pillow, oh I felt dreadful. "Now come on, darling, I know your head feels like a lead balloon," she said almost joyously, "but you need to sit up, or I can't give you your medicine." She popped the cup onto the bedside table and put her hand under my arms to help me up. I groaned in pain as my pounding head responded without mercy to the unwanted movement. My mother, however, managed to prop me up, then sat next to me and began to coax a hot silvery coloured liquid into my mouth. "There we go, darling, try to drink, I promise it'll make you feel better." I stretched out my lips and tilted my head towards the cup. The moment the drink touched my lips, I began to feel as if I were enveloped in comfort and safety. The drink itself didn't taste particularly of anything, but it certainly was effective. It smelt of childhood: cakes baking in an oven, the freshness of the sea and places I had visited on holidays. It took me back to being a little girl

on Christmas morning, excited at 5am to be greeted by a magical tree and a sack brimming with toys. I went from one memory to another, all happy and positive, and experienced the joys of running free like the wind on a bright autumn days, kicking the orange and brown leaves with my red wellies. I felt so warm and safe, cocooned in the comfort that nothing would harm me anymore. Then the muscles of my face began to soften and my jaw began to relax. My frown line began to iron itself out, my body began to let go. "Drink some more, strawberry cup cake," she coaxed, "you'll be up and about in no time." I silently sipped more of the strange liquid, enjoying the relief it brought to my flu-stricken body and after about ten minutes I began to drift into sleep. I could feel my mother lovingly stroke my hair as she began to chant a short spell that's found on the back of the tea packet.

Allow your body time to heal,
Drift away, clear your mind.
No more pain for you to feel,
Just health and happiness you shall find.

Four hours later I woke up refreshed and feeling stronger, I even sat up! My mother was rocking back and forth on the wooden rocking chair reading a copy of Cosmos, with Jupiter 10 snuggled onto her lap.

"Hello, darling, how are you feeling?"

"I feel like I've just had a bad dose of flu," I said as I stretched my arms overhead, "because my legs feel like they've been pounding the treadmill for eight hours, but no more headache and my fever has broken, so I guess I'm on the mend?"

"Bravissima, darling, well done," she congratulated. "Although I must admit you were in an awful shape, darling, when I saw you this morning. For starters, you were the colour of a vanilla yoghurt and your hair looked like strands of deep fried noodles." *Bloody cheek!* "Well you did, darling," she said with a slight chuckle, "still you're all pretty again now, you've actually got a bit of colour to your cheeks. Honestly, darling you looked like you should take up a job haunting houses!" *Thanks!* My mother just giggled again.

"Sorry Jupiter 10, off nanny, she's got to go and run a nice hot Citrus Bang-Bang Boom bath for your mistress, so we can blitz that flu completely out of her system." She then patronisingly told me that I looked about twelve in my PJS and made her way into the bathroom. A few seconds later the flat was filled with scents of lemon, lime, oranges and tangerine, just the sheer smell of that stuff is stirring. "Right, darling," said my mother clapping her hands sharply, "whilst your soaking, I'll get on with changing your sheets, they smell like a stagnant pond from you sweating so much."

"Well, I did have a fever, mother!"

"Yes I know that, darling," she said breezily, "that's why I came over and literally spoon fed you Dr Goombah's, Boo Hoo I've Got the Flu hot drink powder mix!" Adrianna Jasmine pondered for a moment.

"Ah that's it, now I remember; gosh, I haven't had Boo Hoo I've Got the Flue since I was fifteen or something."

"Hmmmm, I know, darling, honestly you were quite poorly when I found you, you were moaning and talking gibberish, I think you were trying to recite a spell. Oh well, that's what mummies are here for: to make their daughters feel better. Now up you get, soak and relax in that lovely bath tub and wash your hair, darling, it looks like it's gone for a cut and blow dry in a lard factory." I didn't say a word. Still feeling fragile, I walked gingerly into the bathroom, slipped out of my sweat-soaked nightwear and edged myself gently into the hot, buzzing water. I lowered the back of my head into the water, so I could wet my hair and allowed the Citrus Bang-Bang Boom to work its magic into my scalp, zapping away dregs of flu. Then I sat up and began to apply shampoo, rinsed it off and massaged Tangle Tamer into my hair and head. I soaked my body in the glory known as Tallulah Toffee. Thirty minutes later I was sitting in fresh pyjamas with my mother lovingly combing and drying my hair.

"Now, darling," said my mother, "you're not doing any work or anything tonight, are you? Because personally, blueberry meringue, I think you should rest." I told her that I had no intention of working and that I'd relax and order a film. "Good idea," my mother agreed, "why don't you order a film off that clever telly of yours?"

"Yes, mum," I chuckled, "I'll order off pay per view!"

"Good, sausage roll, you need a rest, you've been very busy lately, what with all your TV work, cooking for that coffee shop, trying to save every human on the planet, the job at the magazine - which I am very proud about darling - zooming back and forth in that van of yours, yoga, Salsa night and of course getting yourself all in tizzy over your wedding! You're only a witch, darling not a Goddess!"

"Yes mother," I sighed, "you're absolutely right."

'Tall I am young.
Short I am old.
While with life I do glow,
people's breath is my foe…
Now what am I?'
(Anonymous post, Help.com)

Chapter 29
The Riddle

On reflexion, Adrianna Jasmine's flu probably slowed her down for about 24 hours as soon after, she was back to her usual whirlwind self. It was still non-stop and at manic times like these, Adrianna Jasmine dropped to her knees and thanked the Goddess for being a witch. For there was one thing a witch needed very little of and that was sleep. So the hours wasted on sleep could be replaced with more exciting and prosperous activities such as work, cooking and organising a wedding. Her lack of requirement for sleep simply baffled Taylor. He would often wake up in the middle of the night and discover Adrianna Jasmine in the living room performing her way through a sun salutation, or reading some heavy duty book at 4am. *That girl is* not *human*, he would muse. If only he knew!

Due to waiting until they were married, the pair hadn't officially moved in together. The thought of moving in with her husband filled Adrianna Jasmine with mixed emotions of pleasure and dread. Pleasure because she would have her beau on tap, and dread because she would not be able to cast spells quite so freely. During their courtship, Adrianna Jasmine spent more time at Taylor's flat as there was less chance of him discovering her secrets. With a heavy heart Adrianna Jasmine had transferred all her magical artefacts, including her beautiful altar, into the spare room and safely locked the door behind. However when Taylor did pop over for the evening, it would often result in the same question, time and time again.

"Why do you keep that door locked?"

One evening Adrianna Jasmine ran out of excuses, or patience, and she cast a memory block spell on him so he would forget to ask her every time he entered the building. She felt terrible about it, but what other choice did she have? Still, the witch ended up being punished for that one by the threefold law. She banged her head really hard whilst unloading her van at the coffee shop one drizzly morning, thus resulting in a trip to A and E. Well, you know what they say: an eye for an eye, or in this case a head for a head!

The cackle, this time including Sarah, had just returned from their annual Halloween trip to Burley, and of course, a magical experience had been enjoyed by one and all. Sarah had managed to wangle her way out of working on the coffee shop's busiest day of the year, by persuading her mother to hire her beau, Sergio Draganoff in her stead. Apparently, the long haired Latvian with the smouldering eyes went down a storm with the ladies. He had rocked up dressed as some new romantic 18th century vampire prince, causing the hypnotised women to swoon in lust.

"Ooh, to be seduced by that," a young woman was heard saying, her eyes wild with sexual desire, "I'd go back to your castle any night of the week, turn me, turn me!"

The kids adored him, too, which only added to his ever growing popularity with the mothers. He entertained them by telling stories about his vampire family back home, his castle on the top of a dark mysterious hill amongst the deep dark forests of Latvia and how he came to England to seek his eternal bride. Totally fictional of course! Blair was nothing but impressed by Sergio and made it no secret that this alluring six-foot Latvian was a far more superior employee than her daughter.

"Where is the loyalty these days?" Sarah had asked in solemn dissolution to Adrianna Jasmine, "bloody cheek!"

It was an early Friday morning in November and Adrianna Jasmine was busy making vanilla sponge cakes in the coffee shop. The time was 6am and the witch was eager to finish her work by lunch time. She was meeting her mother and Kristobella at the Harrods wedding department to embark on the quest for the perfect dress. She was excited although had no idea what she wanted, or even the colour of the bridesmaids' dresses. She only knew that when she saw it, she would know. The witch had only been in the kitchen about half an hour when a strange chill ran through her blood, causing her body to shiver. She felt a presence behind her back and turned around sharply.

"Goddess," yelled the witch, her heart thumping, "you gave me a fright," The Mystic Odessa was standing about five feet away from Adrianna Jasmine, silent, her eyes intense. "Do you want a coffee or something," inquired the witch with a smile, "or some cake maybe…" Adrianna Jasmine trailed off; the Mystic Odessa appeared to be in a trance, she just stared at the witch with black, dead eyes. Adrianna Jasmine began to feel a little uneasy. She was aware that Odessa was an odd one, but she looked creepy, something was wrong. Tentatively Adrianna asked, "How did you get in?" The front door to the coffee shop was still locked, Adrianna Jasmine had come through the kitchen entrance and the Mystic Odessa had not been presented with a key by Sarah's family. There was no answer. As her senses heightened, Adrianna Jasmine could feel her natural protective barriers build up around her. Her hands began to feel increasingly hot with a surging energy in her fingertips; Adrianna Jasmine's eyes had transformed from chocolate softness to dark and terrifying. She heard nothing but the beating of Odessa's heart, slow and regular and saw only the target ahead. Adrianna Jasmine's fingers were twitching, she was certain Odessa was about to strike. Adrianna Jasmine remained focused on the target ahead, her senses on par with that of some great predator, hunting in the dark. Then Odessa struck, unleashing an energy; not of the physical force but that of wisdom. She simply began to speak. Not losing sight of her target for a second. Her hands still ready to unleash magic, Adrianna Jasmine listened to the Mystic Odessa's now strange, high pitched and inhuman voice.

Black or white
Darkness or light
The law of three
Loss of sight

Death and birth
Breath or choke
Love and hate
Lost in smoke

Red of blood
The softest rose
Ying and yang
Sorrow flows

Touched by love
The choices made
The warmest bed
The coldest grave

For a while there was nothing but silence, just the beating of two hearts and then the cold chill that had been so apparent only moments before, dispersed and the two women re-entered the realms of reality once more. A form of sickness overwhelmed Adrianna Jasmine's body and she dropped to her knees, retching in a cold sweat. The mystique Odessa remained standing, she too felt sick, but was for some reason able to handle the overwhelming bilious sensation far better than that of the young witch. For a good thirty minutes the sickness was intense, but surely and slowly the ghastliness subsided and the witch was able to stand and pour a glass of cool water. As Adrianna Jasmine sipped her water the two women didn't say anything. Odessa had nothing else to say and Adrianna Jasmine felt too bewildered to ask any questions. The strange riddle was circulating around her head like a waltzer: what the hell did it mean? One thing was for sure; the riddle was inauspicious and as a result, put a fear into the witch that she couldn't quite comprehend. For a few moments Adrianna Jasmine turned away from the psychic in order to decode the riddle. When she turned back to her, she had vanished. The strange atmosphere that had been created lingered, until Blair and co. burst in through the kitchen door, unaware of the activities of only moments ago.

"Goddess," said Blair, "you look like death, are you ill or something?"

Adrianna Jasmine nodded. "I've just had a funny turn, felt sick and overcome, I'm alright now."

Blaire looked concerned. "Ok, well take it easy; you're not pregnant, are you?"

Adrianna Jasmine shook her head. "No," she smiled, "not pregnant." Then she excused herself and decided to phone her mother, strangely there was no answerer.

At 10 am, Adrianna Jasmine decided to drive to Hammersmith to find her mother. She didn't start work until one on Fridays and could always be found at home, catching up on her house work. Sicily had not replied to any of her messages and therefore the witch couldn't help but feel on edge. Something was wrong, she could feel it. Not only had the Mystic Odessa's strange riddle set her mind into a paranoid overdrive, but her own natural instincts were warning her that something evil and dangerous was about to pounce and bite. Adrianna Jasmine reached over to her phone, which was set up in front on the dashboard, and scrolled through to find her mother's number. She pressed the green phone symbol and switched to loud speaker. Shockingly she was informed that the phone had been switched off and to please try again later. That was it, Adrianna Jasmine was more freaked than ever, her mother never switched her phone off. Flat battery perhaps? Then her phone began to ring. She glanced over at the screen to see what number had flashed up, but there was no number, it just said "unknown." Adrianna Jasmine pressed the answer button.

"Hello. Adrianna Jasmine speaking."

"Hello, Adrianna Jasmine," an unfamiliar and slightly chilling voice filled Adrianna Jasmine's van. "You don't know me but, my dear, I certainly know you and more importantly, I know your mother." The voice was female, cruel and slow. It was the sort of voice that toyed with your fears, the voice in your nightmares.

"Who is this?" she asked, trying desperately to stay calm and to suppress any rising fear. The voice chuckled playfully down the receiver.

"I'm an old friend of your mother's," came the wiry voice, "she and I are catching up! You see, my mother knew your mother; it's rather like a reunion."

"Pan's daughter," breathed Adrianna Jasmine in horror, her blood pressure began to rise dangerously high, she could feel herself starting to panic. She trod carefully, her voice shaking slightly,

"That's good... well perhaps I could join up with you two for a coffee, or a bite to eat?"

More chuckling, "that would be splendid, Adrianna Jasmine," her voice was verging on psychotic. "I'll tell you where we are."

Adrianna Jasmine took in a deep breath, she had no means or ability to write down an address. "Remember," she said to herself, "remember, remember."

"We're at the old abandoned warehouse in Whitechapel, my dear, you know the one!" Adrianna Jasmine's eyes were stretched to their limits, "what...why are you there?" The voice on the other end of the line honed in on her fear and more chuckling followed. "Oh don't be scared, little one," she soothed with all the compassion of a twisted killer, "your mother is quite alright, but she could be better, why don't you come here ASAP and join the party, it won't be the same without *you*," she laughed again then hung up. Poor Adrianna Jasmine felt her head spin and her ears scream like a demented train whistle. The traffic seemed to float and oxygen appeared to be sparse. *Calm down,* thought the witch, *don't panic,* and she reached her shaking hands over to her phone. She called the one person she knew would know what to do.

Kristobella, Bella Bell, Carolina Plum, Clementine, Sarah, Blair and old Mrs Berry were all huddled together in a circle in Adrianna Jasmine's bedroom. They had literally dropped everything when they heard the news of Sicily's plight and raced over to be with Adrianna Jasmine. There had been a mixture of fear, panic and anger as the witches discussed how to tackle the dreadful crisis. Questions were asked that couldn't be answered, assumptions made and opinions cast. But they all agreed that Sicily's kidnap was the result of a well thought out plan by Pan's daughter, Richenda. Kristobella had come to the conclusion that Richenda had planned to trick the cackle into believing that it was Adrianna Jasmine who had been the target, in order to throw them off the scent, and when Sicily was at her most vulnerable, she pounced. The witches had all nodded in agreement but were not sure why the demented witch had requested Adrianna Jasmine's presence.

"That's easy," stated old Mrs Berry, "she knows Adrianna Jasmine is the most precious thing to Sicily and causing harm to Adrianna Jasmine in front of Sicily will give nothing but pleasure to Richenda. Or the other way round!"

"What do you mean?" gasped Sarah who then reached out and protectively clutched onto Adrianna Jasmine.

"Well, can you imagine the pain Sicily would feel if she knew her daughter was subjected to watching Sicily hurt, or worse killed, either way she is going to use Adrianna Jasmine as some sort of a tool."

"You mustn't go, Adrianna Jasmine," Sarah yelled, "you mustn't go to White Chapel." Adrianna Jasmine said nothing, her thoughts were dancing wildly, and then she spoke.

"Well… maybe I don't exactly have to?" Old Mrs Berry looked at the young witch with intrigue; she appeared to have inkling where Adrianna Jasmine was going to take this.

Over in White Chapel, Sicily was sitting on a filthy floor shivering with cold. She couldn't move and her head hurt from where she had been struck by an object that had knocked her unconscious just as she was about to open her front door. She wasn't sure who had struck her, or where she was, or the reason why she had been brought to this filthy place. Although one thing was for sure, she was in danger and she feared more for her daughter than ever. She felt a presence loom in on her and breathe on her face. She breathed quickly.

"Who's there? Where am I?" Sicily gasped, a small torch had lit up a face, just centimetres from that of hers. "No it can't be," she breathed aghast, "you're…"

"Dead?" interrupted the voice with contempt. A chuckle followed suit, "unfortunately for me, *yes* the person you are thinking of *is* dead."

"But you look so like her," exclaimed Sicily, the woman looked fierce now and her eyes decreased to mere slits.

"Well, I suppose I would look like her, Sicily Poppleapple, seeing that Gunnora was my mother." Everything then became clear to Sicily. Sicily expelled air from her lungs and shook her head.

"You're the daughter, aren't you? I knew it was you." Richenda nodded silently, her eyes never once leaving Sicily. "You will lose, Richenda, just like your mother did," warned Sicily as she looked straight into her old enemy's daughter's eyes, "evil never conquers over good." Richenda's eyes were like stone, she was eerily still, then "whack." A great blow from the back of her hand struck Sicily across the face, causing the witch to fall back. It was a nasty blow, full of hate and wrath, it had shaken Sicily to the core and the pain made her eyes water. Richenda loomed over her once more,

"I am not evil," she screamed, "nor was my mother." Sicily shook her head in disbelief and began to laugh at the deluded witch. Furious that Sicily was mocking her, Richenda clenched her nails deeply into the palms of her hands, drawing blood. "Stop it, you bitch," she yelled and kicked Sicily in the right shin. Sicily screamed in pain and rolled onto her side, her mouth resting on the disgusting floor. "She was not evil!" Richenda screamed defiantly, "she just wanted to punish those who deserved to be punished and you killed her for it." Sicily screamed once more, although not a scream of pain, but a scream of pure frustration and a purple light shot from her hands forcing Richenda to shoot backwards off her feet and land heavily on her back. As Richenda fell, Sicily attempted to stand, but fell down like a sack of bricks due to an almighty head rush and the overwhelming pain from her shin. Richenda, slightly dazed from her sudden flight, leapt up and took four stones from her coat pocket and threw them at Sicily. Sicily instinctively shielded her face and curled up into a ball to protect her from the blows. But no blow came. Instead, the four stones landed in an organised circle around Sicily.

"No!" screamed Sicily, but it was in vain, the stones had connected and Sicily was trapped inside an energy circle. She wouldn't be able to escape unless a stone was dispursed by Richenda herself. Sicily fell back onto the floor, exhausted and beaten.

Back at Adrianna Jasmine's, the witches were sitting about in a circle; Adrianna Jasmine was sat on her rocking chair with Jupiter 10 snuggled in her lap.

"You ready, my darling?" asked Kristobella gently. She looked into her niece's eyes and saw nothing but fear. Carolina, too, saw this fear and Sarah's eyes began to fill with tears.

"Come here, my sweet," Carolina urged soothingly and held out her arms. Adrianna Jasmine placed Jupiter 10 onto the floor and lowered her body down towards Carolina's. Carolina opened out her arms and took Adrianna Jasmine into her magical wings and hugged and hugged until the young witch's anxiety and fear was replaced with courage, coolness and love. "You're ready my sweet," whispered Carolina Plum stirringly, "now go and save our Sicily."

(The answer to the riddle was A CANDLE!)

'Most people have good intentions most of the time. They want to get along, do their work and succeed. Yet personal upsets can make good people into monsters.'
(L. Ron Hubbard)

Chapter 30
Purple light

"Ah, she's arrived," announced Richenda, holding a small church candle in her blood-soaked hands, "this should be...interesting." The candle gave just enough light for Adrianna Jasmine to familiarise herself with her surroundings. It was a cold and lifeless room, stinking of piss and neglect, and with large splintered beams that hung precariously across the ceiling. An abandoned wheelchair, which had fallen onto its side, lay near where the demented witch stood. "And if you're wondering why I'm not contorted with sickness, let's just say when one is unconscious, your worst nightmare can do anything!" with a sinister grin she looked down at Sicily sitting with her knees pulled to her chest. She looked up to see her daughter, but it was just too painful. Her head slumped to pray,
"Oh, Goddess keep you safe, my beautiful child."
Richenda had noticed Sicily's reaction.
"Why don't you look at her, Sicily?" she asked cruelly, "I know it's dark but I can just make out her beauty, she looks like you, well, how you used to look. How frustrating daughters can be." Sicily didn't react, neither did her daughter. "Bold and beautiful," Richenda continued with her torture, "a pity, and soon, a waste." Adrianna Jasmine, unperturbed by her menacing tone, walked closer towards the duo, her facial expression was blank and her eyes dead. She seemed to glide as opposed to walk and air didn't seem to be a relevant life source. Sicily was trying to keep calm; she sneaked a peak at the vision in front of her, beautiful and strong, full of everything that good stood for. Richenda, without taking her eyes of Adrianna Jasmine, placed the candle gently onto the ground and took a wand out of her coat pocket.

"I can't quite make you out," she said with a smile on her face, "you're hard to read, aren't you? Still, I know you've come with some sort of magic up your sleeve, but I warn you, it will seal your mother's death if you dare to use it." To Richenda's surprise, her fiery words stirred nothing in Adrianna Jasmine's face; she simply continued to stare at her enemy with the same blank, breathless look. This unnerved Richenda slightly, why was she so calm? What magic was she about to use? Richenda said nothing for a moment and stared deeply at Adrianna Jasmine, she flicked her eyes quickly towards Sicily, whose face was still buried deep into her knees. Careful not to disturb the stones and still pointing her wand towards Adrianna Jasmine, Richenda entered the circle and grabbed her enemy by the hair yanking Sicily's head back with an aggressive force.

"Look," she snarled, "look at your daughter." Sicily who looked like death, sporting a bloody nose, cut lip, unkempt hair and ripped jumper, stared out towards the vision ahead. A small curl of a smile appeared on Sicily's painful mouth.

"Yes," she said her heart filled with pride, "I agree, my daughter is very beautiful." Richenda forcefully released Sicily's hair and stood up straight. Her smile had now deserted her and her playful enjoyment appeared to have somewhat dwindled. She stepped from the circle towards Adrianna Jasmine with heat and hate in her eyes.

"You dare to mock me," she screamed, "show your feelings, girl. Is this your plan, to say nothing, to act dumb? Well, I'm sick of it, sick of it, you either speak or die!" Still nothing came from Adrianna Jasmine's lips, "so be it," screamed Richenda and shot her wand towards Adrianna Jasmine. A red light blasted from her wand, shooting straight through Adrianna Jasmine's stomach. Sicily screamed and Richenda laughed demoniacally, her eyes dancing wildly. Adrianna Jasmine stood still, a giant hole burnt into her stomach from the red blast, yet still no expression, no sound, no fear. Richenda's face fell.

"What?" cried Richenda, "what sort of magic is this?"

"The oldest, most respected," roared Sicily, and with that, Richenda screamed out in agony, dropped her wand and began to dance wildly about, knocking a stone from the circle.

"Get off," she screamed, "get off, you piece of shit." Blood was pouring from her face and her left eye had been skewered by what seemed to be a claw. She clutched tightly onto the creature that was determined to dig into her flesh and tore her fingers into the hot skin and silky fur that resembled none other than a cat. Richenda, with all her might, managed to take a fair grip, ripped the claws from her scalp and threw the cat far and wide from her presence. Meanwhile, Sicily leapt from the circle, picked up one of the stones and threw it as hard as she could at Richenda. The stone struck Richenda on her right ear, causing the evil witch to fall to her knees in pain and shock. Bewildered, she looked up at where Adrianna Jasmine was standing. "What are you?" she asked through clenched teeth, and like a television programme that had lost signal, the vision in front of her simply faded then disappeared. "No!" she grunted, "no!" She scrambled about to find her dropped wand, "I'll get you, bitch, just see if I don't... ahhhhhhhh!" A strike, hard to her stomach, caused Richenda to scream out in pain and fall to floor; she looked up and saw a naked and highly charged Adrianna Jasmine standing above her. Richenda tried to talk, but due to the blow and being winded, was rendered speechless. The fact that moments later a blunt object was hurled at her mouth, didn't help matters, either. For Sicily threw another stone at her tormentor, causing the evil witch to lose her footing again. Now, Adrianna Jasmine was ready to strike, determined to finish Richenda off, to avenge her mother and wipe the slate clean. Naked as the day she was born; her hair was strewn long and wild over her breasts that were hardened from the cold. Her eyes were black as jet, determined and strong she was ready to finish it once and for all. The witch screamed out a spell towards the now beaten and terrified Richenda.

By the powers stronger than that of me,
Hundred times stronger than the power of three,
Do your will to avenge me
And protect my mother Sicily.

The fate of this evil and punishment,
Earth Mother it is your decision.
Do what is right your judgement is just.
I leave it you to complete this vision .

Terrified of her fate, Richenda screamed and threw her arms protectively over her face as a flash of purple light appeared from Adrianna Jasmine's finger tips. It headed unremorsefully towards the petrified witch. Wind then began to whirl, carrying dust and debris in its wake; the air turned colder than a tomb and cries of terror from Richenda flooded the room. Her body twisted and writhed in agony,
"I'm sorry, mother," she cried, "I'm sorry… ahhhh!"
Dismissing her pain, Sicily ran over to her shivering daughter and shielded her from the noise, wind, and cold. Just as she did, Richenda aggressively shot up into the air and began to whirl around and around with the strength of a tornado. The two witches held onto each other tightly as a destructive wind swept violently through the warehouse, never once did Adrianna Jasmine lose sight of Richenda Pan. The evil witch tried to yell out, but was prevented by the force of the swirling air, soon she could no longer breathe and moments later she was dead. The hurricane lasted for three minutes exactly, before a clear silence was left in its wake. Mother and daughter sat still in each other's arms, before gaining enough confidence to let go of one another.. Unbelievably, not a mark was on the body. A neat and tidy death, no coroner would be able to decipher the cause. Except that her heart had stopped beating.
"Thank Goddess," cried Sarah, who had just run into the room holding out a large red blanket and UGGS for Adrianna Jasmine, "you're both OK! I don't know exactly what happened, I've been out in the car this whole time, but the rest of cackle could see it all from your flat." She threw the blanket around her friend and dropped to her knees to put the UGGS on Adrianna Jasmine's blue, cold feet. Sarah then threw her arms around Sicily, who yelped a little from her injuries, but was generally comforted by the warmth from Sarah's embrace. "As soon as you shape shifted from Jupiter 10 back to yourself, Kristobella phoned to inform me that Operation

Jupiter Claw was in full swing and I prayed like a nut case to the Goddess to protect you both."

"Meow, meow, meow."

"Oh, Jupiter 10!" said Adrianna Jasmine with relief, he was slowly slinking his way over to his mistress, blurry-eyed and sleepy, "My hero!" She picked him up lovingly and buried her face into his silky black fur. "Thank you," she whispered gratefully to him, "thank you for giving up a life for us today."

"The car is still out on the street," said Sarah, slightly breathless, "but we've got to be careful so no one catches us walking out. After all, there is a dead body in here."

"That's no problem," said Sicily coldly, "this was the perfect murder, no one will ever know."

The women turned and walked silently to the car, parked about five minutes from the warehouse on a quiet, dark road. Once they got in, Sarah turned on the engine to the little Toyota Aygo Blue and drove mother and daughter back to Adrianna Jasmine's flat. On route Sicily was the first to speak. "I take it the hologram of Adrianna Jasmine was Mrs Berry's doing?"

Sarah nodded excitedly, "Yes, she conjured up an exact copy of Jazzy at the flat and went into some sort of a trance from there. It was so Mrs Berry could see through the eyes of the hologram and tell it where to go and what to do from her mind. Then," Sarah continued hurriedly, "Jazzy shape-shifted into Jupiter 10 and jumped onto the back of Whiz. I followed your black, slinky butt over to White Chapel, but I couldn't see you,, lost in the shadows of the night and invisible to the naked eye!" Sarah was breathing heavily as she spoke. "It was all rather James Bond, Mission Impossible and Hocus Pocus rolled into one. I tell you, you couldn't make it up! Kristobella kept me informed with what was going via text and phone calls, but we knew when you'd shape-shifted back into you, because Mrs Berry apparently yelled out, we think that bitch tried to kill her with an energy blast or something." Adrianna Jasmine nodded, deep in thought.

"Yes, Pan shot out an energy blast, but of course it went straight through my hologram and made a gaping great hole in my tummy!" The witches chuckled.

"Well, that was when I decided to leap onto her," explained Adrianna Jasmine, "Pan realised she'd been tricked and basically there wasn't a moment to lose!"

Sicily was nodding. "Yes, you did well, apple tree, you acted just at the right moment, she hadn't quite twigged, had she? And she was confused."

"Still it was all incredible," said Sarah holding back the tears, "I'm so proud of you Jazzy, but thank Goddess you're both still alive. She wanted to kill you. Kill you both!"

"I'm sorry, Richenda. I'm so sorry, I knew I'd be useless, they were too strong, I knew the young one was different, I didn't even see the black cat and... oh Goddess, what a mess, what a mess." Hazel sat there in silence kneeling over her cousin's body; she shook her head as she cried uncontrollably. "Why did you involve me? I knew I would simply freeze, I couldn't move. There were others you could have asked and now look, you're dead and I'm alive and alone and..." She began to wail now, screaming out to anyone who could hear. "Give me the strength, Richenda. I know you can, even in death you are stronger than the rest, help me, help me!" Traumatised and stricken with grief, she began to clutch at her hair, yanking it out from the scalp and bit down hard on her bottom lip, not stopping until she felt the taste of her own blood. She proceeded to punch herself in the face. She hoped that the external pain she was causing to herself would dull the internal pain that was burning her very soul.

It was late, 12.45am to be precise, and Sicily was worried about Henry.

"I'll call him when I get back to yours," she said to Adrianna Jasmine, "he'll be anxious and wondering where I am and... oh Goddess," she cried throwing her arms up in into the air, "I have a feeling that my bag is sprawled outside the house, I dropped it just as that evil cow clobbered me over the head, she didn't even have the decency to use magic!"

Adrianna Jasmine shook her head angrily: what could have happened didn't bear thinking about

"What are you going to tell dad about your appearance?" inquired Adrianna Jasmine, "how're you going to explain the cuts and bruises?" Sicily sighed.

"I'm going to have to tell him I got mugged."

Adrianna Jasmine was just about to say, "don't be ridiculous mother," but then again, what else could explain the sprawled out bag on the pavement, cuts and bruises. "OK," Adrianna Jasmine nodded quietly, "we'll say that your mobile was thankfully in your coat pocket and that you telephoned me straight away as soon as you came to!"

Sarah pulled a face, she wasn't wholly convinced that the 'mugging' would stick; besides, shouldn't the police have gotten involved? "I think we should use our heads a bit more," she suggested, Sicily sighed, her *head* had had enough for one day. "Obviously if worst comes to worst we can always use a bit of magic to appease his questions," said Sarah with a good-hearted smile, "but I'm thinking rather on the lines that... yes, Sicily was doing a spot of shopping at the supermarket at tea time, when an irate customer slammed into Sicily's shin, which will explain the nasty bruise, which in turn caused her to stumble backwards in shock and pain, before tumbling into a stack of baked bean cans, that fell on top of her, to explain the cuts and bruises on her face before knocking her out!"

"Don't tell me you just conjured that one up this moment?!" asked Adrianna Jasmine.

Sarah shrugged, "Hey, I can think on the spot when I need to!" There was silence in the car for a few moments whilst the witch's stewed upon the story.

"Well anything's got to be better than explaining to my father that an evil witch called Richenda kidnapped my mother, and that I shape-shifted into my faithful cat in order to save her before hopping onto my broomstick, commonly known as Whiz, and rescuing her from a fate worse than death. So yes, I think we'll go for it, what do you think, mother?"

Exhausted, Sicily nodded. "Yes, I think we should."

'Honey is a great natural antiseptic'

Chapter 30
Healing Wounds

The three witches were met by a warm and thankful reception when they returned to the flat. There were hugs from Carolina Plum and wise words of wisdom from Bella Bell and the amazing Mrs Berry. Clementine began running a bath filled with Tallulah Toffee Yarrow and Marigold Healing oils, with extracts of lemon balm, mint and St John's Wort which would appease Sicily's wounds. Kristobella set to work on making a magic tonic from valerian, citronella, sage and rosemary to promote sleep and calm the nerves. As she stirred the herbs in a medium sized pot with water, she silently chanted a spell.

Protection from harm,
Wrap thee in care.
Protection from pain,
No more despair.
Blessings and thoughts to heal your woe,
Brightest of prayers love doth flow.

After her chant, Kristobella left the tonic to simmer for three minutes then ordered both mother and daughter to drink a hearty tablespoon each. The two witches took their medicine like good girls, preparing themselves for a nasty taste. However, even though the tonic was a revolting shade of green, the two witches licked their lips in appreciation, for the tonic tasted absolutely delicious and reminded them of fresh summer cherries. Grateful for her sister's potion, Sicily then went off to soak in her enchanted bath whilst being comforted by the two eldest witches, Bella Bell and Mrs Berry. As Sicily was soaking, there was a knock at the front door; it was Henry Forthright Punch looking a frightful shade of grey. Visibly distressed threw his arms around his daughter,

"It's OK, Dad," soothed Adrianna Jasmine, "she's fine, she's having a nice bath and her bruises are being dealt with."

"She should be in hospital!" fretted Henry Forthright Punch, "what if she's got internal damage or something. A mountain of baked bean cans falling on top of you is highly dangerous, she should be checked more thoroughly!" Adrianna Jasmine gently shook her head.

"She's with Mrs Berry who used to be a nurse, so don't worry, she's in good hands. Here, have a hug from Carolina." At first Henry Forthright Punch looked a little baffled at the suggestion that he should have a hug from the Plum whilst his wife was soaking her wounds in his daughter's bath. However, for some reason he liked Carolina's hugs and soon enough was accepting a warm embrace. Moments later all his worries and concerns melted away and he began to feel light and free. Later, after a quick cup of tea and a little chat through the bathroom door to his wife, he kissed his daughter goodbye and went back home. Sicily was then helped out of the bath and dressed in Adrianna Jasmine's bathrobe. She was propped up on the couch and her poor leg, which had been kicked by the monstrous Richenda, was elevated on the little coffee table. Kristobella had soaked a flannel in the remaining tonic, wrung it dry and draped it over Sicily's throbbing shin. Instantly the pain began to dull and Sicily feltl more comfortable. Now it was Adrianna Jasmine's turn for her enchanted bath. Clementine ran it for her whilst she disrobed and chatted to the other witches. Five minutes later, a steaming tub with Toffee's Marigold and Yarrow Healing Oils was ready. The heat from the water warmed her to the bone as she laid back, soaking her hair and allowing the water to lick her neck and soothe her shoulders. Clementine sat on the loo next to her, chanting spells to try and calm her cousin's nerves. In the end, Adrianna Jasmine yelled at her to shut up, as she was making her nerves even worse, before slapping down on the water in frustration: she just remembered she hadn't called Taylor!

"Clementine, can you please bring me my mobile, it's in the kitchen, I need to call Taylor?"

"What about the chant? I can't just stop mid flow!" Adrianna Jasmine bit down onto her lip.

"Oh yes, you can," she hissed, then with tiredness to her voice, asked the sulky Clementine to fetch her phone once more. With a huff Clementine got up and reluctantly went to retrieve the phone.

"That bloody Clementine is getting too ripe a fruit for her own good," muttered Adrianna Jasmine to herself.

"Here you are," tinkled Clementine, "and here's a towel to dry your hands."

"Thanks," said Adrianna Jasmine and dried her hands before scrolling down to find Taylor's number. As she did, she could sense that Clementine was still hovering over her. "Can I have a little privacy please?"

Her errant cousin clicked her tongue, rolled her eyes and sashayed out of the bathroom. Taylor's phone rang five times before a sleepy voice answered.

"Hello, Adrianna Jasmine?" *Oh Goddess*, thought Adrianna Jasmine, *I didn't realise it was so late.*

"Hi, sweetie, yes it's me, I'm so sorry I didn't call you today." She could tell he was not compos mentis and sprinkled in sleepy dust as his voice was all cute and dozy.

"I called and called you," he said lazily, "but no answer. I didn't know what to think, I was really worried about you." Adrianna Jasmine closed her eyes and desperately tried to stem hot tears welling up in her eyes.

"Oh darling, I'm so sorry, but we had a bit of a family crisis, but don't worry it's all fine now." At the word "crisis," Taylor became a little more alert.

"What do you mean?" he asked with trepidation to his voice.

"Shhhh," soothed Adrianna Jasmine, "don't worry about anything, it's all fine, I'll tell you about it in the morning."

"Okay," said Taylor with a yawn, "I was just worried because you always call when you say you will." Adrianna Jasmine smiled down the phone, it was true.

"I know, foodie I know, now go back to sleep."

Taylor let out another languid yawn. "Okay, honey, I love you."

"I love you to"

"Yes, I am a dreamer. For a dreamer is one who can only find his way by moonlight and his punishment is that he sees the dawn before the rest of the world."
(Oscar Wilde)

Chapter 31
Dresses and Dreams

The next morning Adrianna Jasmine woke feeling refreshed and optimistic. The tonic had definitely served its purpose. She had slept dreamlessly and the horrors from the previous evening seemed a million miles away. Her mother also slept well and her bruises looked as if they were already a week old, not fresh from the night before. Clementine had taken it upon herself to stay over and slept next to Adrianna Jasmine in her bed. However, due to Clementine's favoured starfish sleeping position, Adrianna Jasmine woke up to find herself balancing on the edge of the bed, it was miracle she hadn't fallen out. After breakfast and morning showers Adrianna Jasmine drove Sicily home to Hammersmith then threw Clementine out at the tube station before making her own way to Covent Garden; she had a great deal of baking to do.

During the course of the morning, Adrianna Jasmine baked a mouth-watering batch of rich chocolate brownies, a Baileys infused chocolate sponge cake, a caramel banana tart, crumbly shortbreads, a moist coffee and walnut cake, a white chocolate cheesecake and mini apple and blueberry crumbles. She had beaten, whipped and baked relentlessly right up to 2pm when she decided to call Taylor. *Blast*, she thought as it went to answer phone. Frustrated after the sixteenth attempt, she made her way into the café and asked for a double shot hot chocolate and treated herself to one of her chocolate brownies. She sat down quietly reading a paper that had been left by a previous customer, chatted to Sarah and sent a text to Taylor. After draining her cup and sticking the brownie crumbs to her fingers before placing them onto her tongue, she sashayed back into the kitchen to clean up before going home again. As she began to bustle around throwing pots and pans into the dishwasher, her mobile rang off.

"About time!" she said when she answered the phone.

"Hello, angel." Taylor's smooth, warm voice sent shivers of pleasure through her soul, "you got a hot chocolate and piece of pie for me?"

Adrianna Jasmine smiled with happiness down the phone; Taylor genuinely was the love that allowed her body to function. He stood for everything that made her complete.

"Sure, when do you want it?"

"How about in five minutes?"

Adrianna Jasmine felt her tummy flip excitedly. "You're near the coffee shop?"

"Yep, just walking down now, I decided to take the afternoon off and come in and see you."

Feeling rather silly, Adrianna Jasmine could feel tears welling up in her eyes, *Goddess, I can't go through what I went through last night again*, she thought, *it's too much for my emotions,.* She managed to pull herself together.

"Lovely, I'll have your treats ready and waiting." Taylor hung up and Adrianna Jasmine set about lovingly preparing her fiancé's sweet goodies. She was feeling happier and more positive, yet something didn't feel quite right. Perhaps she was still in shock from the night before, after all, it had been a highly traumatic experience. She was aware that Carolina and Kristobella had not slept that evening, as they had opted to chant spells deep into the early hours of the morning. When Adrianna Jasmine had woken up, she found the two witches deep in conversation over a cup of coffee. They, too, admitted that something wasn't right, as if there were unfinished business in the air. They made Adrianna Jasmine promise to be vigilant at all times, after all, massive powers had been borrowed from mother earth for that fateful evening; something may need to be returned. The comment chilled Adrianna Jasmine to the bone. Surely ridding the world of such an evil chain of witches was a blessing? Still, the Goddess moved in mysterious ways, nothing was unsurprising in the world of witches and magic. Her thoughts were broken when a pair of strong arms tenderly wrapped around her slim waste. She smiled and closed her eyes. Taylor kissed her neck.

"You smell delicious," he oozed. "You're an intoxicating blend of cream, butter, sugar, chocolate and that gorgeous perfume you use. I could eat you up."

Adrianna Jasmine turned to face Taylor and snuggled deeply in his chest.

"It's good to see you," she said still fighting back the tears again, *he mustn't see me cry*. "What do you want to do today? I've finished for the day now."

"Well... I definitely need some sugar," he teased, "and then I was thinking about wrapping up and going for a nice walk, perhaps popping into a gallery, then dinner and a DVD?"

"Sounds perfect," Adrianna Jasmine cooed. "Sit down and I'll fetch you a nice cake and hot chocolate. Now what do fancy? I've got white chocolate cheesecake, brownies, coffee and walnut cake...?"

Taylor shrugged his shoulders, "a bit of everything!"

Adrianna Jasmine giggled, "OK, one plethora of sugar and cocoa coming up!"

That night Adrianna Jasmine endured an unsettling sleep. Strangely enough, the witch had experienced her first nightmare since the age of five. Nightmares were not a common experience amongst witches as they are able to fight them off, a skill introduced by an elder and conquered by an early age. Adrianna Jasmine's ability to fight off a nightmare was due to conjuring up a spiritual warrior who would rid a nasty dream within seconds. Adrianna Jasmine's warrior held a very strong resemblance to The Lady of The Lake. She was a tall beautiful woman, adorned with long white hair, dressed in soft white chiffon, strong and able, and full to the brim with magic. She brandished a strong, heavy sword which she would use to attack Adrianna Jasmine's nightmares and protected her mind with a powerful shield. Her strong lady would always be standing in front of a castle (the castle represented Adrianna Jasmine's mind) and attacked any dark thoughts trying to invade her happy restful night. This particular night, the lady for the first time ever, almost failed her. She had fought hard to prevent the darkness entering Adrianna Jasmine's castle, yet elements had crept into Adrianna Jasmine's sleeping mind. There had been noises that resulted in Adrianna trying to cover up her ears, sounds so horrendous that the witch began to sweat with fear.

"*My Lady please fight back,*" she urged, "*stop these thoughts in their wake.*" The Lady did indeed fight back but it was not an easy fight and it took many minutes for the darkness to subside. Once it did, the lady was rendered breathless and a little shocked that her fight had not been an easy one. Usually nightmares were crushed within seconds; this one was different, it was strong.

Over the course of the next month, the nightmares continued and the Lady continued to struggle to fight them resulting with the Lady beginning to look withered and tired. Rippling sounds of twisting metal, shouts of horrors and disturbed feelings of sorrow exploded past the helpless Lady and trickled like a rancid poison into the tormented Adrianna Jasmine's castle. Many a night Taylor woke up hearing her screams, soothing her and coaxing her back into trying to settle once more in order to sleep. However it was not an easy task and soon Adrianna Jasmine was beginning to feel apprehensive when the land of nod beckoned. Sleep was making her crazy. It was something that she simply couldn't understand, why was The Lady failing her? She knew that The Lady was working like a Trojan in order to fight off the evil monster but the night terrors still came, perhaps it was time for a new weapon? *Pity* she contemplated with a heavy heart, The Lady had been with her since the age of five, she was family. She decided to keep her on but if the torture continued, a stronger and potentially larger weapon would be required to replace her.

On happier thoughts, Adrianna Jasmine and her family enjoyed shopping for wedding dresses and by the end of November, thanks to a trip down to Bournemouth, she found her dream dress. She had, like most brides, trundled around dozens of shops, tried on copious amounts of lace and satin until she had found "The One." It was discovered in a little bridal shop in an area called Pokesdown, nestled amongst antique and bric-a-brac shops just a stone's throw from the train station. The women bustled about, helping out mother and daughter, offered them a refreshing glass of champagne and lots of encouragement to try on whatever took their fancy. It was fun and when "The One" was discovered, Sicily couldn't help but crumble like a rich vanilla chocolate and pistachio nut cookie.

"Oh my goddess," snivelled Sicily tearfully, "you look like Ava Gardner in that old Hollywood film, *A Touch of Venus*, you're exquisite."

Adrianna Jasmine breathed in and smiled.

"I feel magical."

She stepped in front of the mirror and slowly turned around. The dress was the style of a Greek Goddess gown, a fitted yet billowing floor length ensemble, adorned with Swarovski crystals gathered around the waist, that sparkled like millions of tiny stars. It was the most perfect style the witch could possibly wear; it was spiritual, natural, fit for a goddess…and black!

After paying the deposit, which Sicily insisted on paying herself, mother and daughter began searching for bridesmaid's gowns: one for Clementine, Sarah and Taylor's cousin's eight-year-old little girl, Violet.

"You need a striking colour to compliment the black," advised the sales woman, a rather robust lady with horn-rimmed glasses and a tape-measure around her neck. "What about a dark vibrant pink?" The two witches pursed their lips in thought.

"Perhaps…" Adrianna Jasmine mused, "but I was kind of thinking of the bridesmaids in ivory, perhaps with a black satin sash to compliment *my* dress." The woman looked thoughtful.

"I see, playing about with the tradition. I like it, and I think I might be able to help." She disappeared for a few moments and returned holding an ivory, below the knee, bridesmaid's dress with a boned bodice, a black ribbon tie and corsage for added elegance. It was sensational and perfect for the girls, even the little one.

"I love it," squealed Adrianna Jasmine in excitement, "the girls will look perfect in it, what do you think mum, mum?" she looked around and found Sicily sobbing into her champers. *Honestly, call yourself a hard witch,* she thought, *one little wedding dress and you're reduced to marshmallow and mashed banana.* "I'll take them," said Adrianna Jasmine professionally, "they're perfect." She handed over the measurements of the girls to the woman.

"Oh, I feel so happy," cooed Sicily as she breathed in a deep gulp of Bournemouth sea air. The witches had opted for a little trip to Bournemouth pier before their return to London and had decided to catch a taxi from the dress shop to the famous tourist attraction. "I do love the sea, it makes one feel so alive, so vibrant. Why, it reminds me of the time I was a dancer on the QE2..."

"Hang on," said Adrianna Jasmine slightly confused, "I thought you danced at the Moulin Rouge in gay Paris, how on earth did you have time for a jig on a cruise liner as well?"

Smiling radiantly Sicily gave her answer. "Youth, darling, that's how!"

Adrianna Jasmine took in a deep breath of fresh sea air.

"Anyway, changing the subject. I think the bridesmaids will look beautiful in those dresses and I love the head pieces I chose."

"Ye,s I agree, and your dress, I have to say, is extra special, why, you'll look like Venus herself on the big day. In fact, far superior," she added with pride.

"Thanks, mum. I'm looking forward to seeing the girls faces when they see their dresses, although I don't recall asking Clementine to be my bridesmaid; she kind of presented the role to herself *and* she's organising my hen party,"

Sicily looked up sharply. "She's organising your hen party, poppet pie?"

Adrianna Jasmine nodded with a worried look in her eye. "Yep, she sure is."

Sicily snorted. "Well good luck with that, let's hope it's in plenty of time for you to recover, or return, for that matter."

"Return? What do you mean, return?" Adrianna's voice was tinged with panic.

Sicily looked on out to sea. "Well, knowing Clementine, it won't be any normal hen do, you know, like spending a few days in a health farm or a trip into town dressed up as cheerleaders or super heroes. Oh no, you can guarantee she'll be planning something far more original."

Adrianna Jasmine sighed heavily. "Hmmm, well, we'll see. I don't really want too much fuss. Perhaps a nice meal or trip down to Burley..."

"Look, don't worry," soothed her mother, "I won't let her go too over the top. Mummy will make sure of it," she then winked at her daughter and as she did, a strong gust of wind blew right into their faces. "Oh, so invigorating," Sicily sang over the wind, "the spray from the water is like the kiss of life. I feel it rehydrating my soul."

"Yes, it's great, mother," shouted Adrianna Jasmine over the wind, she was beginning to feel very cold. Her mother chuckled sensing her daughter's discomfort from the bracing sea air.

"Come on, walnut whip, let's go buy ourselves a hot chocolate and warm up the cockles before they fall off."

"That sounds good to me," Adrianna Jasmine said shivering, "let's go here." She pointed at the cafe on the end of the pier, "and perhaps a slice of cake?"

"Hey, beautiful," said Taylor as Adrianna Jasmine entered the living room, "I missed you. Did you have a fun day in Bournemouth?" He wrapped his arms warmly around his fiancé's waist and kissed her hungrily.

"Yes, very much," she said after his dreamy kiss, "we saw the sea!"

"You did!" exclaimed Taylor through a beaming smile, still holding her in his arms.

"Yes," she confirmed, "and look, I even brought you a stick of rock." She reached into her handbag and pulled out a giant, bright pink, stick of rock with the word Bournemouth printed through the middle.

Taylor chuckled. "Wow, that takes me back to childhood, I love it. I'll have piece after dinner."

Adrianna Jasmine smiled and breathed in his after shave. Oh he smelt so good.

"What are we having for tea, then?"

"Marks and Spencer's are doing that dine in for two," said Taylor, "so I brought steak Dianne, new potatoes a bottle of red and chocolate torte."

"Yummy," said Adrianna Jasmine with approval, "excellent choice."

"Well in that case, my lady," said Taylor with a little bow, "I insist you sit down, put your feet up and I'll get cracking with dinner, here's the remote."

He handed Adrianna Jasmine the remote control as she kicked off her shoes, curled up like a cat on the sofa and began to flick through the endless list of channels as her fabulous fiancé prepared dinner. As Adrianna Jasmine flicked aimlessly, her eyes began to feel heavier and heavier. She decided to leave it on Charmed, a series about three witches called the charmed ones. It was an episode where one of the witches called Prudence is lured in to the back of a frosty ice cream van by demonic children, *not scary at all*. As she watched the witches fight off evil demonic children, she began to close her eyes, sinking deeper and deeper into sleep. Her breathing began to thicken and soon she was fast asleep. Then the noises came, first the sound of screeching metal and cries from tortured souls, then the overwhelming sense of sadness causing salt water to well up in her eyes.

"My lady," she cried helplessly, "stop it coming, please."

Her lady was fighting off a great black swirling mass of energy with her giant sword, but her white robes were torn and dirty, and the lady appeared tired, old and weak as she drunkenly waved the sword to defend Adrianna Jasmine's head from wicked images. There was no way she would last much longer, the lady wasn't strong enough anymore to fight off Adrianna Jasmine's nightmares. "Ahhhhh," she cried and wailed as she beat her fists into the air, "get back get back..."

"Hey, sweetheart. Hey, wake up, come on, darling wake up. Adrianna Jasmine you're having a nightmare, wake up, you're safe, it's me." A startled Adrianna Jasmine woke up, staring wildly into Taylor's eyes, she looked terrified. "You're OK," Taylor soothed, "that nasty nightmare won't hurt you now." He held her tightly as he continued to calm her down. Her breathing was heavy and her neck was wet with sweat. "Shhhh" he soothed, "you're OK. It's all gone now. Shhhh. Shhhh."

Adrianna Jasmine remained silent, her eyes out on stalks it was as if she were temporarily immobilised, then she began to sob. Taylor continued to soothe and rock his darling Adrianna Jasmine whilst she cried and came to the painful conclusion that her Lady would have to be replaced with something much stronger.

After dinner, the pair snuggled up on the sofa and watched a film together. By eleven thirty, Taylor decided to turn in for bed.

"You coming?" he enquired gently, Adrianna Jasmine nodded, "in a minute."

Taylor looked at her with concern. "You don't have to worry honey, you won't dream that dream again. Besides, I'm right next to you."

Adrianna Jasmine smiled warmly. "I know and thank you but I won't be too long."

"You won't?" he almost pleaded.

"I won't," confirmed Adrianna Jasmine not once leaving his eyes, "I'll be in really soon."

Taylor's eyes were now locked with his fiancée's, he couldn't blink if he tried.

"You are so tired, my darling boy," she sang with the sweetness of a cherub, nestled on a fluffy cloud, clutching a golden harp.

Time for bed and a soft scented toy,
Cuddle and warmth blankets provide.
Tuck up quickly it's cold outside.
Dream of hope love and joy.
Give in to sleep my, darling boy.

With that, Taylor leant forward and kissed Arianna Jasmine good night and stumbled into the bathroom to clumsily clean his teeth before heavily collapsing into bed.

Once Adrianna Jasmine was satisfied that Taylor was asleep, she called her mother. Something wasn't right.

"A nightmare, darling? How ghastly for you, why, you shouldn't be having nightmares. I haven't had a nightmare since I was a child and even that was just the one. Why hasn't your lady been protecting you?"

"I don't know," answered her daughter honestly, "that's why I'm calling. I need opinions, advice!"

"Hmmm, well, the first thing you need to do is, sadly, sack the lady and replace her with something a little gutsier. Although, it is odd, darling. Your nightmare gauntlet lasts forever, it never gets old or decrepit like we'll end up one day," she added with a sigh, "your lady should stay as fresh and lovely as the day you conjured her up!"

"So why is she deteriorating?" asked Adrianna Jasmine, *a straight answer would be helpful.*

She heard Sicily sigh on the other end of the phone. "Well, it's not common but sometimes you can outgrow them."

"Outgrow them?" Adrianna Jasmine echoed.

"Yes, pac-a-mac, you can. Especially as one's brain develops and becomes more brilliant, your nightmare barrier sometimes doesn't grow with you and therefore isn't powerful enough to ward off nasty nightmares anymore." Adrianna Jasmine mused over this for a few moments; it made sense and she was fully aware that her magic had become stronger over the past few years. Why, she could manipulate the weather if she wished to. "Anyway darling, I think you should hire a new barrier, think of something highly powerful and set it to work straight away; perhaps have a nice Float Away Holiday bath so you can at least rest your eyes for half an hour, which Goddess knows, is perfectly adequate for a witch your age. Why when I was your age, I went without sleep for an entire week and was perfectly fine. However, in the meantime mummy will cast a little spell and try to figure out what this nasty black stuff is doing in my toasted tea cake's head."

Adrianna Jasmine nodded down the phone. "You're right. I'll get to work on finding a new representative then have a bath. Taylor is fast asleep, he won't notice when I get into bed thirty minutes before he wakes up."

"That's it, monster munch. So get to work on your new guard and call me in the morning. And darling?" she added, "just a thought, but why don't you choose a Goddess or God of some sort to protect you, just to be... extra safe?"

"A Goddess or God?" repeated Adriana Jasmine, slightly confused, "bit dramatic."

"Don't be ridiculous, darling your head is very important and precious. No, I insist that you conjure up a Goddess or God. I'd feel much happier if you did."

"Why?" asked Adrianna Jasmine suspiciously, "what do you know?"

"Nothing, darling," tinkled Sicily, "except that you're my daughter and I only want what's best for you. Besides, your brain is obviously more gifted than we could possibly have imagined, so it would only be fitting that a powerful source should protect it." Adrianna Jasmine sighed and agreed with her mother. She would have to think of a famous icon for the role of her new guardian, like Zeus or something! "And I'll get to work on my spell, too," sang Sicily with all the energy of a five-year-old prior to consuming a tub of flumps and blue Smarties. "Nighty night!"

Crazy lady she muttered under her breath before switching on the internet to search for powerful Gods. Meanwhile, back in Hammersmith, Sicily was frantically gathering ingredients for a spell that she hoped she would never have to cast.

Here's a tip to keep you happy in mind and spirit:
"Just stop keeping up with the Joneses. Relinquish living a lifestyle that you cannot afford."
(Sarah)

Chapter 32
Happy Times

December was a wonderful month, Adrianna Jasmine had been inundated with work due to the nation falling in love with her. She was constantly making appearances on daytime TV, demonstrating the art of easy cake baking and invited to stylish functions with Taylor. They were steadily becoming a couple of high-fliers. To cap it off, her nightmares were under control. She had chosen the Egyptian Goddess of motherhood, magic and fertility, Isis, to fit the role as her nightmare gauntlet - and by all accounts she was doing a pretty good job. Of course the nightmares came knocking at the door every time she fell asleep, but Isis, strong and true, barely batted an eyelid as she warded the dark poison off. One example happened to be when Isis yawned in boredom and the powerful exhalation basically blew the nightmare into oblivion. Sicily thought this was hilarious, however, omitted to share her concern that even though the nightmares were fought off successfully by the brilliant Isis, they kept returning relentlessly, night after night. Why?

On December 19th Adrianna Jasmine and Taylor went along to Taylor's Christmas do at the Park Lane Hotel. Fantastico Banquetto shared the party with other magazine companies from all walks of life; editors, writers and TV personalities. On their table was the flamboyant Luca Placidi, who was in fine spirits due to copious amounts of *liquid* spirits and champagne that he'd knocked back from the moment of arrival. Archie and Lorraine Soams, Taylor's boss at Fantastico Banquetto and his 6'4" e-model wife; Dorian Summerby, an editor, and his girlfriend Maggie Malone, a fitness instructor and wannabe television personality; top celebrity chef Royster Dirk; his partner, painter Polly Floss and restaurant critic Hugh Topps accompanied by his politically active feminist wife Toni Ford Topps. The night was filled with fun and frolics but, of course, Adrianna Jasmine and Taylor were the talk of the table, and the whole party, it seemed. Everyone wanted to meet them and talk to them. It was strange, pondered the witch, she was only a baker on the telly, two a penny, really, and certainly not a veteran like the great Jane Asher. Moreover, the lovely Jane was a fine actress. *Oh, she was as wonderful as Jane Seymour,* sighed Adrianna Jasmine, in thought. Nonetheless, people from all sorts of celebrity greatness came over to shake their hands, exchange business cards and pay their compliments. Perhaps the witch's feel good telly had touched the lives of the rich and famous, too, and had made a great difference to their mental state? The glitzy affair went on until the early hours and the pair giggled as they witnessed big bosses making unwelcome advances on girls almost half their age; when two women turned up in the same outfit and were trying to out-dance one another on the dance floor and of course, laughing at Luca falling asleep under a Christmas tree. Adrianna Jasmine wasn't too impressed when a well-known chef made a beeline for her while she was ordering drinks from the bar, especially when he began to breathe heavily on the back of her neck.

"Ohhh," he sighed drunkenly, "you smell like a cross between cupcakes and angels" *Ewe,* she thought and discreetly moved away from his head, his breath was hot and horrid.

"And you, my good man, smell like a cross between Jack Daniels and Windowlene," she said tartly before disappearing back to Taylor. She smiled to herself at her quirky comeback. Poor guy, she didn't even rate his cooking that much. She carried back two glasses of champagne through the maddening crowd and with relief reached her table. As she placed one of the glasses in front of Taylor, she noticed Archie Soams had mistletoe hanging from his belt buckle and before he could ask the inevitable she stated a firm, "No!" He roared with laughter, shrugged then threw his arms around her and gave her an almightily bone-crunching hug. Who needed a chiropractor, hey? As the night drew to a close and people were leaving to fall into taxis and be sick, Taylor and Adrianna Jasmine retreated to a room in the hotel. As a treat, Taylor had booked him and his fiancée into the beautiful hotel for the evening so they could enjoy a large double bed, fresh sheets, giant bath and a sumptuous breakfast in the morning. Oh, life was bliss.

Christmas Day was fabulous, Taylor and Adrianna Jasmine invited both their families to Taylor's flat in Shepherd's Bush and, of course, Adrianna Jasmine made the lunch. She cooked for her parents, Clementine, (recently fallen out with her mother due to certain black magic disputes) Taylor's parents and enough food and drink for when Sarah and Sergio arrived in the evening.

"And who could forget you, my darling," she said kneeling down to stroke Jupiter 10, looking very smart in a red velvet collar, "there's plenty for you to eat, too." Jupiter 10 purred and rubbed his head against Adrianna Jasmine's arm. He was very content in the stylish apartment and enjoyed the large size rooms to explore and sleep in. He also liked Taylor and felt very comfortable sitting on his lap and being stroked. Yes, Jupiter 10 pondered, he had bonded quite well with his mistress's fiancé and apparently Taylor felt the same. Many a time Taylor had commented on how impressed he was with the slinky black cat, especially with his impeccable toilet habits, immaculate meal times and his ability to "ask" to be let out for the night. *Honestly*, thought Taylor, *that cat is more respectable than a human!*

After the fabulous Christmas lunch, the merry party were fit to burst. The splendid feast had been a triumph. The roast goose, homemade cranberry sauce and potatoes cooked in goose fat, salt and rosemary certainly had tantalised the taste buds. The creamy cauliflower cheese, sprinkled with fresh grated nutmeg, had set taste buds alight; the sweet carrots and garden peas were simply poetry on the tongue; the lightly spiced red cabbage with juicy sultanas was so good it was almost torturous. The Brussels sprouts and sweet chestnuts were so amazing that even the most notorious Brussels sprout hater would have begged for seconds; the joint of tender roast beef simply made the mouth water and the perfect homemade Yorkshire pudding and two types of gravy caused mild hysteria amongst the guests. *Well, who would have thought of anything less!*

For pudding, the witch conjured up an array of scrumptious desserts. Of course there was a fabulous flaming Christmas pudding which made everyone cheer in delight as she brought it to the table, a raspberry pavlova topped with thick Jersey cream, Baileys chocolate cheesecake and an apple crumble with homemade custard. It was probably far too much but everyone found room to sample at least a little of all of the luscious delights, and besides, there was always Boxing Day to eat what one couldn't manage on Christmas Day. In the evening, the jolly group ate more food, drank homemade Sangria and played on the Wii. Taylor's parents were a little shocked at how competitive Clementine was during the ski-jumping - at one point Austin thought the crazy blonde would leap out the window, she was launching that high off the balance board, despite frequently being reminded by Sarah that you shouldn't lose contact with the now-battered surface and launch oneself like a missile into the abyss. She had become quite irate as the oldies, meaning Sicily and Taylor's mum, were battering her on the score status. If it hadn't been for the fact that everyone was finding Clementine's raging frustration quite hilarious, Adrianna Jasmine would have cast a calming spell on her dear cousin, but it was far too entertaining for that. However, a chant was put by just in case! At midnight they all drank a glass of pink champagne to celebrate such a wonderful day and then slowly, one by one, everyone began to make a move. Sicily, Henry Forthright Punch and Clementine were all staying over for the night, whilst Taylor's parents were going home then returning for lunch the next day. Sarah, her parents, and, of course, the dark and mysterious Sergio, would also be dropping by, so Adrianna Jasmine was preparing for a full house once more.

At 12.45am the guests had finally gone and Sicily and Adrianna Jasmine began to tidy up. Clementine and Taylor were on the couch watching an old black and white movie starring a British comedian named Frankie Howerd, (about a bus that got stuck in a fog) whilst Henry was asleep on the couch

"Fabulous party, darling," cooed Sicily, "you really are a splendid cook. No wonder you're on telly, to think, my little girl! I'm so proud, darling, really, I am."

Adrianna Jasmine smiled. "Thank you, mother," she said beaming, "it was rather tasty if I do say so myself. I think everyone enjoyed themselves."

"I'll say! Anyway, once I've helped you with this, I think I'll settle down in front of the telly. After all, there's a few hours left until dawn and I fancy watching the Strictly Come Dancing Christmas special. You did record it, didn't you?"

Adrianna Jasmine nodded, "I think they're watching a film at the moment but it shouldn't be on too long."

Sicily shrugged her shoulders. "That's fine. I'll read a magazine or something until it's over, let them enjoy their film."

After the dishes, Adrianna Jasmine began to make a start on the Boxing Day feast. It was now past one in the morning but she felt more alive and vibrant during this part of the day and could continue cooking and moving until dawn if she wanted to. So she began to remove what was left from the goose in order to make a mouth-watering curry; mashed all the remaining vegetables together to create bubble and squeak; wrapped dates in bacon; made a salad with grated carrot and fresh beetroot, pistachio nuts, then squeezed the juice of an orange combined with white wine vinegar and maple syrup to make a vinaigrette. She boiled potatoes for a giant creamy mash; whipped up a healthy Greek salad and sliced the beef artistically on a plate to be enjoyed with pickles, crackers and fine French and English cheeses. At three in the morning, she decided to turn in and woke Taylor up, who had fallen asleep on the couch during Strictly, so they could climb into bed together. She slept soundly and woke at seven, ready to cook, entertain and spread magic and happiness to those who she loved and adored.

January, for some people, is a depressing, grotesque month filled with gloomy weather and gloomy bank statements. February isn't much better. When people think of these months the colour grey springs to mind and a craving for blue skies and warmth. However, the woes of the people of Great Britain did not reflect upon the lives of Adrianna Jasmine and Taylor Jameson: they were racing to the stars at an almighty speed. The pair had been very fortunate as work was being offered to them from every corner of the country and the money came pouring in. Even the States had fallen in love with the beautiful, enigmatic witch and her beau, so much so that there were talks that even Oprah wanted her on the show! Everyone did. The pair were guests on chat shows, radio shows and offered tickets for the glitziest events in town; they were hot property and everyone desired their company.

"It's because you give people what they crave," Sarah told her friend one cold February morning whilst the pair of them were making a batch of chocolate chip cupcakes.

"Oh, what's that exactly?" enquired the witch who was sprinkling chocolate chips into a gooey cake mix.

"Happiness," said Sarah matter-of-factly, "you could make a dying, disease-ridden dog feel like the most special being on the planet if you knelt down beside it during its last final breaths. It's your aura, it's so pure and strong, the sun shines wherever you go."

"That's a bit extreme, Sarah. I think my *magic* has something to do with why people unknowingly feel happy. Besides, I used spells in the magazine articles and telly series which is why people felt the way they did."

Sarah shook her head defiantly.

"That's rubbish. You don't cast a happiness spell every single day do you?" Adrianna Jasmine shook her head, *too exhausting*. "And you don't cast feel good spells before you leave the house every morning, either?" Again Adrianna Jasmine shook her head. "Well, I rest my case, you're oozing at the moment Adrianna Jasmine with love and kindness and warmth..."

"Whoa there, Sarah you're getting a bit over excited with my so-called gifts. I'm still me, nothing more nothing less. People obviously connect me with how they feel when they read the articles or when they saw me on the telly, I don't carry the magic with me during everyday life."

"I disagree, there's a permanent happy glow about you and it's infectious. Maybe you don't know that you're doing it, but you are! Goddess, even *I* can feel it."

Adrianna Jasmine looked thoughtful as she poured the cake mixture into individual moulds; come to think of it, it was true! She did hold a certain power to calm aggressive behaviour, to bring hope to the disillusioned and a sound mind to the crazy, but how? Before, in order to do these things, she would have needed to have cast individual spells to help unfortunate souls through their woes. She thought back to the last time she had actually cast a calming spell for some anxious stranger she felt sorry for, and couldn't recall it. When was the last time she had actually combined fresh grass, camomile tea leaves, lavender and rose petals in her cauldron, blended with three drops of olive oil, gently heated for three minutes before closing her eyes and inhaling the blissful scent whilst focusing on the anxious being as she breathed in restfulness and breathed out the person's gloom? *Hmmm*, she thought, *how peculiar.*

"You see, don't you?"

Adrianna Jasmine nodded. "Yes, I certainly do, but why?"

"Perhaps you have reached a higher state of spiritualism, you know, like a goddess or something."

Adrianna Jasmine began to laugh. "That's the most ridiculous thing I have ever heard," scoffed Adrianna Jasmine, "utterly unbelievable."

Sarah firmly placed her hands onto her hips. "Now listen here, missus," she said matronly, "I had Kurt Cobain play me my own personal concert last month in my living room and you're saying that *my* suggestion is unbelievable. We're witches, Adrianna Jasmine, anything is possible, like having a dead legend play a personal concert in your own home."

Adrianna Jasmine looked thoughtful. "I suppose so but I don't think I'm a Goddess, Sarah. Perhaps, like you said, I've simply elevated to a higher state of spiritualism which means one thing and one thing only."

"Oh?"

"I need to talk to my mother!"

"You do that," stated Sarah firmly, "because the next thing, you'll become so powerful you won't even need Whiz to fly on, or Jupiter 10 to shape-shift. Which is probably a good thing," she added with a wink. Adriana Jasmine chuckled. *Goddess forbids*!

The goddess within you has the power to remember. All things are possible when you claim your goddess self. Imagine you are a goddess. Now, be the goddess you imagine.
(Abby Willowroot)

Chapter 33
Oh to be a Goddess!

Later that afternoon, Adrianna Jasmine called her mother.

"Ha ha," came the cheerful laughter of Sicily down the phone, "how exciting, darling. To think, my daughter, a goddess! "

Adrianna Jasmine huffed in frustration. "No, mother," she explained. "I don't think that I *am* a Goddess for one minute but strange things have been happening and Sarah said..."

"Oh don't be too hard on yourself, darling," said her mother, pooh poohing the remark. "You're a regular Venus De Milo, except made of flesh and blood instead of marble, which would be bad, darling because if you fell on the floor you'd break into a million pieces, which would be such a waste..."

"Mother!" yelled Adrianna Jasmine down the phone, honestly her mother was so frustrating and weird! "Please stay on track here!"

"Okay, pocket watch, I will but what I said is true. Anyway, why do you think you're a Goddess?"

Adrianna Jasmine explained to her mother how she seemed to be casting spells without actually casting them, in the traditional sense through potions and chanting; how she effected people's moods and that magical materials, such as candles, herbs and even a wand, were no longer necessary.

"Well that's no biggie," chuckled Sicily merrily, "you were doing that when you were a baby, even that Clementine did, it's just to do with personal strengths. Magic is a strange thing, angel fish. Some of us need equipment to strengthen a spell; some of us don't. Clearly you don't."

"Hmmmm," contemplated Adrianna Jasmine, "so I'm not a goddess, then?"

"Well, to me you are, butter ball but to triple make sure, let's do a little test, shall we? It'll be fun and we can do it over the phone."

"We can? OK, let's do it." A sense of relief began to sweep over the tetchy witch.

"OK. What excites you more: the witching hour of midnight or the Goddess hour of dawn?"

"That's easy," said Adrianna Jasmine without hesitation, "the witching hour."

"OK, one point to witch, zero to Goddess." Adrianna Jasmine felt a sense of relief. She liked being a witch, maybe she could be a witch goddess if worst came to worst. "Now, question two. Do you have everything you desire?"

Adrianna Jasmine thought carefully. "At the moment life is wonderful but I suppose I will never be fulfilled. I'm still bursting with adventure, plans, hopes, dreams..."

"OK," answered Sicily with a slightly more serious tone, "a goddess will have everything she wishes; so far you've been very successful, darling, and when you apply yourself to something, you jolly well succeed, so I'm going to present a point to goddess." *Boo*, thought Adrianna Jasmine, she felt a sulk coming on. "Now, do you always have occasion for the important and significant things in life, like mummy, for example?"

"Yes," answered Adrianna Jasmine feebly; Sicily tinkled a laugh once more.

"Ha ha, another point to goddess. Oh, isn't this fun, darling?!"

"No, it isn't," spat Adrianna Jasmine tartly.

"But why? It's great to be a goddess or isn't that rustic enough for you, darling?"

"Just ask me some more questions, mother, please." She wasn't in the mood for a pick me up.

"Do you receive compliments with a tasteful thank you, or does it make your head swell?"

"Do I need to answer that one?"

"OK, another point to goddess!"

The questions came thick and fast each time ending in the same result: "point to goddess." Adrianna Jasmine felt as if her heritage were slipping away from her. She was a witch, darn it!

"Although you are a humble witch darling do you or do you not recognise the good that you do and the good that you're achieving?"

Adrianna Jasmine shrugged her shoulders. "I guess..."

"Another point to goddess," chimed Sicily, "my, my they are totting up, aren't they."

Indeed, mused Adrianna Jasmine, this was becoming very painful. After a few minutes the test was complete.

"Okay, all done," tinkled Sicily, "and I can honestly say, what an interesting result."

Adrianna Jasmine grunted unattractively down the phone. "Well, it's hardly interesting, is it? I mean, it's totally obvious what I am, that's no mistake. What on earth do I do now? Will I have to defect to another realm, planet, learn how to play the harp, wear a toga?"

Sicily burst into fits of laughter.

"Oh, caramel frappe, you are funny," she was laughing so hard she could hardly breathe. "No, darling, you just carry on as normal."

Adrianna Jasmine felt angry, not only had she just found out she was a goddess, but her mother thought it was side-splitting.

"Normal. How can I be normal? I'm a goddess for goddess sake, I have responsibility, a calling a..."

"A what darling?" and with that Sicily broke down in hysterics once more. "Oh, ha ha, oh my... it's... too... funny. Ha ha." Tears were streaming down her face. Adrianna Jasmine was becoming angrier by the second at her mother's disrespectful behaviour.

"Stop it, stop laughing, it's not nice, mummy," she cried. "My whole world is about to come tumbling down on top of me because of this bombshell and all you can do is laugh, this is a major disaster...a catastrophe! Don't you see what this means? I'm a goddess, for goddess sake and I don't want to be!" With that Adrianna Jasmine began to cry dramatically.

"Oh, don't be ridiculous, darling," said Sicily dryly.

"You're not a goddess."

Adrianna Jasmine's sobbing came to an abrupt stop. "What...do... you... mean? How can I not be?" Her voice was thick with tears.

"Well, what was the very first question I asked you?"

Adrianna Jasmine had to think for a moment before she remembered. "Do I become more excited during the witching hour of midnight or the hour of the Goddess?"

"And what did you say?" asked her mother, the epitome of calm.

"I said the witching hour."

"Well there you go, you're a witch."

Adrianna Jasmine was confused. "But the point system," she said through snivels. "Goddess received higher points than witch, so I'm a goddess, right?" she began to cry again; Sicily rolled her eyes.

"Wrong, darling! Although nineteen out of twenty points went to Goddess it means absolutely nothing. The most important question to determine whether you are a witch or goddess is to ask the confused person are you inclined to sway towards the witching hour of midnight or hour of the Goddess. And we know what you said, so there we go!"

Adrianna Jasmine heaved a sighed. "Thank Goddess, she breathed, I really thought I would have to start paying for harp lessons." Sicily chuckled down the phone; Adrianna Jasmine dried her tears and began to take in deep breaths of air. "Oh that *is* good news. I really didn't fancy being a Goddess."

"*Really*, darling?" said Sicily, her voice dripping with sarcasm. "I would never have guessed." Adrianna Jasmine allowed herself to laugh at the silliness of it all. What a waste of nervous energy, how utterly pointless... then she realised something.

"Hang on, why did you put me through those hellish questions when I'd already answered the million dollar question right from the start?"

"Oh, I thought it would be fun, darling," Sicily answered breezily. "I found them all in a survey from this month's cosmopolitan. The survey's called, *how much of a Goddess are you*?! I thought it would be fun for us to do, darling."

"Goodbye, mother," said Adrianna Jasmine sharply and hung up the phone, leaving Sicily on the other end in fits of giggles at her practical joke.

During spring plant seeds and flowers, grow a magical herb garden, take long walks and drink in the pure magic of the natural surroundings.
(Adrianna Jasmine, 2010)

Chapter 34
Spring is in the Air

March 21st and Adrianna Jasmine's world was teeming with life. Firstly, Sarah and Sergio were engaged and Sarah was planning a large party to honour the occasion; Clementine had made FHM's top ten sexiest women, although was devastated to have been placed ninth after Jessica Simpson due to her obviously being more well-known - sore loser; Sicily had been offered her own column for the magazine, Mind Spirit Fusion, due to mentioning to the editor at a charity luncheon that she was a fan of natural remedies and only ate organic food. Apparently the editor was highly impressed with Sicily and duly sacked Magic Maud Evens, who was actually a trained psychologist and prominent Wiccan, that afternoon via text. Inaccurate, dated and boring were the words used. He had appeared very determined to get rid of the poor unsuspecting woman, who had been a long and loyal employee of the magazine for almost ten years! Hmmmm, must have been something Sicily had said. Now Sicily answers emails and letters during the dead of night - well it's the only time she has to do it - from lost and confused souls searching for answers to improve their spirit, health and general wellbeing. Could be dangerous! Henry Forthright Punch was doing particularly well as the orchestra pianist for the critically acclaimed show, Chicago, and was debating whether or not to accept the offer of a three month contract with the Broadway cast in New York.

"Do it, darling," encouraged Sicily enthusiastically. "It'll be lovely. I can come with you; I can write my column from the big apple!" She seemed to momentarily forget that she had a full-time job at the college and that her daughter was planning a wedding. Henry didn't take it, anyway, on the grounds that his daughter was getting married, but if the offer ever came up again, he would be more than happy to accept. Then, of course, there was Taylor. He was currently in Morocco, filming a series about North African cuisine to be aired during the ghastly winter months, brightening up miserable, cold Britain with images of flaming spices, yellow sand and a glowing sun. Adrianna Jasmine missed him dearly but was due to visit him shortly and, of course, was very much looking forward to the trip.

"I've always loved Morocco," sang Sicily one afternoon whilst the two witches were walking up Hampstead Heath. "Oh I could tell you some stories, darling about Morocco." Adrianna Jasmine rolled her eyes; she knew another account of her mother's sordid sex stories from when she was young and nubile was on its way. "When I was a dancer at the Moulin Rouge, the Moulin Rouge, darling, can you believe it? My friends, Pippy, Svetlana, Googie, Jo Jo, and I were invited by a very handsome, rich Arab to spend three nights in Morocco and personally entertain him and a few of his chums." Adriana Jasmine's face was a picture.

"Oh, mother! Please don't tell me you went for it?"

"Yes, darling, of course I did. What girl wouldn't?"

Adrianna Jasmine shook her head in disbelief. "Err, respectable girls, frightened girls or any girl with half a brain cell, perhaps?"

Bafflement spread over Sicily's face. "Don't be ridiculous, darling, this world is for living, not for allowing opportunities to pass you by. I couldn't let a little thing like fear put me off something like that, this was a great opportunity."

Adrianna Jasmine snorted. "Yeah right, for the dirty old men."

"Dirty *old* men, darling, dirty *old* men? I'll have you know they were not old! Dirty, yes! But not old." She began to chuckle.

"Ugh, mother must you share these stories with me, your daughter? I find them quite disturbing."

"Oh, darling, you're such a prude," said her mother dismissively, "I don't understand it, did I not raise you to celebrate your body, to dance naked under the full moon once in a while, to openly explore your sexuality - because you never know, darling -

and to remember that your beauty and body is a gift to all men; they should worship you for it?"

"Yes, yes and yes," sighed Adrianna Jasmine."

"Well then, what's the big deal?" asked Sicily, almost sounding exasperated. "You're a natural entity, a witch, a true soul of the earth: instinctive, raw and heaving with sexual energy. Goddess, if I were you, I'd be out there, darling, exploiting my cupcakes with whipped cream and cherries!"

Adrianna Jasmine stifled a giggle; she would not let her mother make her lose focus during the debate. "I know, mother, and I have done all of those things that you have advised me to do, but unlike you, I don't like to shout out about them. I like my secrets, they keep me warm at night."

"Piffle, darling. If you can't tell me your secrets then I suppose we are not as close as I thought. I'm actually quite hurt."

"Oh shut up, mother," snapped Adrianna Jasmine, "you're not hurt, you're just bloody nosy, that's all." Sicily went to argue back but then closed her mouth in defeat. "Ha!" said Adrianna Jasmine triumphantly, "I knew it."

Sicily began to sulk. "Well, it's because I'm interested in you, darling, and it does wind me up when everyone else has a nice little gossip with me and my own daughter digs in her heels and won't spill. I'm only interested in you. I don't really care about anyone else!"

"That's rubbish as well," answered Adrianna Jasmine firmly.

"Oh alright, I suppose it is, darling. But I do like to know about you. Anyway," Sicily carried on, unfazed, "we ended up having such fun in Morocco and all we had to do was perform a few well-rehearsed routines for a couple of hours a night and we each went home with three thousand pounds in our pockets!"

"Three thousand pounds? Wow, just for performing a few well known routines? Goddess, talk about money for old rope. I'm actually stunned."

"I know, crazy, isn't it? And we stayed in a magnificent 6 star hotel. Why, we each had a suite, how about that! Oh it was plush. Everything was gold, gold taps, gold bath, why, even some of the servants were painted gold!"

Adrianna Jasmine raised her brows, she was impressed, not about out the people who had been cruelly painted gold in the manor of an abused Bond girl, but the fact that her mother hadn't undertaken anything racy. "And all you did was dance a few numbers, nothing else?"

"Nothing else, darling," said Sicily proudly.

"Really?" asked her daughter, she could feel herself softening. Perhaps that was all her mother had to do, after all, the routines at the Moulin Rouge at the time were very sexy and the girls were scantily clad to say the least, so perhaps that was enough for the men.

"Absolutely, darling," confirmed Sicily, "that was all we did."

Adrianna Jasmine heaved a sigh of relief.

"Except, of course, when we were offered to indulge in a few heavy sessions of hubbly bubbly, perform lesbian acts and join in the largest orgy I've ever seen in my life, darling."

Adrianna Jasmine immediately sped up her step in style of Olympian going for the fasted walker trophy. *Ugh now I have images of my mother naked sucking on a hubbly bubbly. Great!*

"I can't believe you're getting married, Sarah," said Adrianna Jasmine excitedly to her chum who was sitting in Adrianna Jasmine's kitchen enjoying a glass of pinot grigio blush ,whilst munching into a bowl of cracked black pepper-and-lemon peanuts. "It's just so wonderful to think you and I are tying the knot, virtually together!"

"I know!" answered Sarah enthusiastically, "the next thing is we'll be expecting at the same time."

Adrianna Jasmine giggled. "Goddess, what a blessing that would be! Just think, going through the pregnancy together, the indigestion and weird cravings, antenatal class, the birth! Play dates the birthday parties and the cakes!"

Sarah smiled. She was glowing with happiness. "Hey, thanks for all this tonight, Jazzy. I really appreciate it, thank you."

Adrianna Jasmine went over to her friend and kissed her on the cheek, she had planned and prepared a wonderful girly party in honour of her friend's engagement and, of course, the food and drink was simply divine. "What else are friends for?" said Adrianna Jasmine sincerely. "Come on, let's go and join the others. I believe my smoked salmon rotolos, Szechuan pepper chicken with homemade tomato chilli jam and Mojitos are good to go." They entered the living room to a throng of cheers from the girls who certainly all appreciated a bit of salmon rotolo and a potent Mojito or two!

"Wey hey," sang Clementine smacking her hands together as she clapped her eyes on the Cuban rum treat. "Let's get this party started!" All the women cheered as Sarah handed them all a drink and Adrianna Jasmine popped delicious food onto their plates. There were twelve women all in all: Clementine, of course who was dressed in white tight-fitting jeans and a navy blue figure hugging T shirt with a picture of Marilyn Monroe on the front; Sarah's mother Blair and Blair's two sisters Anuk and Claudia, who both had inherited the red hair gene and poor magic ability. Kristobella, Sicily, Carolina Plum, Bella Bell, Sarah's cousin Sky, who was the daughter of Claudia and her other cousin, Megan who was the daughter of Blair's brother, Eric; Sarah's granny, Flora May, who was 72 and didn't look a day over fifty, acted like she was thirty, drank like someone who was twenty and had a liver like Captain Blackbeard, the pirate.

"OK, who's up for a bit of Madonna?"

"Oh, I love Madonna," cooed Sarah, "go on, put her on. I fancy a bit of a sing-song." Adrianna Jasmine winked over at Clementine who smiled back knowingly at her cousin. Three minutes later there was a gasp. "Oh-my-Goddess," squealed Sarah," Madonna is in the house!" Cheers went up like a box of fireworks as the lady herself appeared in a white lace wedding dress and crucifixes dangling from her neck and arms, belting out Like a Virgin. "It's her, it's really her. I can't believe it, whose CD is it?" Adrianna Jasmine pretended to look at her nails. "Oh, you naughty girl, Adrianna Jasmine. That was meant to be your gift, you wanted Michael Jackson."

Adrianna Jasmine shrugged. "I couldn't decide in the end, so I decided to wait and use the CD for a special occasion and what better an occasion than my best buddy's engagement party?"

"You're the best," squealed Sarah, nearly squeezing the life out of her friend as she gave her a massive hug.

"No worries," choked Adrianna Jasmine, "come, enjoy. This is all for you."

Of course, Madonna was marvellous and sang a plethora of her all-time favourites. She changed into iconic outfits, danced, entertained and threw a jolly good concert for the twelve women, all in the comfort of Adrianna Jasmine's home. Sicily particularly enjoyed Vogue and couldn't help but stand up and do the actions. Clementine rather enjoyed Justify My Love; Flora May rather liked Material Girl and sang along with the queen of pop whilst Kristobella and Carolina showed off their line-dancing skills to Tell Me. Bella Bell, who was also a fan of Madonna, particularly enjoyed the queen of pop's rendition of Papa Don't Preach, and took everyone by surprise when she leapt onto the couch and began to dance about frantically to her favourite song. Sarah's cousins just sat astonished for almost two hours as Madonna sang and danced right before their eyes. They were not used to such wondrous magic as their skills were rather limited, they were as mesmerised at the mind-boggling sight just as much as any non-witch Madonna fan would be. Madonna closed with Express Yourself, Music and Hollywood, before shouting out, "Thank you and Goodnight." Then she faded like a sunset before their very eyes. The witches cheered and clapped, stomped their feet and buzzed like bees on E colourings.

"Right," said Adrianna Jasmine clapping her hands together with a loud smack. "Who's for more food and wine?" There was nothing quite like a good feed after watching a concert, all the witches' hands went up enthusiastically. "Okay, I'll be back in a jiffy."

"I'll come and give you hand," offered Carolina Plum, "I need some air, anyway." She followed a grateful Adrianna Jasmine to the kitchen. "Well done, my darling," praised Carolina as they entered the witch's kitchen, which was peppered with trays of delicious food, "you've done a splendid job." She reached over and hugged Adrianna Jasmine warmly. Adrianna Jasmine began to feel all the most wonderful feelings of happiness the universe could offer, wash over her like some giant wave.

She sighed with pleasure. "Thanks Carolina. I needed that."

Carolina chuckled. "Anyway, what can I do to help?" Adrianna Jasmine asked Carolina to salt the margarita glasses, then cut the homemade rocky road into bite-size pieces so Adrianna Jasmine could get on with the margarita cocktails. She then heated up a batch of homemade chilli before ladling it over nachos and adding grated cheese over the top.

"Okay, I think we're done," said Adrianna Jasmine with a satisfying nod. "Come on, let's get this out. The natives are getting restless." Once again Adrianna Jasmine was greeted to the sound of appreciative cheers from the girls upon entrance.

"Ooh, I love margaritas," cooed Clementine as she took a hefty gulp.

"Now, now, Clementine," teased Sicily, "the margarita is to be enjoyed and savoured; not knocked back like some tacky shot in the uni bar." Clementine didn't even look up at Sicily, however, Adrianna Jasmine saw Clementine mumble something. Seconds later there was a sharp cry from Sicily as the margarita glass shattered into tiny pieces and the cold, alcoholic slush, went all down her front. A startled silence swept across the room as the witches took stock. Once they all realised what had happened, movement stirred and soon everyone was up to assist the now angry, yet shivering, sticky Sicily. She didn't say anything but she knew exactly why her glass had shattered and pretended to play dumb for the moment. In fact, so did her daughter.

"Be a darling and get mummy a cloth, won't you, pom pom? Mummy's a bit sticky." She tinkled a laugh whilst glancing over at Clementine who was stifling a laugh, her head buried in her margarita glass.

"Come into my room, mum," encouraged her daughter, "you're soaked through. You'll need a change of clothes."

Sicily nodded. "Actually, yes, that's a good idea, pumpkin pie. I am a trifle wet and it's trickling into my knickers, so get out the tracki botts, darling. I'm in the mood for comfort." She got up clutching a towel over her body.

"Careful, everyone, there's glass afoot," warned Flora May

"Don't worry, I'll get the hoover," offered Kristobella, "you sort out Sicily, Adrianna Jasmine and I'll clean up in here." Adrianna Jasmine nodded and directed her mother to the bedroom.

"Did you see that, darling?" seethed Sicily. "That little witch. Why, I'll cook her, I'll fry her, I'll bake her in the oven like the witch in Hansel and Gretel. She will rue the day..."

"Shut up, mother," snapped Adrianna Jasmine. "You shouldn't keep goading her. Why you do, I'll never know. Clementine is not on a white path at the moment, she's destructive and experimenting with the dark stuff. She mustn't be provoked; otherwise it's an excuse for her to try out the spells from the shadows."

Sicily scoffed. "I don't care for the certain protocol required around that stupid girl, if she's into the dark stuff, more fool her. I will not pitter patter around her. Why, if she wants to play, I'll play and I'll win. I'll win without even doing anything! The threefold law will take care of that. Actually... threefold law, strong and true, do your will and no time to queue. A lesson is ripe, waiting to be told and remember what she did; it left me cold!"

"Oh, mother!"

"Well, she needs to learn, sweetheart. Now where's that fruity tracksuit that I like? It's very comfy and apparently that Jordon girl is a big fan of the label. I like her, she's got a bit of spunk."

Adrianna Jasmine sighed in frustration. "It's juicy, mother, juicy!"

"Yes, she is, rather. I read the papers; I know all about her cheeky exploits." Adrianna Jasmine opened her mouth to speak, but a piercing scream stopped her before the words could come out. The scream had come from the living room.

"Oh my Goddess!" came the terrified cries from Sky and Megan. "What's happened to Clementine?" The two witches, who were clearly not used to the magical exploits of their cousin's world, began to shake and quiver with fear. Moments later, Sicily, clad in a bright tangerine tracksuit, burst into the room and burst into a fit of laughter.

"Oh, Clementine, won't you ever learn?" Adrianna Jasmine nudged her way next to her mother and gasped in horror. Clementine's skin appeared to be turning from sun kissed caramel to a very unflattering shade of icy blue. Her hair was becoming brittle as if it had become wet then exposed to sub-zero temperatures, her body shaking violently with cold.

"It's not a laughing matter," said Adrianna Jasmine firmly as she pushed her way through the sea of startled eyes.

Megan was actually crying, "she could actually die, she looks positively hypothermic." Kristobella, like her sister, was chuckling, but unlike Sicily, Kristobella had the decency to mask her amusement.

"Mother, do something. I don't know what to do."

Sicily simply shrugged. "Don't be silly, darling, what am *I* supposed to do? It's simply the way of the threefold law, nothing to do with me."

"But she could die, mother. Look, she's beginning to convulse. Her heart could stop at any moment." Adrianna Jasmine's eyes were desperate as she implored her mother, but Sicily's face was stone cold and hard.

"It's the way," she repeated her voice heartless. Adrianna Jasmine glowered up at her mother; she wanted to yell at her, to say it was her fault, that she pressed the threefold law to punish Clementine for smashing the glass and causing icy margarita to spill all over Sicily. However, she didn't, she couldn't. Not in front of the other witches, she couldn't betray her mother, even though she didn't agree with what her mother had done.

"Mother," implored Adrianna Jasmine through gritted teeth and fiery eyes, "help her." Adrianna Jasmine's voice was serious and as hard as diamonds. "Do... it...now." The tension in the room began to tighten as the room became deathly silent except from Clementine's frantically chattering teeth. The cackle could sense from the way Adrianna Jasmine was looking at her mother that something wasn't right. Sicily was stood, rooted to the spot, her jaw was set, her eyes emotionless, she was not going to budge.

"Oh, for Goddess sake, give her to me." Everyone looked over to see Carolina Plum take the now semi-conscious Clementine from Adrianna Jasmine's arms and cradle her like a baby. "My Goddess, she's close to death," she whispered in shock. Adrianna Jasmine took in a much needed gulp of air. "Everyone join hands and call the elements for their support," beckoned Carolina, "this is going to be tough."

"Come, everyone," advised the wise Flora May, "let us link hands to strengthen Carolina's skill." Everyone leapt up and immediately linked hands in a circle around Carolina and the dying Clementine. Sicily was prepared not to move, but her daughter literally yanked her into the circle and forced her to hold hands with Kristobella, who in all fairness, was about the only witch in the room prepared to do so. Carolina held Clementine tight and began to rock and kiss her like a baby.

Oh Goddess within, shine bright through me.
Triple my powers with the power of three.
My embrace is healing, my touch does heal
Before your feet I do but kneel.
Bring warmth to her body through my bones and skin,
Heat her with fire, deep from within.
Soften ice, melt away the cold;
Heel her quick through my gifted hold.
Blessed be.

The witches could barely look as Carolina chanted her spell and soon they too were saying it with her. Their voices were sturdy and powerful, as if they were conjuring up the very roots of the earth, the deepest minerals of the sea, the nutrients from the air and the very heat from the fire. The room was positively electric with power and magic, it crackled with energy and ran through their very veins.

"Keep chanting, witches. I can feel a change in me," shouted Carolina, strong and true. "Keep going, more passion, more will, I can..." The witches gasped as they witnessed before their very eyes, Carolina glowing like flame. A certain peace came over them and quietness and serenity took charge. The witches automatically dropped to their knees and bowed their heads in honour of the Goddess as they watched a true miracle form.

"Look," whispered Flora May in awe, "she's...melting."

There was a stir from the cackle as they all witnessed Clementine being brought back from near death. Her hair began to defrost and droplets began to drip onto Carolina's chest and arms. She cradled Clementine's head and delicately placed kisses upon her cheeks and forehead. As she did so, Clementine's skin began to adjust itself from ice blue to a healthy tan. Her breathing became steady and regular and soon her eyes began to open. She lay still for a few moments as she became familiar with her surroundings. She was confused. Why was she being held in the arms of Carolina Plum as if she were her daughter? And why were the cackle circled around her on their knees? And why were Sky and Megan crying? Clementine's eyes searched for answers; she saw Adrianna Jasmine peer furiously over to Sicily whose face was blank and unreadable. She saw Kristobella shake her head and glower over at her sister before fixing her eyes upon Sarah who was clutching onto her mother.

"What happened?" she whispered. And why were her clothes wet?

"Err, we're not sure," said Carolina gently, careful to not overwhelm. She discreetly glanced over to Sicily, "but you suddenly became very cold and for a moment we thought we would lose you." Clementine's eyes began to fill with tears. She felt afraid. One moment Madonna was in the house, the next she was enjoying a margarita, and the next, darkness. Where did those missing minutes go? "Oh, hush you're safe now, little one," assured Carolina and she hugged Clementine tightly. Immediately Clementine's fears and woes began to appease, and a few minutes later she was tucked up in Adrianna Jasmine's bed with a cup of hot chocolate.

"What the hell happened there?" said Carolina sharply to Sicily after Clementine had been put safely to bed. "You stupid woman. I know you dislike the girl but you nearly killed her, I'm warning you, Sicily Poppleapple, your antics over the past couple of months have been too much to bear, what with..."

"Err, okay. That's enough, thank you. I'll deal with my sister."

Luckily, Kristobella intervened and broke up the torrent of verbal abuse from Carolina's angry mouth. "Come on, Sis. Let's go."

But Sicily stood her ground. "I'm not going anywhere," she said breezily. "*I've* done nothing wrong."

"Just go," said Carolina sharply. Adrianna Jasmine gasped, she had never heard her so mad.

"I will do nothing of the sort," said Sicily firmly. "This is my daughter's home and I will not leave until my daughter asks me to." At once all eyes were focused on Arianna Jasmine, *great!* She knew her mother did wrong but she couldn't abandon her, so she said the first thing that sprang to mind.

"How about a nice cup of tea? Tea fixes everything, you know!" Carolina looked at Adrianna Jasmine as if she were mad.

"Tea? TEA! Sicily nearly killed that girl and all you think of is offering tea. If we were regular people, I'd say call the police." Carolina was spitting daggers.

There was a gasp from the cackle, Sicily's face was indifferent. "I did nothing of the sort."

"No?" Carolina bit back hard, "because from where we're all sitting, the evidence is pretty clear that it was!"

"Don't be ridiculous," said Sicily almost sounding bored, "I never touched her."

"You don't need to touch her, Sicily," shouted Carolina enraged. "You could cause harm to her by just wishing it, thinking it, dreaming it, in fact. But I'm warning you, the law of three will have something to say about that."

With that, Sicily's eyes darkened and the lights in the room began to flicker.

"Watch your tongue," said Sicily, her voice low and menacing. "I know all about the threefold law and we have already witnessed its power tonight, so get off your high horse and thank the Goddess for saving that little witch's life, because from where I've been inappropriately kneeling for the last half hour, no-one has." And with that, Sicily picked up her bag and swept out of the flat, leaving an icy chill in her wake.

Rose Petal Cupcakes

150 g softened unsalted butter
150 g caster sugar
3 medium eggs, at room temperature
150 g self-raising flour
1 tbsp rose water
100 ml milk
1 packets instant royal icing
rose petals or silver balls, to decorate

Preheat the oven to 190C/gas 5. Line a 12-hole muffin tray with papers. Cream together the butter and sugar and the eggs. Fold in the flour, followed by the rose water. Next, start adding the milk - you may not need it all. Spoon the mixture into the muffin papers and bake in the oven until cooked through and golden, about 20 minutes. Turn out onto a rack to cool. Make up a big batch of royal icing and spoon onto the cakes. Leave to set before decorating with rose petals.

Chapter 35
Rose Petal Cupcakes

It was last week of April and Adrianna Jasmine and Sicily were enjoying a cup of coffee and a rose petal cupcake in the coffee shop.

"So, when are you going to pick up the phone and call Carolina, mum?" enquired Adrianna Jasmine. "It's been almost four weeks since you two have spoken, when is all this silly nonsense going to end?"

Sicily shrugged her shoulders nonchalantly. "When she apologises," she said with a sweet smile and airy tone.

Adrianna Jasmine rolled her eyes. "I don't think *she* is the one who should be apologising, mother, and after all, you were the one who almost froze Clementine to death."

"Oh, piff puff, darling. She was never going to die. Unfortunately," she added darkly.

Adrianna Jasmine became angry. "Right, so that's it, is it, with you and Clementine?" Sicily looked indifferent. "Come on, it's got to be something huge, you've disliked that girl for years now, and you make a point of making it obvious not only to her but to other people, too."

Sicily huffed. "Oh, can't you just drop it, toffee crisp? Talking about that little witch is such a bore."

"No, I won't," snapped Adrianna Jasmine sharply, "you need to tell me right now because I'm finding it very hard to cope with the fact my mother almost killed my cousin, intentionally."

Sicily chuckled. "So dramatic, darling." By now, Adrianna Jasmine was furious; her mother was certainly pushing her patience buttons today. She took a deep breath and tried to calm her twisted nerves.

"Is it because you're jealous of Clementine?"

Sicily nearly choked on her coffee. "Don't be ridiculous, darling."

"I don't believe I am being ridiculous, I've been trying to figure out the reason why you hate her, and well, this is what I've come up with."

"Then you're not as intelligent as I thought," replied Sicily. "I'm actually quite shocked at your naivety."

"I am not naive," said Adrianna Jasmine tartly.

Sicily shrugged nonchalantly, "Well your process of elimination has truly failed, darling, and unfortunately you have come up with the most flimsy excuse as to why sometimes a person dislikes another person."

"Oh, do explain, then." Adrianna Jasmine couldn't wait to hear this one!

"First of all, darling, I am not the sort of woman to dislike someone just because they have long legs and a cute face; I'd like to think that I try to perceive myself as a much deeper soul than that. Secondly, one of my pet peeves is when a person uses the excuse that people do not like them because of the colour of their skin. What the whiny person fails to realise is that the reason people dislike them so much, is simply down to the fact that they are a nasty piece of work. And that brings me to the real conclusion as to why I dislike Clementine and it is not because she looks beautiful in a bikini, but because she's simply a nasty piece of work."

Adrianna Jasmine sighed deeply as she took stock. "Okay... why is she a nasty piece of work, in your opinion, is it purely because she's experimenting with dark magic?"

"Yes," hissed Sicily her eyes turning dark, "that's precisely it."

"Oh, mother, she's only experimenting and I've spoken to her about it. I'm sure it's just a phase."

"It's not a phase," said her mother darkly. "She's on a dark path, that one, and she will never steer off it, never."

Adrianna Jasmine screwed up her face. "No, I don't believe that. Clementine is a good kid, a bit confused, but a good kid. She wouldn't go too far."

"Naive, naive, naïve, darling. I thought you were more intuitive than this, why, you used to be able to see into the future when you were little, perhaps it's time to reawaken the talent a little"

"You know I don't like looking into the future, its wrong and frightening. Besides, we've got the mystic Odessa over there; she keeps me updated with any future events."

Sicily chuckled lightly. "Well, I can understand that, tear drop, but sometimes future predictions come to us whether we like it or not."

Adrianna Jasmine lowered her voice. "You mean, you still read the future?"

Sicily nodded solemnly. "Yes, but not intentionally. The art of divination was always one of my strong gifts, but like you, I don't really agree with it and it's something, for safety reasons, I like to keep quiet." Sicily's face became serious and thoughtful. "But the predictions come to me when I least expect them. For instance, when I'm asleep." Sicily thumped the table in frustration. "Cursed sleep, I've never agreed with it, it's a filthy waste of precious time. Or when I'm alone, meditating or reading a book, it's very annoying, darling."

"So, what have you seen?" asked Adrianna Jasmine quietly, "what have you seen that scares you so much about Clementine?"

Sicily sighed heavily, "I've seen her fall deeper and deeper into the darkness, I've seen her hook up with unsavoury creatures that use their craft to harm and punish the innocent. I've seen dark spells that harm and punish, come from her very own hand. And I've watched in vain as good witches, such as you, Mrs Sparrow, *Carolina*, try to steer her into the light. But it's no use and one day she will cause havoc and pain; even kill."

The two witches sat in silence for a while.

"Are you sure, mother? I mean, how can you be absolutely sure?"

Sicily sighed tiredly.

"I can't be sure for certain, jammy dodger, they're only predictions. They're not concrete proof but so far they've come true and unfortunately she has already taken to the path, she will naturally have to come to the end. I was aware she wouldn't die that night, I've seen her alive far into the future. Besides, I knew the spell to cure her and believe me, it didn't involve all that ludicrous piffle Carolina conjured up."

Adrianna Jasmine raised her eyebrows in disbelief.

"Oh, for Goddess sake, mother!"

Sicily smiled cheekily. "I know, I know. All she needed was to be rubbed down by one of us with a chilli pepper along with a request to the element of fire to warm her up a bit. There was absolutely no need for that dramatic rubbish from Carolina Plum!"

Adrianna Jasmine took a bite out of her cupcake. "So what do you think should be done with Clementine? Is there no hope?"

"Is there hope for heroin addicts? At some point that girl will be no different to an addict who is in so deep that they end up stealing from their own family to feed their filthy habit. No one will get through to her, she will become a locked door, a force of pure evil and, quite frankly, I'm very worried, puffer fish."

"So what should be done?"

"She should be killed," said Sicily her voice void of emotion. "But it will not be from my hand directly, although, and this is for your ears only, Adrianna Jasmine," said Sicily, her voice low and serious, "I give my word to the Goddess that if and when I can be any assistance to the threefold law to hurry the process up, I will."

"Hen parties are not about control, make sure all the girls are comfortable and happy with what is to be expected. Go with the flow, relax and enjoy!"
(Clementine)

Chapter 36
Hen Party

"This is totally amazing," squealed Sarah in absolute delight. The sun was hot and delicious as she tilted her head skywards. "I can't believe we're all here for five days of fun in the sun!"

Adrianna Jasmine felt a pang of excitement as she stepped off the plane. It was her hen party and Clementine had arranged a five day trip, staying in a five-star hotel in Tenerife's up-market Playa Adeje. She had managed to arrange an all-inclusive, luxury holiday for almost next to nothing, thanks to a wealthy admirer she had met at some party, who just so happened to own a rather large and elite travel agency. The smitten, although married businessman, arranged for Clementine and eight of her pals to stay at The Hotel Glorious, virtually free. All they had to do was pay for their flights and twenty percent of their bill and, hey presto, a five star luxurious holiday for the price of a 1 star B&B in Blackpool. Fabulous! The witches all hurried excitedly through passport control, giggling and chatting enthusiastically as tourists and officials stared in awe as the wondrous women oozing with magic, charming scents and strong physical beauty, swept past.

"Right, are we all here?" enquired Clementine professionally, as the cackle reached passport control. She was dressed alluringly in white designer shorts, blue and white nautical inspired fitted top and gold wedged sandals. "I'll just do a quick head count," she was looking very efficient with her clipboard, pen and soft leather briefcase. "Adrianna Jasmine, *the mother*," she said with just a hint of sarcasm to her voice, "Kristobella, Sarah, Carolina, Sky, Megan, Bella and of course, me! Great, everyone is here." She then penned a tick mark next to everyone's name in the manner of, albeit a very sexy, school teacher, taking a group of fifth- formers away on a field trip. "OK, ladies, once we retrieve our luggage, go to the main entrance and there should be two white limos under the name of Poppleapple waiting for us." There was a chorus of oohs and aahs from the witches.

"Wow, this keeps getting better and better," exclaimed Sarah. "I wonder if we'll see anyone famous."

Adrianna Jasmine squeezed her friend's hand. "Maybe." She was feeling so happy and excited, if only she could bottle her feelings to remember them forever and ever. Oh wait, she could if she wanted to. She looked down at her beautiful red maxi dress, Kristobella had given her to wear for the journey, teamed with an enormous, tan leather sling bag, police aviator sun glasses and pretty diamante sandals from Dune. Yes, she was looking and feeling absolutely perfect.

The cackle made their way through passport control, collected their luggage from the carousel, then it was off into the sunshine once more and straight into two glistening, air conditioned, white limos.

"Right everyone, AJ, Sicily, Sarah and Kristobella take the first one, everyone else with me." One by one the witches sidled into the limos, every witch was smiling with glee.

"Ooh," cooed Sicily as she languished lazily into the soft leather seats, "how very sensual. Why, it reminds me of the time I was driven around New York by a very wealthy businessman called Mario, he owned theatres, shops and restaurants, oh, it was fun, we ate caviar, drank champagne, saw all the sights and a few more, if you catch my drift." Kristobella turned her nose up in disgust.

"Must you?" she said, "just for once, can you please leave out your sordid stories from the past?"

"POP!"

"Oh, wow, champagne," cried out Adrianna Jasmine in excitement, "perfect timing."

Sarah poured the champagne into everyone's glasses to a chorus of giggles and cheers.

"To Adrianna Jasmine, Taylor and a fabulous holiday!" enthused Sicily with a huge grin on her face.

"To Adrianna Jasmine, to Taylor and to a fabulous holiday," the witches all chorused and with that they drank their fill and tucked into a box of beautiful chocolates.

"Oh my goddess," breathed Adrianna Jasmine as she stepped out of the limo and gazed up in awe at the wondrous hotel standing before them. "It's like something out of a fairy tale." Sicily gasped, and Sarah clapped her hands in sheer excitement.

"Oh yes, this is us," said Kristobella. "I think we'll be very comfortable here."

With that, the second limo pulled up and the rest of the cackle spilled out onto the sun-drenched stone floor. As expected, excitement bubbled and fizzed through their veins as the newcomers to the group drank in the impressive hotel, all sparkly and white.

"Right everyone, follow me." Clementine with clipboard in hand took control once more and began to lead the witches into hotel reception. "Leave the luggage, it'll be taken up to our rooms by the porters." The witches merrily followed suit, enjoying the VIP experience.

"Oh I feel rather like Jackie O today," said Sicily.

"You're as old as her," mumbled Clementine under her breath.

"I'm really starting to connect with her, I think it may have something to do with…"

"The oversized glasses and hat?" cut in Adrianna Jasmine; Sicily chuckled.

"Well, I do agree that her unique and timeless style has inspired my overall look today but the real connection is the way I'm feeling, darling,"

"Oh?" inquired her daughter, "how is that?"

"I'm beginning to understand her, butter ball. I'm beginning to connect with her spiritually and actually understand what it's like to be admired by the masses, to be incredibly rich and iconic." Adrianna Jasmine raised her right eyebrow.

"Since when have you been incredibly rich and iconic?"

"Right now, darling. I'm surprised you even ask such a thing." Adrianna Jasmine wanted to say that writing a column in a monthly magazine didn't make her filthy famous and a virtually free holiday didn't make her filthy rich, but filthy lucky! However, she decided to keep quiet and allow her mother to wallow in her Jackie O moment.

Of course, as the witches entered the hotel, the holiday-makers and staff all stopped and marvelled at the sumptuous specimens gliding with grace and loveliness towards the reception area.

"Party under the name of Poppleapple," said Clementine, full of wealthy confidence.

"Ah yes, we've been expecting you," said the handsome, tall, dark receptionist. He was probably in his early fifties, slightly greying and impeccably dressed. Kristobella couldn't help but offer him a little sexy smile. "Please make your way out onto the terrace for welcome cocktails, canapés and cool towels. Rodrigo!" Moments later a young Spaniard, with chocolate brown, melt in the mouth, eyes appeared from out of nowhere and into the chic black and white marbled reception area.

"Ladies, if you would be so kind to follow me," said the dashing Rodrigo with a courteous bow. Megan and Sky giggled girlishly, Rodrigo was a stud muffin just longing to be bitten into.

"So far so good," said Sicily with a cheeky grin. "And the hotel's not bad either."

"I'll say," added Kristobella who winked playfully at the receptionist. He blushed ever so slightly. The cackle followed Rodrigo out of the reception area and onto an enormous terrace that looked to an enchanting blue sea, peppered with very expensive yachts.

"Senoritas, please make yourselves comfortable." Rodrigo gestured towards a choice of sumptuous looking sofas made from the softest, creamiest, white suede one had ever seen, scattered with plump luscious cushions. The witches, smiling in delight, gracefully placed their grateful bottoms onto the plush, sensual fabric. Immediately their grateful bottoms let the whole world know just how satisfied they were via a chorus of praise from the witch's vocal chords.

"Ooh this is positively dreamy," cooed Kristobella.

"Ooh exquisite," sang Bella Bell, "I could spend the next five days right here. I wouldn't mind. And oh look!" She gasped, "I can see the ground below me."

The witches simultaneously looked down towards their feet. It appeared that the terrace's floor was made from some sort of Perspex glass and beneath was a beautifully manicured garden.

"I do hope no one can see up my dress," said Sicily chuckling with amusement, "after all, I am a lady."

Clementine couldn't help but snort a little at the remark, which in turn evoked childish giggles from Sky and Megan.

"That will not be possible," said Rodrigo politely. The witches all looked up and gawped like lovesick kittens at the handsome hunk. "The garden below is out of bounds to guests so your modesty is protected senorita." He gave a little bow and for the first time ever in her life, Sicily actually blushed. Adrianna Jasmine couldn't help but smile a little as she witnessed her mother ever so slightly lose her cool to a sexy young man.

"Ah Champagne," tinkled Sicily as a waiter from nowhere appeared with a tray filled with tall, elegant glasses, dancing with fizz and bubbles. "I could do with a drink." The witches graciously accepted their sparkling treats and helped themselves to delicious seafood canapés and sweet petit fours whilst languishing on soft white sofas, gazing out towards the sparkly blue sea.

"Oh, this is the life hey, girlies," said Kristobella to Sky and Megan who were both grinning from ear to ear whilst drinking in the wonder of it all. "Have you ever received five- star luxury treatment like this before?" The girls shook their heads.

"We've been to Magaluf and Cyprus together," said Megan, "but it was a bit of budget holiday, really, and the accommodation was pretty basic."

"Although, don't get us wrong, we had a great time," added Sky enthusiastically. "But I must say, this is totally amazing. I never dreamed we would actually experience, well... this!"

Kristobella sighed in satisfaction. "Well, get used to it, you two, because with your lovely looks and talents, you shouldn't expect anything less. So no more budget holidays for you, my girls, its high flying, five-star and cocktails all the way." Sky nodded eagerly.

"Although I'm not sure how we could afford to live up to this lifestyle, Kristobella, after all, this is almost a freebee holiday. I wouldn't like to know how much a holiday like this would cost for real!"

"Three and half thousand pounds per person," the three witches looked over towards Clementine, who was busily texting someone.

"You're joking," asked Sky, "what, for five days?"

"Ah ha," said Clementine not even bothering to look up, "so enjoy it, girlies. Things like this don't come along every day." She then looked at her watch and jumped up theatrically. "Right, I'm off to meet... an old friend. Rodrigo has been instructed to take you to your suites in about thirty minutes, then perhaps spend the rest of the day around the pool. I'll meet you there a little later, and remember, order anything you desire, it's all on the house."

The witches couldn't help but smile.

"Who is this friend, Clementine?" enquired Adrianna Jasmine, trying to sound nonplussed. Clementine said nothing but gave her cousin a cheeky wink.

"I'll see you later," she said and as she turned her back, Sarah and Adrianna Jasmine exchanged glances.

"What's the guessing it's a man, he's very rich and he organised this whole trip?"

Adrianna Jasmine nodded. "I would put money on it, Sarah."

"Oh, I'm so thrilled we've got interconnecting suites, what fun. To think, the midnight chats, the gossip, the popping in and out in between getting ready, oh it's wonderful, lemon pips." Adrianna Jasmine and Sarah raised their eyebrows.

"Yes, wonderful," said Adrianna Jasmine trying to match her mother's enthusiasm. Somehow Adrianna Jasmine and Sarah had been given interconnecting rooms with her mother. *Goddess, there will be no peace from the old witch.*

"Oh, you haven't eaten our complimentary praline truffles yet, they're absolutely delicious," exclaimed Sicily. She was diving towards the box before anyone could stop her, "you must try, rainbow drops!"

"Well, we will if you don't scoff them all, mother," said Adrianna Jasmine trying not to sound irritated. Sarah decided to keep well out of it, she liked Sicily but she was also a tiny bit petrified of her.

Sicily tinkled a laugh. "Of course I won't, darling, but I shan't promise anything. Now, you two, hurry up and get your cozzies on, there are rays out there that need to be caught." With that, Sarah began to undress and change into her bikini as if she'd been magically sped up. Adrianna Jasmine and Sicily stared at her in shocked silence.

"What on earth are you doing, Sarah?" enquired Adrianna Jasmine. "It's not the who can change into their bikini the fastest championships 2010, what's up with you? It's like you've been injected with some sort of amphetamine or something." Sarah began to glow red and Sicily began to chuckle.

"I'll leave you two alone, darlings," and with that, she was gone through the interconnecting door.

Sarah, with her bikini top not quite covering her left breast, looked up and slightly shame-faced met Adrianna Jasmine's perplexed eye. Adrianna Jasmine shrugged her shoulders, "Well?"

"I'm sorry," sighed Sarah, "it's just that your mother really freaks me out as of late, she's all dark and scary. She never used to be. Well, not as much," she added as she adjusted her top, "but she makes me feel, she makes me feel..."

"Unnerved?" offered Adriana Jasmine.

Sarah nodded, "Yes, very much so." *Goddess*, thought Sarah, *at last a chance to offload my feelings*. "I'm sorry, Adrianna Jasmine. She's your mother and I do love her, hell, I've known her most of my adult life but she's changed, and that episode with Clementine at my party has really made wary of her."

Adrianna Jasmine couldn't help but nod in agreement.

"I know," she said slumping onto the king-size bed, "I feel the same, although I don't feel scared. I feel more worried. I don't know why, but I feel that my mother is harbouring a secret and the weight of it is driving her a bit mad."

"Have you spoken to her?"

"No," said Adrianna Jasmine standing up and walking towards the balcony to gaze out towards the twinkling sea, "but I will. It's just going to be tough because I don't think she wants to talk about it and therefore, unless I cast some sort of truth spell on her, which I wouldn't do, I won't squeeze out any information, and by then it could be too late."

Sarah walked over to join her friend.

"Hmmm, it's a tough one. Just keep an eye, something isn't right, I can sense it."

Adrianna Jasmine nodded. "I know," she said trying to lighten the heavy mood, "anyway, come on, as the old witch said. Let's get out the bikinis as there's rays to be caught." Moments later the witches were outside their front door talking and laughing with Sky, Megan, Carolina and Kristobella. The rest of the cackle followed suit and off they marched to the pool looking like something out of a glamour magazine.

The cackle decided to settle around the Lenpora Pool which was situated at the foot of a six-tier garden. They laid their sun-starved bodies out on luxurious, king-size sun loungers whilst sipping scrumptious cocktails and listening to ultra-relaxing tunes from Cafe Del Mar.

"Oh, this is the life," cooed Bella Bell who was slathering herself with Tallulah Toffee's fruity fruit salad, factor fifteen, sun lotion. "I think this trip will recharge me for about six months. The sun feels amazing." Kristobella and Carolina Plum both nodded in agreement.

"I'll say," said Carolina. "Clementine has most certainly outdone herself and oh look, talk of the devil, there she is."

"Hello ladies!" The confident and assured voice of Clementine hit the sound waves as she sashayed towards the cackle. She was wearing a white, floor length, halter neck dress that barley covered her boobs, and some impressive oversized Chanel sun glasses. "Are we all having a tremendous time?"

A torrent of yesses and words of praise for Clementine poured from the witches' mouths, they couldn't have thanked her enough if they tried. Megan and Sky even *cheered*.

Clementine gave a humble bow. "Oh please, it was the least I could do," she said modestly, "anyway it's nice to do something nice once in a while." Luckily, Sicily had her giant Cavalli sun shades that she had purchased from TK Maxx, covering her eyes, because if a picture could paint a thousand words, Sicily's eyes could paint a million.

"Oh, please," she mumbled under her breath.

Clementine coolly sat down next to Carolina Plum and engaged in conversation with the merry witch.

Splash!

"Oh, there go Sky and Megan," Kristobella chuckled to Adrianna Jasmine, "making the most out of the pool and what lovely figures they have." Adrianna Jasmine nodded in agreement.

"Yes, they do, and I'm so pleased they came with us, what a lovely experience for them both."

"I'll say. I'd have killed for an experience like this at their age. How old are they?"

"Eighteen/nineteen, I think. They look like Sarah, don't they."

Kristobella nodded. "Yes, they do but unfortunately their magical abilities mimic the weak Flash Barron trait, no offence to Sarah."

Adrianna Jasmine smiled. "She wouldn't be offended, she knows full well her magic isn't exactly up to par but she's comfortable with it."

"That's good," commented Kristobella, "there's nothing worse than being self-conscious about one's magical disability. Still Sky, I have to say, although not brilliant, appears to have some potential."

Adrianna Jasmine looked interested. "Go on."

"Well, I happened to get chatting to Sky on the plane, on the way over here and she confessed that she can tell if a person's soul has left their body by looking at a photograph of them."

Adrianna Jasmine raised her eyebrow in surprise. "Really? That's a rare gift to have. I only know one witch to have that gift and that would be me!"

Kristobella let out throaty laugh. "I know, Adrianna Jasmine and I have to admit you're the only one who I know to be soul sensitive... until now."

Adrianna Jasmine paused for thought. "It's not a nice gift, mind."

"I wouldn't imagine it is," agreed Kristobella. "I mean, it's not particularly pleasant when a picture of a missing child is splashed all across the front pages of a newspaper and you know instantly that they are no longer alive simply because you cannot see their soul!" Kristobella shuddered. "It's awful, a curse more than a gift."

"It's highly irritating, too," added Adrianna Jasmine, "because all you want to do is call the police and the wretched parents to let them know that their precious babies are no longer in this realm..."Adrianna Jasmine swallowed hard, "after all, who would believe me?"

Kristobella shook her head, "It must be horrendous. What do you do when you see a child, or a missing person's picture, for that matter, minus their souls?"

Adrianna Jasmine looked down towards the floor and her eyes appeared sad. "I cast a spell to appease their souls and guide them into the Summerland's eternal peace."

Kristobella nodded her head, "That's all you can do, I suppose. But to think all of those relatives still wondering if their loved ones are dead or alive, never experiencing closure, life is very cruel." The two witches remained silent for a while until laughter and splashes from the pool broke the sombre mood. "Perhaps you could advise Sky at some point about her gift?"

"Sure," said Adrianna Jasmine with a shrug, "or warn her."

At six o clock the witches decided to withdraw from the swimming pool and return to their suites to enjoy a cocktail whilst getting ready for an evening of fun, food and fashion! Sarah swiped her key card and the pair walked into their luxury suite. It truly was breathtaking, what with the crisp white decor, alluring sea views and personal hot tub on the balcony. It boasted two double bedrooms, both en suite, a steam room and living area with a gigantic plasma TV and squishy white leather sofas.

"It's a dream," cooed Sarah as she sank into the hot tub with a raspberry mojito. "To think, if you hadn't fallen in love, none of this would be happening."

Adrianna Jasmine agreed. "It's true, so, to love!"

The pair chinked glasses and sipped the delicious liquid.

"Hey, I wonder if we'll get to meet the owner." pondered Sarah, Adrianna Jasmine shrugged and sucked on her straw absent-mindedly, she was feeling a little tipsy. "He must be very rich, I mean, just look at this place, a brand new hotel, all that marble and landscaped gardens, gorgeous hand-picked staff, from catalogues it seems and to be able to afford nine borderline alcoholic witches to stay virtually for free for five nights. Well, he must be loaded!"

Adrianna Jasmine nodded; her head was buzzing from the alcohol. "Do you know his name?" She asked speaking slowly, careful not to slur her words. Goddess, this should be her last cocktail for at least thirty minutes.

"Well, his name's Lenni, I believe."

"Lenni? How do you know? Did Clementine tell you?"

Sarah shook her head. "No, when she popped to the loo earlier she left her phone on my sun lounger and when it bing-bonged the screen lit up with the name Lenni."

"So?"

Well, have you noticed the name of our suite and the name of the seafood restaurant that we're dining in tonight? Plus, the number one cocktail that they sell here, which we must try, is the flaming Leonidas and our suite is called the Leonidas suite. But what really made me make the connection is the name of the piano bar, it's called Lenni's bar."

"Ah! I see, good snooping!"

"So, to Lenni, I think," said Sarah and the pair chinked glasses once more.

"Coohee, darlings."

"Oh Goddess," sighed the pair of witches.

"Just popped in to ask what we're wearing tonight." Adrianna Jasmine and Sarah were both laying out a couple of dresses on their beds each debating which ensemble to fashion. "Oh, this is fun, I love being able to pop on in and out." Adrianna Jasmine and

Sarah smiled weakly. "Anyhoo, I'm sure what you both decide to put on will look fabulous. By the way, what time are we meeting the others; I heard Clementine's bringing Crystal!" Sarah gasped.

"You're joking? Crystal, oh my Goddess, that's like £500 quid a pop!"

Sicily looked unimpressed. "Hmmmm, well it's ridiculous if you ask me. Don't get me wrong, I am a great admirer of all things expensive, fancy and French, but that sort of money for a bottle of plonk is obscene."

"I don't care," said Sarah through excited smiles, "I can't wait to sample it, ooh Crystal!"

Sicily shrugged, "Well, we'll see. Anyway, must fly, I think they're all arriving in here at 8.30pm which means, my beauties, you have half an hour to get ready." With that she was gone.

POP, POP went the corks, fizz went the champagne and "hurray" went the witches as they drank the delicious liquid gold.

"To Adrianna Jasmine," they all chorused with aplomb as they toasted the bride to be. Adrianna Jasmine blushed, she was wearing a beautiful black and white Alexander McQueen cocktail dress, courtesy of Kristobella, and her friends had put a bride- to-be sash over her shoulder.

"I wish I was a little more tanned, though," she confessed, "I do feel pasty." The others all agreed that they, too, felt a little under tanned and wished that they had perhaps applied a little fake bake before flying over.

"Well, darlings..." said Sicily mysteriously. "I was waiting for such a perfect moment to present you all with these." The witches all exchanged looks of bewilderment as Sicily momentarily left the room via the interconnecting door, only to return with eight silver sparkly gift bags. She handed them over one by one to the excited girls. Adrianna Jasmine looked sceptically into the bag; Megan and Sky were simply bursting with excitement.

"Oh my Goddess," squealed Sarah in delight, "don't tell me it's, its..."

After removing various objects, such as detox tea bags that you place onto the souls of your feet to draw out the body's impurities, baby bottles of Moet and hair dye that lasts for up to six months, the witches located their star gift.

"Yes, it most certainly is," cried Sicily with animated enthusiasm, "Dr Goombah's latest and greatest invention, Golden Dream Pill." There was a stir of excitement throughout the room.

"What do you do?" Sarah whispered, her whole body was fizzing with glee.

"You simply swallow it with liquid," shrugged Sicily, "and then you wait for about two minutes and watch how your skin transforms from pasty to tasty!"

"Hang on," cut in Adrianna Jasmine her voice etched in caution, "how dark will we go?"

Sicily smiled in order to appease the now shifting mood of doubt back to excitement. "It's all okay, witches, *this* pill will only produce a light tan for all of us, I didn't want us to look unnatural or raise suspicion, after all, we've only been here half a day. No, no this pill will produce what is known as a healthy looking glow, without the worry of skin cancer."

Sarah shrugged her shoulders. "Well, I'm game!" And with that, she popped her pill into her mouth and washed it down with a hearty gulp of Crystal. Soon everyone watched in awe as one by one, everyone in the room began to take on a subtle skin transformation.

"Oh my Goddess," gushed Kristobella once she caught sight of her new skin colour in the mirror, "Sicily, my sister, you have most certainly outdone yourself. I look healthy yet completely natural, and look, my skin ever so slightly shimmers."

There were a chorus of oohs and aahs from every direction.

"Well, come on then, ladies let's get this party started," whooped Sicily, "and remember our little secret lasts an entire three months!"

"Three months! Ugh Katie Price would kill for these pills," said Carolina with a chuckle.

"Ughhhhhhhhh, my head. I need Citrus Bang-Bang Boom right now. Ahhhhh, my head, its pounding, make it stop, make it stop."

Adrianna Jasmine tried to peel her eyes open and search for Sarah. Ugh, why was the room upside down? Oh no, it wasn't the room, it was her. She was on her back hanging off the edge of the bed. *I'm surprised I'm still alive*, she thought. The upside down room was spinning and the witch felt sick.

"Must turn over," she grimaced and tried to roll onto her front but slid off the sheets into a pile on the floor. She landed with a thump. "Ouch," she moaned, "where am I? Sarah, why can't I see you?"

"I'm here, Jazzy, you need to open your eyes."

"I'm afraid; I think my head will explode if I do."

"Oh Goddess, what a night," groaned Sarah. "I can't believe we were so... frolicsome, drunk, uncouth, unladylike and rowdy. I will be surprised if none of us aren't booted out of the hotel, and what was your mother thinking?" Adrianna Jasmine tried to remember and it hurt! "It's all very well getting up and snatching the microphone from the hotel entertainments crew and singing a rendition of Johnny Cash's Ring of Fire, but to set the piano alight and try to put it out with £500 quid's worth of champagne is just unimaginable." Adrianna Jasmine winced at the thought, it was all flooding back to her as she lay there in a pathetic pile of sheets and false eye lashes. "Oh, Goddess, what about Bella Bell, who actually does that? You know! Who throws up in the laundry bin and falls asleep in the bath tub? The maid's going to have the shock of her life this morning when she finds Bella comatose under a dripping tap and her puke amongst the dirty towels."

Adrianna Jasmine crawled to the side of the bed, pulled herself up to a seated position and heaved a sigh. The room was spinning like a merry-go-round.

"Oh no," she moaned as she buried her face into her hands. "It's too embarrassing for words, why did we all get so drunk?"

Sarah shrugged from under her covers, "we were all just merry and excited to be here, it was our first night and we let go of our inhibitions silly, silly, silly, I need Tallulah and I need her now!"

Adrianna Jasmine nodded, "Ouch, that hurt." She had had a thought. "Hey, did you see Clementine last night after the ring of fire incident?"

"Was that before Sky and Megan went skinny-dipping with Rodrigo in the Rock pool?"

"Err, after."

"But was it after we caught Carolina snogging Rafael the receptionist."

"Err yes."

"Then no, I didn't."

"Hmmm interesting," mused Adrianna Jasmine.

"Why?"

"Well, I couldn't be sure last night, I was so dizzy from drink that I thought I was dreaming, but I could have sworn I saw Clementine looking rather cosy with... a woman."

Sarah sat bolt upright then regretted it immediately. "What do you mean, a woman?"

"Well... kissing, canoodling, that sort of thing."

Sarah looked shocked. "Who was she, was she someone we saw in the restaurant?"

Adrianna thought hard as she crawled over towards her make-up bag to retrieve Tallulah Toffee. "No, it wasn't but I distinctively heard Clementine call her Lenni."

"Lenni?"

Yes, Lenni! I think we should put this in the Jacuzzi. I don't think I've got the strength to stand under the shower."

"You can't do that, the bubbles will go mental."

"I don't care," said Adrianna Jasmine as she crawled to the outside hot tub, "we can clean it up when we feel better." Sarah sighed and slithered out of her bed. Every step was torture. "I won't put too much in, anyway," promised the hung over witch and she proceeded to squeeze a fair dollop of the life-saving, lemony, goddess-sent saviour into the water, " we won't put the bubbles on, either."

A few moments later the two witches were submerged in the lemon scented water.

"Hahhhhh," sighed Sarah, "that's better. I can feel life returning to my body, now what were you saying about Clementine and this Lenni character?"

"Just like I said, she was kissing a woman and she called her... Lenni. Oh my Goddess, Lenni is a woman!"

"Yes, we just discovered that, Jazzy catch up."

"No, don't you see?"

"Clementine is gay?"

"What? No, she's not gay! Kinky, experimental and probably bisexual when it suits her but no, not gay, no, it means Lenni, female Lenni, is the owner of this hotel.

Sarah allowed her brain to whirl and buzz for few moments as she took it all in. "Yes of course, it all makes sense, no wonder she was so coy!"

"Yes," agreed Adrianna Jasmine, "and I spotted lots more names, too, like the Leonardo restaurant, the Lennington pool. Our suite is called the Leonora Deluxe!"

"Cool!"

"I know!"

"Coohee, darlings!"

"Oh goddess," chorused the witches simultaneously before both ducking under the water."

"Its mummy! How are my little party goddesses? Oh stop being silly, you two, come out from under the water." Sicily sat on the edge of the hot tub. She was as fresh as a daisy and happily dipped her fingers into the hot lemon water. Adrianna Jasmine was the first to pop her head out. "Goddess, darling, you are hung over aren't you," she said with a chuckle, "and ah ha, here is Sarah!" The witches just about managed to muster a smile between them.

"Morning, mother."

"Morning, Sicily."

Sicily beamed from ear to ear; it was most annoying. "Do I detect a whiff of Citrus Bang-Bang Boom?" She pronounced "whiff" like "hwhiff" which utterly grated on her daughter. Sarah nodded her head.

"Good idea, you two, however, I took a couple of Dr Goombah's Over with the Hangover Milk Thistle and Mortilla Chilli Drops before I laid down for a quick half hour, just before dawn. Why, I feel as fresh as the morning dew." The two witches grimaced and inhaled the lemon steam. Luckily, it was beginning to kick in. "Would you like to take Dr Goombah's Over with the Hangover Milk Thistle and Mortilla Chilli Drops, Sarah? It will plug you back into the mains if you do." Sarah nodded feebly. "And you, Adrianna

Jasmine would you like to take some Dr Goombah's Over with the Hangover Milk Thistle and Mortilla Chilli Drops?"

"Yes, mother," seethed Adrianna Jasmine through her teeth, "I would like to partake in the consumption of Dr Goombah's Over with the Hangover Milk Thistle and Mortilla Chilli Drops."

"Well then, I shall go get you my Dr Goombah Over with the Hangover Milk Thistle and Mortilla Chilli Drops; you'll soon be feeling right as rain, darlings." With that she punched down on the hot tub bubble button. The two witches gasped in horror.

"No, mother! Don't..."

But it was too late. Sicily had pressed the bubble button and within seconds the pool began to produce masses of foam and froth that would shame a foam party out in Ibiza.

"Oh dear, what's happening here?" inquired Sicily coolly as she watched the bubbles erupt like Mount Vesuvius on a bad day.

"It's the Citrus Bang-Bang Boom," cried the girls, "we put it in here without the intention of putting on the bubbles because, well... this would be the result."

"Bit silly putting it in there in the first place. Really! Anyway, I'll get you your Dr Goombah's Over with the Hangover Milk Thistle and Mortilla Chilli Drops"

Ahhhhh!

That evening the girls sat down to a more civilised meal. The hot tub fiasco had been resolved due to Kristobella suggesting that the girls add soap to the bubbles, which enabled the bubbles to disperse and disappear, back to the bubbly world which they came from. Everyone had had a drop or two of Dr Goombah's and was feeling more compos mentis. Bella Bell managed to clean up the laundry bin before the chamber maid had any nasty shocks and Carolina was aglow due to her sexual awakening with Rafael. Kristobella, on the other hand, was looking slightly stony faced. She was just about to surrender herself to the handsome receptionist in one of the hotel beach tents, when she had this horrid sensation that he was married. She soon found out that he was, so she cast a quick sleep spell on him to punish him for his adulterous ways. He was found, earlier on that day, by a guest and as a result, fired with immediate effect.

Megan and Sky were in fine spirits as they had caught the eyes of two rather good looking premier footballers and had been plied with champagne and cocktails all night. Although, being two very sensible witches, the pair had only opted for a kiss or two from the two ball jugglers and a promise to see them again the following evening. Sicily was full of joy as she recalled the shenanigans from the night before and pleased that she managed to wiggle her way out of taking the wrap for setting the piano on fire. How she did it was anyone's guess, but let's just say it included a chant, a banana, a cup of milk and brown sugar!

"Try switching from traditional tea to herbal teas to calm the mind, body and spirit."
(Megan and Sky)

Chapter 37
Great News, Darling!

Adrianna Jasmine was sitting peacefully on her couch enjoying a lemon cupcake when she nearly jumped out of her skin.

"Ahhhhh, mother!" she cried as crumbs flew everywhere. "Will you stop doing this?"

"Doing what, darling?" her mother asked innocently.

"This! Barging in unannounced, it's most distressing. I could've been in the middle of something."

Sicily gave her a daughter a saucy look and laughed. "Don't be ridiculous, darling. Besides, this news is worth interrupting *anything* for, it's so huge, so gigantic, so earth shatteringly magnificent, you'll understand, darling." Adrianna Jasmine got up, brushed the crumbs from her lap and made her way into the kitchen. "That's right, darling, crack open the champagne, this calls for a celebration."

Adrianna Jasmine huffed with frustration, "I'm not getting any champagne, I'm getting a cloth, you made me knock over my hot chocolate when you burst in on me. I'm going to attempt to rescue my rug."

Sicily carried on regardless, "Well, hurry up, darling, if I don't tell you my news soon I shall simply burst." *I wish you would*, Adrianna Jasmine thought as she located her carpet cleaning kit from under the sink before trudging back into the lounge. Her mother was hopping about like a demented modern arts performer.

"Well, what is it?" Adrianna Jasmine all but hissed as she began to soak up the dark gunk from her lovely aubergine rug.

Sicily took her stand theatrically and paused for a dramatic silence. "I've got it, darling."

"I know, you said that, what exactly have you got?"

"It! The very thing that I've wanted most in my entire life, darling, except you, of course." Adrianna Jasmine rolled her eyes, *damn it, this was going to stain.*

"What is it?"

Sicily took a long breath, "The gig of a lifetime."

Adrianna Jasmine shrugged her shoulders, *what on earth could it be? The woman dreamed of so many gigs of a life time it could be one of many: working with Madonna, acting on Broadway, a part in Coronation Street?*

"The greatest gig of all, darling." Sicily's eyes were wild and wide and she was breathing heavily. "I, Sicily Mariposa Poppleapple, have been offered the chance to dance on the greatest TV show on the planet. The show with more sparkle than champagne, more glitter than Kylie Minogue and more style than Yves Saint Lauren."

"WHAT?" Ugh, the woman was insufferable.

"Strictly... Come... Dancing!"

Try to look enthusiastic, Adrianna Jasmine said to herself, *go on make yourself smile with joviality, you can do it, you can do it... ah there we go, smile.*

"Wow, that's amazing, mum good for you. I know it's always been your dream."

Sicily bowed her head. "I know," she breathed, "I know, I think I need to sit down, it's just sunk in and I feel a little queer."

Adrianna Jasmine rolled her eyes, "I'll put the kettle on."

"Yes, good idea, Squirrel Nutkins, and I'll have one of those lemon things. I think I need the sugar." A few moments later Sicily was sipping a steaming cup of Earl Grey and tucking into a zesty lemon cupcake. "Much better, darling, oh I felt rather overwhelmed, it's thoroughly deserved, of course, but still, a total shock."

Adrianna Jasmine frowned, "Hang on, I thought you had to be a celebrity to go on those shows and, no offence, mum but you're hardly Liza Minnelli."

"That's because I was never given the chance, darling, but now I have, I shan't blow it. I shall reign as a true dance icon like I should have always been, darling."

381

"Yes but you've missed my point, you're not a celebrity, you have to be one first before you can go on one of those shows, you have to be well known!"

"I am well known, darling. Ok not exactly *well* known but known nonetheless and I shall become even more formidable once I've got my dancing shoes on. The nation will love me and I shall be catapulted into the realms of stardom quicker than you can say Catherine Zeta Jones!"

"Yeah, like you can say that name really fast."

"Don't be facetious, darling. Anyway mummy will do you proud, you'll see. I must begin to prepare and this is the last cupcake for me, so stop giving them to me, darling, I must get down the gym too. I've already booked in for some beginner ball room classes next week, you know, just to give me a head start before I meet my partner. I want to give a good impression."

You'll give him something. "Anyway, who is the lucky chap?"

Sicily frowned in frustration, "That's just it, I don't know, but I'll tell you something: if it isn't Vincent Simone there'll be hell to pay. I simply will not be able to perform my Argentinean tango with anyone else!"

Adrianna Jasmine tried to stifle a laugh. "Mother, all the men are professional dancers, I'm sure they have enough talent to knock out a decent tango."

"*I'm* a professional dancer, lest you forget," Sicily said unperturbed, "I used to dance in the Moulin Rouge, the Moulin Rouge, darling can you believe it? And I will not dance with anyone! No, the lucky pro will fall onto their knees and thank the Goddess that it is me, Sicily who has been picked as their partner."

"Well, I'm pleased for you mum. Well done, I know you'll be unforgettable."

Sicily laughed gaily, "Yes, I will, darling, you mark my words," She then took a hearty bite from her cake. "Ooh this is delicious but once I've demolished it, that's it, it's strictly come dieting and strictly come to the gym for me." She then chuckled to herself at her merry quip, "I'll have another cup of tea, though."

Tip for the bride on her wedding day:
Make sure you enjoy a big hearty breakfast on the morning of your wedding as you'll be needing lots of energy to mingle and boogie woogie later on!

Chapter 38
Wedding daze

"I can't believe it's the day of your wedding, Adrianna Jasmine. Oh my Goddess, you must be so excited."

Adrianna Jasmine, who had just emerged from a steaming bath of Drift Away Holiday, smiled leisurely at her friend.

"I know, it's come around quick."

"I'll say, anyway, I'll have a quick bath myself then I'll be all yours."

"Take your time, we've plenty of it, why, it's not even 5am yet."

"Have you slept at all?"

"Uh huh, from about 1am to 3.30am so not bad really."

Sarah agreed. "So what are we going to have for breakfast?"

"Two soft boiled eggs, two slices of linseed and soya bread, toasted, smothered in butter, and a pint of organic full fat milk, no crash carbs for us today, we want to stay on a steady path of constant, slow, energy release."

Sarah nodded approvingly. "Good idea. OK, I'm going to pop into the bath now."

"Don't forget to rinse out the sand."

"Toot toot, little star, where's my little bride to be?" It was six am and Sicily energetically burst into the flat carrying an array of pre-wedding items. She was holding her dress and shoes, a large makeup case, bottles of champagne and a picnic hamper. "Let's get this party started!"

A few minutes later Clementine and Carolina Plum arrived, also looking fresh and full of beans. They too were holding pre-wedding tools.

"Morning, everyone," said Adrianna Jasmine happily as she kissed and greeted the women, "great to see you all. Now, I know its early but shall we partake in a little glass of bubbly!"

"Rather!" trilled Sicily, "it's never too early for champagne. Why, when I was in the Moulin Rouge, the Moulin Rouge, darling can you believe it, it was as natural to drink the stuff for breakfast as it is tea the for Brits!"

"Alcoholic," mumbled Clementine, she had still not forgotten or forgiven Sicily for almost killing her at Sarah's engagement party. The feelings, on the other hand, were mutual and Sicily simply chose to ignore the blonde harlot for the sake of her daughter's happy day. Anyway, Clementine would get her comeuppance soon, she was sure of it.

Carolina went over to Adrianna Jasmine and gave her a beautiful hug. Immediately the younger witch sighed as the soothing effects from the magical embrace overwhelmed her senses.

"Well, if I did have any signs of nerves, I don't now! Anyway, that was lovely."

"My pleasure," Carolina answered graciously.

Pop!

"Here, everyone, champagne is served." Sicily poured the champagne and handed out the glasses just as Sarah entered the living room. "Ah perfect timing, Sarah," chimed Sicily, "now we're ready for a toast. To Adrianna Jasmine, Taylor and a perfect day!"

By 11.30 am the flat was pandemonium. Aluino, the hairdresser, with his assistant Toby, and Pepper the makeup artist, were working up a whirl in order to make the witches look nothing short of perfection. Aluino swept and curled, blow dried and sleeked, whilst Pepper highlighted, emphasised, brightened and softened. Aluino managed to set finger waves to Clementine's blonde pixie hair so by the time he'd finished, she looked like a 1920s film star. Sarah had somehow transformed into Julia Roberts after her thick red hair had been washed, combed through and set in big, hot rollers, resulting in big bouncy curls spiralling down her back. Then, of course, little Violet, Taylor's nine year-old niece whose lovely long blonde hair was simply washed, dried, straightened and decorated with petit rouge noire roses. The girls looked nothing short of beautiful. Sicily emerged looking about 39 years of age by the time Aluino sleeked her hair into a sexy 1920s bob. She was wearing an emerald green, one shoulder sleeved, full length gown.

"Okay, darlings, are we all nearly ready? I want to take a photo of you all."

"Almost, Mrs Poppleapple Forthright-Punch," called Aluino from the bedroom, Pepper is just finishing off Adrianna Jasmine's eye makeup she won't be two ticks."

Aluino winked at Adrianna Jasmine who was looking nothing short of radiant as her hairdresser and makeup artist worked their supernatural talents on the bride to be.

"OK, beauty, I think you are what I would call, perfection." Pepper expertly scanned Adrianna Jasmine's exquisite face from the tip of her eyelashes to the corners of her mouth. "He will faint when he sees you."

Adrianna Jasmine giggled. "I hope not!"

"Oh Christ, can you imagine if he did," flapped Aluino. "It does happen, you know. I've seen it on Caught on Camera, you know when it's all too much for the groom, or he's still sozzled from the night before and the blood pressure plummets like a lead balloon; the next thing the bride is catching her husband-to-be in a mass of white lace and froo froo." There was an awkward silence for about a second or two. "Err, not that that's going to happen to Taylor. No no, he's far too controlled." Adrianna Jasmine chuckled and Pepper glowered at Aluino. "Anyway, I think we better get going, it's now twelve o'clock and we've got to get over to Hotel 78 for one o clock. Toby, start packing up, I'm about announce the bride."

Adrianna Jasmine stood up and stared at herself in the full-length mirror and liked what she saw. Not because of her flawless makeup, beautiful gown and hair but for the first time in her life, she was right where she should be. The glowing witch had just spent the last four hours making a great effort to look breathtakingly beautiful for the man that she loved. Loved! *I can't believe it.* Adrianna Jasmine Poppleapple Mariposa Forthright-Punch was in love and about to offer herself unconditionally to the man she would die for. How grown up and strong she felt. The witch had taken life by the horns and gone for it. She'd never felt more at one with herself and would cherish the delicious feeling for the rest of her life.

Aluino opened the door and made a quick announcement. "Okay, everyone, hold your breath because here she is, the bride to be, Adrianna Jasmine."

The young witch glided towards the doorway and stood still for a few moments. Her face was glowing with happiness and her smile shone like the stars above. She was holding a cascading bouquet of rouge noir roses and wore a delicate pearl bracelet on her right wrist that had belonged to Henry's mother, Grandma Ruby. The bridesmaids all gasped as they drank in her vision. Little Violet's mouth dropped to the floor when she saw her aunty-to-be standing like the most exquisitely sculpted statue in the universe and Sarah began to well up.

"O.M.G.," breathed Clementine totally taken aback, "you should so go in for the bride of the year contest, the other contenders wouldn't stand a chance! You look breathtaking."

Adrianna Jasmine didn't say a word, she just smiled and scanned the room for her mother. When she found her it was difficult for the young witch to hold back tears. Her mother looked beautiful in her elegant dress but it was her face that touched Adrianna Jasmine. It was a mixture of pure love and pride. No words needed to be said. The mutual adoration and respect was tangible. Sicily walked over to her daughter and kissed her softly on the cheek.

My rose, so sweet you are to go
To a new life with your love
And a new life to grow.
May your days be blessed with happiness and light,
May the stars brighten even the darkest night.
Love is an honour and time is a gift,
Live fully, my child, time can be swift,
I bless you my daughter with the elements of five:

Spirit, earth, water, wind and fire.

"Thank you mother," said Adrianna Jasmine as she accepted her mother's words, "that's a lovely charm."

"Indeed it is, my daughter, my mother said the very same thing to me on the day of my wedding and her mother before that and her mother before that and one day if the Goddess smiles upon you, then you will say the same to your daughter, too."

Adrianna Jasmine smiled, "That's why I love our family, mother because we have traditions to carry on until the end of time."

Sicily nodded, "I couldn't agree more, now, where's that handsome husband of mine? Henry, come out here and look at your beautiful daughter."

"Did someone call?"

As mother and daughter looked up, Henry Forthright-Punch walked from the kitchen towards the two lovely creatures standing before him. His face lit up with joy.

"Oh, my Adrianna Jasmine you look incredible. I don't believe I have ever seen you look quite so beautiful." He took her into his arms and gently kissed his daughter, trying carefully not to spoil her makeup or hair. "And Sicily, my goodness, you look like a young Liz Taylor, breathtaking. I still love you as much now as I did when I first met you."

It was all too much, Sarah began to wail, which in turn set Aluino and Pepper off.

"Oh stop it, you lot, come on," warned Clementine in her no nonsense way, "do you really think we can afford to have mascara running down our cheeks, red eyes and swollen noses?" Sarah looked up and blinked plops of tears down her face whilst her nose was running and dripping onto her cleavage. "I say, no!" Clementine then proceeded to pull out some tissues from a box and wiped the salty liquid off Sarah's chest with one clean swipe, ordered her to blow her nose, apply some new lippy and wipe away the revolting eye liner dribble. "We are about to walk down the aisle and hundreds of pairs of eyes will be looking at us. It's our moment to shine. So, I say, are we ready to glide?" A cheer from the wedding party erupted. "Then let's get going!"

Henry Forthright-Punch was impressed. "Clementine, have you ever thought of running a boot camp, or leading motivational workshops, it would be a great career choice."

Clementine chuckled, "You never know, Uncle Henry, you never know."

"Toot toot."

"Oh, the cars are here, everybody," informed Sicily, "I heard the toot! Right, everyone, let's get going, have we got everything? Pepper, do you have all the extra makeup supplies?"

"Check, Mrs P M F P"

"Aluino: hair tongs, hair spray and curby grips?"

"Check, check, check!"

"Right, ok then, I think we're ready Henry, lead the way with Adrianna Jasmine, you two are in the Rolls, bridesmaids with me, we're in the Bentley; Pepper, Aluino and Toby, you're in a black London Cab."

The hired help faces dropped like lead balloons.

"Oh, don't look like that, you lot, I have at least *ordered* it. Crumbs, did you really think we'd make you book it on your own!"

"How you feeling, mate?"

Taylor Jameson turned towards his older brother Mark; they were enjoying a quick livener in the bar at Hotel 78. The pair both looked incredibly handsome in their dark grey tailor-made suits.

"Good, really good. I can't wait for this girl to be my wife."

"I don't blame you, bro, she's one in a million, that one. I can honestly say I've never met anyone quite like her, you're a lucky man."

Taylor smiled and shook his brother's hand, "Yes, she is. I feel so blessed right now, it's almost surreal."

"I'll say, that girl is good luck, not only has she made you personally content but look at your career: you're a celebrity, a famous food critic on paper and screen, constantly on TV; you're being offered everything from book deals to presenting and travelling all over the place. You're living the dream, brother, living the dream."

Taylor looked deeply into his brother's blue eyes and nodded thoughtfully.

"I know, it's all happening, I just hope the bubble doesn't burst."

"It won't, not with a charm like her, she's amazing and Violet loves her. Mind you, everyone does."

"Yeah, I heard she really enjoyed her dress fittings with Adrianna Jasmine and her family."

"Well, she especially liked Carolina Plum, I have no idea who or what a Carolina Plum is, she sounds more like something from a fairy tale, but I can't wait to meet her myself."

Taylor laughed, "You'll like all her family and friends they're all... unique in their own way, they all possess their own sense of magic."

"I can't wait. Hey, are any of her friends single?"

Taylor smiled; it had been a while since his brother had mentioned an interest in the ladies. "I think so, my good man, and they're all cracking!"

"Good. I feel like having some fun now the divorce is finally over."

"You deserve it, too. I know it's not really appropriate talking about your divorce just as I'm about to get wed, but after the way that woman treated you and Violet, it's time lady luck shone on you."

"It will. Anyway, I heard she's moved in with Goodwin and they're about to move to Qatar."

"What about Violet, she's not going?"

"I'll make damned sure of it that she is not. There is no way she's moving to the Middle East."

"But has Madeline requested that she go?"

"Oh yes, but I won't let her, besides, *she* had the affair, *she* left me and I've got full custody because of it. Besides, the fact that I'm a barrister and she was nothing more than a mere Pilates instructor, not that I'm disrespecting Pilates instructors, Pilates is an important part of one's fitness regime and imperative for good back care, but honestly, she didn't stand a chance."

"So why did she do it? You're a catch, Mark: good looking, rich, you've got a celebrity younger brother!"

Mark laughed at his brother. "That's funny, you being all famous. It should have made me so much more appealing to her, I can't understand it!"

"Well, her loss and besides, soon she will be melting in the heat of Qatar, imprisoned in her air-conditioned apartment for two and trying to make a new life as a self-employed Pilates instructor to all other expats. She'll be climbing the walls and wondering where it all went wrong. What does Goodwin do, anyway?"

"Surveyor."

"So long hours working, then."

"Most certainly."

"Hmmmm, I give three months, tops."

"Well when it all goes Pete Tong I won't be there to pick up the pieces. Anyway, we'd better finish off our drinks and make our way down to the ballroom. It's almost one o'clock!"

The ballroom Reception looked utterly magical. The room was exquisitely decorated with white and black floor tiles, giant chrystal chandeliers and dark wooden furniture adorned with rich plum coloured cushions. Bunches of Adrianna Jasmine's favourite rouge noir roses had been placed at each table, accompanied with tea lights pressed into glossy red apples. The place looked nothing short of spectacular.

"It looks beautiful," whispered Taylor's mother as she and her sister went round and inspected the room for one last time. "If Adrianna Jasmine were a room, this would be her."

Her sister, Sandra, laughed, "Yes, I suppose it would be, dark and rich, beautiful and elegant, yes, it's very her, and I love these roses. I've never seen them before, are they black or are they red? I can't quite tell."

"They're called rouge noir, apparently, whilst coming out of Harrods a few months ago, Adrianna Jasmine found a beautiful flower stall on that corner by Rigby and Peller and instantly fell in love with them. But I have to say, I've never seen them before, either. Spectacular, aren't they?"

Sandra agreed as she gently caressed the velvety petal from one of the arrangements, "They do make a beautiful couple, Patty, their babies will be just darling."

Patty felt a shiver of excitement, "Oh grandchildren! Wouldn't it be lovely? And little Violet would adore a young cousin, yes, let's hope they try instantly!"

"I'm sure they will, Patty. After all, they've achieved so much already, it's not like they need to find adventure or live a little first. I mean, just look at their wall of fame over here." The two sisters went over to a giant canvas that was covered in pictures of Taylor and Adrianna Jasmine. There were pictures of them as babies, toddlers, teens, you name it. "Just look at all the places they have travelled to, the fun they've had, together and apart, all their experiences. You mark my word, the next adventure will be children."

Patty squeezed her sister's hand tightly, "Here's hoping."

The 1930s room was buzzing with excitement. Taylor and Mark were seated by the altar which was decorated with horse shoes, candles and roses, going through last minute details in their heads. Taylor's father, Austin, had just handed his sons a fine Cuban cigar each which was to be enjoyed later that day with a good glass of whisky and a couple of words of wisdom. The registrar, Daphne Dune, a pagan priestess, was dressed in a dark red twin set with pearls. She didn't look like a regular pagan priestess, who would traditionally wear long loose robes. She appeared more like a sufficiently reliable headmistress at a top girls school. However, due to Adrianna Jasmine's family wishing to keep their magic ability's a secret, Daphne was kindly asked to tone down the ceremony, her traditional robes and to perhaps discreetly, add magical influences as and when she could. Luckily, Daphne understood the predicament as the Poppleapples's were of unusual stock, their spells actually worked! No, this wasn't some far-out, New Age couple who had found Wicca as their new way of life; this family truly were magic in all senses of the word and the groom had no idea!

"Just some last minute details, everyone, if you please." Daphne was now addressing the wedding guests. She had a sweet voice, almost childlike, and made one feel pleasant and relaxed. "Just to inform you I have word that the bride and her entourage have entered the building." There was a stir of excitement amongst the congregation. "So, if you could all make sure mobile phones are switched off, cameras and tissues are on the ready. Taylor and Mark," she said turning towards the pair of brothers with a warming smile, "would you please stand and wait for the bride?"

Taylor and his brother both stood simultaneously, followed by the rest of the guests. Taylor looked at his brother who settled his nerves with a wink and within moments the beautiful aria from Puccini's Madame Butterfly, sang by the now world-famous Chrystal Rose, began to fill the room. The doors gently opened and the congregation turned towards the back of the room. The first person to enter was Sicily in her green gown. She walked like a queen and smiled like a true Hollywood star as she made her way towards the altar. Everyone agreed she looked awe-inspiring and so young for her age. Next, the bridesmaids. Little violet took the lead looking like a flower fairy from a fairy tale by scattering a selection of pure white and pink rose petals onto the ground from a white wicker basket. She was followed by the delectable, ice blonde Clementine who looked tall and sinewy in her fitted cream Grecian gown and the mouth-watering Sarah simply delicious and voluptuous. Her thick red hair tumbled over her creamy breasts and her eyes sparkled with radiance, they all looked beautiful. The bridesmaids made their way slowly down the aisle drinking in the moment and lengthening out the aria for the perfect moment, when Adrianna Jasmine would stand in the doorway. The moment soon came, just as Chrystal Rose hit the high note, the witch, in all her splendour, stood at the door. The congregation literally gasped at the wonder. There stood the epitome of perfection. Adrianna Jasmine breathed deeply, her adrenalin was through the roof.

"Well, my angel, shall we?"

Henry Forthright-Punch squeezed his daughter's arm gently as he gallantly led his daughter towards the man she would soon call her husband.

Taylor couldn't quite believe the vision approaching. He knew his fiancée was beautiful and believed that many a times he had seen her at her very best but he couldn't quite understand how she could be even more so. His face was a picture, a mixture of awe, pride, excitement and unconditional love. *Hurry to me*, he thought, *become my wife.*

She looked so radiant, so happy, she smiled as if she were powered by the stars themselves. They never took their eyes off one another. Mark, on the other hand, couldn't take his eyes of Clementine; sadly neither could Lenni, Clementine's latest and highly controversial squeeze.

Henry Forthright Punch kissed his daughter tenderly on the cheek thus causing Sicily to shed a small tear. Carolina and Kristobella had already lost it the moment they saw Adrianna Jasmine appear in the doorway. Henry Forthrigh- Punch handed his daughter over to Taylor and took his stand next to his wife, whom he kissed before taking her hand. Thankful for the gesture, she squeezed his hand tightly, he was a pillar of strength during this incredibly beautiful and moving moment.

"Please be seated," gestured Daphne. "Friends and nearest and dearest, fasten together with me in the merriment of the unification of Adrianna Jasmine Poppleapple Mariposa Forthright-Punch and Taylor Daniel Jameson, as their souls now unite to become a singular galaxy of love and affection."

The Poppleapple/Forthright Punch clan found the opening speech from Daphne moving and patriotic; the Jameson's found it a little strange but then again they were aware that Adrianna Jasmine was a colourful soul and somewhat earthy, anything could be possible during this ceremony.

"You are both conscious of the authenticity of the vows you are about to speak to one another and of the duty that comes when a partnership is fashioned. If there is any rationale within your hearts that this ritual should not persist on this occasion, I charge you to voice it now, as marriage is based on truthfulness and faith, and only with those things can you successfully create a partnership."

The pair looked at one another with nothing but pure love in their eyes, "We do not," they both said, as clear as day.

"Then we shall proceed. I believe your Aunt Kristobella is going to read a poem to you both?"

Adrianna Jasmine nodded. Kristobella stood from her seat and walked calmly towards the altar. She was wearing a lovely pale and dark blue gown that fitted into the waist and spilled out into a long flowing skirt as soft and serene as the sky on a summer's day.

"I would like to read a poem: Shall I compare thee to a Summer's Day, by William Shakespeare."

> **Shall I compare thee to a summer's day?**
> **Thou art more lovely and more temperate.**
> **Rough winds do shake the darling buds of May,**
> **And summer's lease hath all too short a date.**
> **Sometime too hot the eye of heaven shines,**
> **And often is his gold complexion dimmed;**
> **And every fair from fair sometime declines,**
> **By chance, or nature's changing course untrimmed.**
> **But thy eternal summer shall not fade**
> **Nor lose possession of that fair thou ow'st;**
> **Nor shall death brag thou wand'rest in his shade,**
> **When in eternal lines to time thou grow'st,**
> **So long as men can breathe or eyes can see,**
> **So long lives this, and this gives life to thee.**

(Shall I compare thee to a summer's day, Sonnet 18, William Shakespeare)

Kristobella stepped down and went back to her seat.

"Thank you, Kristobella," said Daphne sincerely. "A beautiful poem. "Now, Taylor, what symbolic gift did you bring your wife-to-be today?" Taylor looked over to Mark who immediately stood and carried over a white satin pillow, upon which laid a scroll and a star. Adrianna Jasmine became excited. "Taylor, please explain to Adrianna Jasmine why you have chosen this particular gift for her."

Taylor turned to face a glowing Adrianna Jasmine. "Adrianna Jasmine, no one in my eyes shines quite like you, so for my symbolic gift, I wish to present you with your very own star." He then handed her crystal star from the pillow. "The star is called

Jasmine and when you read this scroll it will explain to you exactly where she lays in the nights sky, so when you look up into the night, you will see her in all her glory." He then kissed her tenderly on the cheek.

"Thank you," she whispered, "I love it."

"Now, Adrianna Jasmine, what symbolic gift do you present to your husband-to-be today?"

Adrianna Jasmine looked over towards Clementine who then stood up holding a black present bag. She handed it to Adrianna Jasmine and kissed her on the cheek before sitting back down. Mark couldn't help but swoon as he eyed the lovely ice blonde. Ah, it was good to be single!

"I have a few gifts that I wish to offer. The first rose quartz stone I give it to you as a symbol of my love and appreciation." Adrianna Jasmine began to giggle as she lifted out the second gift. "A bottle of mojito mix." The wedding guests began laugh with her. "To commemorate our first date where we drank Mojitos together; here's to drinking many more."

Taylor, too, was laughing, "Thank you, I'll enjoy that later!"

"And..." Adrianna Jasmine teased, "two tickets for next year's Six Nations." There was a whoop of cheer from Taylor's mates. "Because I know you love rugby and I wanted to buy you these tickets for you and a friend to enjoy." Taylor kissed her, smiling from ear to ear.

"I take it you are both happy with your symbolic gifts?" inquired Daphne. The pair nodded eagerly. "Then let us proceed, I believe we now have Adrianna Jasmine's father and special guest, Chrystal Rose, who will now perform a special rendition of The First Time Ever I Saw your Face."

Henry Forthright-Punch stood up and went over to a stunning baby black grand piano followed by an elegantly dressed Chrystal Rose. Henry gallantly waited until she had taken her stand next to him then proceeded to sit down, open his music and waited for her nod.

First Time Ever I Saw Your Face

The first time ever I saw your face
I thought the sun rose in your eyes
And the moon and stars were the gifts you gave
To the dark and the empty skies, my love,
To the dark and the empty skies.

The first time ever I kissed your mouth
And felt your heart beat close to mine
Like the trembling heart of a captive bird
That was there at my command, my love
That was there at my command.

And the first time ever I lay with you
I felt your heart so close to mine
And I knew our joy would fill the earth
And last till the end of time my love
It would last till the end of time my love

The first time ever I saw your face, your face,
your face, your face

(Written by singer/songwriter Ewan MacColl)

There wasn't a dry eye in the house: Henry had played exquisitely and Chrystal Rose had sung from her very soul.

"Thank you," mouthed Adrianna Jasmine, "as the pair both took their leave and went back to their seats. Henry blew his daughter a kiss.

"Thank you for that beautiful song," said Daphne who was finding it difficult to keep herself together, in all her years as a high priestess she had never felt quite so overcome with emotion. "It is believed that the virtues of our soul work in conjunction to the cardinal directions; East, South, West and North. Honouring tradition, a blessing will be offered dedicating the bride and groom's honour to the four corners. Blessed be this union between these two people, by the powers of the East to assist communication and new beginnings. Blessed be this union between these two people, by the powers of the South to lend a hand in the warming of their home, igniting their everlasting passion and bringing light into darkness. Blessed be the union between these two people, by the powers of the West by washing away any negative energy that may accumulate over time. Blessed be the union between these two people, by the powers of the North by creating a strong foundation for you to build your lives and home. May you always have a home to return to and remember, dear couple, that although the elements are here to assist you through your married life, it is up to you to make your lives complete. Now I ask members of the congregation to take their stand and with perfect love and purity in your hearts, to light a candle for Adrianna Jasmine and Taylor. Upon doing so, ask the great earth mother for one act of goodness to shine upon the happy couple."

The congregation stood and formed two lines towards the altar, which was covered with tea lights, ready to be lit. Some prayed for their health, some prayed for financial happiness and some prayed for the blessing of children. All in all, the prayers were heartfelt and untainted.

"What a lovely thing to do, the candles and the gifts," commented Austin to his wife, "I don't actually understand the ceremony or its origins, it's certainly not traditional, but all the same it's very, very nice."

Patty agreed, "Well, it's designed specifically for them, so much more meaningful, don't you think?" Austin nodded enthusiastically. However, he couldn't be more wrong about the ceremony not being traditional; this ceremony had taken elements of traditions well before the birth of Christianity.

"It could certainly catch on!" he said.

"Now it is time for the bride and groom to take their vows." There was a stir of excitement form the guests. "Would the ring bearers please present themselves with the symbols of their eternal love." Mark and Violet took their stand and handed over the rings.

Adrianna Jasmine kissed Violet on the cheek, "You look beautiful," she whispered to the little girl.

"Thank you." Violet smiled and as proud as punch, went back to her seat next to Sarah, who was crying violently into her Kleenex. Mark then handed his ring to his brother.

"Thank you," he said as Mark gave him an encouraging wink.

"Taylor, it is now time for you to say your vows."

Taylor turned towards Adrianna Jasmine who greeted him with a smile.

"It is because of you my life is complete. You are the reason that I laugh, smile and dream of a future. The thought of spending the rest of my life with you fills me with nothing but joy, you are my everything, my universe. I look forward to the roads ahead, the adventures we will experience. But most of all, I pledge to be true and faithful, live to care and protect you through sickness and health, through light and through dark, for as long as we both shall live." Taylor then slipped the ring onto Adrianna Jasmine's finger resulting in wet eyes from most of the women in the room.

"Adrianna Jasmine, it is now time for you to say your vows."

"My love for you is pure and I wholly give to you everything which is mine. I understand that we are free spirits, therefore I will honour and support the dreams you may desire with encouragement and care. I will honour you above all others and promise to always use the art of communication to keep our relationship quarrel free. In times of hardship, I will support you, in times of sickness, I will care for you, in times of hunger, I will feed you and in times of coldness, I will keep you warm." Adrianna Jasmine then placed the ring onto Taylor's finger.

"Blessed be," said Daphne, "now it is time for the traditional act of handfasting." She took out a cloth ribbon from her pocket and began to tie it around the couples entwined hands. "This ribbon represents a binding commitment between two loving souls. The commitment is as deep as a bottomless valley and as binding as a handshake between two Gods. Without a doubt, a handfast can last eternally, so long as love continues unconditionally. This commitment is so strong that even death cannot end a handfasting unification; there is no 'til death do us part' in this ritual."

Before the non-magical congregation had a chance to allow what she had just said to sink in, music began to play in the background.

"Oh, how lovely," remarked Sicily to Kristobella, "Venus by Gustav Holst. When I was dancing at the Moulin Rouge, the Moulin Rouge, darling can you believe it?! I played a sea goddess, all naked and sinewy, coming out of a giant clam and this was the music I performed to!"

Kristobella rolled her eyes, "Great, now I've got visions of you naked, with a bad mermaid wig on, bursting out of a sweaty clam shell. Nice!"

Sicily ignored the remark and continued to listen to the music and reminisce times past, as she watched her handsome new son in law kiss her daughter, the bride.

"If you wish to clear out any negative energy try carrying a piece of Black Tourmaline around with you. It keeps you well rooted and helps release nervous tension."
(Carolina Plum)

Chapter 39
Her

Adrianna Jasmine, who was seated at the head table next to her new husband, looked out happily towards her family and friends. The energy in the room was buzzing; everyone was thoroughly enjoying themselves. People sat where they wished as Adrianna Jasmine hadn't bothered to do a table plan, and all around you could hear happy chit chat and laughing. Rick O' Shay played merry Celtic music which made even the most hardened non-dancers tap their feet under the table. The food, of course, was a triumph, expertly served by the waiters, complimented with ice cold Lanson Champagne, simply perfect. The flavours were also a success. The ladies certainly appreciated an Adrianna Jasmine homemade red velvet cupcake topped with white chocolate cream cheese, accompanied with a miniature bottle of Jo Malone lime basil and mandarin body lotion. The men had been presented with a miniature bottle of Glenfiddich whisky and a chocolate beer cupcake with beer-infused butter cream, topped with crushed pretzels. Yes, Adrianna Jasmine felt very content as she scanned the room.

She looked towards Carolina who was wearing a yellow 50s inspired dress, Kristobella, Bella Bell, Mrs Sparrow and old Mrs Berry and Sarah. Unfortunately her fiancé, Sergio, was not present at the wedding as he was in Latvia with his father where he usually spent the summer months. Nonetheless, he had sent Adrianna Jasmine an enormous box of chocolates from Thornton's and a pair of Lion King Tickets. Thoughtful! She snuck a peak at Clementine and her latest controversial squeeze, Lenni, Archi Soams and his wife Lorraine, Luca Placidi, who couldn't keep his eyes off the provocative Clementine and her sultry girlfriend and two of Taylor's old schoolmates who were not married but happily dating. They were bringing their latest squeezes to the night-time bash. She looked out towards Taylor's family, his aunt and uncle from his mother's side, Violet, his cousins and his father's brother, Bo, who unfortunately was widowed. His son and family were not present as they had emigrated to New Zealand four years earlier. Further back from the front was Megan and Sky, more friends of Taylor, Pepper, Aluino, an unfamiliar blonde woman with the palest skin ever witnessed, Hannah and Angelo, Chrystal Rose... Hey? Adrianna Jasmine looked over towards the pale woman again. She didn't recognise her. She was not one of Taylor's family or friends and Adrianna Jasmine had most certainly never laid eyes upon her in her life. The witch looked from one side of the room to the other, no one had noticed her yet how could they not? The woman was wearing a cream chiffon floating gown slashed down the middle of her belly button, barely covering her breasts. She wore a large, heavy gold necklace and her hair was long and wavy, it reminded Adrianna Jasmine of mermaid's hair. The strange woman was staring at Adrianna Jasmine with intense violet eyes, they burnt like embers. She was smiling but not in a kind way, her smile was cruel, almost menacing like an evil cat just waiting to pounce. Adrianna Jasmine began to feel unnerved; she looked over to her mother who was merrily chatting to Taylor, no doubt about the Moulin Rouge. She looked over towards Kristobella who, too, was engaged in conversation; in fact everyone in the room was deeply and intensely conversing. Clementine was talking to Lenni; Luca talking to Lorraine and Archi; everyone talking, talking and talking. The room began to feel unbearably loud and Adrianna Jasmine felt quite queasy. Her heart rate and breathing quickened, and although she was in a room with over eighty people, she felt completely isolated. What was going on? She looked over at the woman who was still staring, burning, smiling. Adrianna Jasmine swallowed hard: she wanted to call out to her mother but what could she do? The room was filled with non-witches and magical folk, she couldn't cause a scene but then again, could she, if she tried? The witch felt as if she were disappearing. No one looked at her or spoke to her. It was as if she no longer existed. Then her body felt cold and she started to shiver.

"Oh Goddess," she moaned through chattering teeth, "I feel like I'm about to die." Her skin was turning a deathly shade of white and her lips an unflattering shade of blue yet still no one noticed, it were as if she was floating in some goddess-forsaken nightmare. She could feel her body temperature dropping below 35°C; her level of consciousness began to flounder. *Please don't let me die alone*, she begged the Goddess, *my family are here but they cannot see me, they are not aware...* Fear overtook her mind as her blood vessels began to shut down in her feet and hands and from that moment on, she couldn't move them. *Help*, she was calling in her mind, *help*! But no one did. She painfully raised her eyes to look at the woman who she now realised was the cause of her terrifying ordeal. The woman was still smiling her cruel, malicious smile, enjoying the hold she had on the witch. *Who are you?* thought Adrianna Jasmine, *why... are... you.. doing... this...to...me?* Her emotional cognition was beginning to fail her and soon, she was sure, she would surrender to the powers of hypothermia.

"So cold," she murmured, "must have heat, give me heat." The noise around her was deafening, the laughing, the clatter of plates, the music... Then like a lightning bolt, Adrianna Jasmine realised what is was she had to do. "The candle," she slurred, "look at the candle." It was a small chance but one of the little tea light candles that was pressed into a glossy red apple; it could just be the chance she was looking for. She stared hard into the candle's flame. It was only little but even the smallest of flames was powerful enough to burn a giant building to the ground. It would have to do.

"I call upon Brigid," she said silently, "the Celtic fire goddess to help me bring light and heat into my hour of darkness and to ignite this spell with her association with fire."

> *Fire fire the element of fire, melt this evil and immortal desire*
> *Warm my bones warm my flesh for I am far too close to death*
> *Fire fire the element of fire, melt away this curse and spell*
> *Warm my soul bring me back to life*
> *Give her husband back his wife*
> *Fire fire the element of fire burn and blaze flame and burn*
> *Thaw this freeze from my fingers and toes*
> *Heat and passion from the blood red rose*
> *Basking in sun soaking up its rays*

Give me back to the sun-filled days
And harm none

A few moments passed and Adrianna Jasmine felt no change but slowly and surely, the noise in the room began to filter out and the witch suddenly began to feel part of her world once more. She looked over towards the woman whose once demonic smile had now been replaced with an angry snarl. Her eyes burned like hell itself towards the witch who now was beginning to feel confident that Brigid had heard her plight and was fighting for her. She began to breathe more easily as a delightful warmth spread deliciously through her body. Adrianna Jasmine wiggled her fingers and toes, blinked her eyes, before reaching over to a glass of red wine. She took a hearty gulp and felt the immediate pleasure of the sweet rich liquid trickling through her tummy warming her internally. She took a couple more to encourage internal warmth.

"Yes, the Moulin Rouge darling, the Moulin Rouge, can you believe it?! I was there for four years, I danced for princes, queens, film stars, oh it was magnificent."

"Your mum's been telling my dad all about her days at the notorious Moulin Rouge. I don't think he's quite ready for it," joked Taylor.

Adrianna Jasmine didn't answer, she just blinked a few times and looked a little bewildered.

"Sweetheart, are you alright?"

Adrianna Jasmine didn't answer straight away, she was still in shock. Only moments ago she thought she was actually about to die. She reached out and squeezed Taylor's hand; it felt good to feel his touch. His hand was incredibly warm and she used it to aid her quest to defrost. She took another hearty sip of wine and kissed his cheek.

"Yes, I'm fine," she eventually said as convincingly as possible. "I just need to go to the ladies room."

She stood up feeling a little woozy. As she did, she scanned the room for the woman. The woman had disappeared.

"Mum, come and help in the powder room," Adrianna Jasmine said to her mother as she walked past.

"Of course, darling. Stay there, Austin, I simply must tell you about the time I met a very shady character from the former USSR, who apparently adored my act which involved an umbrella, body oil and chamois leather! TTFN."

As Adrianna Jasmine stood, she made eye contact with Kristobella and Carolina and discreetly beckoned for them to follow her to the ladies. Realising something was afoot, Clementine, Sarah and Bella Bell immediately followed suit.

Once safely in the ladies room, Adrianna Jasmine poured out her story and when she'd finished her mother went berserk.

"I'll kill her," she hissed, "I'll rip her to shreds. I'll turn her inside out, her blood will evaporate quicker than the speed of sound by the time I get my talons into her. Her! That thing, who is she? How dare she come here, today of all days, she is dead, dead, dead!" There was an uncomfortable silence in the room "And where are Sparrow and Berry?" shrieked Sicily breaking the Silence, "they're here, aren't they? Oh they're too busy stuffing their decrepit faces. How could they not have noticed the abomination that's just happened and right under their noses?"

"Mother!" exclaimed Adriana Jasmine.

"Well, it's ridiculous, darling, they *claim* to be the most powerful witches of our time and yet they were totally unconscious to your plight!"

"Well, in all fairness, we all were," said Clementine.

Sicily turned slowly towards the voice that had dared to speak. Her eyes began to blacken and her face looked positively fearsome, possessed even. Then the lights in the room began to switch on and off and taps sporadically shot out water into the sinks, splashing the mirrors above them. Sarah began to feel scared. *Oh goddess,* she thought, *please Sicily calm down.* Sicily turned sharply towards Sarah as if she had heard her very thoughts resulting in Sarah cowering behind Bella Bell.

"I think someone needs a hug," suggested Carolina softly amongst the chaos and with care and, some may argue, absolute bravery, she went over to Sicily and placed her arms around the witch. She was like a statue completely still yet crackling with wrath.

Carolina was cautious, Sicily was as volatile as a stick of dynamite. Nonetheless she allowed Carolina to embrace her and immediately the mother witch began to melt and her anger started to appease. She sighed heavily.

"Thank you, Carolina. I thought I was going to internally combust."

Carolina smiled and looked at Adrianna Jasmine. The poor girl's eyes were like saucers and she had turned a nasty shade of white.

"Come here, my darling," Carolina whispered and took the now close to tears Adrianna Jasmine into her magical embrace. The warmth of Carolina's hug melted and soothed Adrianna Jasmine back into a calm, beautiful bride once more. Carolina then kissed her gently on the cheek before offering her magical cuddles to everyone in the room. She hugged everyone before reaching Clementine who was practically shaking with fear. Clementine now realised that this would be the last time she and Sicily ever met because if not, it would result in the final solution... death.

The wedding breakfast continued without a hitch. This was down to two things: one, great wedding organisation and two, the witches' protection spells placed in front of every door in the hotel in order to prevent any unwanted evil from returning. Of course, Taylor and guests suspected nothing. The champagne flowed and the speeches were a success. The wedding cake, made by Adrianna Jasmine's fair hands, was a triumph and everyone loved having their tarot card read by the Mystic Odessa. From 7pm to 9pm the guests were invited to listen and dance to a group called West End Miracles who specialised in performing all the songs made famous from the shows. Afterwards, champagne and fish and chips were served, followed by more of Adrianna Jasmines delicious wedding cake. Then it was back over to Rick O Shay who filled the room with more tapping Celtic beats. Everyone was merry as they had drank and eaten to their hearts' content. Luca Placidi had struck it lucky with Sky, and Taylor's brother, Mark, was certainly enjoying Megan's company. Although she was a little young for him he was impressed with her maturity and the pair talked over glasses of champagne whilst she read his palm. Taylor's father was taught how to combat basic Irish dance steps by the lovely Sicily, and Patty sat and talked to Henry Forthright Punch about his exciting life as a pianist. The cackle, of course, danced like maniacs as if the unfortunate event of Sicily almost boiling her own head off with anger due to Adrianna Jasmine almost freezing to death, hadn't actually occurred. However, one witch was not present. Clementine had taken it upon herself to get the hell out of there as soon as the lights went down and the disco lights went on. She had made some excuse to Lenni about wanting her more than ever and that if she didn't get out of there soon, she would explode with frustration. Lenni being a hot-blooded Spanish sort and, of course, utterly infatuated with the beautiful blonde, required no pleading from the delicious Clementine, she was out of there! So all in all, the wedding was a complete success.

At midnight, Adrianna Jasmine hurled the bouquet (Carolina caught it) and Kristobella and Sicily placed Whiz onto the ground and encouraged Taylor and Adrianna Jasmine to jump over him on their way out (an old Pagan Ritual) before bidding farewell to their guests and retiring to their bedroom in Hotel 78 to enjoy their first night as husband and wife.

"Don't wait until mother's day to do something nice for your mother, surprise her with a bunch of daffodils in the spring, English stocks in the summer, traditional roses in warm colours for the autumn and a bouquet of holly, ivy and mistletoe for the winter. Or if flowers aren't your style, then a Simnel cake for the spring, Summer Pudding for the summer, pumpkin pie for the autumn and mince pies and Christmas cake for the winter"
(Adriana Jasmine Mariposa Poppleapple Jameson)

Chapter 40
Mother and Daughter Time

"Well, this is lovely, darling, just you and me in our favourite special occasions restaurant."

Adrianna Jasmine nodded happily. Sicily had treated her to a welcome back from honeymoon celebratory luncheon, at the world renowned San Lorenzo Restaurant on Beauchamp Place. They were tempted to go for a traditional afternoon tea at the Ritz, but due to Sicily's Great Aunt Primrose, who used to be a cook at the world-renowned hotel many moons ago, witches found it quite difficult to enter the hotel. Primrose had cast a spell on a rather poor batch of scones to make them appear more appetising which unfortunately resulted in the unsuspecting guests, who had eaten the scones, to think that they were characters from Alice in Wonderland. Chaos apparently erupted thereafter with people believing that they were everything from the Mad Hatter, to trying to squeeze their bodies into a tea pot to hide from the Queen of Hearts. As a punishment, the threefold law put a stop to any witch from setting a toe in the building, and every year Sicily dares to hope that the law has been lifted. Shortly after her spell at the Ritz, Primrose got a job as a cook at Buckingham Palace and as punishment the threefold assigned her to making the Queen's cucumber sandwiches for the rest of her days! Little is known of Primrose these days, or her whereabouts. The two women sat down and excitedly began to look at the yummy menu.

"Can I offer you something to drink?"

The two witches looked up at an impeccably dressed waiter with an Italian accent.

"A bottle of house Rosé, please," asked Sicily, smiling brightly, "and perhaps a bottle of mineral water."

The waiter nodded politely, "Certainly," and off he went to fetch the ladies their drinks.

"So tell me all about the honeymoon, was it wonderful, was it everything you hoped it would be?"

Adrianna Jasmine beamed with happiness, "Oh yes, it was just spectacular. I loved every second of it."

"Well, I must say, darling, you seemed to be gone forever!"

"I know, well we were away almost a month and even though I'm really pleased to be back home and getting stuck into my work, if Taylor said 'come on Mrs Poppleapple Jameson, let's go off travelling right now for a month,' I'd jump at the chance."

Sicily smiled, "Well, I don't blame you, pineapple pop, the world is a wonderful place and needs to be explored. So tell me all about it."

"Excuse me, ladies, your wine. "

"Hold that thought," said Sicily,

Mother and daughter sat patiently as the waiter expertly poured a little of their wine into a gleaming glass for Sicily to taste, she took a sip and then nodded her approval. The waiter continued to pour then left the remainder of the bottle in an ice bucket. "Are you ready to order?"

"Yes we are," answered Sicily assuredly, "Adrianna Jasmine?"

"The melon and Parma ham to start, please, followed by Spaghetti Marinara."

"And for you, Madame?"

"The same to start but spaghetti Vongole for my main course, thank you." The waiter nodded, retrieved the menus and made his way towards the kitchen. "Cheers," said Sicily and the pair chinked their glasses and drank a toast to happy marriage. "So you were about to tell me all about the honeymoon."

Adrianna Jasmine took a deep breath. "Well we stayed in Paris for three nights and had the most spectacular time. We visited all the sights: the Arc de Triumph, The Eiffel Tower, the Louvre and The Moulin Rouge!"

Sicily squealed with glee, "Oh, was it fabulous?"

"Oh yes, it was, we loved it, especially when this half clad woman did an underwater performance with a boa constrictor."

Sicily nodded seriously, "Yes, it's quite alarming, some of the things the performers get up to with snakes."

Adrianna Jasmine coughed politely. "Then, after three wonderful nights we caught the *Orient Express*, courtesy of my mother and father, to Venice." As their wedding gift to the bride and groom, Sicily and Henry had paid for a two night trip on the Orient Express.

"Oh what was it like, darling?"

"Eloquent, stylish, romantic, beautiful… everything you would expect. I loved it; the food was delicious, the service impeccable and our little cabin adorable and very cosy."

Sicily giggled, "Good, darling, well I'm pleased you enjoyed it. And how was Venice?"

"Ah Venice," said Adrianna Jasmine floating off into a trance, "magical, beautiful and historical. We stayed at the Luna Baglioni and it had its own private canal entrance. I tell you, it was really something. Mind you, the city was so expensive, never go for a cup of coffee in St Marks' square, it'll set you back about ten Euros!"

Sicily nodded, "I know, darling, but hey, it's a once in a lifetime ten euro cup of coffee."

"Then we caught a train from Venice to Bologna, where we stopped for two nights and had a bowl or two of spaghetti Bolognese, then continued travelling down to Florence which was breathtaking."

"Was the art exquisite, darling?"

"Oh yes, stunning. Thank goddess we spent three nights there, otherwise there was no way we'd have seen the amount that we did. Then, of course, we travelled down to Rome, although we only stayed for the night as Taylor and I were there not so long ago. But it was lovely to stay in the Regina Baglioni again."

"Brought back some wonderful memories, I'd imagine," said Sicily with a light-hearted sigh.

Adrianna Jasmine nodded, "And we revisited Flavia's restaurant and guess what, the people who worked there recognised us!"

Sicily smiled. "Well, you two are hard not to remember."

"Then we caught the train at about ten o clock the following morning and headed down to Naples, then caught a coach to Sorrento, which is probably one of my most favourite places in the whole world."

"Did you visit Capri?"

"Yes."

"Did you visit the Grotta Azzurra?"

"Uh huh, stunning."

"And what of Sorrento, what made it so special?"

Adrianna Jasmine sat back into her chair, a warm smile spreading across her face as the memories washed over her. "Relaxed cafes and restaurants where you can sit at pavement tables and watch the world go by; the sun, the atmosphere, the people, the energy, the panoramic views. It's just... Italy in a nutshell."

Sicily took a long hearty sip of wine, "Oh wonderful, darling and how long were you two there?"

"Five days. Actually, Sorrento was a bit more relaxing. We lazed about by the pool and enjoyed nice walks into the town and people-watched."

"Don't blame you, honey pot, after all, walking around sight-seeing and all that travelling does tend to wear one out."

"I'll say, and well, Taylor needed it, really, he was exhausted, bless him."

Sicily chuckled, "Hmm, he wouldn't be able to keep up with you darling your energy is like the sun itself. Ah, our food!"

The two witches immediately began to tuck into their starter, talking in between mouthfuls.

"And what of Greece, was it glorious?"

"Oh mum, you and dad should really go, we visited two islands after departing from the mainland."

"Which two did you do again?"

"Poros and Spetses."

"Magical?"

"Picture postcard magical. Poros is just so pretty and the food! Calamari, tzatziki, beautiful salads, mussels, chicken, oh my goddess..."

"Sounds glorious again. And what of Spetses? You stayed in that beautiful hotel, didn't you?"

"The Possidoneon? Oh, it was breathtaking, an architectural beauty that somehow recaptures the old elegance of the 1960s. It just oozed style, and the view from our room was simply awe-inspiring."

"What did you see, butterfly wing?"

"A statue of the famous Boobalina and the glorious sea."

"Ooh lovely, I am envious."

"Well, you and dad should go, you know, for a second honeymoon or something. It would be well worth it, and besides, you two have lots to celebrate at the moment, what with dad doing so well with Chicago and your career is going from strength to strength, and of course, what with your little girl all grown and married..."

"I know we should do, darling, and yes, perhaps a little trip would do the pair of us the world of good. I'll find out when he can spare a week away from the West End, in fact, I'll go on the internet later and have a little look-see."

"Good for you and the climate, mum, it's just exquisite. Oh to just walk out in the evenings and not have to wear a jacket..."

She then trailed off

"What is it, Ferrero Rocher?"

"I just remembered a few times whilst on my holiday I felt an overwhelming sense of cold."

Sicily stiffened slightly in her chair, "Cold, darling, what do you mean?"

"It was strange, just like I experienced at the reception but... different."

"How was it different, peach pie?"

"Well, when I felt that awful cold during the wedding, the reason behind it was due to... her."

411

"The woman that no one else could see, even though I totally believe that you did see her, darling, because you're a witch and you see all sorts of things that others just aren't susceptible to."

Adrianna Jasmine thanked her mother for her support. "Err, yes and I obviously realised that she must be the reason why I felt so Goddess damn cold."

"Well, you were hypothermic, darling, that's a little bit more than just cold!"

Adrianna Jasmine sighed, "Well, it was rather frightening and infuriating really, as I had to deal with the problem as discreetly as possible due to being in front of eighty-odd people who were none the wiser."

"You were magnificent, darling, but what I want to know is what exactly was or is she, and why was your chilling experience on your honeymoon different from your wedding?"

Adrianna Jasmine paused for thought. "Well, she wasn't a ghost and she wasn't human, that's for definite, but she was very real, but why couldn't anyone see her except me?"

Sicily shook her head in bewilderment. "What sort of energy or emotion did you receive from her?"

Adrianna Jasmine took a deep breath, "Well, she reminded me of... death"

Now it was Sicily's turn to feel cold and she swallowed hard. "Like the Grim Reaper?" Sicily was trying desperately hard not to shake, she reached over to her wine and took a few hearty gulps in order to calm her quaking nerves.

"No, the Grim Reaper is a psychopomp, a person who manages spirits or souls to the other world. He's just a person, or entity I suppose, that takes life when it is the person's time. He wouldn't be caught dead, pardon the pun, toying with the victim for fear of the victim cheating him and escaping death. No, this woman wasn't the Grim Reaper she was toying with me and enjoying it to boot."

"Well, that's all very well and good, darling, but this still doesn't help us solve what she is, pop petty pooch, and why was the experience different from that of the honeymoon?"

"Because I only felt cold, I didn't actually see *her* again."

Sicily smiled a wry smile. "That's because we all cast a bloody good spell on you, darling, to protect you from her evil."

"I know, thank you and I must thank Mrs Berry and Mrs Sparrow for involving themselves."

"Oh I shouldn't bother, sweetheart. It's any excuse for them to cast a spell or two, in fact, your plight probably did them a favour, they don't get out much these days."

"Oh good! Pleased I entertained them with my plight."

Sicily laughed, "Oh, darling, it's not like that. They just get a good buzz from casting spells, that's all and anyway, you're goddess damned lucky to have them casting spells for you, after all, they're the best at what they do... apparently"

Adrianna Jasmine huffed, "Anyway, although much appreciated, the spell, or spells or whatever they did, only watered down her power, she still managed to infiltrate me which resulted in me having to a cast my own spell in order to get her to back off."

"So what did you do, darling?"

"Well the first time..."

"The first time! You mean she tried to get at you more than once?"

"Oh yes, three time's altogether, one when Taylor and I were on a Gondola!"

"On a gondola, darling? How very inconvenient."

"I'll say. The gondolier was right in the middle of singing O Sol O Mio, when I experienced the icy blast. Poor Taylor thought I was coming down with pleurisy or something!"

"What did you do, Dorset apple cake?"

"I used the sun."

Sicily smiled knowingly, "Ah yes, good thinking, I bet the Italian sun soon melted away her evil chill."

"It took about three minutes to execute, and bear in mind I had Taylor constantly asking me what the matter was and the Gondolier in my ear, so it made it all rather challenging."

"Bravo, darling, at the end of the day you did it. You said there were other times?"

"Uh huh, once in Sorrento and once on Spetses but I just had to do the same thing and use the sun to my advantage!"

"Luckily it didn't try anything at night."

"Well, if it did my nightmare gauntlet would have put a stop to it penetrating my dreams."

"And have you experienced anything else since?"

Adrianna Jasmine shook her head.

"Well, that's a blessing at least, darling." She then looked up, "Ah, the main course, perfect timing."

"Make time for each other, have a date night, laugh at each other, communicate and celebrate each other's body".
(Sicily)

Chapter 41
Married Life

July 2010 and Taylor and Adrianna Jasmine were enjoying a crisp glass of wine with their dinner. The food and drink tasted even more delicious that evening as the pair had just finished moving all Adriana Jasmine's possessions into Taylor's apartment, in Shepherd's Bush.

"To home," toasted Taylor as the pair chinked glasses on their balcony. Adrianna Jasmine leant forward and kissed her husband tenderly on the mouth. "The place has never looked so good," he said with a smile, "and I love all the little knick-knacks you've brought."

Adrianna Jasmine smiled with satisfaction; she had brought her throws and cushions, rugs and shabby chic furniture, pictures, linen, kitchenware, books and book shelf. The place now looked like a contemporary modern home with elements of a modern, yet firmly rooted, witch living there. In addition, Jupiter 10 had also successfully moved into his new location without much fuss and was quite comfortable with his new living quarters. In fact, he was a little relieved that Adrianna Jasmine was finally living with a man and a non-magical person as it meant that it would make life very hard for her to shape-shift for fear of getting caught. He liked living and didn't want to be snuffed out quite just yet.

"This place has never looked so complete as it does with you here, my lovely new wife."

Adrianna Jasmine smiled adoringly, she still couldn't quite grasp just how much she loved him, she could honestly say that she would die for this man.

"Thank you," she answered whilst gently scooping a spoonful of homemade strawberry ice-cream into her mouth. "I like living here and Jupiter 10 likes living here, too."

Taylor looked over towards the little black cat that was nestled on the sofa, purring gently as he slept. "I've not had a pet since I was a boy," said Taylor, "it's rather nice, actually, caring for something, like giving him his food and letting him out for fresh air. Hey, shall we get a dog?"

Adrianna Jasmine nearly spat out her ice cream. She liked dogs but they weren't a witch's best friend. "Err, well they tend to be a little harder to care for, Taylor," she said carefully. "They're not as independent as cats." Taylor looked thoughtful. "Besides, what will we do when you're away travelling with work and I'm out and about baking and on TV, who will walk him and take him out to pee pee?" Taylor spooned another load of ice cream into his mouth, absorbing the information. "They need constant care and attention, at least with Jupiter 10 if he wants to stay in, he'll stay in and if he wants to go out and not return for a week, he will! You see, independent."

Taylor nodded. "Huh, OK. Well, maybe in a couple of years then."

Adrianna Jasmine leaned over and kissed his cheek. "Yes, when we live out in the forest somewhere with a large garden and an AGA cooker."

"I like the sound of that! I've always dreamed of living somewhere other than the city, surrounded by greenery and fresh air."

"It's the way forward, darling, when we make our fortune, that's what we'll do."

"I like the sound of that and I tell you what else I like the sound of."

"Oh, what's that?"

"Me! Smearing the rest of this ice-cream over your delicious body and slowly licking it off."

Adrianna Jasmine giggled and began to strip off, resulting in Jupiter 10 waking up and jumping off the couch like a bolt of lightning. Some things he was not quite able to stomach.

"So where's she gone, Sicily?"

"I don't know, Kristobella, but I'll tell you this for nothing, you don't just disappear like that, she's up to something."

"Hmm, but what? Look, I don't like to make assumptions without knowing the facts, but..."

"But what? Go on, say it."

"Well, she looked scared at the wedding."

"We all looked scared, Kristobella, except me, of course. Carolina said I looked more like a deranged psychotic killer which I'm very pleased about because it meant I didn't look vulnerable."

Kristobella rolled her eyes. "Anyway, what're you getting at?"

"That thing showing up really seemed to frighten her. It was like she knew what it was and how dangerous it was, so her fear was different to ours."

Sicily looked thoughtful, "So you think she knew what it was, then?"

"I'm not saying that exactly but we all know she's been... dabbling."

"I'll kill her."

"Shut up, Sicily," snapped her sister, "it could mean that she read about her in some dark art book, it could mean anything."

"Well, you mark my words, I will hunt her, find her, question her and if I don't like her answer, I will kill her."

"Stop being so dramatic, Sicily."

"So dramatic, she could have killed my daughter!"

"Well, we don't know that yet!"

"And that's exactly what I want to find out; when I know, I'll strike."

Adrianna Jasmine lay next to Taylor, who was sleeping soundly in their bed. She had been feeling good since their honeymoon and was pleased that her nightmare gauntlet was taking care of any unwanted visits from "her." However, the fact that she still relied on the magical gantlet unnerved her. She was being heavily guarded by magic from her cackle which made her feel unsettled, she shouldn't be guarded from anything. Adrianna Jasmine silently climbed out of bed and went into the spare bedroom, she needed to find the source of her problem. That way she could squash it.

She gently closed the door behind her and opened the wardrobe. She pulled out her shoe rack to unveil a secret hatch that she had built one afternoon where she now kept her magical tools and her most prized possession, the book of Shadows. She opened the book, went over to the window which was lit by moonlight and opened the page to find a spell to locate an evil source. The book told her that she needed to think about the evil source, retrieve her atheme, find a white candle and to draw a circle of salt on the floor to stand inside. She would then need to light the candle and cut her hand with a knife to draw blood.

Ugh. she huffed at the thought of having to cut herself. Nonetheless she obeyed the rules. She sighed with thanks as she stared up at the moon. It was full and golden and would enable her to draw off its powerful energy, intensifying the spell. When she was ready she stepped inside the circle of salt.

"May this circle of salt protect me from the evil I must locate." She then quickly slashed her palm with the knife and the blood dripped onto the wooden floor. "May my blood be a symbol of my life force," she said, trying not to whimper. "May this candle be the light to highlight the dark secret I must find." The witch then sat on the floor with her legs crossed and focused on the flame. About half an hour went by and the witch still hadn't seen anything, the flame was still lit and her hand still stung from the deep cut. She remained as calm as she could and concentrated on the face that she had seen at her wedding. The beautiful, yet disturbingly evil face. As time passed, the face became more and more real. The spell was beginning to work. She saw her roaming from different countries, homes and times, effortless in her movements, graceful and light. She was only noticed when she wanted to be noticed and wore fashions that depicted times from as early as the 17th century through to Victorian and present day. She was never seen during the day, only amongst the shadows of night and constantly highlighted by candles and moonlight. Times flew past as if Adrianna Jasmine were watching a film. The mysterious she-devil was now in some sort of tavern, sitting at a table, talking to someone yet Adrianna Jasmine could not see who. They were in deep conversation and the person appeared to be scared. Bargaining chips were being laid and rules set, although not in favour of the person who sat opposite her. *Who are you?* asked Adrianna Jasmine, *why are you here?* The person was reluctant to show their face and tried desperately not reveal themselves. This made the she-devil laugh as if she found the plight of her table companion highly amusing.

Show yourself, willed Adrianna Jasmine, *show yourself to me now!*

Then the witch got the shock of her life, *oh Goddess, no,* breathed Adrianna Jasmine, *you stupid fool!*

"Remember, if you can see someone, they can probably see you, too."

(Jupiter 10)

Chapter 42
Sneaky

"Oh Carolina, thanks for seeing me. I didn't know who to turn to, I couldn't see mum, she'll go potty and I couldn't trust Mrs Sparrow or Mrs Berry. I just didn't feel comfortable..." Carolina took a frantic Adrianna Jasmine into her arms and soothed away her anxiety. "Thank you," she breathed with a sigh of relief.

"You're welcome, now come in, sit down, have a cup of Earl Grey and tell me all about it."

A few minutes later Adrianna Jasmine and Carolina were enjoying a steaming pot of tea and fresh scones with clotted cream.

"Okay, what's the trouble, my darling?"

Adrianna Jasmine took a deep breath and told Carolina about the spell she had cast the night before "Oh, I wondered how you had cut your hand, it makes sense now." Adrianna Jasmine nodded. "So who did it reveal, my darling? It must be someone quite close to our circle because you're in a dreadful panic."

Adrianna Jasmine felt her heart race ever so slightly, "Carolina, it was Clementine." she said solemnly.

Carolina put her tea down then shook her head. "That stupid, stupid girl, what a fool she is, oh Adrianna Jasmine, what has Clementine unleashed?"

"I'm not sure, Carolina but it's dark, very dark."

"Where is Clementine, anyway?"

"I don't know, her mobile is switched off and her flat is in darkness..."

"Perhaps she has gone away with that Lenni, she's probably staying in her hotel in Tenerife. Hold on, let me find a map and we'll try to locate her." A few moments later Carolina was back in her sitting room unfolding a large map of the world onto the coffee table and dangling a piece of string attached to a small pink crystal. "Okay, here we go."

> *Reveal your presence, Clementine, show us where you are*
> *You may be close or maybe somewhere far*
> *Guide us, oh crystal, shine on her mark*
> *Reveal her soul from out of the dark.*

The crystal swirled and whirled about for a few moments before strangely landing on Stoke Newington.

Carolina looked across to Adrianna Jasmine. She shrugged her shoulders, "Does that mean anything to you, Adrianna Jasmine?"

At first Adrianna Jasmine was confused why would Clementine be there and why does Stoke Newington ring a bell? Then fear swept over her, "Oh Goddess, that's where Mark lives."

"Mark, who's Mark?"

"Taylor's brother, he liked her at the wedding, oh Clementine, you little witch!"

"You think she's been shacked up with him? What will you do?"

"I think I need to find out what's going on."

"You are stunning, Clementine and you can stay here as long as you like."

Clementine smiled seductively from under the sheets and kissed Mark hard on the lips.

"Thank you, handsome. I may just take you up on the offer."

"You do that! Now, Violet will be home from school soon, so I don't mean to spoil the mood but..."

"Would you mind if we got out of bed and looked a little more presentable?"

Mark smiled, "If that's okay with you, it's tough enough that her mother's up and left her without having to see her daddy with another lady in his bed."

Clementine waved her hand dismissively, "Say no more, in fact, I'll have a shower then make some tea and crumpets." She kissed the top of his head before running the water.

About half an hour later Violet came in from school.

"Clementine!" She ran over to the witch and threw her arms around her. The little girl had become quite close to Clementine since they first met at the dress fitting. She found the tall blonde exotic, exciting and completely cool. She loved the fact that there was another girl about the house, and so different to her mother. She was more like an older sister than someone trying to muscle in and take over as a parent. "Let me show you what I learnt at dance class last night." Violet dumped her school bag and began to high kick, whirl and jump. Clementine laughed and clapped her hands appreciating the little girl's talents.

"Fabulous," complimented Clementine, "very good."

Mark looked over towards the happy sight. He wasn't going to get his hopes up, but he liked the picture he saw in front of him. His lovely little girl happy in her home, playing with a beautiful woman who he could quite easily call his wife one day. He went into the kitchen and began to fantasise about a future with Clementine. First of all he thought how dating such a hottie as Clementine would infuriate his ex, resulting in the ultimate revenge, then of course, the usual, like going on lovely holidays to the Caribbean, having a strong secure woman in Violet's life, family, meals, outings, wedding and babies! *Ugh get a grip man,* he thought snapping himself back to reality. *You've only known her a couple of months. Plus, she's only in her early twenties. Anything could happen.* But he had to admit, the fantasies were nice.

That evening the threesome sat down and ate spaghetti bolognese, courtesy of Clementine, and watched TV whilst Clementine played with Violet's hair. At eight thirty Clementine put Violet to bed.

"Do you dream, Violet?" she asked the little girl.

Violet nodded, "Yes but they're not very nice dreams."

Clementine felt saddened by this. Obviously the little girl was unsettled inside due to her parents' divorce.

"Well, I bet tonight you have the most magical dreams and tomorrow you can tell me all about them."

Violet smiled, "I won't remember them, though."

"You will."

Clementine began to sing a soothing lullaby, evoking sleep. Violet's eyes began to feel heavy and soon she began to drift and float into a dream-filled sleep.

Hush, hush into a world of pinks and blues
Horses with wings and strawberry chews
Floating on clouds light and white
Protection from a handsome knight
Sweets from trees and treacle sponge
Milk and cookies and a water plunge
Merry-go-rounds and candy floss
Peaches and grapes so sweet so soft
Tabby kittens picture books
A glowing sun and sparkling brooks
Green, green grass rabbits that spring
Angels and fairies hear them sing
The world is yours wonder and explore
Space dust, music and a sea shore

She crept out of Violet's room and went back to see Mark who was on the couch watching TV. The pair drank a glass of red wine, watched a film then turned in about 11.30pm. They both enjoyed one another's bodies for an hour or two before Mark fell into a deep sleep. At 2am Clementine crept out of the bedroom and to the front door. She opened it silently.

"Hello," she whispered, fear enveloping her body.

"Hello, Clementine. Aren't you going to invite me in?" Clementine was reluctant, "Only if you promise not to harm anyone in this house." The woman laughed dryly. "If you don't I can't let you in, I won't let innocent people die."

"Whether you let me in or not I could still kill you, or anyone in this building for that matter, now, Clementine, let me in."

Clementine looked sad and defeated. "Katarina, please come in."

The woman swept in like a chilling wind. "Are they heavily sedated?"

Clementine nodded, "They won't wake until daybreak."

423

"Good, now listen to me, you've played a very dangerous game summoning me and I will tell you now, there will be consequences." Clementine began to tremble; the woman began to chuckle. "Well, what do you expect? It was very foolish to meddle and now you've shown us into your world, we want some of your treasures."

Clementine began to weep. "Please don't hurt anyone," she begged as her tears plopped onto the floor.

"I'm afraid that is unavoidable." Clementine fell to her knees in despair. "Our plan I'm afraid, involves taking lives to achieve our goals. It's a sad affair but..." She came closer to Clementine like an evil spirit waiting to strike and gently cupped Clementine's chin with her hands. She was ice-cold. "It is what it is and nothing you can do will stop me." Clementine shook her head freeing herself from the woman's icy touch.

"You have to stop, Katarina. I've changed my mind. I never thought innocent people would suffer when I summoned you, I was just experimenting, I wanted to see if your kind really did exist, I meant no harm..."

Katarina curled her mouth into a cruel smile. "Oh, I'm very real, Clementine, and perhaps your foolish spell will teach you an important lesson for the future." She loomed in closer towards the terrified Clementine. "Don't meddle."

"Please," begged Clementine, "I didn't mean to summon you, please, we can work something out..."

"I know we can," Katarina toyed, "there are many options to be explored. Especially as I've always wanted to bag me a witch. For some reason your kind have always been unattainable. But then of course, I met you!" Clementine's heat sank. "Now all I need to do is begin the ritual and a new age will begin."

"What do you mean? What ritual?" Clementine was almost sick now with fear.

"Why! The draining of your blood, of course."

At first Clementine didn't quite comprehend. She had heard the words "draining" and "blood" but just as the horrid realisation that she was about to die hit her, Katarina struck and drained the life from Clementine. R.I.P.

When Katarina was finished, she picked up Clementine and carried her as if she were nothing more than a rag doll, opened the front door and disappeared into the dead of the night. Where she took her, no one knew for sure, not even the little pair of eyes that had witnessed everything from the balcony window.

Chapter 43
Disappearance

"Well, I think you were very brave, pumpkin patch, but incredibly stupid, why on earth didn't you tell me?"

Adrianna Jasmine and Sicily were enjoying a cup of tea inside a fitness club in Westfields. Sicily was on a break from rehearsals. She'd been learning a rather vigorous quickstep with her partner Nathanial Lunette, a former French world Latin ballroom champion. She had unfortunately not been chosen to dance with Vincent and for days the witch skulked and sulked, threatening to quit the show, until, that was, she met the beautiful Nathanial. It had been love at first sight; Vincent was nothing more than a passed infatuation.

"Because I knew you would flip, mother, and probably do something extremely hot-headed. Besides, I was quite safe, courtesy of Jupiter 10."

Sicily shook her head, "that poor little cat. How many lives has he got now?"

"Oh, I don't know but I shan't be shape-shifting into him again anytime soon."

"Oh, why's that?"

"Because he's gone walk about, I haven't seen him since the end of August. I think he hates me," she added with a touch of sadness.

"Not surprised, darling. Anyway I still can't believe Clementine submerged herself into something so dark." Sicily then paused for thought. "Actually, I retract that last statement, I *can* believe she would submerge herself into something so dark. Silly little fool, if you meddle, then prepare to face the consequences. And anyway, what exactly did you hear, lemon meringue pie?"

"I couldn't really hear anything, mother, I was behind the window but Clementine appeared to be pleading with the woman from the wedding. She was trembling and sick with fear."

"Hmmmm, interesting that it turned out to be the mystery woman who's been causing so much trouble for you, sticky toffee pudding. I had my suspicions, of course."

"What suspicions?"

"Well, that someone from our circle was involved with your night terrors and although I couldn't prove it, darling, I just knew deep down that Clementine had something to do with it. However, why on earth Clementine got herself mixed up with something *quite* so dark, I'll never know. Have you any idea what the woman is?"

Adrianna Jasmine shook her head as she sipped her coffee. "Unfortunately I'm not sure. Maybe she's a witch or perhaps some kind of sorceress, she was dressed in a long flowing gown and was incredibly beautiful but I tell you, mother, her evil was practically penetrating through the glass."

Sicily looked thoughtful. "So you could feel her darkness?"

"I could indeed. But when I look back at the horrid situation, the woman had something incredibly animalistic about her."

"Oh?"

"There was something predatory about the woman, almost inhuman."

"Go on." encouraged Sicily

"It's hard to explain, but she reminded me of a great lioness and Clementine, the helpless dear who had been stalked, captured, toyed with and eventually slain."

"So you think the woman killed Clementine?"

"I can't be certain but after the woman pounced..."

"Pounced?"

"Yes, pounced! Like some great cat. I know it sounds ridiculous... but that's exactly what she did."

"Then what did she do?"

"Well she proceeded to lie on top of her."

Sicily raised her eyebrows, "Err, and what exactly was she doing to Clementine whilst she was on top of her?" *Goddess, this was beginning to sound more and more risqué by the minute!*

"I'm not sure. The woman's hair was cascaded all over Clementine's face and neck I couldn't really see. But one moment

Clementine was quivering and shaking and the next she became deadly still."

There was silence for a few moments from the witches.

"You think she died?" asked Sicily carefully.

"I believe she did, mother, because when the woman carried Clementine out of the room, Clementine was limp and lifeless. Her skin was no longer a healthy shade of caramel but alabaster white."

"But how can you be sure, darling, that Clementine is actually dead? It could just be that she was so terrified, the entire colour drained from her skin."

"She's not alive, mum," said Adrianna Jasmine solemnly.

"Oh whys that, vanilla cream terrine?"

"Because I was looking at my wedding photos last night and Clementine appears to missing one crucial thing... her soul."

"You mean she's dead darling? Dead and gone?" Adrianna Jasmine nodded sadly and her eyes began to fill with tears. "Well, that *is* a turn up for the books. Hmmmm, it will be interesting to see if you suffer anymore chilly spells."

Adrianna Jasmine sighed, she knew her mother disliked Clementine but her reaction was quite callous. "I suppose we need to inform her family," suggested Adrianna Jasmine.

"Well, yes, darling, because everyone from our world knows you can see if a person is dead or alive through photographs. They may become suspicious if you omit to mention it, darling. However, I'm afraid we'll just have to keep it to ourselves when it comes to non-magical folk."

"Like Mark, for instance?"

"Yes, especially Mark."

"Poor chap."

"He's a fool," snapped Sicily, "did he honestly think a harlot, and a sexually confused one to boot, would ever consider partaking in a stable relationship with him?"

Adrianna Jasmine felt sad, "Well, yes. Since her *disappearance* I've seen quite a bit of Mark and Violet. Mark was most certainly beginning to fall for Clementine and vice versa. Plus the little girl adored her. She had also interestingly told me all about a gorgeous dream she had had the night Clementine vanished."

Sicily scoffed, "So she did a little dream spell for the child, big deal, it means nothing. She probably wanted her to fall asleep so she could have her wicked way with her father."

"Mother! Have you no compassion. Clementine was a good girl, she was just mixed up and who could blame her look at her upbringing compared to mine. She had to suppress her magic, her mother was ashamed of her and all she ever wanted was a loving family. It's all wrong, mum and very unfair."

Sicily shrugged, "Well, I don't see it, there are some things a witch just doesn't do, and besides, if anyone puts my little girl in danger, I will do everything in my power to make sure they suffer to their very core. Speaking of suffering to the very core, I need to get back to rehearsals; this quickstep is very demanding, darling. Nathanial is very good but, Goddess, he's a slave-driver. Toodle loo!"

She got up, kissed her daughter goodbye and with a spring to her step and a gigantic smile to her face, Sicily went back to training. "Ah," she breathed, "at last Clementine is no longer a part of this world."

Sliced Fruit and Toffee Fondue

50g unsalted butter
175g light muscovado sugar
284 double cream
3 apples skinned and cut into wedges
3 pears skinned and cut into wedges
Juice 1/ lemon
Pinch of cinnamon
6 wooden skewers soaked in cool water for at least 30 minutes

Dissolve the butter in a pan and add 100g of the muscovado sugar. Stir until the muscovado has gone. Pour in the cream, bring to the boil and whisk until smooth. Set aside until warm. Meanwhile heat the grill to high. Toss the fruit in the lemon juice, remaining sugar and cinnamon. Thread onto the skewers and arrange in one layer on a baking tray. Grill for 5 minute turning once when golden. Dip into the caramel sauce

Chapter 44
Halloween 2010

Due to Sicily's gruelling schedule and Adrianna Jasmine's hectic workload, the witches were not able to make it to Burley that year for their annual Halloween feast. In addition, the cackle, except Sicily, was most saddened by the unexpected death of Clementine and celebrating didn't seem quite right. Instead, they opted to stay in London and enjoy cocktails in the Blue Room at the world-renowned Berkley Hotel in Knightsbridge. During the day, Adrianna Jasmine appeared on This Morning and cooked up a batch of Halloween treats for the nation, consisting of caramel and fruit fondue, spider cupcakes and pumpkin cheesecake! She then bolted over to Covent Garden to assist Sarah and her family in the coffee shop. Sarah had specifically asked her to make an appearance on the shop floor today to read to the children and meet and greet customers. Basically, she wanted to use Adrianna Jasmine's well-known face to entice customers into the shop. Sarah had created a massive poster with a picture of Adrianna Jasmine and placed in the window saying "spend Halloween with Adrianna Jasmine the princess of Cupcakes!" It also advertised story time and hot spiced cider, free for every adult, along with other delectable treats, such as black velvet cheesecake, pumpkin pie and toffee-apples.

"Hi, Jazzy," said Sarah cheerfully as her friend walked in through the back kitchen door, "how did it go?"

"Really good, thanks, all the camera crew ate the cup cakes and Phil and Holly are just delightful, in fact, Holly loved my pumpkin pies!"

"Oh, I love Holly, so well done you."

"Hello, Adrianna Jasmine."

Adrianna Jasmine looked up and saw Sergio walking towards her with a gleaming smile, "How are you? I haven't seen you in ages." He leant over and kissed her on the cheek, "you look well. Sorry I couldn't make the wedding, and work has been crazy so as it is, it's been impossible to meet up."

"I know, don't worry, hey, we'll arrange a nice night out or something next week, just the four of us and we'll catch up. By the way, thank you for the chocolates and the tickets; I devoured the chocolates and loved the show."

Sergio smiled, "My pleasure, Adriana Jasmine, glad you enjoyed them, right, I need to get into my costume. I'm going to be a werewolf this year!"

As he walked off, Sarah gave out a long languished sigh.

Adrianna Jasmine laughed. "Yeah, yeah, he's a catch, good for you, come on, let's get this party started."

"Okay, well let's start by getting you in the shop, the queue outside has been crazy today and I know it's because the public want to see you. Mind you, have we got enough products to sell?"

"Don't worry, I made plenty. By the way, what paper is coming down?"

"Oh Goddess, I don't know, but there's a few so be prepared."

Adrianna Jasmine huffed, she wasn't keen on being pulled about by journalists and paps! "Ok, well maybe we could put the werewolf on the door to stop anything getting out of hand."

"He's already on the case and my dad is standing on the door, too, by the look of that mob outside, it could be one in one out!"

"Ok, well, I'll go over to my table with my cakes and cook book. What time am I with the children?"

"Four o'clock."

"Ok, that's fine. Hey, Taylor should be down soon."

"Oh my Goddess, they'll go potty!"

The shop was pandemonium. The queue went halfway down the street with people wanting to come in and take a glimpse of Adrianna Jasmine and her husband. She smiled and posed for the cameras, spoke to fans, signed copies of her book, held babies and offered cupcakes and drinks to the customers. She read stories to the little ones whilst local news channels filmed her and even allowed her mother to perform a salsa in the middle of the shop with Nathaniel.

"Well, it's good practice for us, darling! When I was in the Moulin Rouge, darling, the Moulin Rouge, can you believe it?" She told a bedazzled reporter for BBC News, "I danced every style of dance ranging from ballet to burlesque but I must say performing for Strictly is my most honoured role!"

The place was simply buzzing and everyone was thoroughly enjoying themselves thanks to a cackle of witches, a Latvian werewolf and a food critic!

"To a fabulous day, girls," toasted Sicily whilst holding a smoking cocktail called Sex in the City. The cackle of witches was now sitting at a table in the Blue Bar enjoying a round of deliciously prepared cocktails.

"I'll say," added Sarah, "the shop was so busy I thought it would burst at one point."

Adrianna Jasmine nodded, "It was crazy!"

"Oh, I wish I could have come over but work was manic today," said Carolina.

"Same here, I just couldn't leave the shop," added Kristobella.

"Never mind, at least we're all here together and we've managed to celebrate Halloween a little," said Adrianna Jasmine.

"Yes, absolutely but I think we should all toast a drink to Clementine. I know she was foolish and brought her untimely death upon herself but it's a shock nonetheless," said Bella Bell.

"I agree," said Kristobella with a firm nod, "an absolute waste of a life."

"Excuse me, darlings. I've just got to pop to the loo!"

They looked up to see Sicily standing up and taking her leave. "Hmmmm, I guess she doesn't want to toast Clementine then," deliberated Carolina

"I can't blame her," said Kristobella as gently as possible, "after all, she did almost kill our Adrianna Jasmine but the girl didn't mean it, she was just stupid."

They all nodded. "Anyway, to Clementine," said Adrianna Jasmine, "enjoy your new existence in the Summerlands." They all chinked their glasses before Sicily returned to her seat.

433

"OK, ladies, I do have a few gifts to give you but be discreet amongst the mortals," she giggled and handed them all an orange and white striped goodie bag. I'm afraid it's just TT products this year, as I haven't had time to be creative but I think you'll all like what you get."

The witches peaked into their bags and found a jar of Tick Tock Stop the Clock moisturising cream, a small bottle of Citrus Bang-Bang Boom and Cellulite Zap jelly beans.

There was a stir of excitement from the cackle.

"Goddess, I'm going to take mine now," exclaimed Sarah and through a jelly bean down her throat. The rest of the witches followed suit.

"So how long does it take to work?" asked Bella

"About three hours, darlings," trilled Sicily, "good, huh?"

The witches all nodded enthusiastically. *Goddess bless TT.*

"Will you be going out on Whiz tonight, Adrianna Jasmine?" whispered Kristobella.

Adrianna Jasmine shook her head. "I'm afraid not, but I plan on getting out into the forest next week. Taylor's in America for two weeks filming down in Miami so I'll slip out then, mind you, that's if Jupiter turns up."

"Oh dear, is he still on AWOL?"

Adrianna Jasmine nodded unhappily, "Yes, the little so and so, he's really hurt."

Kristobella gave Adrianna Jasmine a sympathetic look, "He'll turn up when he's good and hungry. Anyway, what's Taylor up to tonight?"

"He's with Mark, they've gone out for a drink."

"Oh dear, poor Mark. I hear he was really smitten."

Adrianna Jasmine nodded, "Yes he was."

At 3am Adrianna Jasmine fell in through the front door, she was absolutely sozzled. The cackle had gone off to their favourite salsa bar and danced the night away and drank copious amounts of mojitos. Adrianna Jasmine fumbled and stumbled about in the kitchen as she tried to make herself some toast. It wasn't happening so she opted for a bit of cheese and a slug of milk before stuffing a piece of fruit cake into her mouth. She then went into the bathroom and ran the shower. She just about managed to get undressed and stood under the jet. Moments later she fell asleep upright with the shower still on. Luckily, Taylor had heard all the commotion and decided to check on his wife. He walked into the bathroom to discover his usually demure wife passed out with her head against the tiles and mascara running down her face. He switched off the tap, lifted her to safety, wrapped her in a towel, put her pyjamas on and tucked her into bed. She slept soundly until a raging hangover woke her up.

Chapter 45
The Wrath of the Threefold Law

The next morning Adrianna Jasmine felt terrible. Taylor had already left for work so she ran a Citrus Bang-Bang Boom bath and laid in it until her headache was completely gone. She then got dressed and made her way over to Covent Garden. The roads had been a nightmare due to the underground being in chaos. She walked in through the back door still feeling a little jaded but nonetheless, she got her act together and made a delicious batch of chocolate brownies, a tiramisu, a caramel banana tart, crumbly shortbreads, a white chocolate cheesecake and mini apple and blueberry crumbles. It was just after 2pm and Adrianna Jasmine tried Taylor's phone again. She had been trying to get hold of him all morning and it kept going to answer phone. Frustrated after the sixteenth attempt, she made her way into the café and asked for a double shot hot chocolate and treated herself to one of her chocolate brownies. She sat down quietly reading a paper that had been left by a previous customer, chatted to Sarah and sent a text to Taylor. After draining her cup and sticking the brownie crumbs to her fingers before placing them onto her tongue, she made her way back into the kitchen in order to clean up before going home. As she began to bustle around, throwing pots and pans into the dishwasher, her mobile went off.

Ah, about time! she thought, then realised it was Taylor's parent's house calling. "Hello," she answered cheerily, expecting it to be Taylor, then felt a little taken aback when it wasn't his voice on the phone, but his mother's.

"Adrianna Jasmine?"

"Yeah, hi Patty, how're you?" There was a silence for a few moments, and then the sobbing started. Confused, Adrianna Jasmine asked Patty what was wrong, why was she crying

"Oh, my precious, I'm so sorry to have to tell you down the phone, but, but oh Adrianna Jasmine, oh God, its, its Taylor. There's been an accident and he's… dead." Adrianna Jasmine felt as if the Grim Reaper herself was crushing her windpipe with her cold fingers.

She couldn't breathe and the room began to spin. "Wha...?" she barely whispered, Her knees buckled and she fell to the floor.

"He's dead, Adrianna Jasmine, look, come over, please we need to talk about this together. It's not right you should hear it on the phone, my son, my darling son. Oh God, oh God," she began to wail. Adrianna Jasmine was in shock, she couldn't comprehend what was going on, the next thing, another voice came onto the phone, it was Taylor's father cracked and broken.

"Adrianna Jasmine, its Austin, listen, come over, come over straight away. Just get a cab."

"How did it happen?" whispered Adrianna Jasmine she hadn't blinked since she had heard the word "dead."

"Err, oh Lord," Austin struggled to find the words as tears sprung into his eyes, he was struggling tremendously, "it was this morning, Adrianna Jasmine... the hospital called... we haven't even been to see his body... I... oh, it's so terrible, my son, my beautiful son." More sobbing came and it was hard to make either head or tale of what he was trying to say, but in the end Austin just held it together enough to explain. "Apparently Taylor had been waiting for a tube at Shepherds' Bush and a fight had broken out amongst two men. Taylor was caught in the cross fire. He was accidentally pushed in front of an oncoming train and killed." Adrianna Jasmine at this point dropped the phone and began to rock back and forth like a distressed child. She couldn't swallow, she couldn't breathe and she tried to call out for Sarah but no words would come. She crawled to stand and then the room began to go all fuzzy, then blackness. The next thing she saw was Sarah's face leaning over hers.

"Adrianna Jasmine, wake up, come wake up, honey. You've fainted, what's going on? Come honey, that's it, open your eyes, what happened?" Adrianna Jasmine sat up slowly, her complexion was almost transparent. She still couldn't speak and gestured towards her phone. A little confused, Sarah retrieved Adrianna Jasmine's phone and handed it carefully to her friend. Adrianna Jasmine went to messages and began to punch out words, after a few moments she had finished and handed the phone in a daze back over to Sarah. Sarah scanned the screen then seconds later she too dropped the phone and fell to the floor; she threw her arms around Adrianna

Jasmine and held her as tight as she could. For a moment, there was an eerie silence with Sarah holding her disorientated friend as protectively as possible. And then it came, the cry of pain that no human should ever have to cry. Sarah with tears in her eyes, tried to soothe and comfort, but nothing would pierce through the shell of pain that had now engulfed Adrianna Jasmine's very soul.

"Whhhhhhhhhhhy," wailed Adrianna Jasmine, "why him, why? Nooooo, please nooooo, oh Goddess, help me, please make it stop, help meeeee, ahhhhh."

"I don't know, Adrianna Jasmine," said Sarah through sobs, "I just don't know." The two girls sat on the floor, Adrianna Jasmine wailing and digging her nails into the palms of her hands, trying to create a physical pain that could overpower her emotions. Then she began to beat her fists into her face and started to tear out her hair, crazed and unhinged. Sarah grabbed her friend's hands in order to prevent her from beating herself up. "Stop it, Adrianna Jasmine, stop it, this won't do."

Adrianna Jasmine continued to wail, "No, let me. It helps, it helps," she cried, "Oh Goddess, the pain, oh Sarah, help me, I can't live, I can't, I can't..." Sarah now trying desperately not to break down, took her fiend into her arms and cradled her in her soft bosom.

"Shhhhh, Adrianna Jasmine, shhhhh," She gently rocked her friend back and forth and began to sing to her friend.

Hush now my sweet, love is here
I'll take the pain, fight your fear
Soft and gentle no tears don't weep
Your sadness and sorrow will not keep
Tender flowers colours and dreams
Sunlight, Christmas, strawberry creams

Loving as a mother's embrace
Chocolate spread all over your face
Kisses and wishes will heel your wounds
Cookie dough licked off silver spoons
Stay with me, melt in love
Purer than a snow and the soft white dove

As her friend sang the song over and over again, Adrianna Jasmine's sobbing eventually subsided into fretful hiccups, then silence. She stared out into nothingness. Sarah gently untangled Adrianna Jasmine from her arms, cupped her face and tenderly kissed her tear-stained cheeks. Emotionless, Adrianna Jasmine nodded her head and began to stand up. She then walked over to her bag and pulled out the van keys from within. She took one last look at Sarah, whose eyes were filled with nothing but compassion for her friend, then walked out of the coffee shop kitchen so she could drive to the one person who could explain to her why this had happened.

Sicily was dressed in black. Black slacks, black woolly and black shawl wrapped around her shoulders. She was standing in her living room peering out of the bay windows and into the garden. It had begun to rain and she watched the drops plop into her little pond at the bottom of the garden, it bubbled and splashed. She didn't turn around when she heard her daughter walk into the room, just spoke.

"So who was it that died?" she asked, in a melancholy tone. Adrianna Jasmine said nothing for a few moments; she needed to gather strength to say his name.

"Taylor," she whispered. "It was Taylor."

Full of grief Sicily turned to face her daughter. She looked older than she had ever looked and there was genuine sadness to her eyes. She took a small breath. "It could have been anyone you held dear to you, Adrianna Jasmine, your father, Kristobella, me! But the law chose to take your Taylor and for that, I truly am sorry."

Adrianna Jasmine didn't flicker, her eyes were dead. "So I was punished for killing an evil witch? A witch who was just about to kill you, and possibly myself?"

Sicily nodded shamefully and sighed. "A life for a life, Adrianna Jasmine, a life for a life, the bottom line is that you took a life and the balance had to be restored."

"Restored?" boomed Adrianna Jasmine angrily, "my beautiful soul mate was taken in order to compensate for the death of *that* evil bitch!" Sicily looked down at the floor, it wasn't fair. "And you knew, didn't you mother, you knew that someone would die."

Sicily nodded. "Yes and today I knew would be the day, I dreamt it last night. But I didn't know *who* would be taken, all day I've been waiting for the dreaded message of death. And I'm sorry it was your Taylor, truly I am."

Adrianna Jasmine nodded, "Me too." The two witches were silent for a few moments. Adrianna Jasmine was the first to speak, "I can't do this anymore mum, I just can't." Confused, Sicily asked exactly what her daughter couldn't do, work, sleep, live? "This!" exclaimed Adrianna Jasmine throwing out her arms. "The way we live, who we are, the threefold law we must abide by. Ha, the threefold law!" spat Adrianna Jasmine she felt nothing but pure hatred towards it, "the threefold law has done nothing but turn me into a paranoid lunatic ever since the age of five and killed the most genuine, sweetest, beautiful human being I ever had the privilege to meet."

The tears began to flow once more and Sicily's heart was close to breaking point. "I don't know what to say, Adrianna Jasmine, truly," said Sicily, "I wish it could have been me, I really do mean that."

Adrianna Jasmine looked down at the floor, "It shouldn't have been any of us," said Adrianna Jasmine angrily, "that's the point."

Sicily's eyes began to trickle with hot tears; it wasn't fair, the threefold law had well and truly shown the true nature of its brutal power.

"What's done is done and it cannot be undone," said Sicily, "all we can do is use the gifts we have in order to move on and support those who need it most."

Adrianna Jasmine looked at her mother and scoffed, "What, you think I'm going to use magic again, you think I'm ever going to go near the very thing that killed my partner? You must be madder than I thought! I will never touch magic again for as long as I live, never!"

"You don't honestly mean that, Adrianna Jasmine," said Sicily dejectedly, "you're just upset right now, magic is who you are, what you are and it will always find you."

Adrianna Jasmine shook her head defiantly. "No it won't, I'll make sure that evil force never darkens my door again, I've washed my hands of it, I renounce my status, my so-called gifts, everything."

"Do you mind if I sit down?" Sicily suddenly began to feel quite giddy and unwell. Adrianna Jasmine shrugged her shoulders; she could fall down for all she cared. "Oh Adrianna Jasmine," sighed Sicily wearily, "Richenda had this all planned, you know!"

"Well, we know that!" Snapped Adrianna Jasmine, "even in death she's won, it's almost like she had a backup plan."

Sicily nodded, "Richenda must have known that she would probably die that night but also felt safe in the belief that her death would not be in vain. She knew that whoever killed her would be punished which would cause disastrous events."

"And you were ignorant to this then, mother?"

Sicily nodded in defeat, "I didn't know her plan, Adrianna Jasmine. I thought she was after you and that she wanted to hurt you, we all did. Little did we know that she wanted me."

"That's stupid, you were the one who killed her mother!"

Sicily bit her lip. "Yes, I... we killed her, that is true and..."

"And she wanted revenge!"

Sicily took a deep breath, her daughter's anger was very draining. "I fully believe that she wanted to kill me that night in order to avenge her mother's death. In her eyes her mother was unjustly killed and therefore if she killed me she would be exempt from the wrath of the threefold law. Perhaps she actually believed that she *was* the threefold law." Sicily laughed dryly. "However, she also knew that *you* would try to recue me, and that if she died well she would still win because the law would avenge her death." Sicily then looked up towards her daughter, "and as you can see, it bloody well has."

"So she martyred herself?"

"It appears to be that way."

Mother and daughter were silent for a few moments. Adrianna Jasmine could literally hear the beating of her heart.

"What I don't understand," said Adrianna Jasmine looking blankly down at her hands, "is how in this mortal realm did Gunnora Pan avoid the wrath of the threefold law for such a long time?" She then looked up at her mother, her eyes searching for answers. "You said she spent *years* practising black magic, why did it take the threefold law so long to punish her, well, for *you* to punish her?"

Sicily sighed long and slow, then forlornly shook her head, "I'm not absolutely sure, my precious, but sometimes we're punished for the wrong that we have done immediately and sometimes it takes longer. It's just... one of those things." She looked at her daughter, searching for some kind of recognition, Adrianna Jasmine still looked angry.

"So you're saying that all my life I've been tiptoeing around the threefold law, trying desperately to lead a pure life, use magic with good intentions so that I wouldn't be punished. Yet that bitch was able to get away with dark magic for years and not even receive as much as bump on the head? Then I kill a witch, a witch that was evil, who not only wanted to hurt me but kill you and I have to immediately pay for it with the life of my fiancé! What sort of law is that?"

Sicily shook her head with great sadness and dissolution; there was no rational explanation she could give her daughter, "It's what's commonly known as the Law of Sod." As it stood, life even for witches, was unfair.

'A single death is a tragedy; a million deaths is a statistic.'
Joseph Stalin (1879 - 1953)

Chapter 46
Sicily's Story

"She was the most evil witch of the twentieth century," said Sicily staring at the ground, "killing over two hundred innocents with her black magic. Women, children, no one was safe, she even cursed babies unaware, sleeping in their prams. She was a deranged psychopath, fuelled with hatred and power, a curse on the witching world and what we stand for. Her daughter, on the other hand, was not like her, she was born... pleasant. Richenda was born five years after my birth and was raised by Gunnora's mother, Celia. Her father was an unknown, we believe only used for his... sperm?" Adrianna Jasmine sniffed indignantly and remained seated on the chair, listening but not looking up. Sicily wrapped her black shawl tightly around her shoulders, the wind was beginning to howl outside. She continued on. "I had not really heard much about Gunnora Pan, just snippets. You see, darling, I was 22, living in Paris as a dancer at the Moulin Rouge, the Moulin Rouge darling can you believe it! I had the body of an angel and the face of 1940s silver screen Goddess. I was young and free, living the dream. I was sharing a very chic apartment that had been on loan to us from a millionaire business man... Jean Baptist with a group of equally avant-garde Moulin Rouge dancers. We were very glamorous and sexy, darling, oh yes, men simply threw themselves at our perfectly manicured toes. We drank champagne for breakfast, lunch and dinner, ate at all the chicest restaurants and met all the celebrities of the moment. Well, the Moulin Rouge was *thee* place to go! Oh those were the days," Sicily sighed dreamily. "We danced two shows a day, six days a week, wore fabulous pink diamante thong-type things and poetically sashayed about adorning white ostrich feather fans and gliding into the splits with Frank Sinatra a hair's breath away, oh it was bliss. I slept for an hour about every six days or so," Sicily chuckled to herself, "Goddess these days I need a good four, or I'm practically useless, oh to be young. Well I've never really needed much sleep and in those days I didn't want to miss a minute of my life, you can sleep when you're dead is what I used to say. So it was ironic that sleep was the reason as to why I was summoned to do what I did."

Adrianna Jasmine's eyes flickered towards her mother with interest. "What do you mean, sleep was the reason the threefold law contacted you?" then she realised, "oh," she said quietly, "it messaged you in a dream."

Sicily nodded, "It surely did! Curse it," she added with lament, "I only fell asleep on the balcony for no more than an hour, but that was enough. I didn't really understand it in all honestly. In my dream I found myself walking in line behind three other people. I couldn't make out who they were because they all had their backs to me and we were all wearing dark, long, hooded cloaks. It was twilight and I could feel the crunching of leaves and twigs beneath my feet. We walked and walked and then I woke up. When I woke I was sweating, I was scared. I wanted to call my mother, but convinced myself I could handle it by forgetting about it and basically not falling asleep again!" Sicily then chuckled. "I went for eight days without sleep!" Even Adrianna Jasmine looked surprised, eight days was impressive, even for a witch! "But it all got too much and I fell asleep in a park one lazy summer's afternoon and that was it."

"What was your dream that time?" asked Adrianna Jasmine, she didn't want to admit it, but the story was certainly attention-grabbing. Sicily frowned as she tried to explain.

"It's hard to explain, lemon posit, but it was about me representing the element of earth in a circle of witches and I must say after that dream, I was very frightened."

"Why?" Adrianna Jasmine asked slightly confused, "what's so frightening about that, after all you're a witch, it's what witches do, you know, cast spells in circles!"

Sicily raised her eyebrows, "What, black magic circles, darling?"

Adrianna Jasmine couldn't help but feel a little shocked, "what do you mean, black magic circles, mother? I don't understand and how would you know if it were a black or white situation?"

Sicily let out a frustrated huff, "Come now, Adrianna Jasmine. I thought you were a bit more astute than that." Adrianna Jasmine looked indifferent, "I can sense black magic from ten miles away, I can sense if a black witch knitted a scarf before tying it around my neck, so I should be able to sense a black dream from a white one and so should you!"

Adrianna Jasmine rolled her eyes, "OK, OK, I get it, just get to the point will you," she said grumpily.

Sicily ignored her daughter's tone, "Then it really kicked off," she spat full of bitterness, "the next thing I received a phone call saying that my brother had been seriously burnt in a fire and that I was to return immediately..."

"But you don't have a brother," interrupted Adrianna Jasmine, "or, do you...?" Sicily didn't answer, she just raised her brows at her daughter's idiocy, "Oh...sorry," said Adrianna Jasmine realising her mistake, "the threefold law again... right?"

Sicily again didn't answer, yet opted to turn away and continue, *silly girl* she thought. "I played along with the story and left that very night for England. I can remember feeling as if my body didn't belong to me, like I was in some bad dream and I was just waiting to wake up. But I didn't, and as soon as I got home I realised that I wouldn't wake up anytime soon. When I got home that night, I found Mrs Sparrow, Bella Bell and Mrs Berry in my house waiting for me, my mother was out with Kristobella at some fashion show, they didn't even know I was home. Well, they all explained that they, too, had experienced the same dream, except they had all represented a different element to mine. Mrs Sparrow admitted that she had made the phone call about my burnt brother, hanging on for dear life and apologised, but she simply had to bring me back. She warned us all that something was about to happen, but couldn't quite tell what it was, however advised us to keep within close contact and to communicate regularly. Of course we all agreed and that night Bella Bell, who was five months pregnant with her son, Comet, had dreamed about a woman. Mrs Sparrow asked Bella to describe the woman's face and once she did, the two elder witches, Mrs Sparrow and Mrs Berry, knew exactly who it was she had dreamt about."

"Gunnora Pan!" said Adrianna Jasmine, "it was just a guess!" she added sarcastically.

"Yes, it was Gunnora Pan," said Sicily, "well done!"

Adrianna Jasmine snorted. "Then the next night, we all slept, even me, I can remember feeling the sleepiest I had ever felt in my entire life, apparently we all did and that's when we all dreamed the same dream. We were back in the forest again, although this time we all held… objects. Mrs Sparrow's object was a picture, Mrs Berry's a lamb, Bella Bell's a lock of hair and mine a snake… an adder. Then that was it, Mrs Sparrow realised that we had been chosen to perform a task, a task that would act on behalf of the threefold law. A task to punish Gunnora Pan, the witch who used her magical powers to hurt the innocent."

Adrianna Jasmine let out a huge sigh and shook her head forlornly. "Why you?" she asked, "what did you do to make the threefold law choose you as one of its… weapons?"

"I'm a very, very powerful witch, that's why and so the threefold law chose me to represent its army." Then Sicily's face fell. "You must realise, Pixie Pea, I was 22, living the life of Riley. I didn't ask for any of this, I didn't want to cast a dark spell, I wasn't even that bothered about magic really, I was living the fairy tale, without the hocus pocus! But once the spell had been cast, even though it had been the threefold law's wish, that was it, I was never quite the same again. Plus, when I returned to Paris a month later, I had to leave again!"

"Why?" asked Adrianna Jasmine

"My brother died!"

"Ah, I see," said Adrianna Jasmine, "your service was not quite finished."

"No, it bloody well wasn't," spat Sicily full of anger, "I was sent to blinking Australia, to make sure she was dead. Old Berry had a vision that her death was brought on by swimming into a swarm of deadly jelly fish in Australia, and muggins here, was once again pulled out of the Moulin Rouge and off I went. I never went back after that," she added quietly, "it was over for me."

Adrianna Jasmine was silent for a few moments, deep in thought, "So that's why you made me respect the law so much, then, is it?"

Sicily nodded solemnly. "It was to protect you; I know just how spiteful it can be and how low it will stoop to seek its revenge."

Adrianna Jasmine was silent in thought once more. "So the events of that night," she eventually broke the silence, "Richenda seeking revenge, that was all part of the threefold law's plan to punish you… well, the circle?"

"No," said Sicily sadly,

"Well, what was it then?"

"Personal," said Sicily. "The threefold law wanted Gunnora Pan dead and it simply used my Coven to make that happen, so therefore we were home dry, but the pain it caused to her daughter was not the threefold law's concern, that was a separate matter."

"So she came looking for me to seek her personal revenge on you?"

Sicily sighed heavily, "Yes, I suppose she did."

Adrianna Jasmine thought long and hard; something wasn't right, the threefold law had reacted most out of character. She shook her head hard, she neither had the strength nor the intelligence right now to figure it out, she would put it to bed. Regretfully, there was nothing she could do to rectify the tragedy, the past was in the past, what was done was done and Taylor would always be dead.

*'Be open to your dreams, people. Embrace that distant shore.
Because our mortal journey is over all too soon.'*
(David Assael, Northern Exposure, It Happened in Juneau, 1992)

Chapter 47
New Dawn A New Beginning

"I can't believe that this is the last day you'll be baking for the coffee shop," said Sarah full of sadness, "you sure, you're still going through with it?"

Adrianna Jasmine smiled affectionately at her friend and nodded. "I'm afraid so, I have to go. I can't live here anymore, there's nothing left for me."

Sarah shook her head in disagreement, "Of course there is, Jazzy, everything is here, your career was just taking off, you have money in the bank, everyone knows who you are, you've got friends and family who love you, your little flat, me!"

Adrianna Jasmine reached over and gave her friend a warm and grateful hug. "I recognize all that, Sarah," said Adrianna Jasmine with a tired sigh, "but I'm dead inside, I can't feel emotions anymore. I feel like I'm in a body but without a soul, I can't float around in a dream anymore, I need to wake up and fall in love with the world again and to some degree..." she added sadly, "with me."

"But your work, all your Tallulah Toffee products!"

Adrianna Jasmine smiled. "I've basically quit all my jobs and the Tallulah Toffee products are now yours... if you want them?"

"Really? Gosh thanks," said Sarah, "I can't believe you don't want them," she said, shaking her head in disbelief. "You have nearly every beauty product she ever made. Are you absolutely sure?"

"You know I don't do magic anymore, Sarah," said Adrianna Jasmine turning her back on her friend, it was tough trying to forget about magic when you were still in contact with witches. She hadn't spiked the coffee shop's cakes with magic sprinkles since Taylor's death, she hadn't done anything. All her magic tools, herbs, books, candles and Toffee products had been packed away into boxes and left for the cackle to wrestle over.

"Well, it's a damn shame," snivelled Sarah," "everything is just a damn, damn shame."

It was a cold, wet, Monday afternoon in January and Sicily, Henry Forthright-Punch, Kristobella, and Carolina Plum were all huddled around Adrianna Jasmine at Heathrow airport. Adrianna Jasmine was dressed casually in jeans, purple fitted, long sleeved top, a cool multi-coloured scarf wrapped loosely around her neck and her feet snuggled into a pair of Uggs. She had just checked in her one suitcase, opting to keep her baby blue, Quicksilver rucksack, where she kept her passport, tickets, money, the latest novel from Marian Keyes, ipod and a copy of Cosmopolitan for the trip. She looked so young and beautiful that her mother couldn't bear to look at her, for in a few moments, her precious creation would be gone.

"You got everything?" asked her father with a big smile.

"Yes," said Adrianna Jasmine, "I have."

"That's good then, you'll be fine, have a wonderful time, I think it's marvellous what you're doing, but I will miss you, sweetheart."

Adrianna Jasmine hugged her father. "I'll miss you, too, dad." She then turned to the other three women. "Well, I guess this is it." She hugged Kristobella first, who didn't want to let go and was sobbing uncontrollably. Then she kissed and held her mother for a few moments, breathing in her Chanel no. 5. Sicily, unlike her sister, was not crying, but was, if truth be told, absolutely dying inside. Then Adrianna Jasmine turned towards Carolina Plum, whose arms were open and ready to hug. But Adrianna Jasmine kept her distance and simply blew her a kiss. Hurt Carolina blew one back. Did witchcraft repulse Adrianna Jasmine that much that she couldn't even hug Carolina Plum? Then, inhaling a deep gulp of air, Adrianna Jasmine picked up her rucksack and without looking back, headed towards the gate.

Once on the plane, she felt a little more settled, the hardship from all the goodbyes, the tears, the questions, the organisation, the stress, now felt like a distant memory and Adrianna Jasmine suddenly realised just how tired she actually was. She longed for the plane to take off, so she could fly far away from her past, from the memories, from the magic and start fresh as a new person, as a new soul. Soon her wish came true; the engine rumbled into action, the plane began to speed up on the runway, then the delicious sense of lift, ascension, popping ears, and flight. Soon she was able to recline her seat and drift off to sleep

So tired, she thought, *so, so tired*, and soon she was fast asleep. She woke six hours later, due to a raging thirst. She removed a bottle of water from her bag and drank frantically. She decided she needed the bathroom and asked the chap next to her to move so she might get by. After visiting the tiny room, she sat back down onto the seat and enjoyed a spot of television, food and Cosmopolitan. She succumbed to more sleep and woke just as the plane was about to descend in order to refuel. "Oh, thank God," she thought, "I so need to stretch my legs."

Once the plane had landed and it was safe to do so, the passengers disembarked. Adrianna Jasmine was filled with anticipation and excitement, she felt free and grown up! She was also hungry and therefore headed straight for a restaurant where she treated herself to a sushi platter and jasmine tea. After eating her body weight in fish and rice, Adrianna Jasmine made her way to the ladies in order to freshen up, change her underwear, brush her teeth, wash her face, cleanse, tone and moisturise. Then after an hour of pottering about, was called to board her plane in order to resume her journey to her new beginning. As she re-entered the plane, the overwhelming sense of tiredness hit her once again and she was asleep before the plane took off. Her sleep was filled with dreams, dreams of Taylor laughing and smiling, bathed in sunlight. He was happy, handsome and free, blowing kisses towards her, telling her that he loved her. Adrianna Jasmine could literally smell his aftershave and feel the warmth of his skin; it was so real, so uncanny. She must have been crying in her sleep because when she woke, her neck and cheeks were damp from tears and she felt a little confused as to where she was. Although as soon as the plane touched down on the runway, her muddled mind was appeased.

"Well folks," the captain announced over the Tannoy, "welcome to Australia!"

To be continued...

Additional Stories Shared from A Circle of Witches on Halloween night 2009

Adrianna Jasmine

Well my last usage of magic, which I guess leaves me feeling warm and happy inside, was when I helped a lady at an afternoon tea party that I had catered for. I was catering for about twenty people. The organiser had desired a real English tea party; you know with bite size cucumber and smoked salmon sandwiches without the crusts, homemade savoury cheese scones and sweet scones accompanied with clotted cream and plump strawberry jam. Sky high Victoria sponge cake, devilishly rich chocolate cake and lemon chiffon cake with zesty lemon icing. I think I made a Bakewell tart as well as an apple pie with homemade vanilla custard. I can remember pouring endless cups of Earl Grey from a Victorian tea urn, which I'd purchased at Portobello Market. It was a lovely do actually, very civilised but still quite relaxed. Anyway, I was busy serving the guests when I noticed a woman who was sitting all on her own, not mingling with the other guests and looking so full of sadness. I decided to go over to her and offer her a cup of tea and a small slither of chocolate cake. I poured the tea into the most fragile china tea cup, which unfortunately were not my own but the organisers, honestly they were so beautiful, and popped the cake onto a matching side plate. I took a deep breath and said,

"Excuse me there, but may I offer you a cup of tea and perhaps a slice of chocolate cake?" I stood above her and tried to smile gently, yet pleasantly. I didn't want to come across as pushy or neurotic and waited for her response. After a moment or two she glanced at the cup of tea then at the choccy cake. I could see that her parched lips were longing to be quenched by the freshness of the Earl Grey and for the lovely rich chocolate flavours to spoil her senses, so I said,

"I tell you what, I'll just leave it here for you on this little table." The lady graced me with a flicker of a smile and with frailty to her voice said thank you. Now, in case you are wondering, yes the food was spiked with magic sprinkles, Jolly, in fact, which I thought would be befitting for a English tea party, jolly hockey sticks and all that, but that's not the reason as to why her mood went from dreary to cheery. After about ten minutes I went back over to the lady in question in order to clear up her crockery, but mostly to see if she had enjoyed her treat and tea. She certainly appeared a little more relaxed and there was definite colour to her cheeks.

"I hope you enjoyed that," I said, "and please, if fancy anything else just let me know, we've got lemon chiffon cake, apple pie, thick clotted cream, or if you're more of a savoury person, cheese scones and cucumber sandwiches."

"Thank you, you're very kind," the lady said, "did you make the cake?" I smiled humbly and nodded.

"Well," she said, "it's the most wonderful thing I've ever tasted, truly."

"Thank you," I said and introduced myself there and then, "I'm Adrianna Jasmine, the Magic of Food and may I ask your name?" The woman looked a little stilted at first, but then relaxed and told me her name was Grace and that she was sister to the party's host. "How do you do, Grace?"

"Oh," she said, "not too bad, but I must say your chocolate cake has made me feel the best I've felt in six weeks, maybe I should think about eating more!"

I smiled, "Well chocolate is rich in feel good endorphins, so you never know, how about another slice?' At first the woman shook her head, "go on, you deserve it." I coaxed.

She looked at me a little startled and then said, "Yes, why not. I do deserve it." I popped off and brought her back a fresh cup of Earl Grey and slightly bigger slice of cake. I handed her the tea and popped the cake down on the table, once again I left her to enjoy the treat and came back a few minutes later to collect her plate.

"That was even more delicious than the first slice," she complimented as she licked her lips before sipping her tea. "What did you say your name was again?"

"Adrianna Jasmine," I reminded her.

"You're very good at what you do and I must say, I really do feel better today."

453

I tilted my head to one side and asked, "Oh? Why's that, may I ask?"

The woman smiled and shook her head, then I saw it, a tear trickled from her eye and plopped onto her lap. Without saying anything, I handed her a napkin and she wiped her eyes. After she looked up and more tears silently fell, I crouched down beside her and took her hands into mine and looked deeply into her overwhelmingly sad eyes.

"It's been six weeks," she whispered through silent yet painful tears, "six weeks since he died and I'm in such incredible pain, I don't know how I will ever continue, I miss him so much."

Well, the woman didn't need to say anymore to me, she was experiencing the sort of pain no human being should have to endure, so I took her into my arms and hugged her like she had never been hugged. When I let go of the woman, she looked a little confused, as if to say, what just happened there?! But moments later I could see that the pain and the poison that fills one's body subsequent to bereavement had been released from her body and in its place, peace. She was in pain no more; you could see it in her face, for her skin was now healthy and her eyes swimming with life.

"Who are you?" she breathed.

I answered "The *Magic* of Food."

Clementine Poppleapple

Well, it's kinda bittersweet, my story. basically you know, I used to live on the top level of a renovated police station? Well the family from hell have moved into the lower-ground flat, and my bedroom is above their lounge, children and their tearaway teenage mates. Not only are their voices deafening, they play loud music and there is no evidence of a curfew from their chav parents, and the language! I tell you, it's a f*****g disgrace! Anyway, to make matters worse, they've got this rat of a dog, a chiwawa thing, called Candy, that possesses the most ear-shattering yap of a bark. Goddess, it goes right through you, you know?

    Well, about two months ago I wasn't feeling particularly healthy so I tucked myself up into bed about ten thirty for an early night. It was difficult to sleep because the Lost Boys and co. were round, swearing and laughing, whilst all I could hear from the girls was "Candeeee, Candeeeee," in stupid, high pitched voices. Still, I managed to drift off to sleep by mentally blocking out the noise, when that blasted dog yapped as high as ten decibels. Well, you can imagine, I leapt out of my skin and prior to realising that it was that bloody dog and not the chainsaw massacre in my bedroom, I felt angry, oh I felt so angry, to the point where I clenched my fists and teeth making my blood pressure rise to high risk levels. My body began to elevate off the bed like the exorcist child, and before I knew it an explosion like a large bag of water hitting a wall at 100 miles per hour filled the room, followed by earth shattering screams from the gang down below. Apparently Candy, the dog, had internally combusted and exploded all over the walls! Now I know I shouldn't have lost my temper and I certainly know that I shouldn't have caused a dog to explode, but I promise you I have confronted my anger issues with a counsellor and we are addressing the matter one step at a time. Because the scary thing was, for a few weeks I didn't feel guilty, I was just happy to get some sleep!

    Anyway, a few weeks later I did feel the slightest bit of remorse, so decided to do something nice for them, I decided that they needed a break and to get away from it all, therefore I cast a good fortune spell with the intent that they would win a nice holiday in the sun. Nothing too special because if I sent a family like that to the Caribbean in order to languish in five-star luxury hotels, they would only make fools of themselves due to their common upbringing. Besides, I thought they might feel uncomfortable in the company of wealth and decorum and therefore they would realise just how ignorant they were? So I decided a nice two-week break camping in the south of France would fit the bill perfectly. Not a cheapskate holiday, a really nice holiday park with luxury tents, showers and swimming pool! So off I went and set to casting a good fortune spell. I firstly set about importing thoughts into the mother's head. I wanted her to look for competitions on the computer; like the ones where you can win holidays. I believe this didn't work straight away, as I heard from the neighbours chattering that she had been up the last few nights with night terrors, so obviously I wasn't quite there, but don't worry, I was undeterred and continued with my mission. After a few gruelling weeks, the mum was tapping away on the family computer and entered a competition to win a holiday for four in the South of France at a top camping resort plus £500 spending money. Well, to cut a long story short, a few days later they received a letter in the post saying that they had won and that they needed to go within the next four weeks. Two weeks later the merry group were off to the South of France, to bask in the lovely sun, splash about in the pool, spend their winnings and get over the exploding dog. I think they had a lovely time, they all looked tanned and rested, plus I had two blissful weeks without the ASBO clan. *And* I actually did it again, so they got to travel, broaden their somewhat starved horizons, and again, I managed to get some sleep! Basically, I got to kill two birds with one stone, what do you think of that!

Carolina Plum

Well, my story is a little similar to Adrianna Jasmine's, although for once, it doesn't involve one of my famous hugs, but a kiss! I was invited to a very nice dinner party held by my friends, Alicia and Robert, and four other couples, in their beautiful house in Holland Park. And yes, due to being a single girl, I was the odd one out. However, it didn't matter as they're a great bunch of people and I always feel very comfortable and relaxed in their company. We had a wonderful meal, Bollinger on arrival, giant prawns wrapped in filo pastry for starter, with a sweet chilli dip, followed by an amuse bouche, and then for dinner we were treated to roast loin of pork with crackling and spicy pear sauce with roasted potatoes, carrots, peas and cauliflower cheese. And for pudding... ah yes, sticky toffee pudding and white chocolate ice-cream. Well, as I said, it was a lovely night, everyone was in high spirits, merrily sipping champers, laughing at one another's jokes and of course, the hosts were tending to our every whim.

However, I noticed that something was slightly off with the two. Of course, to the un-magically trained eye, one wouldn't notice, for there was Robert, expertly popping champagne corks and lighting the log fire in the living room, Alicia pouring spicy apple sauce over our perfectly crackled pork and expertly engaging in witty conversation with her guests. So it would seem picture perfect, but I knew something was amiss.

Robert looked somewhat distracted, as if he were standing from the outside and peering in, and Alicia was hidden behind a colourful mask of over the top giggles and frothiness, I believed to hide her true feelings. Anyway, after dinner we retired to the drawing room for coffee, although Alicia was busying herself tidying up the dinner table. Robert took residence in the living room serving coffee to his guests, keeping everyone entertained, that sort of thing. I, on the other hand, decided to help Alicia clear up the plates. When I offered to help usually she tells me to go away and relax with the others, but today she was different, today she accepted my offer.

As we cleared away the remnants of the evening's feast, Alicia began to strike up conversation, quite a personal one, as I recall, about how frustrated she was feeling and how dowdy and old she thought she looked. Now let me tell you, Alicia is most certainly not dowdy and she is most certainly not old, but in the prime of her life, in wonderful shape and extremely attractive. However, she complained that she felt Robert no longer found her attractive and that they hadn't had sex for 18 months! All he was interested in was his work, he's a company director, and thought he could fob her off by simply paying for trips to the beauty salon, wash and blow dries at Niki Clarkes, and buying her gym memberships.

"Ha!" she concluded, "to distract me from sex, because he isn't interested." Then she gasped, "what if it's because he's found someone else, there are a lot of attractive younger girls at his firm who wouldn't mind gobbling him up and it's not like we need to stay together for the sake of the children, we haven't got any!" I told her to not think such things, I was sure he wasn't having an affair, but the sex life crisis needed to be addressed, maybe a little encouragement? "Encouragement!" she screamed, "how much more encouragement does a man need? Do you know I brought a whole set of lacy black underwear from Victoria's Secret, clambered into black heeled stripper shoes, that I'd bought from a seedy back street sex shop in SOHO, along with a whip and set of handcuffs with the hope I'd stir something! Plus, I forked out £400 on a full length black leather coat that looks like something that German bird from *Allo Allo* would wear!"

"He didn't go for it, huh?"

"Ha!" she laughed sarcastically, "By his reaction you would have thought I was dressed up like a telly tubby, it was embarrassing, he fumbled about with my hair, fumbled about elsewhere and in the end I just said, 'forget it' and went downstairs and made myself a cup of tea and a hob nob, well it was the only nob I'd be getting for the evening "

"Oh dear," I said "how odd, there must be something more to this, because I must say I'm picturing you right now dressed in your black lace get up, and well, I can honestly say wow!"

Alicia smiled, "Thanks, oh I don't know, it's bizarre. Come on, forget it and let's join the others."

Anyway, after an hour I decided to leave, kissed everyone goodbye and allowed Robert to walk me out. "Well, that was another fabulous evening by my favourite couple, Robert, thank you very much and the wine you chose to go with the pork was exquisite."

"Thank you," he said, and may you speedily return for another one of our little soirées," He helped me on with my coat and kissed me on my cheek, and then I turned and looked him square into the eyes. He stared at me a little bewildered, then his face went all soft and before he knew it, I had gently kissed him on the mouth. Oh, not for long, about three seconds. When I pulled away he didn't move, it was if he had been hypnotised, well, he had, actually, but don't worry, he snapped out if it when the door shut with me firmly behind the other side. I guess he just shook his head vigorously for a few moments and resumed his place back in the living room. Anyway the next day Alicia called me excited as a schoolgirl.

"You'll never guess what," she said, "but Robert asked me to slip into my black lacy number after you all left last night and ravished me into the early hours of the morning!"

"Never!" I exclaimed.

"True!" she said, "and what's more, he's just phoned me asking me to put on my black leather coat and shoes for when he comes home tonight as he's horny as hell!"

"Wow," I said, "that's great, wonder what brought that on?"

Copyright © Catherine Sabatina 2011
All Rights Reserved
www.catherinesabatina.com